A WITCH'S AURA

BOOK ONE

THE SORENYA CHONICLES

INARA GAGE

Editing by: Wendy Smuts and Emerantia Parnall-Gilbert

Alpha and Beta readers: Tillie Peart, Frances Volkel, Lynda Volkel, Dustin Traw

Cover art by: Order of the Bookish

Hype team: Book Beasties are the best Beasties

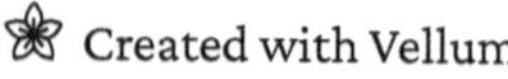 Created with Vellum

CONTENTS

DEDICATION

This one is for my son Gauge.
Who taught me never to give up on myself or my dreams.
Without wax little man.

TRIGGER WARNINGS

This book contains mentions of suicide, domestic violence, teen drinking, pot smoking, and a drunk driving accident resulting in death (only in mention). The book also contains some language and sexual situations that may not be suitable for some readers. This list is not exhaustive and other triggering circumstances or topics may be present within the work without any further warning beyond this point. You are important and your mental health matters. Reader discretion is advised.

PROLOGUE

On the night before her birthday, Shayde Gamic looked out to the street from the window seat of her bedroom. It was the early days in June, and the moon's light was dancing in the street as the wind softly billowed through the trees. The air was still slightly humid from the day, and when a gust of warm air snuck in through the open window and kissed Shayde's face she could only smile inwardly, not having the strength to muster a full smile. It was supposed to be a time of happiness and excitement, she was going to be sixteen, every teen looks forward to turning sixteen, but for members of the Gamic family a sixteenth birthday was especially significant. Apparently, there was something very special that happened to them when they turned sixteen, yet she had no idea what it was or what was being planned. Up until recently she couldn't wait to find out what the big secret was, but now she couldn't muster the enthusiasm, no matter how hard she tried. She had suffered a tremendous loss at the beginning of the year. Her brother, Kain, had been killed when he was thrown from his vehicle after being struck by a drunk driver. He died instantly. The truth was she didn't feel like celebrating anything in her life at the moment.

Kain had looked out for her since the day she was born. Being a year older, he had always been very protective and concerned for her welfare. He had loved her to the moon and back. Kain had been admittedly the best-looking junior student attending Salem High with his tall, muscular build which he loved to work on. He had dark red hair which he wore short and piercing bright green eyes. Shayde too had red hair but it fell to the center of her back and her eyes were the same unusual green but unlike Kain she was not so aware of her effect on the opposite sex. Shayde knew he was very aware of his allure and was sure that every single young woman at Salem High lusted after him. Girls were drawn to him like bees to honey and he took his pick whenever—and however often—he wanted. The times when Kain didn't have a girlfriend by his side, girls would try to befriend Shayde, just so they could get closer to her brother. Having experienced this numerous times, Shayde knew what they were after, and would simply ignore their compliments and offers to hang out with them. It had been more than once that she had been betrayed by her so-called friends, after they had used her in order to get closer to Kain.

Since then, Shayde had decided that no one was good enough for her brother, not that it had stopped him dating. When it came to Shayde however, Kain's protectiveness could be a little excessive, there were many times when boys in school would just try to befriend Shayde, and Kain would threaten them with just a sharp look as soon as they approached. One of Kain's unspoken warnings was enough to deter them from approaching his sister ever again. But instinctively Shayde knew his worry came from a good place. The older he got the more protective he became until last year it was like he could see into boys' minds and read their thoughts; according to Kain they all had their own secret agendas. He seemed to pick out bad guys as if by radar: he knew exactly who would cheat, and who would expect more than a simple kiss on the first date. But Shayde didn't mind not having a boyfriend anyway, she was more interested in doing well at her schooling, graduating, then going on to college and carving out a career for herself, rather than worry about silly teenage puppy love.

Shayde was supposed to have been in the truck with Kain on that final and fateful night. The accident occurred after one of their high school football games. Though Shayde had ridden there with Kain, she decided to ride home with her best friend Alizé who had been very upset as her boyfriend Jeff had suddenly broken up with her.

Unfortunately for Alize, Kain's protectiveness didn't extend to her and when her boyfriend told her that he wanted to see other people she had been taken completely by surprise. She was literally dumbfounded, Shayde and Alizé could only stare after him confused as he walked away. When it finally hit Alizé that she had just been dumped and it wasn't a joke, she was absolutely devastated. Alizé's brother tried to comfort her, but Alizé really needed the moral support of her friend, so Shayde agreed to get a ride home with them instead, telling Kain that she wouldn't be far behind him.

When Shayde had arrived home, she thought it was a little odd that Kain's truck wasn't there as he had left the school well before they did, but she chose to ignore her unease and fondly told Alizé goodnight.

"Call me if you need anything, I'm always here," she offered.

Alizé had looked at her with bleak expression, "Okay," she said reluctantly.

As soon as Shayde closed the car door, she hurriedly climbed the steps to her house and as she entered their front sitting room, she was startled to find her mom, Tara, sitting in the dark by the window.

"Whoa!" Shayde exclaimed as she closed the door. "What are you doing Mom? Are you okay?"

Tara's face was cradled in her hands and as she looked up, her despairing expression overwhelmed Shayde with dread. "Yeah. Just have a bad feeling is all." Her breathing was stressed, as though she was trying with all her might to suppress her anxiety.

Tara was a "sensitive", as Shayde liked to call her because she could find no other word for it. She was able to see people's auras and knew when someone's actions weren't true to their word. There were even a few times when Shayde tried to hide what she thought about something, and her mom seemed to see straight through her. Shayde hadn't liked that at all.

She had merely shrugged her shoulders, knowing her mother would tell her more as soon as she, herself, had figured out what had been making her feel so uneasy. Most of the time it would just be small things such as an incoming storm that would knock the power out for a few hours, or a traffic accident that was holding up her dad, so she decided to just let it be and head upstairs to her room to undress and get ready for bed.

Then the Tara's cell phone rang.

Immediately she'd stopped what she was doing and listened to her mother's muffled voice downstairs. She hadn't been able to make out what exactly Tara was saying, only that it suddenly had become eerily and uncomfortably quiet, the room began closing in on her. Something flashed through her mind that felt almost like electricity from a lightning bolt, she had some sort of hallucination where she saw the cell dropping from her mom's hand and hitting the ground and shattering, but it was only at that moment that she heard the sound of a mobile phone noisily crashing to the floor.

The vertigo had become overwhelming, it affected her so adversely that she lost her balance and was near fainting. With a deep foreboding she'd dropped to the floor and hugged her knees tightly to her chest. Such an overwhelming feeling of sadness and grief came over her being that she could hardly find her breath, it was as though she was suffocating. She had begun to shake uncontrollably at the realization that something had happened to her brother. Just as quickly she went numb and was no longer able to move even a finger. Her mother had come running up the stairs, and as she entered Shayde's room, had found her daughter lying on the floor of the bedroom completely paralyzed. Tara quickly rushed to her child and enveloped her tightly in her arms.

She had experienced these visions before throughout her young life but never so strongly. Neither Shayde nor her mom needed to confirm verbally how the other one had known well in advance that Kain was gone. The only thing that was relevant on that night was that Shayde's closest friend had been taken from her forever.

Saying goodbye to her brother was the hardest thing that she ever had to do. How was she supposed to celebrate her sixteenth birthday with him no longer around to share such an important moment with? It was as though nothing else mattered anymore and everything around her had faded into insignificance.

It had already been five months since they put him into the ground, and yet it still seemed like only yesterday he was in the room next door to hers texting her goodnight. The window seat in her room had become her quiet sanctuary, where she would stare at the night sky and miss everything that was her brother. Even five months on his presence was still missed to the point of pain. She examined the phone in her hand and read the last text message she'd ever received from him.

"Love ya sis."

It was the very message Kain had sent her from his truck as he drove off that night. She would save and cherish it forever. It was as though Kain too had somehow known, had a foreboding of what fate was awaiting him that tragic night, and had felt urged to let her know one last time how much he truly loved her.

At the time, she had just laughed at it, thinking that she would see him at home in twenty minutes and would playfully punch his arm and simply say, "Love ya too!"

But she never saw him again.

There she was again. This was the third time he'd seen her in a single week. Kruise knew who she was, the beautiful Gamic girl, sister of that Kain kid who died in a car wreck in January. He knew her from school. To tell the truth, he had a crush on her, but then who the hell didn't at Salem High? She was absolutely drop-dead gorgeous. Standing at five-feet seven inches tall, her legs were long and toned, and her dark red hair hung perfectly straight, cascading down to the center of her back. Her eyes were the color of the Caribbean Sea right before a storm, tropical green, and framed by dark lashes and brows. They were the first thing that you saw, luring you into the beauty of her face. Her skin looked soft and smooth, reminding him of a delicate silk that tempted fingers to touch it. Both the Gamic kids were down right bewitching in their looks, alluring and beautiful, as though they were the product of someone's delightful dream.

He had sat behind her in homeroom all year and was very aware of her presence, though she gave no sign she knew he even existed. After her brother died, a deep sadness seemed to engulf her and her green eyes had dulled a little from that loss. The glow in her seemed to dwindle, if ever so slightly, as though a part of her had died along with him. He secretly longed to comfort her, to make her smile again and hear her beautiful laugh. Many nights he would spend staring up at his ceiling dreaming about that smile.

As beautiful as she was, Kruise could never find the courage to go up and talk to her—as much as he had wanted to. He knew plenty of guys at school who would have tried dating her, that is, if Kain hadn't intervened. It seemed she turned down every guy that ever asked her out, and didn't seem very interested in dating anyone, which made her all the more interesting. However, from what he could tell she didn't appear to be a shy girl by any means. She had an abundance of friends and just about everyone knew who she was. She seemed to get herself into a lot of fights, but never at school, and not with anyone who didn't deserve it. She defended the nerds, the emos, the nice girls, and the kids with special needs, but behaved like a bully to the bullies, if you will. He knew of a few girls with mean dispositions who had "run into a wall" after they had been very nasty to Colynn; a girl at the school who had Down's Syndrome. Nobody was brave enough to mess with Shayde, and he respected that about her.

Kruise Wright was a very handsome seventeen-year-old, a

tall guy—standing at about six feet, with a muscular build. He had dark brown hair, which he wore short, and his eyes were a hazel color. He had an attitude but only with people he didn't respect; some of the teachers would say it resembled that of a young James Dean. He had his first tattoos done when he was about sixteen and was working on getting both of his arms sleeved. His ears were gauged to double zeros, and he had started growing facial hair when he was thirteen or fourteen, so by the time he was sixteen he already donned full sideburns, much to the annoyance of other guys at school, who could barely grow four hairs on their face. Kruise's casual and indifferent attitude was evident in how he conducted himself towards his peers and his interaction with people in general, the opinions of others made no difference to him. He was a tough guy that didn't know *that he actually was.* Although he didn't go around picking fights, since his teens there were times when he just wanted to pound the faces of some of the dense people that crossed his path, and he did just that, from time to time.

He was born and raised in Salem, Massachusetts, as were his dad and his grandmother, and he had no particular desire to move away to another town. Kruise's mom had died when he was eleven years old. She had always been the positive influence in his world and the light in his life. After she passed away, he began to change and a certain degree of hardness had seeped into him. His indifferent attitude seemed to ever worsen, to the point where he really didn't care about anything at all.

His best friend Jason knew him better than anyone else and had been in his life since they were in second grade. Jason actually lived with him, having come from a broken home himself. Jason's mom had been addicted to meth and his dad had abandoned them when Jason was just a baby. Kruise's mom and dad, Simon and Reanna, decided to take him in when his mom finally lost everything they had. Jay didn't have any brothers or sisters and neither did Kruise, so they were the closest thing that either of them had to a real sibling.

When Reanna died suddenly it tore them all apart. Kruise came home from school one day to find her lying on the living room floor, lifeless and unmoving. It was the strangest thing; how their happy lives had changed so unexpectedly. Everything had been so normal, with not a worry or threat on the horizon, and then one day everything dramatically changed by some terrible whim of nature. The autopsy revealed that Reanna's death was caused by a bite from a Northern Black Widow spider. The fact that a million to one event had caused his mother's death was still inconceivable; it made things even harder to come to terms with, especially for Kruise. Reanna had been the best wife, the most perfect mom, and a truly amazing person. Kruise didn't think they would ever recover from her loss.

Kruise and Jason were out getting some lunch at the local diner that afternoon, when in walked Shayde Gamic and her friend Alizé Ryan. He loved the sound of her name, *Shayde*. It reminded him of a hot summer day when he'd found refuge in the shade of large weeping willow tree. How the cool ground was both welcoming and comforting. The humid air that clung to his skin, the breeze that swept up and kissed the moisture, cooling it instantly and relieving it, if only momentarily. That's how he imagined a kiss from Shayde Gamic might feel.

As the hostess led the two girls past their table a whiff of her delicate perfume was carried on the breeze that swept over him as she passed. The scent of vanilla and jasmine filled his nostrils and he closed his eyes and basked in the delicious aroma.

As the girls settled in a booth down the way, he thought to himself that this was a sign he needed to force himself to go talk to her.

Jason tried to get his attention back to the matter at hand—the weekend trip they were planning to the beach. It was the middle of June, school just ended two weeks ago and they were ready to kick off their summer. Himself, Jason and a few other guys from school, Jordan and Danny, and their girlfriends, were all planning on renting a little cabin in Cape Cod, a beach city two and a half hours away, for the weekend. Their dad, Simon, didn't know that girls were coming, but even if Kruise and Jason had girls to bring of their own, Simon wouldn't care much. He had been a laid-back dad all their lives, more of a buddy than a father but a good dad all the same. He had become even more lenient on them after Reanna had died.

"Dude!" Jay yelled into Kruise's ear, jolting him out of his silent reverie. "Hey bro, I need you to come back to earth man, we gotta figure this trip out."

Jason Hughes was shorter than Kruise, but not by very much. He had reddish-brown hair that he usually wore short, and dark brown eyes. Kruise and Jay were in the same year at high school, though Jay was a few months older, being born in March and Kruise in July; they were both going to be seniors the following year. The two boys had the same style and wore Dickie's and dark shirts with wallet chains and skater shoes of some type. Jay's personality was effusive and funny, and he liked to give everybody grief about everything. He wasn't as thin as Kruise, actually he was more on the chubby side, but it suited him. His belly protruded a little underneath his shirts but his legs were skinny to the point where his jeans were always baggy and sagging off of him, revealing his boxers.

"Wha—huh?" Kruise said, as he clicked back into the moment and out of his daydreams. "Oh, yeah, dude I know, sorry about that. She's just so hot it takes my breath away." He was unashamed of his feelings towards Shayde and Jay knew all about his crush.

"Yeah, I know, you say that about her every single time we see her. I just don't understand why you haven't even asked her out yet." He paused and then, like a light bulb coming on, an idea entered his head and his eyes widened. "Hey, why don't you ask her and her friend to come to the beach with us this weekend?"

Kruise examined him with momentary hope, a French fry frozen in midair before his lips. The hope quickly dwindled. "Oh yeah I'm sure that wouldn't make me sound crazy at all... 'Hey, I know you don't even know I'm alive but my name is Kruise, we go to school together, we even had homeroom together all last year and you never even said hi to me once. But anyways, I was wondering if you and your friend would like to come with me and my creepy friend to Cape Cod this week-end?'—yeah dude, not crazy at all bro," he said, throwing the French fry back down onto the plate.

"It was just an idea, you don't have to be a dick," Jay said defensively, biting into his burger.

"Dude, I know. It's just, well, I don't know. She has turned down everyone who has ever asked her out. I'm pretty sure I am not going to be an exception," he said sadly, taking a sip from his Coke.

"Never know until you try. Just tell her about it, the worse she can do is say no."

Kruise focused on his half-eaten burger and processed what Jay had said. What if she said yes? The thought of her being there on the beach with him was almost too much for him to handle. To be with her for a whole weekend, sitting next to her and getting to know her. Smelling her sweet scent next to him, her finally knowing that he was alive, getting up close and personal with those gorgeous green eyes. What if they even hit it off? The thought of it almost constricted the air in his chest and his heart contracted. His stomached flipped and suddenly he didn't have much appetite.

But what if she did say yes and then it turned out to be horrible for her? What if she doesn't drink and she goes with us this weekend and sees what morons my friends can be when they drink? She'd never talk to me again, he battled with himself.

How bad it could be to at least go up and try? What was the harm in it? He had never talked to her before and the worst thing she could say would be no. If that were the case, he would just continue to admire her from afar and wait for the crush to slowly fade away.

This could just be the chance of a lifetime.

"You're right! I'll do it." Kruise said suddenly, scooting to the edge of the booth.

"Yeah! Atta boy! Go get her!" Jason laughed animatedly and dipped one of his fries in the ketchup, throwing it into his mouth. "I'll Google some cabins down there to see how much we're looking at," he said, chewing loudly. "Oh yeah, and hey, you think Jordan's brother will buy the booze for us, or should we ask dad?"

"I don't know. Text and ask Jordan first, see what he says. If he says no, then we'll ask dad as a last resort."

Swinging his legs to the side of the booth, he took a deep breath and stood. His nervousness appeared to have weakened his knees, he quickly righted himself and with as much nonchalance he could muster he ambled towards them.

When Shayde arrived at the diner, Alizé was already waiting for her, sitting on the edge of the red vinyl benches in the front lobby of O'Reilly's. Shayde opened up the double glass doors and when Alizé saw her, she jumped up eagerly and shoved a big pink gift bag at her and then gave her an ample hug.

"Zey!" Shayde scolded her. "I told you not to get me anything!"

Alizé laughed. "If I told you not to get me anything on my birthday, would you have listened?"

"Probably not."

They shared a laugh as the hostess with a blonde bob and a name tag that read "Lindsay" approached them.

"Are you ready to be seated?" she inquired, her voice edged with a little impatience.

"Yeah. I told you it'd be a minute," Alizé snapped. She had no patience for people that didn't like their jobs, and wasn't afraid to show it.

The hostess seemingly ignored Alizé and turned and grabbed some menus from a cubby in the wall.

"Right this way," she said with a phony charm.

"Sorry it took so long," Shayde whispered as they trailed behind her. "Were you waiting long?"

"Nah. Only a half hour. Nothing unbearable."

"I'm so sorry. You know how the DMV goes."

"I totally understand. I was perfectly fine waiting. She wouldn't seat me until my party was complete and I gave her hell about it. I just wanted a damn soda," Alizé said tersely, not even trying to keep her voice low.

The hostess seemed to be either ignoring Alizé or really couldn't hear her.

As they were walking to their table, Shayde spotted Kruise Wright and his friend Jason sitting in one of the booths. She and Kruise had shared homeroom together all year. Kruise was staggeringly handsome, and interesting. She had always wanted to talk to him but she never knew what to say and she was afraid of he might blow her off.

Lindsay walked them through the diner. It was an American grill, with walls covered with so much 1950's memorabilia not an inch paintwork could be seen. She showed them to a booth that was three or four seats away from where Kruise and his friend sat, thankfully empty tables lay in between.

They scooted into the vinyl-clad seats and Lindsay handed them their menus.

"April will be your server," the hostess said tonelessly. "The specials are on the back." And with a flip of her hair she was gone.

Shayde began to look over the oversized menu and felt a glare coming from Alizé. She put down the menu and saw Alizé gazing at her mischievously.

"What?" Shayde asked innocently.

"Nothing." Alizé snickered. "Well… it's just, funny."

"What? What's funny?"

"That guy Kruise from school is totally undressing you with his eyes. I'm surprised you still have clothes on, the way he's staring at you, you'd think they'd just fall right off."

Shayde felt her cheeks flush scarlet. "Whatever! You're crazy!" Trying to ignore her friend, she put her menu up once again but could still feel Alizé's eyes on her.

"Are you sure?" she said, stealing a glance behind her. When she caught Kruise's eyes, she quickly turned back around, embarrassed.

"What?" Alizé's tone was questioning. "You think he's hot, too! You should see your face, it's so red!" she said teasingly.

"Well, he is, don't you think?" Shayde admitted.

"Yeah, they both are. Why don't you go talk to him?"

"Because! Oh my god, no! No way! I can't, how embarrass-ing! I don't know how to talk to boys!" Just the thought of going up to his table and trying to spit out some words to him made her legs go to jelly. She knew that she would just stumble over them and make herself look like a fool.

"I know you don't." Alizé laughed out loud. "But you should learn really quickly 'cause he's coming over here."

Her heart contracted. "What?" She turned again to see him walking towards their table.

It seemed like wild butterflies had invaded her stomach, meanwhile her heart started pumping so hard that hot tingles ran down to her fingertips. Her legs went numb and suddenly she didn't know what to do with her hands, so she clasped them in front of her and sat there, frozen, as the gorgeous man rapidly approached her table.

She thought that maybe he was just getting up to use the restroom but then remembered it was in the lobby. The only thing in their direction was more tables and the kitchen.

When he stopped at their table, she could swear that the entire room could hear her thundering heart.

"Hey ladies, I'm Kruise," he said. She looked up, right into his hazel eyes, and seemed to tip over her own aura, right into them. "Um, we had homeroom together." He sounded nervous, his words coming out stiltedly as if he didn't know what to say either.

Speak, Shayde, SPEAK! She screamed at herself, but the words were not coming. Her eyes were frozen on his and she couldn't seem to move anything. "Yeah, um, I know who you are, what's up?" was what finally came out. She cursed herself inwardly. She had hoped that something much friendlier would come to her but that was about all she could muster, apparently.

"Oh, not much, chillin', having some grub with Jay. You?"

He sounded more confident now and that made her all the more nervous.

"Same." Her voice was shaky.

"Nice, nice." He glanced out of the window to the street beyond as if something more interesting had caught his attention. Then, as quickly his eyes were back on hers. He shifted his weight from one leg to the other. "Hey, this may sound weird, but do you have any plans this weekend?"

Her eyes widened and she fought the urge to giggle. "Um, no, not at all."

"Cool, well Jay was just wondering if you girls would like to come to Cape Cod with us this weekend? We're getting a cabin on the beach, sort of like, to kick off the summer." He hesitated and glanced at his feet. "I know we don't really know each other or anything but Jason was—"

"We'll go!" Alizé interjected. "Hi, I'm Alizé Ryan. I know you from school too," she said, holding out her hand to him.

Kruise took it in his. "Yeah, I remember your face. Alizé huh? Nice name."

"Thanks. My mom's a fan of Tupac." She laughed. "But we'll go for sure."

"Really?" His eyes seemed to light up as Alizé spoke. "That's sweet! Alright cool, got a cell?" he said, sitting down next to Alizé and fishing in his pocket for his phone.

Shayde watched the two interact from her side of the table. Being so close to him had made her skin feel warm, although it now seemed to be cooling at his sudden interest in Alizé and not her.

He said Jason was wondering, she thought gloomily to

herself. *Jay was the reason he had come over to the table at all. Jason wants me to go, not Kruise and Kruise wants Alizé.*

Sinking back into the booth, she pulled the menu up over her face and tried to hide behind it as Kruise and Alizé flirted.

Alizé Ryan was the same age as Shayde, having just turned sixteen on the fifth of June, Shayde's birthday being on the ninth. She was a little taller than Shayde and had medium length, dark brown hair, that she straightened daily, and big blue eyes. Her body was curvaceous, and she embraced her curves and carried them with a sexy elegance. Alizé was very blunt and didn't mind telling anyone what she thought of them, and god help anyone who wronged her—she would wait years to wreak vengeance on them. She had been Shayde's best friend since sixth grade, more like a sister than a friend.

Shayde listened to the two of them talk while trying to pretend she was carefully mulling over what she was going to eat. When she peeked over at them again, Kruise was holding Alizé's phone in his hands.

"Okay, here's my number," he said, returning her phone. "Text me yours and we'll set everything up later. We're still trying to figure out the details and work out the kinks."

"Sure, yeah no problem," Alizé said, texting Kruise her number. "Sounds like fun!" She set the phone on the table and regarded Kruise again, almost amused.

"Sweet," Kruise said, smiling. "We're gonna try to get a keg and a couple cases, we will be there all weekend." He raked his hands through his short hair and stood up. "So, we'll talk to you soon then, I guess?" Shayde looked up and his eyes were on hers again. She was sure she appeared as annoyed as she felt.

"Okay. Bye then." Her tone was edged as sharp as a razor

blade. She was trying to sound indifferent, but it came out irritated.

"Later."

She averted her eyes from his and he walked off.

After he was back at his table Alizé leaned in and whispered, "Girl, what's wrong with you! You barely said two words to him and what you did say to him was rude."

"Well I froze. And then he said *Jason* was the one who wanted me to go and he showed more interest in you than in me," Shayde snapped sulkily.

A girl with short brown hair in a multi-colored uniform was suddenly at the end of their table.

"Hi girls, I'm April," she said, setting coasters down in front of them. "I'll be your server today. Can I get you started on something to drink and an appetizer?"

"Sure, yeah I'll take a Coke and these cheese sticks sound good," Shayde said, pointing to the item on the menu. "Um, and then—I'm ready, if you are Zey."

"No, I still need a few, but I'll take an Iced Tea and um—" She inspected the menu, her eyes scanning the pictures. "This artichoke dip sounds good."

"Right on, cool I'll go put that in and grab those drinks," April said and she trotted off.

"What the hell are you talking about, more interested in me? It's because I was the only one being nice to him and actually giving him the time of day," Alizé said in a retaliatory tone. "He probably used Jason as a cover to come over and talk to you. Besides, I think Jason is way hotter than Kruise."

"First of all, you are nuts! And secondly, why didn't he sit down next to me and ask me for my number?" She knew that she was being childish but it was her first real crush and she was jealous.

"Like I said, you were being rude to him." Alizé didn't even make eye contact with her as she read over the menu. "He probably was afraid that you would bite his head off if he sat down next to you. You didn't even tell him it was your birthday," she said, putting it down as she scrutinized her.

"It's not that big of a deal to me." She paused. Looking down she said, "Was I really that bad? I wasn't trying to sound so rude; it's just that I got so nervous. Do you think I just messed it all up?"

"I don't think you did girl, just next time, relax and be yourself, you have nothing to be worried about."

The way Alizé was talking made her feel a little better. In that moment, it seemed as though it was Alizé that Kruise wanted, but maybe Alizé was right. Maybe he was just using Jay as a cover. It was funny, before they arrived at the diner, she hadn't really even thought about him, aside from the times that she would see him in school. Now, suddenly, he was her crush and she cared who he was trying to flirt with. Funny how one moment can change a person.

She had always thought he was attractive, but something about the way that he looked today made her insides melt. The way the butterflies rose up in her stomach when he approached their table told her that she really did have a crush on him; she just hadn't admitted it to herself—until now.

April approached with the drinks and set them on the table. "Ready?" she asked, pulling out her pad and pencil.

"Yeah," Shayde said, distractedly. "I'll have a bacon cheeseburger with no onions and some fries please."

The waitress turned to. "And for you?"

"I'll just take this chicken sandwich please. Thanks."

"Sure thing," the waitress smiled, taking Alizé's menu from her. "The apps will be up shortly."

"Thank you," Alizé said.

"Sure." She turned and walked off.

"So," Shayde started, returning her attention to her friend across the way, "we're really doing this then, yeah?"

"Damn straight! It's gonna be so much fun Shayde, think of it as an escape. I mean, you haven't left Salem since…" She trailed off. "It will be good for you to get out of town and let loose. You need it. And, you may even end up with your first real boyfriend!" She chuckled.

Shayde's heart galloped at the thought of being away with Kruise, and being so close to him that she could get lost in those hazel eyes. Being in a cabin with him for a whole weekend, away from everything familiar, sounded welcoming and might give light to a world that seemed lately to be shrouded in darkness. The question was, would her mom go for it? There was nothing that she couldn't tell Tara, and even when she had tried to lie to her about something, Tara always seemed to know when Shayde wasn't being honest. Telling her mom the truth was non-negotiable.

"Okay, well I'm gonna have to tell my mom what I'm doing. Ever since—you know—she has been super overprotective. I don't even know if she will go for it."

"Just tell her that it's me and you and some other girls. Don't tell her there's gonna be booze and boys. Tell her we planned this for you for your birthday."

The server appeared again, appetizers in hand.

"Yum! Thanks." Shayde said as the plates were set down on the table. Shayde glanced over her shoulder to see if the guys were still there, and they were. She heard them laughing and she could just imagine Kruise's smile. His perfect lips curling at the edges, revealing his straight white teeth, his left incisor slightly protruding further than the others; a slight imperfection in an otherwise flawless face, but something that suited him perfectly. "Should I go over there and apologize for the way I acted?"

"Nah; let him suffer. Guys fall hard for women who play hard to get," Alizé said, dipping a piece of bread into the steaming hot artichoke dip.

Suddenly, bright light flashed at the back of Shayde's eyes, she could see Alizé still, but it was as if she was a few minutes ahead in time. She saw Alizé biting into the piece of bread, the steaming goop burning the roof of her mouth, making her drop the piece of bread, spit out the contents onto the plate, and shriek at the top of her lungs.

Alizé put the bread up to her mouth and bit down.

"*OOHH,*" she screeched and fanned her mouth with her hands as if it would help. "*Hot! Hot!*"

"You didn't see that happening?" Shayde laughed at her friend. "You're a retard!"

"I couldn't help it, it looked so damn good! I just burnt the crap out of the roof of my mouth. That is really going to hurt later. Ow," she said, still inhaling rapidly to cool off her scorched mouth.

Shayde couldn't help but giggle and Alizé laughed right along with her.

Taking a drink of water, she started to calm down. "So anyways, you think your mom will go for it?" she continued.

"I don't know. All we can do is hope that she does."

"Yeah. So, what have you gotten for your birthday so far?"

"My parents got me the car I wanted even though I never mentioned it to anyone. It was really weird."

"Huh," Alizé said as she blew on her next bite. "What they get you?"

"A sea-green convertible bug. It is so cute, I love it!"

"That's awesome! Was that all?"

"No, they have something planned for tonight that they are being really secretive about."

"Maybe it's a surprise party."

"I hope not. I hate surprises."

THREE

K ruise was so lost in thought as he drove down the road that he was barely able to pay attention to the traffic. He'd finally got up the nerve to go up to Shayde and speak to her, and all it got him was her bizarre behavior. That strange, beautiful creature with the bright green eyes.

Maybe she was a vampire or a werewolf, like in Twilight. He laughed at himself.

Really, he didn't have anything to go on, being that he had never tried talking to her before, but still, there was something about the way she had talked to him that told him she was annoyed. Yet the look hiding behind those gorgeous eyes when he first went up to her told him that she knew who he was. It hadn't been a simple glance; it had been as though she took a running leap right into his soul. He had been so nervous, tripping over his words and trying to play it cool at the same time. Maybe she had been just as nervous as he was and that was the reason for the coldness. The way she reacted was not what he wanted, but at least the effort he had made had gotten her and her friend to agree to go with him and Jay for the weekend. His his stomach flipped at the thought of her actually being so close to him, and for longer than just a class—where they never had the chance to actually talk and get to know one another.

"You alright, bro?" Jay asked from the passenger side, pulling him up out of his reverie.

"Yeah, just thinking," he replied, stopping at a traffic light. "That was so weird; I—I don't really know what to think."

"What was? Your chick?"

"Yeah. It just seemed like she didn't really even want to come. Like her friend was forcing her to or something. She barely even spoke two words to me. Alizé was the only one that kept the conversation going, so of course I had to talk to her. And now I think they think I'm interested in Alizé and not in Shayde."

"Dude, who cares. They'll find out this weekend who you are interested in." He paused. "Hey, I have an idea... You said you got Alizé's number, right?"

"Yeah..."

"So, text her and ask her about Shayde. Ask if she's seeing anyone and what her type is and stuff, and what is really up with the strange broad," Jason chortled.

That could work.

"Alright," he said, pulling his phone out from his pants' pocket. "What should I say?"

"Um, say…" Jay was looking out the front windshield, apparently deep in thought. "Just say 'hey' first and see what she says back."

Finding Alizé's number, he began to text but when he looked up, the light had turned to green. He handed the phone to Jay. "Will you do it?"

Jay took it and texted the word into Kruise's phone for him.

"Thanks. So did you check Air B&B about those cabins?" Kruise asked, turning onto their friend Jordan's street.

"I did. I found one that is only a hundred and fifty for the weekend. It's only two bedrooms though."

"That's cool; we'll just give the bedrooms to Jordan and Hannah and Danny and Amy. I seriously don't think either you or I will need them!" Kruise laughed.

"Dude, speak for yourself, I'm gonna totally try to flirt with Alizé. I heard she gets down sometimes," Jason said just as Kruise's phone alerted him that there was an incoming text message.

"Yeah, with her boyfriends, dumbass!" he said playfully. "What's it say?" He inclined his head towards the phone resting on Jay's lap.

"You never know. Maybe with a bunch of beer and some pot, she'll think me the sexiest man on earth!" Jay said, rubbing his belly with one hand as he clicked the phone on with the other. "It says '*Hey!*' with an exclamation point. Good sign!" Jay said derisively.

"Sweet. Alright now what do we say?" Kruise said as he

parked his black Toyota in front of Jordan's parents' house and killed the engine.

"Um, what's up? I don't know dude this is your conversation. Here, take it," Jay said as he tossed the phone back to Kruise who grasped at it clumsily. "You take over now; it's your damn phone!"

"*Thanks*, bro," he answered, steadying the phone in his right hand. "You could've told her it was you and start putting the moves on her now to sweeten her up for the weekend."

"Yeah, true. Just tell her I think she is hot!" He laughed.

As they climbed out of the truck and started to walk towards the house, Kruise was trying to think of something clever to say. He wanted to make sure that Alizé knew he was interested in her friend, not her, but didn't want to come right out with it in the first text. Deciding on something simple, he put,

> What you guys up to?

and hit send as they approached Jordan's front door and knocked.

The storm door was open and through the screen door they could see Jordan appear at the back. "It's open," he shouted. "C'mon back."

Jordan's parents were currently out of town, which was common in the summertime. They had a boat that they would often go out on for weeks at a time, leaving Jordan home alone. Kruise knew that Jordan didn't mind at all because he would have his girlfriend, Hannah, over as much as he wanted. He wasn't sure if Jordan's parents knew this or not, but if they did, they didn't seem to mind. It had been the same way last summer too.

Jordan Black was a tall, bulky fellow standing at about six foot three, with white blonde, unkempt hair and bright blue eyes. His skin was a pale white but his cheeks were often red and his eyebrows and eyelashes were the same color blonde as his hair. He was a year older than Kruise and Jay but had been hanging out with them since junior high school. Jordan was the type of guy that was cynical about absolutely everything, and Kruise didn't think he had ever heard Jordan say something positive about anything the entire time he'd known him.

"What you guys up to?" Jay asked as they reached Jordan out on the porch.

Hannah, Danny and Amy were already there, relaxing on the couch under a large green and black awning.

Hannah and Amy were both short blonde girls, except Hannah had shoulder-length hair and angular features while Amy had longer hair with a chubbier, cherub-like face.

There was a little white radio blaring music from its post on the grill, a blue cooler at its side, which no doubt was loaded with beer—knowing Danny—and they were passing around a joint.

The covered porch was at the foot of a large green lawn, which spanned out at least three hundred feet each way. The yard was bordered by a chain-linked fence, beyond which was a dense park that was criss-crossed with bike trails and large, looming trees. Kruise enjoyed going over to Jordan's house during the summer to relax on the couch with his friends, with not a worry in the world except laughing and people watching. It was one of his favorite pastimes.

"What's up fellas?" Danny greeted them warmly. He opened the cooler and handed them each a beer. "What you up to?"

Kruise grabbed the beer and popped it open with a loud crack. "Not much. Just got done with lunch." He took a large swig. "We figured out some stuff for this weekend. Speaking of which, Jordan, did you talk to your brother yet?"

"Nah, not yet. I texted him but he's at work 'til five. He'll probably get a break and be able to meet us before then though. I'm sure he'll do it though, you know Mike," Jordan said, leaning against one of the awning's posts.

Kruise's phone vibrated with a chime in his pocket and he pulled it out. There was one new message from Alizé. It said that she and her friends were at the docks getting their toes done. After reading it he said, "That's cool," to Jordan. "We found a cabin that was only one-fifty for the weekend, right on the beach. It only has two bedrooms though, which can be for the couples of course. But split between eight that's only like twenty bucks apiece."

"Eight?" Danny exclaimed, sounding surprised. "Who are the last two?"

"Two hot chicks from the diner!" Jay blurted out loudly and laughed at himself as he took a hit off the joint and passed it to Amy.

Hannah rolled her eyes as Amy took the joint from Jay. Hannah and Amy had a difference in opinion when it came to the boys' talk of females. Amy didn't mind it at all and Hannah always took offense to it. Hannah didn't like when they called girls by demeaning terms and corrected them every time they said "chicks". It seemed as though this time was not going to be an exception. As she began to lay into them and the discussion started, Kruise decided to tune it out and respond to Alizé's text.

After hitting send, he interrupted Hannah's diatribe on sexism to fill in the blanks from Jay's outburst. "Yeah, um, you know Shayde Gamic and Alizé Ryan?"

"SHAYDE GAMIC?!" Danny burst out as he grabbed the joint from Amy. "Damn! She's smoking!" Amy's annoyed expression made it known that she was not at all pleased by his observation. She might be unfazed by the boy's terms for females but fancying other women was another matter. "Uh, I mean she's alright," he muddled on, trying to recover and avoid evoking Amy's predatory notice. But her eyes were fixed on him, yelling at him with her stare, and Kruise knew that she didn't buy his evasive correction. That was just how Dan was though, very blunt and most times he never thought about what he's going to say before he said it.

Danny, seemingly ignoring her, tried to pass the joint to Kruise. Holding up a passive hand Kruise shook his head. "None for me right now. Gotta drive." He watched Dan pass it to Jordan and looked back at Amy, who was still staring at Danny. "It's cool Amy," he said to her reassuringly, trying to get her gaze to lighten a little. "He only has eyes for you!"

Dan Lawson was the most spontaneous of the guys in the group. There was a certain boldness and candor about him that either made him either really likeable or real easy to hate. His forwardness with people was frequently aggravating to Kruise, as he had the tendency to just say whatever it was that was on his mind, no matter who it hurt. He was smaller than the other guys and as thin as a stick, even though he could eat whatever he wanted without gaining a pound. Being erratic and crazy were just some of his traits and he never thought through his decisions. He was diabetic but still drank like a fish and would eat whatever he wanted. Amy had been his girlfriend for a few years and, honestly, Kruise didn't know why she stuck around because his treatment of her was not the best. Even though he said he loved her deeply, he often broke plans with her to go drinking with his friends. They fought three or four times a week and no one really knew why they were together still. Breaking up with each other was a common factor in their relationship too, they seemed to break up and get back together more than anyone else Kruise knew.

When Kruise's phone sounded again, a current of excitement surged through him. It was Alizé. He had asked her if Shayde was single and she countered that she was and then asked whether Jason was single.

Jay had been dumped by his girlfriend of three years recently. This had hurt him deeply and he had found it difficult to trust girls since then, nor did he ever want to be hurt by one again, but Kruise knew he wouldn't pass up an opportunity to flirt with Alizé.

Relief washed over him, now that Alizé knew he was interested in Shayde not her, and that Shayde was available. The realization that Jay's interest in Alizé was not unrequited also played a part in deepening his excitement for the upcoming weekend. It seemed Jason also had a chance at flirting with a girl he was crushing on. He responded by asking her what type of guys Shayde liked.

"That's craziness," Danny resumed, taking a drink of his beer. "Have you talked to her before or was this the first time?"

"It would have been his first time, if he had actually talked to her and not her friend!" Jay snorted letting out a deep belly laugh as he grabbed the joint from Jordan.

Kruise's cell beeped again.

Alizé told him that he was Shayde's type.

She has a funny way of showing it, he thought inwardly.

> So, why didn't she talk to me at the diner?

he texted back, then stood up to sock Jay on the arm. "Yeah, only cause she was being weird at first."

"How was she being weird?" Hannah asked, she was now interested in the conversation.

"I don't know, she just barely talked to me, and what she did say was almost snappy like she was annoyed."

"She was probably just nervous," Hannah offered. "I don't know that much about Shayde but what I do know about her is that she's very unsociable with the guys. Her brother practically blocked every guy from getting to her, so she's probably not that used to it."

Kruise knew that Shayde and Hannah weren't exactly friends, but Hannah knew the people that Shayde knew, so was more on the in than he was.

He clicked his phone on when it chimed once again.

She was nervous and feels pretty bad about it. If it helps, she's super excited about this weekend if her parents let her go. Her number is 978-744-9125. You should text her and give Jason my number and tell him to text me. Maybe then we can start talking to who we really want to!

"Yeah, you're right," Kruise said to Hannah. "Her friend just told me that she was." He turned back to his phone and told Alizé that sounded good and then glanced at Jay, who seemed to be lost in thought, staring at an ant on the ground. Smiling, he said, "Hey bro, Alizé wants you to text her. I'll send her number to you in a message."

"Sweet. So, what's going on tonight then?" Jason said, changing the subject.

"I think we were just gonna drink over here," Dan answered, stubbing out the last of the joint into the ashtray on the ground. "You guys down?"

"Nah," Kruise replied. "I gotta work tomorrow morning, bright and early."

As he talked, he plugged Shayde's number into his phone. Staring at her name in digital letters on his cell phone, he thought about how to approach her and what to say. He settled on just saying hello. No more than what seemed like two seconds later, his phone beeped loudly in his hand. It was her. His heart raced.

Hi

she said.

Sorry about earlier.

"What about you, Jay?" Dan asked, surreptitiously pulling Amy down off the arm of the couch and into his lap. "Are you gonna kick it tonight?"

"Um, I'm not sure," Jay said. "I'm supposed to get up early and go look for a job. Doesn't do much good for me to be hung over, I'm pretty much worthless when I'm hanging."

"Then don't get wasted retard. Just have a few," Dan retorted.

"Right! Jay only have a few! HA!" Kruise laughed again as he typed in his next message to Shayde. He told her that he understood that it was nerves and that he was pretty nervous himself.

Jason threw a pebble at Kruise. "Sometimes I can, ya dick!"

"Sure thing Jay!" Kruise snickered sarcastically. "So did you reserve that cabin, then?"

"No. I should probably do that. I'm on it," he said, pulling out his phone and walking off towards the yard.

Kruise's phone sang to him again.

Why would someone like you be nervous? You probably have tons of experience with the ladies LOL.

The thought of her texting him made him smile. There she was, sitting somewhere, thinking of him. So many times he had sat in class, day dreaming about moments like this. Though it was only text messaging, it was the most that they had ever communicated and every text he got felt like opening a gift at

Christmas. No matter how short, he knew that they were steppingstones to far greater things. He could just imagine her beautiful green eyes glowing and her smile as he told her how gorgeous she was. He imagined sitting on the dock with her, their feet in the water, staring intently into each other's eyes. How he longed to caress her beautifully soft face and lean in for the sweetest kiss—

"KRUISE!" Jason's obnoxious voice pierced through his wonderful daydream. "Yo man, where'd you go? We need a card to hold the place and you know I don't have that kind of money in my account," he said, phone frozen in the palm of his hand with the Air B&B screen up.

Kruise reached in his back pocket, pulled out his wallet, and retrieved his Visa debit card. "Everyone's gotta pay me by this weekend though. One fifty's all I got in that account."

"No problem," Jordan said, pulling out two twenties from his wallet and handing them to Kruise. "Here's our share."

"Yeah, here's ours too," Dan said, handing him a fifty. "Keep the change."

"Right on, thanks guys," Kruise said as he shoved the money into his wallet.

Turning his attention back to the conversation with Shayde, he pondered on what to say to her next. It was hard to find the right words to say to someone so beautiful. What *were* the right words to say? What if he spoke the wrong ones? New beginnings were always as hard as they were exciting.

His fingers began to press the keys as if they had their own free will. When he looked down, what he read was,

Well, with someone as beautiful as yourself, one finds it harder than one thinks to find the right things to say.

It was as though the words had chosen themselves.

"Alright, here," Jay said, shoving the card back at Kruise as he stared at the last message as though it was typed by someone else. "It's all set, we're ready to rock. Now all we need is for someone to get us liquor. What time is it?" Jay asked the air as he looked at his phone. "Four-thirty," he announced to himself.

"Yeah cool," Jordan said, grabbing another Pabst from the cooler and popping the top. "Mike should be getting off of work soon and then he'll get back to me. But I'm saying, I'm sure he'll do it, he's a partier, and he remembers what it was like being our age and not being able to buy beer."

Mike was Jordan's brother. He was older than they were and bought Jordan alcohol whenever he wanted. They used to hang out with him a lot, but his drinking had gotten out of control and nowadays he was a sloppy drunk who was annoying. Sadly, they just used him to buy beer for them whenever they needed it.

"How's he doing lately?" Jason asked Jordan. "I haven't seen him in a while."

"Oh, you know the same. Pretty much drunk whenever he ain't workin'," Jordan said quietly. He didn't like to talk about it much. They had tried to get him help before, but he wouldn't go and then they figured after his DUI he would slow down, but he never did.

"That's too bad," Dan said, taking a drink of his beer.

Dan wasn't really one to talk; the diabetic that drank as often as Mike did. Getting too drunk to remember to take his insulin and going into diabetic coma was something that had happened more than once. They tried to get him to slow down too, but he insisted that he was fine, a free bird doing whatever he wished, no matter who it hurt. He was only sixteen too, which was the saddest part. He didn't seem to realize that as he got older, the drinking would slowly put him in his grave. Not even Amy was able to get that through his thick skull. He was lucky to have her; she had saved his life more than once. After not responding to her text messages, and knowing that he sometimes got so wasted that he forgot to check his blood sugar, she had tracked him down and found him unconscious. She had checked his glucose levels and injected the appropriate amount of insulin into him accordingly, then put him some-where safe to sleep it off. No one really knew why she kept putting herself through it.

Kruise's phone beeped again.

Shayde replied that he was sweet.

Benny's was the local breakfast place.

"Yeah bro," Jason interrupted. "He's cool though. He still has his job you know. I'm sure he'll quit drinking eventually." It was clear that Jason had noticed Jordan's apprehension and was trying to make him feel better.

Jordan's phone beeped seconds later.

"If you speak of the devil he shall answer," Jordan announced. He read over the message and then relayed it to them. "Says he's going away for the weekend too, so if we want liquor, we better meet him now because he's leaving tomorrow morning."

"Cool, let's go then, shall we," Jay offered. "Kruise'll drive since he's only had half a beer!" He laughed as he volunteered his friend.

Kruise was eyeing him discontentedly, about to protest when his phone loudly interrupted. Distracted, he read the message instead. Shayde had responded that she still had to ask her mom, but she was pretty sure she'd be able to go. As he stood back up and stretched, he clicked the phone off. "Oh, okay let's go then." He didn't feel like arguing, he was too happy.

Dan chugged the rest of his beer, as did Jordan.

"Not everyone will fit in his truck," Hannah said pointedly, slipping on her flip-flops. "I can drive too."

"Okay cool. We'll meet you there," Kruise said as they began to file into the house.

As they walked, Kruise sent another text to Shayde asking her if there was anything she wanted from the liquor store. As he was climbing into his truck, she responded saying to get her anything that he thought she'd like and also asked if he needed any money. Quickly responding with a no, he turned the keys and started the engine.

Jay climbed in next to him. "Sounds like it's going well so far. Your phone's going off more than it normally does!" He laughed.

Normally, Kruise would have a clever come back but his

head was in the clouds. He just smiled and answered, "Yeah, it's going well so far. She said she was just nervous at the diner. What about you? You text Alizé yet?"

"Yeah, I have been talking to her," Jay affirmed as he rolled down the window. "Told her we got that place and asked if she wanted anything from the L-Q. She said she just wanted some beer and asked if we needed any money."

"Yeah, that's what Shayde said too. I told her no. I also told her to meet us at Benny's on Friday at eight for breakfast before we head out. Does that sound good?"

"Yeah, that's cool." Jay paused after his phone chimed loudly. "Hey bro, did you know its Shayde's birthday today?"

"No, I didn't know that at all."

When they stopped at a light, Kruise made sure to tell her happy birthday.

They sat in silence the rest of the way, both sporadically texting the girls they had basically just met earlier that afternoon, lost in thought.

Kruise wondered if Shayde's mom would actually let her go on such short notice, and the thought of him getting his hopes up for nothing nearly constricted his chest. She had to be able to go, she just had to. There were so many things that he wanted to find out about her, and finally begin to get to know the personality behind the beauty. He was a pretty good judge of character and could normally tell the difference between a girl who just had looks and no personality at all, and a girl who had a personality that matched the exquisiteness of her face. Shayde was one of those girls. The kind of girl that was flawless, breathtakingly so, yet he had no idea how beautiful she actually was. Thoughts of her preoccupied him as he drove towards Mike's. When they were almost there, his phone sounded again.

It read,

> Let me guess, Alizé told Jason.
> Awesome. Thanks though, that's very
> nice of you!

He was smiling from ear to ear as they arrived at Mike's building and parked next to Hannah. Even though they were simple little texts, each and every one of them made his heart jump. It had been a long time since he had been this happy.

He killed the engine and wrote her back asking her what her birthday plans were. Jordan appeared at his window.

"So, money and list of what you want," he said bluntly.

Kruise pulled out his wallet again and handed him the two twenties Jordan had given him earlier. "Let's do a case and put the rest towards the keg."

Jordan took the money. "Cool, Jay?"

Jason pulled out his wallet and produced a twenty. "Just a case. I only got another twenty for the cabin. You guys don't mind me not pitching on the keg do you?" He looked at them with his big puppy-dog eyes.

"Nah, it's cool bro," Jordan answered as he reached across Kruise and yanked the money out of his hand, "but you should really get a job soon. Shit's getting old."

Kruise knew that he was just being sarcastic, as he was with everything.

"Screw you dude!" Jay called back to him grinning, as Jordan turned and walked towards the apartments.

Conveniently the liquor store was right next door to Mike's

apartment complex, which was both bad and good. Bad for Mike, being that he was an alcoholic and lived so close to the resource, and good for them that they didn't have to make two trips.

Kruise's phone beeped again.

> My parents have something big planned for me and I have no idea what it is. I'm pretty nervous and excited about it. What about you, you have any plans?

> Nah, I have to work in the morning. But how exciting for you, I wonder what they have planned. You will have to keep me informed.

he replied.

The gentle click of fingers pressing buttons were the only sound in the cab of the truck. Kruise knew that Jay was talking to Alizé as he was never on his phone that often.

"What you guys talking about?" Kruise asked him.

"Oh, just about this weekend and stuff. She seems pretty cool, she likes to party," he said, finishing his text and setting his phone down on his lap.

"Awesome, you two will get along famously!" Kruise laughed.

"I know right!" Jay responded.

Kruise's phone went off again and Shayde told him that she'd keep him posted, and then asked where he worked.

he responded immediately.

As he hit send, he looked in the rearview mirror to see Mike and Jordan emerge from the liquor store with an attendant who was wheeling a dolly with the keg on it. Seeing the keg and knowing who he would be with next time he saw it, sent hot waves of excitement surge up inside of him.

He jumped down from the truck and helped them load the keg. As soon as the attendant was out of sight, Kruise held his hand out to Mike.

"Thanks, man. We really appreciate it," Kruise said as the boys exchanged handshakes.

"Sure, not a problem. What you guys doing this weekend?" Mike asked, leaning against the back of Kruise's truck as he popped open a beer that he had in his pocket.

"Got a cabin in Cape Cod for the weekend," Jason replied, emerging from his side of the truck. "Gonna lay on the beach and get drunk all day!"

"Nice, that sounds like fun!" Mike chimed back and loudly slurped down half his beer. "Well you guys have fun and be safe. We're going to Atlantic City tomorrow to do some gambling and to climb Black-out Mountain!" He guffawed loudly.

"Sweet dude, sounds like a blast," Kruise said despairingly. Mike seemed oblivious to the sarcasm.

"Oh it will be!" He laughed.

"Well, have fun," Jordan told his brother. "Be safe bro and

thanks again." He held out his hand and they shook with a hug to complete it.

"Will do lil' bro, you too. Later guys," he said as he turned and started walking back towards his apartments.

"Later," they all said in unison.

"Back to my house?" Jordan asked. "We'll put the keg and the other cases in the kegerator to stay cold for this weekend."

"Sounds good, see you there," Kruise said and climbed into his black truck, shut the door, and started it.

He awoke the phone by pressing the side button as Jay climbed in next to him. A little envelope on the home screen indicated that he had one new message. It was her. Without even reading the message, little fireflies lit up in his heart.

She said

> That's awesome that you have a job. I'm thinking of getting a job as like a waitress or something. Sometimes I would just like to focus on something else, escape from my thoughts and do something mundane.

Reading her text something dawned on him, like a spark lighting up the dark. They both had something pivotal in common. The escape that she was talking about was getting away from the memory of losing somebody. They both had suffered tremendous loss, her with her brother and he with his mom. He had never made that connection until then.

Simon had helped him get the job at Quimby's when he was eleven years old, the year his mother had died. It had got him out of the gloomy house and get his minds off things. He hadn't really thought about it in that way before but he supposed work was a sort of escape.

Kruise backed up and started down the road towards Jordan's house.

For sure, that is exactly how I see it. And it is nice to buy the things that you want without having to ask your parents for money.

he responded to her while they were at a stop light.

When they pulled back up to Jordan's house, Kruise hopped out and he and Jay unloaded the keg while Jordan ran in and opened the garage door for them. They stuck the keg and the cases of beer in the fridge and what they couldn't fit they just laid on the ground next to it.

"We'll get some ice sometime this weekend," Jordan said, closing the door to the mini fridge. "What's cold should last us the first day and a half hopefully!" He laughed as they headed out to the back porch.

"Just make sure that you guys don't drink it all before then!" Kruise said, punching Dan in the arm, directing the last comment to him personally. He knew that Dan would if he had the chance.

Dan bent down and opened the blue cooler. Grabbing another beer, he opened it, took a drink and burped loudly in Kruise's face. "I won't dill hole!"

Smiling, Kruise took a seat on the couch out back just as his phone began vibrating again in his pocket, he tried to quell the grin on his face anticipating who it was from. He pulled it out and opened it.

He didn't want to seem like a last text freak so he thought he'd leave it for a while. He figured he would text her later on in the evening and find out what the big surprise was that her parents had planned for her.

The group sat around and chatted for hours.

When the sky began to turn to violet, twilight whispered that it was time to go home. He had to work in the morning, and if he were to stay any longer the bowl that was being passed and the beers in the cooler, would start calling and he would end up staying up way too late for his own good. Five a.m. came fast when he stayed up passed twelve.

"Alright," he said, standing up. "I gotta get. Jay, you coming or staying?"

"I'm gonna chill for a while," Jay responded from his spot on the couch, reclined with his feet stretched out and a beer resting on his belly. "If these guys are too drunk to drive me home later I'll just walk."

"Alright cool," Kruise said, holding out his hand.

Jay took Kruise's hand with the one that was not on the beer. "Later."

"Later guys," Kruise said,

He left through the darkened house and made his way out to his truck. Their house was not far from Jordan's so he wasn't worried about Jay. If Jay drank too much, which he had the tendency to do, he could walk.

When Kruise got into his truck, it was about ten 'til nine. He thought about Shayde, wondering what she could be up to. He wondered if he should text her now and see how she was doing or if he should just wait for her to text him first.

Turning the ignition on, the truck revved to life and he began his drive home.

Although it had been quite awkward at first, they had really hit it off in their text messages, and he was excited to see where things were going to go. All that was on his mind now was her. As he advanced down the road all he could see was her bright green eyes, her long red hair, and her soft, sweet lips. He couldn't wait 'til the next time he saw her, he secretly hoped it would be sooner than Friday.

When he thought about the upcoming weekend his heart rippled at the thought of being alone with her. Just thinking of her sent a charge through his skin, rippling through his layers and to prickle at his center. He had heard of things like this, from his friends and in movies, but he never considered it to actually be real. It was the very essence of a fairy tale. Normally he didn't believe in that kind of thing but when he thought of her he suddenly felt different about the world, as if it was getting smaller and less complex. Things just made sense when he thought of her, as if his mind was becoming clearer, that he was coming out of the fog that the loss of his mom created.

And he liked it.

FOUR

After lunch, Alizé and Shayde were driving down Main Street in Shayde's new bug, top down with the warm summer air blowing their hair wildly in the wind. Alizé was excited about the coming weekend and kept asking Shayde what she thought Jay was like in person. Shayde's replies were short, she was distracted; worried that her parents wouldn't let her go on the weekend getaway and trying not to think of what would happen if she didn't go. Would it be her last chance with him?

Courtney, Dawn and Cherie, some of her other friends, were waiting for them at the docks. There was a nail salon in the harbor that they all liked to go to for pedicures and they were treating Shayde for her birthday. She was looking forward to spending the day with her friends but couldn't shake the miserable feeling that her mother was going to say no. For the most part, she tried keeping the smile on her face as Alizé excitedly talked about the trip, hoping she wouldn't see the uncertainty that Shayde felt was clearly written on her face.

She pulled the little bug into a spot across the street from the salon and put the top up. The two young women got out and waited for the pedestrian light to turn green. Crossing the road, they spotted the girls waiting for them by a newspaper stand.

"Shayde!" Courtney exclaimed, running up to her and hugging her. She had a pink, polka-dotted gift bag in her hands that she handed to her. "Happy birthday!"

Courtney Daniels was the same height as Shayde, but skinnier. She was almost three years older than her, turning nineteen in November and had just graduated high school two weeks earlier. Shayde had met Courtney at the middle school they attended together and they became friends.

Courtney dyed her hair so often that they really didn't know what color it was naturally. She wore it prettily though, short to her shoulders and she straightened it all the time. Lately it was dark black with bright streaks in it, which were supposed to be red but had turned pink. She was so beautiful that she pulled it off. Courtney had tons of clothes and dressed the best out of all of the girls. Shayde didn't think she had seen her in the same outfit twice. And shoes, the girl loved shoes more than she loved boys. Oh, but did she love boys too. She changed boyfriends more often than she changed her hairstyle. But aside from her fickle heart, Courtney was a loyal, loving friend. She would do anything for anyone she loved and would be there for them no matter what.

"Oh Court, you shouldn't have!" Shayde smiled, taking the bag.

"Maybe I shouldn't have either!" Dawn said, handing Shayde the purple and brown gift bag that she held in her hands.

Dawn Smith was the prettiest one of the girls, in the opinion of most observers. Having turned seventeen that March, she was over a year older than Shayde. Standing at five three, she was of Spanish origin and was always a soft tan color all year around. Her eyes were bright green, framed by perfectly sculpted eyebrows, and her hair was dark, which she wore long and straight. Not only was she gorgeous, she was funny and had the most beautiful personality. Shayde and Dawn had the best time when they were alone together and laughed like it was going out of style. They saw eye to eye about a lot of things and their personalities were the most similar.

Shayde reluctantly grabbed the bag from Dawn. "Oh, you guys! I told you that the day with you girls was my present and not to get me anything else!" she said, hugging Dawn with her free hand.

"Oh, here, me too!" Cherie said, pulling her away from Dawn and handing her a smaller, but equally thoughtful gift. Giving her hug as well, Shayde's hand touched Cherie's back. Dread filled her; she had the feeling that there was something Cherie was dying to tell her, and she couldn't shake the feeling of impending doom.

Cherie Grey was a year older than Courtney, about to turn twenty that July. They had met at the call center they both worked at, and Courtney had introduced her to the group. Cherie was the most independent of all the girls, having moved out of her parents' house the weekend after she graduated high school, and she'd had the same job since she was sixteen. She was a little heavier than the rest of the girls but she was, by far, the sweetest. Her hair was incredibly long and red with blonde streaks. The red of her hair was different from Shayde's though, hers was more the color of a Caribbean sunset. Cherie's personality was as beautiful as her face and it was this that made her attractive, but she lacked confidence perhaps because she wasn't as skinny as the other girls; however, they could never really get to the bottom of it. The girls tried to reassure her more than once that she was just as beautiful, if not more so than they were because of her bubbly personality, but it never did any good. She was so lacking in confidence she would fall in love with a guy just because he gave her a bit of attention, no matter if they were a bad one.

True to form, Cherie had fallen in love with the wrong guy. His name was Nate. She met him at work at the call center. At first, they just started off as friends; Nate had a girlfriend who actually lived with him. When they started hanging out a lot, it was apparent that they had started a love affair, though not one of the girls would call it real love. He began to stay at her house frequently, unbeknownst to his girlfriend. It was clear to everyone but Cherie that he used her for things; money, rides, and other things of that sort, yet Cherie was oblivious to it. She was constantly at his beck and call even though he was never there for her in return. He told her things, when it was just the two of them, that made her swoon and then as soon as the sun came up and there were other people around, he would treat her as someone he just simply knew.

Nate was a manipulative, twisted individual, and she was putty in his hands. At one point he even persuaded Cherie to befriend his live-in girlfriend Liz and the three of them would go out together. Liz had no idea that the two of them were actually sleeping together behind her back. Shayde had accompanied Cherie to the movies one night along with Nate and Liz. He had sat between Cherie and Liz with a smug look on his face and Shayde had been disgusted with both of them. She couldn't believe that Cherie could do that to some innocent girl, but it was as if Nate had bewitched her. She would do anything for him.

This had gone on for a few years, Liz had come and gone as did so many others, yet he refused to ever make Cherie his one and only, keeping her at an arm's length. She would know of the other girlfriends, yet they would know nothing of her.

So many times Shayde just wished that she could get her friend away from this spoilt boy that didn't even have the right to be called a man, but no hopes or wishes would ever do any good. Cherie was entranced by him.

Cherie was holding the door open for the circle of friends and they began to file into the salon. Just as Shayde was about to enter, she grazed Cherie's arm with her shoulder. The feeling of impending doom hit her once again like a static shock and she eyed Cherie imploringly.

"Hey girl, you okay?" she said as the other girls went in and put their names down.

"Sure, Shayde, why?"

"I got this strange feeling when you hugged me. Almost like

there is something inside you that you are dying to tell me," she said, studying her friend.

"Shayde, you are too weird at times!" Cherie laughed and then she sighed. "How do you always know these things?"

"I don't really know Cherie. It's like... like auras speak to me or something. My mom's the same way."

Letting the door swing shut, leaving the others on the inside, Cherie dug in her purse for her cigarettes, took one out and lit it. "I'm late," she said, taking a big drag. She leant her head back on the salon's wall.

"Oh no. Did you take a test?"

Cherie stared at her with tortured eyes. "Yeah, six of them. All positive." She took another drag and blew it out slowly, sadly.

"So, what are you gonna do? Did you tell the girls anything? Or *him?*" She couldn't hide the dislike she had for him.

"Oh god no. I did tell Court though, she was actually the one that went with me to the clinic after all the other tests came out positive. I don't know how to tell him. I know he's going to hate me."

"Who cares what he thinks hon, it is your body and ultimately your decision. I will have your back no matter what you decide," Shayde said adamantly.

Shayde knew that Cherie didn't do it consciously, but also knew that she wasn't completely innocent when it came down to it. Cherie hadn't used any protection the last time they had had sex, she could read it in her eyes.

The ability to read people's eyes had always been a part of her life. Not that she could see what they were thinking because that would be weird, but she was able to sense people's emotions and their agendas. She knew when people were lying to her and she knew when someone was hurting inside. People show a lot more than they realize in their eyes. What was stranger was that she also could see a person's aura, a sort a glow a person has surrounding them. Shayde often knew if a person had bad intentions as their auras tended to be darker shades of grey. Positive people had multi-colored auras and sometimes she could even discern the type of person they were by the colors in their aura. She hadn't told a soul about it, but she found it very interesting though sometimes a little disconcerting. She's learned to somehow turn off when she was younger, and most of the time she just ignored it.

Cherie took another drag off her cigarette; a tear fell from her eye and trickled down her cheek. "Thanks, Shayde. You don't know how much that means to me. I don't know what to do right now. I don't know when or how to tell him, my brother and sister, my parents. I'm just so much at a loss right now, it's like my world is falling apart."

Shayde's heart went out to her friend. So many times she had wished that she could save Cherie from that bastard. And now, if Cherie decided to keep the baby, he could quite possibly, be stuck in Cherie's life forever.

Shayde shuddered at the thought.

"When did you find out?"

She took one final drag of the cigarette and stubbed it out against the wall, flicking it to the ground. "Yesterday."

"Oh wow. Okay, well sweetie you don't have to figure everything out right now. Take your time and really think hard about things. Make sure that you make the decision for *you* not for anyone else," she said as she wrapped her arm around Cherie.

"I know, I will. Let's not dwell on it today though. It's your day!" She looked crestfallen as she hugged Shayde back.

The door opened and Alizé emerged from the salon.

"C'mon you guys, they can start on three of us right now. And Shayde has to go first!" Alizé said, waving them into the salon. "Oh yeah and Shayde, your crush is about to text you!" She giggled, disappearing back through the door.

"WHAT!" There was a hint of forced cheerfulness in Cherie's voice but it was quickly replaced by the real thing being excited for her friend. "Shayde has a crush? On a boy!? Do tell!"

Shayde blushed. "I will inside," she smiled and started to walk in, patting Cherie on the back. "If you need me, I'm always here."

Cherie sighed. "Thank you, friend. I'm sure I'll need you soon."

The salon was a brightly lit parlor, lined with shelves of nail polish and pictures of beautifully manicured hands. Nail stations took up the front, behind the cash register and parlor chairs for pedicures were in the back. They walked in and sat down on the couches in the lobby, a table of magazines before them. As soon as Shayde sat down, she received her first text message from Kruise. When she heard the music for her phone's text message notification, little butterflies soared throughout her entire body. It was such a funny, amazing, new feeling and she loved it.

Clicking her phone open. It read,

Hi. It's Kruise. What's up?

Her primary concern was that she apologize for the way she acted in the diner. She typed it in and hit send.

From the very first message she received from him, blood rushed like an erratic current beneath her skin. Excitement flooded her as she realized that she may not have messed things up by acting so cold to him at the diner. Even though flirtatiousness wasn't really her style, she still could've been a little less sharp towards him. But that didn't matter anymore. All that mattered was that from now on she was going to do her best to be friendly and charming. Being new to this whole "dating" thing, she didn't know how to show she was interested and remain nonchalant at the same time, it wasn't helped by the fact that a part of her wanted to meet up with him that instant and wrap her arms around his sexy body and sift her fingers through his silky hair.

These thoughts were interrupted when the salon attendant informed them they could go through. Alizé, Courtney, and Shayde walked up to the three empty parlor chairs. Shayde flung off her flip-flops and sat down, submerging her feet in the hot water while setting her phone on her lap. Cherie and Dawn took were seated a little further along.

"So?" Cherie said as they got settled in, pressing Shayde to continue.

Shayde blushed again. "SO!" She cleared her throat. "We ran into Kruise and his friend Jason at O'Reilly's today when we went for lunch." She jumped as the old Asian lady grabbed her left foot and started to massage it.

"Ooooooh!" Dawn cooed. "How'd that go?"

"He just came up to our table. I was so nervous; I didn't know what to say or how to say it. I mean, you all know me; I have absolutely no idea how to talk to boys, especially one so hot. You know my brother, he never let any of the boys talk to me at school. He always said that there were more mature guys who would treat me right, waiting for me at college." She paused and looked down, realizing she hadn't thought of him that day.

"She was a bitch to him!" Alizé teased, interrupting her silent contemplation of her lost brother.

"Atta Girl!" Courtney laughed. "Nothing hooks 'em like a girl playing hard to get!"

"What did you say?" Dawn leaned in, interested.

But then Shayde was distracted by another message.

> No problem at all. I totally understand nerves. I was pretty nervous myself.

She felt herself grow scarlet, remembering how nervous he had made her. Drawing her attention back to Dawn, she said, "Not much of anything really. My voice was shaky, my mind went blank, I said very little to him at all."

Alizé chuckled loudly.

The little Asian lady working on her feet looked up at her strangely and then said something to her co-worker in her native tongue. Shayde knew they were talking about her and her friends but paid no attention to them.

"He asked her," Alizé answered for her, "if she had any plans this weekend and she just said no. Then he was like, 'Well Jay was just wondering if you girls wanted to come to Cape Cod with us this weekend,' you know how we all say it's our friends who were wondering and not us, when in all actuality it *is* us and we are just afraid of rejection?" Her hands moved wildly, dramatizing her story. "Well, Shayde here thought that it was Jay who wanted her to go, not Kruise so she got all pouty. SO... I was like 'HELL YEAH we'll go,' and he sat down next to me and gave me his number to work out the details. That made her think he was more interested in me and she got all quiet and wouldn't even look at him!" She laughed and looked at Shayde consideringly. "You are so sweet and innocent Shay, it's sickening!"

"Well, you guys know me, I'm new at this," Shayde retorted, her tone tinged with embarrassment. She stared at her phone, avoiding pressing eyes as she replied to Kruise.

"Don't get upset Shayde, we love you and we are happy that you finally found someone that you like. We're just teasing you." Alizé winked at her. "We were beginning to think that you were going to be single forever."

More embarrassment swelled up inside of her. "Thanks for the vote of confidence guys... I thought so, too though," she admitted, squirming as the Asian lady started scrubbing her foot.

"So, are you guys gonna go with them this weekend?" Cherie asked.

"If my mom says it's okay. I know she won't let me go if she knows there will be boys there but there's no way that I can't tell her."

"Why not?" Courtney asked.

"That's what I said," Alizé declared. "I told her she should just tell her mom that us girls are doing it for her birthday."

"Because you guys, you don't know my mom," Shayde

frowned, switching feet as instructed. "She knows when I'm lying, she always has."

"So tell her then," Alizé insisted. "Your mom has always been cool with stuff like that Shay, you know she digs it when you tell her the truth, and she might even consider it if she knows you haven't hidden anything from her. You've never given her any reason not to trust you. She knows that you're a good girl."

Her phone sang again.

"Is that him?" Dawn asked, intrigued.

She clicked her phone to life. Butterflies were wildly leaping in her stomach. "It is," she said with a smile. "He just called me beautiful!" she added, answering their questioning eyes. She clutched the phone to her heart and gazed at the ceiling.

Alizé rolled her eyes. "Oh my god! You're such a retard!"

"But you do have a point, Alizé, about telling my mom," Shayde acknowledged. "Maybe tonight I will tell her exactly what's going on and let her know that she doesn't have to worry, that I'm a big girl and I plan on doing nothing wrong. Maybe if in my head I truly believe that it's completely inno-cent, then she'll see it that way." It seemed she was trying to convince herself more than her friends.

Alizé's phone buzzed too. Either it was the first time it had gone off or just the first time Shayde noticed, she'd been more interested in what Kruise was going to text next.

"Who are you talking to over there?" Shayde asked. "Everyone you talk to is in this room!"

"Jason just texted me. He's just seeing what we are up to," Alizé said shortly, Shayde saw that she didn't want to talk about her situation, and she wanted the focus back on Shayde.

"Well that's good Shay, I think she'll totally let you if you go about it that way. Parents always respect honesty."

Courtney laughed at Alizé, "She sounds like she's reading from a soc ed textbook," she said wryly to the rest of the girls.

"Yeah, I think you're right Zey," Shayde interjected before Alizé could retort, she saw the tell-tale sign of a rising temper in her eyes. "I'm so excited! I think this might just work!"

As she began to think she might actually be able to pull the weekend off, her heartbeat quickened as she imagined being with Kruise in a different city. Under the moonlight, the ocean ebbing and flowing over their feet as they walk along it hand in hand, was the most beautiful fantasy she had ever had. Surely it was all too glorious to actually be possible.

Frowning, she looked at the last message from him, and unable to think of what to say in return, she handed the phone to Alizé with the message pulled up. "So, what do I say back to this? I can't think of anything. I'm so bad at flirting, it's ridiculous." She turned to Courtney, "you need to school me on flirting." She laughed.

"My pleasure! Come to my house tomorrow for a lesson in flirting one-o-one," Courtney smiled, though she knew Shayde was kidding.

"Just say, 'You're too sweet'," Alizé advised, handing the phone back to her. "It's simple, straight to the point, and puts the ball in his court."

She took it, typed it in and hit send.

"I will for sure," said Shayde. "I don't have anything going on tomorrow, I don't think."

"Cool. I don't have work tomorrow. Any time after ten. It's my day off and I like to sleep in."

"Okay cool," Shayde said as the phone loudly chirped in her hands.

"Damn! That was fast!" Alizé teased.

"What's it say?" Dawn asked.

"It just says that everything is set for the weekend and do we want to meet them at Benny's at eight for breakfast Friday before we take off." She peered at Alizé. "Does that sound okay with you?"

"Yeah it sounds good. You may want to tell him you still have to ask your mom though, to save him the heartache if she does say no."

"Okay, I'll tell him right now."

"So tell us about this weekend thing, what's going on, who's all goin'?" Cherie questioned, getting comfortable in one of the chairs across the way.

"Well, as far as I know," Alizé offered, "it's Shayde and me, then Kruise and Jason, and then a couple of their friends and their girlfriends. They got a cabin on the beach in Cape Cod. We'll leave early Friday morning and come back Sunday night. Just a bunch of us lying around on the beach with a lot of beer. Bonfires, stories, swimming, make out sessions... The works!"

Shayde's message notification sounded.

> Right on, sounds good. Going to get the LQ now, anything in particular that you want?

Kruise's message asked.

> I like anything. Just get what you think I'd like. You need some money?"

she responded. She hoped he would say yes so that she would have an excuse to see him before Friday.

"Jay wants to know if we want anything from the liquor store," Alizé directed at Shayde.

"Yeah Kruise just asked me the same thing. I just told him to get anything. I'm not picky. I asked if he needed any money too."

"Okay, I'll text Jay the same thing." She pounded away on her phone.

"Well that sounds like it'll be a lot of fun you guys," Dawn gushed.

"Shayde, I am so excited for you! There is nothing like a first crush, a summer romance, a beachy fling! Ooooooh, you have to tell me all about it when you get back!" Cherie grinned excitedly.

Alizé's eyes were on Shayde. "You definitely will remember it for the rest of your life. Everyone remembers their first kiss."

"You've never even been kissed before?" Cherie asked, taken aback by the revelation.

Shayde felt her cheeks flush. "No... Never... Kain always screwed it up for me. There were never any guys that he liked enough to let into my life. He swore every guy had their own agenda. Made it hard for me get close to anyone at all but I know it was just 'cause he didn't want me to get hurt," she said regretfully.

"I'm sorry Shayde," Alizé said. It was all anyone said. The entire room grew uncomfortably quiet until she cleared her throat. "Well that's what this weekend is going to bring, my sweet friend. You have your first real crush, he likes you, you like him. You have never been kissed and you guys are going away for the weekend together! How exciting!"

When her phone beeped again, the dismal mood fell away from her. Kruise wished her a happy birthday. Though she frowned a little when he said he didn't need any money, and she wouldn't get to see him before Friday, he was still texting her and that was all that mattered. "Yeah... " she said, more to herself than the group. "I have a really good feeling about this." After she thanked him, she stared indignantly at Alizé. "Did you tell Jay it was my birthday?"

"I might've!" Alizé replied through giggles as the attendant vigorously scrubbed her left foot.

"Zey!" Shayde exclaimed but another message from Kruise diverted her.

"What's he saying now?" Alizé asked.

"He just asked what I was doing for my birthday," she said as the attendant looked up and asked her what color she was going with today. She decided on a French manicure.

"What about you Alizé, you like Jason now or what?" Courtney asked her with a slight edge to her voice.

Courtney and Alizé didn't see eye to eye on a lot of things. In fact, they didn't see eye to eye on anything. They were like oil and water, they just didn't mix. Shayde winced, she had to deal with this sort of thing all the time. She loved both the girls equally but in different ways. She found it extremely difficult to do things like this altogether, without one of them saying something that rubbed the other girl the wrong way. She just wished today that they would sugar coat it so that they could all have a good time. She gritted her teeth as she anticipated Alizé's answer.

Maybe Alizé picked up on her wish, because instead of getting snippy with Courtney for the tone of her question, she just answered sweetly. "I think I do. I mean, I've seen him before in school and I always thought he was good looking. I like his attitude: he seems a lot like me. Just the way things happened, it seems as though we were meant to start talking, you know. It seems normal. I mean, I'm not like Shayde here, with the tingly stomach and what not, but he seems like a cool dude and I'm enjoying getting to know him."

After Jeff had broken her heart on that fateful night she never forgave him. He had told her over and over again that he had no idea what had come over him, that he loved her and wanted her back badly, but she saw it as a sign and never went back to him. Since then, she hadn't shown any interest in anyone—until now.

"Aw that's cool. I hope you guys hit it off too," Dawn said sincerely.

"I hope so too. I think this weekend will be fun regardless."

Shayde sent a message back to Kruise telling him about the big surprise her parents were planning and asking if he had plans. Then she asked, "What about you, Court, you seeing anyone these days?"

"No, just taking some time off to figure myself out. The last one took its toll on my heart," she said, sounding a bit doleful.

"I think that's a good thing for you to do," Shayde said reassuringly. "You're a wonderful person; you don't need a guy to define you. I think if you stop searching so hard for Mr. Right he'll come along."

When her phone's alarm sounded again, he told her he

didn't have any plans as he had to work the next day. She replied, asking him where he worked.

"Easy for you to say," Courtney retorted. "You just found yours... literally!"

Shayde laughed, realizing she was right: Kruise's last name was Wright. "No but I'm serious," she continued. "I think if you just took your time and focused on what else was going on in your life, the right guy will find you."

"I know" Courtney said. "It's not like I try to find these relationships. I attract guys who want to be serious and then I fall for them. I can't help it. I wish it wasn't that way. But when one comes along and it feels so right, it feels wrong to push them away, especially if they might be Mr. Right. You know what they say; 'It's better to have loved and lost than to have never loved at all.' It's true." She sounded like an old professor concluding a lecture.

"It is true," Dawn stated, "but maybe this time you could refrain from getting into a relationship so soon after a break up. You know, at least a couple of weeks."

"Very funny Dawn!" Courtney's tone was defensive. "Like you're one to talk. You have a different boyfriend every week!"

"No I don't! I've had the same one for a year, where have you been?" she snapped.

Dawn really had been in the same relationship for the last year. Her boyfriend's name was Brayden and he was a sweetheart. Though he was older than her by four years—which is a big difference to teenagers—their relationship seemed similar to everyone else's around them. He treated her well and made her happy and that was all that mattered to her friends.

"She's just trying to say that you being single for a while

would probably be good for you," Alizé defended Dawn. "I swear, the minute you stop looking for love it will find you, it's the way it always works."

"Okay, okay, anyways, what should we do after this?" Shayde said, trying to change the subject and avoid a heated discussion. Courtney tended to get aggressively defensive if she felt like she was being criticized.

"I need to find a new bikini for this weekend," Alizé answered. "The only one I have is from last year and I think my boobs grew because it doesn't fit anymore!"

"Yeah, I would like to find something cute to wear for the weekend too!" Shayde smiled; glad she succeeded in getting the attention off Courtney.

"There's a cute little shop on the boardwalk called Tulip and it has some cute clothes and swimming suits and stuff. It's my favorite store," Dawn suggested as Shayde's phone sounded again.

Kruise explained that he worked at a local fish market. Sometimes she wished that she had a job herself. It would give her time away from that sad house, an outlet to get her mind off the things that haunted her every day. The loss of her brother had cut into her in ways no blade ever could. "That sounds perfect!" Cherie said, cutting short Shayde's depressing train of thought. "And then, top the day off with sun tanning on the beach?"

"You know it sister!" Alizé said.

"Yeah, it sounds like the perfect day my friends!" Shayde exclaimed. "Thank you for spending my birthday with me."

"Wouldn't miss it for the world Shayde," Alizé replied

lovingly. "You are a good friend, and we would do anything for your happiness."

"Don't make me cry you guys!" she said, fighting back tears. "I love you all too and you girls make me happy. I couldn't ask for better friends."

As the girls' toes were finished, one by one they started to trickle out of the salon into the nice warm June air. Shayde and Alizé were the first ones outside and Alizé lit up a cigarette. Then out came Dawn, Courtney and Cherie. Their toes looked beautiful in the funny little sandals the salon gives out after a pedicure. Courtney and Cherie lit up as well.

Shayde didn't smoke cigarettes, never had. She didn't mind the smell as long it wasn't it in a house or car or somewhere that it would smother her. Dawn only smoked when she drank, and that was usually only on the weekends.

The last message that she had received from Kruise said that he knew what she meant by a job being an escape. She hadn't heard from him since. The idea on whether to press the matter and send him another text anyway fought with the tugging feeling telling her no. The latter idea won, she would leave it be for the time being and wait for him to text her. He was probably busy with something anyways.

As the girls smoked their cigarettes, they walked down the boardwalk towards the little shops that lined the beach. The cloudless sky gave the sun a glorious playground and it shined warmly upon the town. They arrived at Tulip and the girls stubbed their cigarettes out in the ashtray out front.

Upon entering, a multitude of racks clad with brightly colored clothes greeted them. Sundresses and tank-tops, halter-tops and skirts, bikinis and shorts, were strewn out in abundance throughout the store. Shayde tried on a variety of different clothes, trying to envision herself in them next to Kruise. She purchased three new outfits for the weekend, a new bathing suit, three different pairs of sandals and a new beach towel. With each outfit that she picked, she imagined what she might be doing in them the next time she had them on.

Shayde and Alizé parted from the group for a second to put their new swimsuits on in the gas station across the street. When they emerged, they made their way back across the road to the beach. The hot summer sand embraced Shayde's toes and the lullaby of the sea's retreat and return, sang to her in the soft melodic voice that only the ocean could sing. The water was a dark blue, reflecting the azure afternoon sky, its cool refreshing waves beckoning her to come out and play in the luxurious water.

As they approached their friends, Shayde noticed that her other friend Eric was there as well, with another boy she assumed must be his new boyfriend. Eric was just another one of the girls.

When he saw her, he ran up to her with glee. "Hey Shay, happy bee-day!" he said, and gave her a kiss on the cheek. "This is my man, Paul. Paul this is my girl Shayde."

She shook Paul's hand. "Nice to meet you."

"Nice to meet you too. Happy birthday."

"Thanks so much!" Shayde smiled broadly at him.

Flinging her new towel down onto the beach with her drink resting steadily in the sand, she stepped out of her sundress and sat down to cream up.

"Have you heard from lover boy lately?" Alizé asked as she sat down next to her.

"Lover boy?" Eric declared delightedly. "Shayde's got a boy? Oh happy day!" he said, clapping his hands together. "Spill, spill, who is he, what's his name?" he said as he laid his towel down on the hot sand and took off his shirt.

"Kruise Wright," Shayde said, rubbing lotion on her legs.

"OOOOH, I know him, he's so hot!" Eric proclaimed. "So, how long have you two been talking?" he asked, taking his lotion out and rubbing it on his arms.

"About two hours," Shayde laughed shyly. "We were texting all afternoon and now he hasn't said anything back to me. I think he got bored of me," she said dejectedly.

"He's probably just busy. Don't ever read too much into a boy's silence," Eric reassured her, finishing up with the lotion and handing it to Paul.

"Yeah, he's probably just hanging with his friends and forgot," Paul told her, as he lathered himself up with the goop. "Boys have short attention spans."

"Really?" Shayde questioned, gazing out to the ocean. "Should I just leave it alone or should I ask him what he's doing?"

"Who sent the last text?" Eric asked as he lay down and settled in.

"I did."

"Then wait," he affirmed. "You don't wanna sound desperate, you wanna be aloof. Make him wonder about you, make him think you don't want him, that drives boys crazy."

"Okay. So wait for him to text me, even if he doesn't for the rest of the day?" she said apprehensively. She didn't want to wait until tomorrow to talk to him again. He intrigued her.

"Yes, but he will, don't worry," Eric consoled her. "He's probably thinking of you right now and doesn't know what to say. When you're first getting to know someone, it's sometimes difficult to keep a conversation over text going for too long. You run out of things to say and don't wanna force things, whereas if you were talking in person you would find something to talk about to kill the awkward silence. Texting is such a fraught thing," he explained.

"Yeah because you can't hear the tone in someone's voice when they say something," Alizé added. "So you don't know how to take certain things. You can't see someone's eyes when they say it, so you don't know if they're being sincere. You can't read their body language, which speaks so much louder than words, the list goes on," she said as she finished rubbing lotion on her legs and lay down on her towel.

"This is so complicated," Shayde said, her eyes still fastened on the ocean.

"I know, dating is the most infuriating thing in the world," Eric said. "It's like you can't just say, 'Hey, I like you, I think we should be together.' It turns into this huge dance where, if you make the wrong move you lose the guy. It sucks."

"I hate dating," Cherie said with disgust from under her big sun hat, sitting on the other side of Courtney. She had stuck a beach umbrella into the sand and was lounging beneath it in a folding chair, watching the local kids playing beach volleyball.

Eric sat up and leaned over, looking around Courtney to laugh at her. Eric and Cherie had a love/hate relationship. They loved to hate each other, but they loved each other so much it was funny. Seeing them spark off each other was always a good time.

"What'cha doin' over there Cher?" he laughed.

"Bite me bimbo. Don't call me Cher," she lashed back with a smirk on her face. He loved to tease her and she hated it but thought it was amusing at the same time.

"Dating is seriously overrated," Courtney said. "It's such a waste of time."

"Great, you guys, this sounds like so much fun," Shayde said sarcastically. She lay down and closed her eyes and let the warm sunshine wash over her body. Her purse wasn't too far out of reach so she would be able to hear her phone if it went off, but then this made her feel more uncomfortable because she didn't want to feel that needy. She fought with the idea of just turning her phone on silent so she wouldn't know if it went off so she wouldn't text back right away if he did decide to text her and she would appear more aloof than she was feeling.

"Aw, Shay, it's not that bad, really, and the stress is worth it," Alizé said. "You have no idea the rush you are gonna feel when you're next to him in the darkness, sitting on the beach with him, being just inches away from his face. How your stomach will tingle in anticipation, him being so close to you, knowing he wants you, you wanting him, that your lips are gonna touch soon and you don't have any idea what to expect. It's a feeling you have to experience to understand and once you experience it, you will never forget it. From then on, little scents will remind you of that moment; certain songs will trigger that memory and spark it back to life. The moment will never leave you,"

Shayde feel better about the whole thing again. It actually sounded like something she could handle.

Everyone was quiet after Alizé's speech, as though they were all reliving their own first kisses.

THEY REMAINED LOUNGING ON THE BEACH FOR THE REST OF THE DAY, making small talk and soaking up the sun. Most of them went swimming in the ocean while Cherie just stayed under her umbrella and thought quietly, a million miles away.

As bright, fluffy white clouds started to fill the sky, the setting sun colored them with bright oranges, yellows and pinks. Lavender spilled out over the horizon, melting into the blue atmosphere and as the colorful clouds danced within it, attenuated the sun's rays, Alizé stood and brushed the sand off her.

"Well, I better get going," she said as she folded up her beach towel. "It's starting to get dark."

"Yeah, I probably should get home too," Shayde seconded. "It's getting close to that time."

"What are you doing for your birthday tonight, Shay?" Eric asked as he stood as well, putting his shirt on and starting to pack up.

"My parents have something planned, I have no idea what though," she said, grabbing her beach towel and shaking it out.

"Well, that sounds cool; you don't have any idea whatso-ever? Do you think that it's a surprise party or something?"

"I don't know. It's something weird. I'll keep you guys posted though okay?" she said, slipping her sundress on.

"Yeah do for sure. Happy birthday!" Eric gave her a kiss on the cheek and a hug, and Paul followed suit.

"Would you guys wanna drop me off at the diner?" Alizé asked Eric and Paul. O'Reilly's was on the opposite end of town from Shayde's house.

"Sure," he said kindly. "Not a problem at all."

"Awesome thanks. Give me a hug Shay," she said, opening her arms to her. "I love you mama. Happy birthday! Text me after you're done with your parents' stuff."

"I will, love you too," she said as Alizé turned to go. She swung back to her remaining friends on the beach. "What are you girls going to do?"

"I'm gonna go meet Brayden for dinner," Dawn said.

"I've gotta go home and start packing," remarked Courtney. She was moving in with Cherie that weekend.

"I'm gonna go lay down," Cherie commented.

"Well, that all sounds very fun. Thank you all for your presents and I love you all very much," Shayde said, giving every one of her friends a hug.

"Love ya too. Happy birthday!" Dawn replied. "Call me later after your birthday thing."

"I will. And I'll text you girls later. See ya tomorrow Court?"

"For sure. If I don't hear from you tonight I'll hit you up tomorrow when I'm up and then you can head on over."

"'Kay sounds good. Later," Shayde said, walking back across the beach towards her shiny new car.

"Bye," they called after her in unison.

When she climbed inside, she pulled out her phone and checked to see if she had somehow missed it going off.

No new messages.

Feeling a little sad, she put the phone back in her purse and started her car. She tried not to let it get to her and then remembered all the things her friends had told her and her worry melted away.

CHAPTER
FIVE

When Kruise pulled up to his house, his dad's motorcycle was in the driveway and so was Jason's little green Ford. His dad owned a Toyota that he drove in the winter, but in the summer he drove his most prized possession; the chopper he built with his own two hands. Kruise loved that bike and planned to build one for himself someday.

Simon was a machine operator at a local plant that made materials for sports; major league baseball hats, soccer uniforms, football jerseys and other things of the sort. There were only two companies like it in the world. He was a hard-working man, working about six days a week from sun up until four in the afternoon. He had been in the job for going on fifteen years. Obviously, Kruise got his work ethic from his father.

Pulling his little black truck into the driveway, he killed the engine and pulled out the keys. When he stepped into the house his dad was sitting in the living room watching a baseball game.

"What's up kid?" Simon asked him as he came in the door.

"Not much, just been chillin' at Jordan's. What's up with you?" Kruise sat down on the couch next to his dad and put his keys on the center console.

Simon handed him beer from the cooler in the couch. The black leather sofa wrapped around two walls in the living room, ending with two recliners on both sides. In between the two recliners was a consul with cup holders, but underneath was a little compartment for storage. Simon used this storage as a cooler.

Simon was a good-looking fellow; he stood about six-two and had light blonde hair that he wore in a long ponytail. He was the biker type, often dressed in jeans, a black shirt and leather of some sort with a bandana around his head. He had the same hazel eyes as Kruise, but Kruise had gotten his dark features from his mom.

"Nice, that where Jay is?" Simon asked, eyes fixed on the game.

"Yeah. He'll probably be there all night. Told me to tell you not to wait up."

"That's cool, make sure to tell him if he needs a ride home, though, I'll go get him." He took a large swig of his beer.

"You can text him, too, you know," Kruise joked.

"I know. But you'll probably talk to him before I do."

"True. If he texts, I'll tell him, cool? You hungry?" Kruise said, as he stood and started to walk towards the kitchen.

"Yeah, there's a frozen pizza in there that I was gonna make. The oven should be pre-heated by now."

"You sure you don't want something else? I can make us burgers on the grill or something. We always have pizza."

"Sure kid, burgers sound good."

"Cool, I'll get on that."

Kruise went into the kitchen and turned the oven off. Going into the freezer, he pulled out two burger patties and stuck the pizza back in. After the hamburgers were separated and laid out on a plate, he put them in the microwave to defrost a little.

Shayde flashed into his mind again.

A little glint of regret hit him suddenly when it dawned on him that he hadn't got back to her. He hoped she didn't get the impression he wasn't into her.

The microwave hummed, and though his eyes were fixed on the rotating plate, all his mind saw was her. He wondered what it was that her parents had planned for her and what she ended up doing for the rest of the day. What was she doing right now? He abstractedly pulled out his phone and began to text her.

What you doing?

he typed

He opened the spice cabinet and pulled down a shaker filled with mesquite seasoning. The microwave beeped, he pulled out the plate and sprinkled them generously. Leaving the plate on the counter he headed out to the back yard, flicking on the porch light before he thrust open the sliding glass doors.

His Great Dane, Guido, came happily trotting up to greet him as he turned on the barbeque. They had adopted Guido after Reanna passed, as a loving distraction from the pain. Although the void was too large for anyone but Reanna to fill, Guido was still an excellent addition to the family and he was the most loyal and loving dog that they could have asked for.

As the grill sparked to life, the phone vibrated in his pocket and a tingling sensation ran through him at just the thought of her.

> Just got done at the beach. Headed home to shower. You?

her message said.

He sat down on the lawn chair to respond.

> Getting ready to cook me and my dad some dinner. How was the beach?

he replied.

Thoughts of the weekend consumed him once again, hoping beyond all hope that she would be able to go. When he thought about the chance that her parents might not let her go a tightness gripped his chest and he had to quickly divert his thoughts to repress the ache.

She must look amazing in a bikini, he thought. After all, he was a guy and she was one incredible looking woman. His sanity would be in question if he didn't think of a beautiful girl like that scantily clad in swimwear.

His phone beeped again.

The whole day was amazing. I have awesome friends. What did you do all day?

I just hung out at my friend Jordan's. Not really much of anything

he typed in as he checked the grill to see if it was hot enough. Satisfied that it was, he returned to the kitchen to get the burgers from the counter.

Simon was still in the same position in the living room, eyes fixed on the television set.

With the plate in hand, he doubled back to the grill, grabbing a spatula on his way out the door. He laid the burgers on the grate and they sizzled in response. His phone beeped to life again. Laying the spatula on the attached shelf, he sat back down and pulled out his phone.

Shayde said that she liked to hang out and do nothing with her friends as well.

So did you have a nice birthday so far? You get anything cool?

From his post on the lawn chair on the porch, he watched twilight seep away into the horizon, being consumed by the night. Thoughts of her were so severely invading him that he jumped when his phone buzzed on his lap.

I've had a really good day so far. I got a new car, my license, and got to spend the day with my girls. I still don't know what else my parents have planned but I hope it's not big, a car is enough.

That's cool that they got you a car. What kind of car did they get you?

They got me a new little green bug that's a convertible! I love it, it's so me!

As he stood again to flip the burgers he imagined her long, dark hair streaming wildly in the wind against the bright green of the car, her eyes almost the color of the car itself.

Nice. I can't wait to cruise in it with you this weekend =)

he replied.

Me neither. This weekend is going to be so much fun, I just know it.

Just the thought that she was looking forward to hanging out with him in return made him ecstatic. It was the first time that he had ever felt this way about a girl that he barely knew. Little crushes he was no stranger to but this was not a simple little crush. There was something about this girl that pulled at him like gravity and left him wanting more.

More than you know sweetheart. And it's just the beginning

he wrote. He shuddered and little chills ran the length of his arms and legs just thinking about what that meant.

Even though the last message might have been too honest, he was just so confident that this was going to be much more than a weekend fling. He sensed that she would be more than just a high school romance. The feeling was rooted deep within his bones. The more that they talked, the more relaxed he felt and he knew that he could open up to her. So far she seemed like she was very level-headed and down to earth.

She was special.

> I know. I have such a good feelings about you too

she replied, like she knew what he was thinking.

Before he had the chance to respond, she wrote back.

> I just got to my house and have to shower before the birthday festivities commence so I will text you back as soon as I have a moment, okay?

> Sure thing. Let me know what they had planned for you, I'm all curious now!

> I promise the minute I get done I will.

He couldn't help but smile.

The burgers were done, so he turned off the grill and tipped them on to the plate with the spatula. Calling Guido to follow him, he went back inside and set them on the counter. He grabbed the buns from the cabinet, the condiments from the fridge, as well as lettuce, cheese, and tomatoes, and made the burgers for him and Simon. Adding a dollop of potato salad that was left over from the barbeque they'd had over the weekend, he grabbed paper towels from the roll and headed into the living room, where the family had eaten since he was eleven, and handed the plate to his dad.

"Aw man, thanks! Smells delicious," Simon said, taking the plate from Kruise.

"Welcome." He sat down next to his dad. "Who's winning?" He inclined his head towards the TV and took a bite of his burger.

"Rockies," his dad answered, setting his beer down in the cup holder and taking a bite.

"So," Kruise started, playing with the potato salad with his fork, "I think me and Jay and some of the fellas are going to Cape Cod this weekend to kick the summer off. That cool with you?"

"Sure kid, I don't mind. Do what you do. You wanna take the jet skis and the boat?"

"Yeah Dad, that would rock! Are you sure?"

"Yeah, I trust you. Take 'em, have a good time."

"For sure. I'll take good care of it. You won't have to worry at all."

"I know son. You're a good kid. I worry more about Jay," Simon snickered.

Kruise laughed too. "Me too, Dad, me too!"

They sat in silence for the rest of dinner, watching the baseball game. After they were done, Kruise grabbed the plates and walked into the kitchen, rinsed them off and stuck them in the dishwasher. He went back into the living room to say goodnight to his dad. Normally, he didn't go to bed until later, but he had to be up exceptionally early and didn't like to be tired.

"Alright old man, I'm hitting the hay," Kruise told him, holding out his hand.

"Workin' tomorrow?" Simon asked, looking up at him. He slapped his hand then took another drink of his beer.

"Yup. Bright and early."

"Right on, well thanks for cooking. 'Preciate it."

"No problem pops. See you tomorrow."

"Alright, later."

After climbing the steps to his room, he took a quick shower and prepared for bed. When he was nice and clean and all dried off, he checked his phone's alarm, making sure it was set at the correct time and on. Satisfied, he plugged it in and set it on the nightstand. He flicked the light off and crawled into bed, the cool sheets welcoming to his hot skin. Even though the beginning of June wasn't as sweltering as the middle summer months, the humidity had been awful today and he and his dad had not yet installed the air conditioners for the summer. Even after his shower, he still felt sweaty and uncomfortably hot.

He flipped the pillow over to the cold side and stared at his phone on the bedside table, wondering when she would text him again and what she would say. If she texted in the middle of the night, he knew he probably wouldn't hear it—he was a very heavy sleeper and often times needed three alarms to wake him up—but if she did, he would have something of her to start his day off with in the morning.

The thoughts of her devoured him completely as he drifted off to sleep.

CHAPTER
SIX

. * . * . ☾ . * . .

Sitting at a stop light on her way home from the beach, Shayde's phone sounded inside of her purse from the passenger's side, indicating that she was receiving a text message. Turbulent bubbles of anticipation rose up in her as she tore through her purse to find the phone. By the time she finally found it, the light had turned green and she was being honked by the guy behind her. She jumped at the sound and dropped the phone into the gap between the driver's seat and the console. Cursing under her breath, she let out the clutch and pressed her foot onto the gas pedal, moving the car forward while ruminating on who the message was from. She was nearly home when she finally caught another light. Fumbling with shaky hands, she frantically tried to find it before this light turned green as well. When she finally retrieved it, she felt sick from the anticipation.

It was Kruise, just as she had hoped. He asked her what she was doing.

As she texted him that she was heading home, she was so focused on him, she hadn't noticed that the light had turned green again. Another annoyed honk came from the car behind her and unluckily for her, it was the same car she had held up the last time. She hastily set the phone on her lap and lurched forward, stalling the little bug at the intersection. Outraged, the person in the car behind her laid on the horn, flashed their lights and passed her screaming obscenities as they did so. Shayde laughed at how impatient people could be over a two-second delay.

Still amused, she continued to drive at a slow pace, taking her time getting to her house. As soon as she arrived home she would have to forget about her phone for a while, as she was not allowed to text during family dinners, family discussions, or any family events. Her parents found it rude and thought that it made people feel like they weren't enough for someone's full attention. Her parents said they would help her pay her phone bill on the condition was that when she was with them, she was with them and not on her phone the entire time. She respected that and didn't argue with it at all, deciding that she would probably have the same rules for her own children.

When she arrived at her gate she punched in the code, it opened and she continued slowly down the road to her house.

As soon as she pulled up to the front of her home and parked, she finished her message to Kruise by asking him what he was doing and hit send. She put the top back up and turned the car off. She became nervous at the thought of what her parents were doing in the darkened house. It looked as though no one was home. All the lights were off and they parked in the garage so it was not easily ascertained whether they were there or not. And if they were, what in the world would they be doing in the dark?

Shayde and her parents lived in a gated community on the nice end of town. Her dad was a Vice President at a software engineering company and her mom was a Drug Addiction Counselor, specializing in family interventions and teen addictions. Their house wasn't as big and flashy as most of the houses in the community and was probably the least expensive. Shayde had no idea how much her parents were really worth because they never talked about things like that with her. They both loved what they did and didn't gloat about their wealth. Shayde had to work for the money they gave her too, doing chores and helping out around the house. She didn't have an unlimited credit card courtesy of them and they didn't shower her with everything and anything that she wanted. They lived simply and honestly, as they always had.

The house they had in the community hadn't always been their home. Her parents were both in college when Kain was born so money was tight. They grew up on a normal street, in a plain two-bedroom house where she had to share a room with her brother, even though she hated sharing rooms with a boy. Tara worked and went to school part-time so she could devote more time to their kids, while Dustin studied and worked almost every moment to pay for his education. He literally started at the bottom as a janitor at his company and worked his way up. It was his ambition that had been an example to

Shayde; he was exactly how she wanted to be when she grew up. Well educated, with a decent job that she loved, happily married and successful, and wealthy yet modest about it. Even if she found out that the trust fund was worth a couple thousand, she would invest it towards school so she could make it grow. Should a day ever come that she found herself rich, she would still live the way her parents lived; as though she wasn't rich at all.

Tara started working as a Drug Addiction Counselor because she had known a few friends in high school who were addicted to drugs and she watched them destroy their lives. Through Tara's work, Shayde had made a conscious decision to never use drugs. She drank a few times in her life and her parents knew that she had, though she didn't know how—like she told her friends, her mom had caught her in every lie she had ever told. They had a long conversation about it and her parents were okay with it as long as she didn't do it often, didn't let it get in the way of her schooling, and this was the most important one—she never, ever got behind the wheel. Of course she never would, considering the way her brother had been taken from her. Tara worried about Shayde drinking but she would have been a hypocrite to tell her not to, she had done far worse things than that when she was Shayde's age.

The only things that Shayde ever kept from her parents was the fact that she could read people's eyes, see their auras, and how sometimes her dreams would tell her of things to come. They were strange little coincidences and it was stupid to tell anyone about them. Aside from that, Shayde told them everything.

Sitting outside in the twilight, her phone alarmed once more and she clicked the phone open.

> Getting ready to cook me and my dad some dinner. How was the beach?

Kruise's text said.

She replied and they continued to text while she sat in her dark and silent car. The only sounds that pierced the silence were her rapidly beating heart and the music from her phone informing her of a new message from Kruise—which caused her heart to race even faster.

What she gathered from his messages was that he had been with his friends all day. There had been no reason to be worried at all and she felt a little dumb, having mulled over the fact that she hadn't heard from him for a while. Relief cleansed all the worry that had soaked her all day and she was pleased that she hadn't tried texting him again and made herself look desperate. As she sat in her car and talked to him, she wondered if her parents were looking out the window at her, wondering what she was doing. Giggling to herself, she mused if she would soon get a text from them asking her. The oddness of her sitting in her car outside in the dark was definitely going to demand some sort of explanation.

Shortly after the thought, her phone went off twice in a row.

The first one was Kruise asking what she got for her birthday and the second one was from her mom.

> What'cha doin' out there Shay?

It wasn't surprising to her that her mother had texted her

right after she thought about it. What was odd was that it had been happening more often than usual. Most times, these little "visions" only happened once, maybe twice a week. It had happened twice today, not including in her car on her way home when a song popped in her head and two seconds later it came on the radio.

She responded to Kruise first and told him about everything she had received for her birthday. Then to her mom she said,

> I'll be there in a min Ma, just finishing up a conversation.

Kruise responded asking her what kind of car she'd got and she explained, not wanting the conversation to end but knowing that her mom and dad were waiting for her inside. She would've been content sitting in the car talking to him until the sun came up.

> Take your time sweetie pie. Just wondering what you were doing out there.

Tara answered.

Talking to a gorgeous man, she thought inwardly. She could just imagine his bright eyes looking over at her from the passenger seat as they cruised down the highway with the top down. His warm, succulent lips saying something to her and not being able to hear him, his beauty so spellbinding that it left her deaf. It was usually hard to describe a man as beautiful, but to her, he was. More so than she had ever realized before.

As if he had read *her* mind, he wrote back,

Nice. I can't wait to cruise in it with you this weekend =).

Me neither. This weekend is going to be so much fun, I just know it.

Almost immediately his response was,

More than you know sweetheart. And it's just the beginning.

She looked at the message for a long time, hoping to discern the depth of feeling behind the words. She shivered as knowing in her heart that this really was "the beginning". The anticipation of new things was always exciting, but when she thought about *this* new beginning, it put her in a cloud so far above nine that she didn't know if she would ever come back down, or even if she wanted to. It was nice up here. And if this was the way she felt over just text messages, what were the feelings she was bound to feel when she really got to know him?

It was almost hard to process what this strange day had brought into the light, and that it all happened on her sixteenth birthday. It was like it was meant to happen this way, like it was written in the stars. Shayde had known Kruise from school and thought he was attractive, but today he became someone more... something special to her, and they hadn't even spent time together. Was this just some phase that all teenagers go through? They think they feel so strongly about a person they hardly know, then the feeling is gone as quick as it came. Something in her heart told her that this was far from true. This was going to be more than just a simple "fling" and she didn't know exactly what it was or what it was going to be, all she knew is that it was something deeper.

> I know. I have such good feelings about you too

she replied, glancing up at the house just as her parents' heads disappeared behind the lace curtain that covered the front door. She had better get inside, they were obviously anxious for her to come in.

She sighed as she sent the last text to him and put her phone in her purse.

As she prepared to get out of the car she had to re-evaluate her surroundings. It was as though she had been in another world while talking to him. It strangely didn't even feel like her neighborhood or her block, and it was hard to adjust to the plainness of it all. As she had been talking to him, the world seemed to get smaller and more beautiful and things just made more sense. Now that he was gone for the moment, it was as if it all became very dull—or maybe it was always bright and beautiful, it just took knowing him to realize it.

She sighed and grabbing her presents from the back seat she got out the car.

When she stepped inside she saw that there was a light on, but it was in the kitchen in the back of the house, so she couldn't have seen it from the street. Her mom emerged from it, nibbling on something and wiping her hands on her pants, her dad followed close behind, with their dog, Knotti, tailing him. She was relieved that they hadn't been planning a surprise party.

"Shayde! You made it!" Tara teased her. "I thought you

were going to fall asleep out there and that I was going to have to come out and get you!"

Shayde resembled her mother, inheriting her long red hair and green eyes, but Tara was slimmer than Shayde and less curvy. Kain had also looked more like Tara than their father. Dustin was stauncher with dark brown coloring and dark features, not to mention that he was covered in tattoos.

"Very funny Mom," Shayde smiled at her, not offended by her teasing. "I was just talking to a friend."

"You could've come in honey, I don't mind if you're finishing up a conversation just as long as you don't keep it going on my time."

"I know, I just... felt like finishing it outside," she looked into her mother's eyes and saw instantly that her mother knew about her crush and was happy for her.

Bemusedly, Shayde cocked her head to the side at the strange incident. This had never happened before. There was never a time that she had been able to read Tara's eyes, she had tried it a few times after she first learned of her strange gift but to no avail. Kain's eyes had been very readable though, and sometimes she wondered whether he could read hers, she even tested his ability, provoking him with her eyes, just to see if he could. He never acknowledged it and neither did her mom.

She composed herself and turned towards the stairs. "I have to put this stuff away real quick and take a shower, is that okay?" she asked, moving towards the staircase.

"Sure honey, go ahead," Tara said, so nonchalantly, it was as if nothing had passed between them. "Dinner's not quite done yet. I hope you're hungry, I made your favorite."

"Chick Parm?" she asked, grinning largely.

"You bet, Shay," Dustin replied merrily. "It's your birthday and you always get what you want on your birthday."

"Awesome," she said, holding up her hand for them to high five. "I can't wait! I'll be right back."

With a smile, she bounded up the stairs with her bags in her hands.

"Okay sweetie," Tara called.

When she arrived at her room, she threw her things on her bed and sat down. Putting her elbow on her knee, she cradled her chin in her palm and tried to process what had just happened between her and her mom. Maybe there was more to her little abilities than she thought. Questioning whether or not she should try and talk to her mom about it, she decided to delay it for a bit, take a shower, clear her mind and think about it later. It was her birthday and her parents had a nice dinner planned.

After her gifts were put away, she gathered up the clean clothes she intended to dress in after her shower and went to the bathroom. When the water was at the ideal temperature, she undressed and stepped in. The soothing water ran down her in rivulets. As she dipped her head back into the stream and closed her eyes, all that was there behind them was Kruise. She raked her hands through her long hair as she washed it, with nothing but that image in her head.

When she was all clean and dry, she dressed and put her sandy clothes into the hamper in her room. She took her phone out of her purse and plugged it in, laying it on the nightstand by her bed.

The whole house smelled delicious as she climbed down the steps and headed towards the kitchen. As she arrived, Tara was bent over the oven, pulling out succulent chicken breasts with melted parmesan blanketing them.

"Perfect timing, my lovely," Tara said.

"Smells so good, Mama, I can hardly wait." She leaned over Tara and eyed the food. "Can I do anything?"

"Nope. Just get your butt in the dining room," Dustin said smirking as he drained scalding hot water from angel hair pasta into a strainer in the sink. "There's glasses filled with ice here, grab one and get what you want to drink."

"Okay," she responded as she grabbed one of the crystal glasses filled with ice cubes and filled it up with tap water.

A cool summer breeze was sweeping up through the open windows in the dining room, blowing around the scents of the ocean as well as the delicious food. Their wedding china was laid out at the far end of the table by the open windows, atop a lacy white tablecloth. Candles had been lit, the reflection of their flames dancing on the surface of the wine glasses that were set out beside the elegant china.

Shayde sat down at the head of the table with her back to the open windows; her parents sat either side of her. The food was served; two gorgeous golden brown chicken breasts—drizzled with marinara and topped with melted mozzarella—sat beside a colorful salad and a pile of angel hair pasta. Steam was rising off of the chicken but it looked too delicious to wait for it to cool. She cut a piece of the chicken and blew on it quickly, then put it in her mouth. An ardent sting bit the roof of her mouth and scorched her tongue, causing her to spit the food out as fast as she had stuck it in.

"Are you okay?" Tara asked her.

"Yes I'm fine," she laughed. "Alizé did the same thing earlier and I called her a dumbass for it."

"That's karma for you," Dustin laughed.

"Don't I know it," Shayde said, breathing in the cold air to soothe her aching mouth.

"So how was the day with your friends?" Tara asked, pouring herself a glass of wine.

"Today was really good. It was a day filled with lunches, pedicures and a hot, sandy beach. It was the perfect day."

"That sounds cool," Tara said, taking a drink of her wine. "Did they get you anything?"

Shayde cut a piece of her chicken and blew on it. "Yeah I got a bracelet from Alizé, some lotion, a candle, a book… " She trailed off, trying to think of everything.

"Nice," Tara added. "That's really sweet. I'm glad you have good friends."

Shayde tested the chicken's temperature with her tongue this time and decided it was cool enough to put in her mouth. She put it in and bit down. "Me too," she said, tonguing the chicken into her cheek as she talked.

Forking a bite of salad onto the utensil, she tried to determine whether now was a good time to bring up the weekend getaway or not.

"So," Tara started, speaking before Shayde had the chance to ask. "Have you met anyone special lately?" The tone of her voice had an affected casualness yet it seemed edged with a side of deeper knowledge.

"I may have," she said shyly, twisting the fork around in some dressing. "I don't know yet. We have only texted so far. That's who I was talking to out there."

"What's his name?" Dustin asked, his voice soaked with fatherly concern.

"Kruise Wright. He's going to be a senior at Salem next year." It was slightly embarrassing bringing him up to her parents when they hadn't even hung out together yet. It would be even more so if it didn't go anywhere, but they brought it up and she couldn't lie to them.

"What's he like?" Tara asked, sincerely interested. Shayde had never had an interest in anyone and she knew her parents must be slightly surprised at the notion.

"I don't really know that much about him yet but so far he's really sweet." She felt her cheeks flush scarlet talking about him and awkwardly stuck a bit of salad into her mouth, hoping to avoid any more questions.

"Are you guys going to hang out soon?" Tara asked, taking a bite of her chicken.

Her heart thundered in her chest and she asked herself what she should do in this situation. Tell them or don't tell them?

Then in her mind, in a voice as clear as her own, she heard; **Tell them**.

"I don't know," she answered when she had swallowed her food. "He invited me to something this weekend but..." The sentence hung in the air like smoke from a fire. She was at a loss at how to tell them.

"But?" Dustin asked when she didn't continue, leaning over his plate and eyeing her intently.

Nervousness strangled her and she was starting to think that this was a bad idea. There was absolutely no way that they would ever go for this. "But," she began, trying to find the right words. "A bunch of people are all going."

"Going where?" he asked, his gaze cutting into her like little knives.

"To Cape Cod, for the weekend." She looked down at her plate, twirling some pasta onto the fork, avoiding her father's eyes.

"And you want our permission to go?" Dustin asked, completing the thought that she had left unfinished.

There it was. They now knew about the trip and knew that Kruise was going to be there. All that was left was for them to say no and for her to begin her grieving period for missing the opportunity of a lifetime.

Anxiously, she watched him, chewing on her lip. "Yes, but so are like six other people. Alizé will be there too. She and I get one of the rooms in the cabin." The last part she didn't know if was true or not but had to give them something other than her going away for the weekend with a boy that she had technically just met.

She studied her dad apprehensively.

Dustin said nothing at first, only took a large drink of his beer. After the beer was set down, he cocked his head to the side. Tara was watching her husband intently, nodding imperceptibly. Puzzled, Shayde took a drink of her water. After what seemed like an eternity of silence, her dad finally made eye contact with her.

"Okay," was what he said, although it shocked her so much that she didn't know if she had heard him correctly. "But under one condition."

Shayde could not believe her ears. She noticed her mom

was smirking slightly while her dad was straight faced and serious. "Sure Dad, anything."

"You keep your phone on, fully charged, and on you at all times. You check in when you get there, after breakfasts, lunches, and dinners. You answer our texts and phone calls immediately and if you don't, you will return home and be grounded for the rest of the summer. You make sure that you get one of those rooms and you are to be in there with Alizé only," Dustin said firmly.

Tara giggled a little. "That's like ten conditions, babe."

Dustin frowned, not amused. "I don't care how many there are, they are my rules and they will be followed."

She was astounded. "Of course, Dad, anything. I promise I will be good, you have nothing to worry about."

Something was very aberrant about the whole situation. On any normal day, there would have been no way that her parents would've gone for it. Especially after losing one child, they were agreeing to let their only remaining child go away for the weekend, to a town two-and-a-half hours away, with a boy that they have never met before. It was insane.

She couldn't wait to tell Alizé.

And *Kruise.*

"And absolutely no drinking and driving young lady," Dustin added, his voice raised an octave. "Nobody is to drive that car but you and if any of you have a drink and get behind that wheel, or any wheel for that matter, I WILL find out about it and you will be grounded for the rest of your life."

"Dad, no, of course not," she affirmed. "I will not let anyone drink and drive and you can trust me, I would never do that to.

Believe me." That part was absolutely true. It was unimaginable, thinking about putting her parents through that twice.

"I know, honey, I trust you," Dustin said. "That is why we are letting you go. We know that you're a good kid and you wouldn't do anything stupid. You have never given us a reason not to trust you and as hard as it is for me to say yes to this, I can't tell you how proud I am that you were honest with us about it. It truly makes us proud as parents. You could've easily lied to us and told us that it was you and a bunch of your girlfriends. But you didn't. You chose to be honest with us and tell us the truth. It means the world to me, Shay, it really does." His voice was shaky and it almost looked like a little tear was welling up in his eye. But he cleared his throat, looked down at his food, started cutting his chicken, and the tear was gone.

Shayde's eyes welled up. She was glad that she was honest with them; it made her feel so much better. The tension in her chest was gone as she breathed a sigh of relief and took another bite of her chicken.

"How exciting Shay, I can't wait to hear all about it!" Tara exclaimed.

Shayde smiled. Excitement started to overflow in her chest and she wondered what Kruise was doing right now. The urge to excuse herself from the table to go text him was getting harder to control but she composed herself and stayed put. "I know! Me neither!" she said happily. "Thank you so much you guys. I can't tell you how much it means that you trust me. I won't let you down."

As dinner was eaten and conversation flowed in abundance, Shayde finished all that was on her plate. Satisfied and full, she stood up and helped clean up the dinner and dishes.

She was rinsing off the last dish when her mom appeared at the counter and sat on the bar stool.

"So," she began. "There is something really important that we all have to talk about."

And there it was. Shayde searched her mom's eyes for a glimmer of anything that would clue her in, but there was still nothing. "Okay Ma, what is it?"

"Not here."

"Okay, where?"

"Downstairs."

"In the game room?" She was confused.

"No. Just come with us." Tara started walking towards the basement door, grabbing a flashlight from the counter on her way.

Bewildered, she placed the last dish into the dishwasher and shut the door. The only thing downstairs, besides the game room, was emptiness, a guest room and bathroom, and storage. After she dried her hands on a towel, she went around the island and waited with her mom while her dad locked all the doors and blew out the candles.

Mystified, she followed them down the stairs to the dark basement.

When they arrived at the landing, Dustin shut the door behind her and locked it. She never knew that the door could be locked from the inside. Silently, they went past the game room to the south end of the basement. They passed the laundry room and headed straight for the storage area under the stairs. Dustin started moving the boxes out from under it and with every box removed, Shayde could see another door being uncovered, a door that she hadn't known was there.

Apparently, they didn't want anyone to know about it. Dustin reached into his pants' pocket and pulled out a key ring with an assortment of keys. He unlocked the door, opened it wide and motioned them to enter. Tara went first and Shayde followed. What lay behind the door was another darkened staircase. They waited as Dustin closed the door behind them and locked it as well, engulfing them in darkness. Tara flicked on the flashlight and it eerily illuminated the dark staircase. It smelled damp and muggy, like an old root cellar. The walls bordering the staircase were dirt, cut right into the earth, looking as though someone had dug it out themselves. As they reached the bottom, Tara flicked a switch; its metal casing was attached to a tall wooden post that looked like a ceiling support. Wiring exited from the top of it, and ran the length of the post and across one of the beams that supported the ceiling, to power a hanging bulb above their heads. It illuminated the small room they were standing in. The wire continued along the ceiling and disappeared over the top of a thick, wooden door that looked like it had been taken from a room in a castle. The wood looked very old, its hinges were made of thick iron and it was adorned with a tarnished brass handle that had an old-fashioned keyhole beneath it. When Dustin reached them, he examined the key chain and singled out an old-fashioned black one. He placed it in the keyhole and then he turned around to face Shayde.

"I know you will have a lot of questions, Shay," he told her, his brown eyes the only thing comforting in this strange new world, "and they will all be answered, but right now I just need you to stay quiet and listen. We will explain everything to you."

Secret staircases and strange doors which led to unknown

rooms, the questions were mounting in her mind and yet no words would form anyway. She simply nodded and waited.

Dustin turned the key and pushed the door open.

It creaked heavily on its large black hinges. As it opened, Shayde noticed the wiring for the light bulb continued on into the next room but what she saw next still surprised her.

The primitive wiring disappeared into a modern ceiling to illuminate several silver teardrop light fixtures. These were suspended in four rows, dripping down like silver water. The room was enormous and the entire floor was covered with white tile. It was stunning but it was so white that it almost hurt her eyes to look at it. All along the circumference of the room were wall-to-wall cedar bookshelves, some so high there was a ladder on rolling casters that was used to reach them. In the southeast corner sat a large antique mirror. It was made of thick mahogany and had abstract designs carved into the frame. It was held securely in place by two sets of carved, clawed bird's feet, clutching and balancing on what looked like crystal balls.

Along the shelves were hundreds of books. Some of them looked like they were hundreds of years old, all faded colors of red, green, blue, black and brown. The top shelves held taller, wider books, the next row down contained yet smaller books, and so forth. Along the north wall, the bookshelves continued but then ceased at a gigantic black marble fire place that almost covered the entire wall. It should have looked incongruous in the sea of white, but strangely it made the room look all the more avant-garde. Above the fireplace was another mirror, this one long and plain.

In the northwest corner of the room there was an old

wooden table with four chairs. Opened books were strewn about on its surface. Beyond it, the bookshelves continued all along the west wall, but the shelves now contained jars. Little jars, big jars, bottles of all shapes and sizes which were all labeled and they contained curious substances. Some looked like spices, others looked like liquid. There were also little wooden containers that looked like tea boxes, placed intermittently amongst them. Shayde finally noticed that a door lay recessed in the wall. It was slightly ajar and she could see a decent sized bathroom beyond it, all accented in black and white.

In the center of this vast room, were four black couches placed facing each other in a square, each flanked by tall candleholders. Above them, in the ceiling, was a vent that Shayde vaguely registered must be for ventilation. What was the most peculiar realization of all, however, was that hanging beneath the vent, in the middle of this strange room, was a massive black-iron cauldron, imprinted with what seemed to be *signatures*.

The closing door clattered and echoed in the silence, making Shayde jump at the noise. As she turned around, she noticed that this side of the door had two vertical holders made of the same thick iron as on the other side, and as Dustin slid a very large piece of wood to rest within their grooves, she was reminded of a portcullis made to keep intruders out.

It was very medieval looking.

Dustin walked past them towards the fireplace, flicking a switch on the wall beside it that made it spark to life.

"Come on sweet pea," Tara interrupted Shayde's thoughts and motioned her to follow. "Let's go sit."

Shayde followed her mom to the couches in the middle of the room and they sat down, Dustin soon followed and sat on her other side. Shayde could see now that she was closer to the cauldron that there *were* names impressed within it.

"Okay, I know this is a lot to take in," Tara said, stealing Shayde's attention back and turning off the flashlight before setting it on the ground. "Okay, like your dad said, try to hold your questions 'til I'm done. There is much to explain and it's easier to get through it first, and many of your questions may be answered as we go. If there is something you feel is imperative to know now, just stop me to ask, but if you feel like it can wait, please do.

"Okay," Shayde said, utterly lost.

"Okay. Here goes... There are a lot of things that you don't know about us, about yourself, your family, and the world. As you know, there is something that you get on your sixteenth birthday but the significance of that gift it is somewhat difficult to explain, so I think it's best to let me start at the beginning." Tara stood and walked over to the bookshelf. She climbed a few rungs of the ladder, grabbed one of the biggest books on the top shelf, and returned with it in her hands. As she sat back down next to Shayde, she put the book on her lap.

It was an extremely old looking book, the cover was tattered and torn and the binding was coming undone. It was the size of an atlas but much, much thicker and the cover was faded black. Written in gold letters in an old English font were the words: The Magic Sorenya.

"Before I explain *our* past, I need to give you a history lesson." Tara took a breath. "When Christianity first arrived in Europe, Paganism was the oldest and most dominant faith. In the beginning, Christians and Pagans co-existed with each other. But because of the fundamental difference of beliefs between them, this made conflict inevitable. The bible says there is only one God—a male entity—and that it was a sin to worship any Gods or Goddesses before him. In contrast, Pagans worship nature in many forms, and so to Christians this made any deity, God, or Goddess they worshiped demons. Even now some conservative Christians believe in the literal truth of some biblical passages and any non-Christian religions are regarded as forms of Satanism. In the early years of Christianity, the Christian Church had convinced followers of the old faith to convert but even when they did, many of the old Pagan ways were still followed.

"Anyway it wasn't until the middle ages that problems in this uneasy co-existence came to a head. By this time the Christian Church had grown very powerful and Christians were strong enough to declare that anyone who continued to practice the old Pagan ways were witches who worshipped Satan. Paganism was an evil and unorthodox religion and anyone who practiced it was working for the devil. They began to root out any Pagans who refused to convert to Christianity, banishing them from their villages and towns, and in the worst times, suspected Pagans were even burned alive or hung for what they believed in. Any member of society caught practicing the Pagan faith, would be tortured and killed."

Shayde looked confused, "I thought it was only witches that were killed."

"Ah, that's a common misapprehension; the Old English term for the Pagan faith is Wicca but to most people it is known as witchcraft, but witchcraft isn't what people are led to believe. Wicca is solely a religion that worships everything in creation and sees all nature as sacred. Wicca worships a male and female deity who together created everything in the world. In fact, all Wiccan holy days follow the cycles of nature and the changes in the seasons. They do not believe in the Christian God, the Devil, heaven, hell or anything of that sort. They believe in reincarnation, an interconnected universe, eternal energy, the sacred feminine as well as the sacred masculine. Pagans believe in the Goddess just as much as the God, but our views of them are very different from that of Christianity. We believe that every living entity has a spirit that is interconnected to and part of every other spirit. Humans are a part of nature; nature isn't a part of humans. Divinity establishes itself through all living beings.

"In the past anyone who used the knowledge of the old ways, exhibited their sexuality openly, or celebrated the lunar cycle, were seen as a threat to the established Church and were accused of worshipping and selling their soul to Satan. The followers of Wicca were forced so far underground that most thought they no longer even existed. Over time witches became the fairy tale villains of bedtime stories told to little kids to scare them straight. A witch was the old hag covered with warts who liked to take little children from their parents and eat them for dinner. When people keep believing the same irrational stereotypes and presumptions over hundreds of years, it somehow gets accepted as truth. Although there are rumors that people of our faith practice black magic and dance with the devil, it is untrue. Anyone who practices that magic and worships the devil, is not of Pagan culture.

"The casting of spells has become misconstrued as well.

The Pagans worship all the elements of the earth and believe that everything is interconnected. Like a thread that makes up a sweater, if you pull one thread the whole sweater can fall apart. Everything you do in your daily life is projected into the energy around you. The good deed you do today may benefit you or someone you love at the least expected time. If you never see the consequences of the deed, at least you will have made the world a better place. If you want good things to happen to you, do good things for people and you draw positive energy towards you. Our faith does not believe in evil, we do not worship the devil—the devil is of Christian origin—and none of our spells are used for personal gain or harm. Casting spells is to conjure up positive energy and should be used wisely. For instance, if one wished for financial gain and came to a Wiccan for help, the Wiccan would not put a spell on them to make them rich but rather give a gift to the energy surrounding them and tell them to do a good deed for someone with money. This would make their energy more appealing to the forces at work, would attract better, more positive energy, and as a result good luck would come to them. Witches have a rare knowledge of the world, an understanding that makes them more able to control energy and work magic.

"A Pagans main rule of behavior is that they are forbidden from harming people, including themselves, except in some cases of self-defense and sacrifice to a worthy cause. The most modern form of our faith is Wicca, which is a very decentralized religion. Many Wiccans develop their own rituals, beliefs and other practices. There is but one main idea that has been the same for thousands of years and it is this; The Laws of Enchantment or The Wiccan Rede that rules that a witch may engage in any action, so long as their actions harm nobody, including themselves, and that it is carefully considered. Witchcraft is also ruled by the Threefold Law, which is the belief that the effect of any action taken by any witch against another person, will return to the witch threefold whether it be harmful or good."

"Okay," Tara paused. "Now begins our tale."

Shayde just nodded.

Tara opened the book. On the first page was the title: **"THE MAGIC SORENYA."**

Then on the second page there was an old drawing of a beautiful woman and beneath it, elegant and flowing script which Tara began to read:

"Our ancestor Aenya Duggan was born on March 13th, 1658 in County Cork Ireland," Tara began, pointing at the picture. Then she continued. "During that time, there were great religious wars raging. The Pagans who remained in County Cork that escaped persecution had begun practicing their beliefs in secret. Aenya and her family were part of this group—Pagans forced into seclusion in fear of being killed for their ways. Aenya longed for the old days when they were free to worship openly, but she still devoted a great deal of time perfecting her craft behind closed doors. She would spend all hours of the day reading books, studying the faith and casting spells; it became an obsession for her.

"Aenya possessed a ring that had been in her family for generations—longer than anyone could remember—but family legend said that it was forged in the time of the Tuatha, a race of people in Irish mythology. It held a beautifully cut diamond that had a faint purple tint seen in no other diamond before. It was said by her ancestors that it emanated power and would protect whoever wore it. She used the power from the magic ring—along with all her blood, sweat and tears—and called upon the winds, the rain, the northern lights and the southern sky, the earth, the water, the fire and the air. She intertwined herself within the universe so much so that she re-discovered the old faith, the magical kind and Traditional Irish Magic was reborn.

"Traditional Irish Magic is not a form of witchcraft, nor a religion or a belief, it is an art. Aenya learned to manipulate the energy surrounding her. She successfully pulled a gathering of energy together so powerful and full of light that she gave it a name. She fittingly gave her energy the name "Aura". The day she did this, Aenya's eyes began to glow.

"As Aenya grew, so did Aura, and so did her magical ability. The more energy that she gave to Aura, the more good energy they could, as a team, draw from the universe. Aura was so strong, in fact, that by the time Aenya was in her thirties, Aura took on the form of a beautiful young woman who resembled Aenya—a gorgeous witch with blood-red hair and piercing green eyes—she was still only energy though and didn't have a solid form, her appearance was transparent and undulating, like heat rising off a hot surface. She could even materialize on her own, without Aenya calling on her.

"Eventually Aenya fell in love and married. Together, she and Aura were able to ignite the magic blood within her non-witch husband, Eamon, and teach him the craft. Even though Aenya was much more powerful, he was still able to learn it with ease. When she married him she took his last name and became Aenya Guard and when he took her faith, his eyes began to glow.

"They had five children and as the children were born, Aura would look deep in their eyes into their soul to see if they had gained Aenya's magical gift just by growing inside her. When Aenya's last child was born in 1683, her little infant eyes were glowing slightly—more so than the other children had—and she had a birthmark on her back that was shaped like a Lily. Aura saw it as the mark of a true witch."

Tara paused to explain, "Now most people see the Lily as a symbol of the Virgin Mary, but in fact originally the Lily represented fertility and life in the Pagan religion. Christians have done what they've always done: If they couldn't get rid of a symbol or festival—like the mid-winter feast or the Lily in the celebration of spring—they adopted it as one of their own. Ironically, people accused of witchcraft were sometimes branded with the symbol of Fleur-De-Lis: the lily, as a talisman to protect against their power.

"Anyway," Tara continued reading, "Although *all* of Aenya's children had magical abilities, this child had powers far deeper than Aenya's and had gained them by just growing inside her. Aura picked a powerful name for her: Breken. In ancient Ireland the name meant 'Magical Being'.

"As Breken grew, Aura would tell her tales of ancient Ireland and other people like her. By far the most interesting of her tales were those of the people that formerly inhabited Ireland, the Tuatha de Danaans.

"In old Irish traditions there is much mystery about them. They were often described as more than men, more like Gods and fairies. According to the legend, they arrived in the sky on a ship of dark purple clouds.

"Magic was always attributed to the Tuatha, and it has been said that they were just as wise as they were magical. Being able to cure ailments with water, travelling on the wind with wings that could appear at will, and shape-shifting into anything they desired, were just some of their magical gifts."

Tara paused, and picked up a small box that sat on a table beside her. She carefully opened it and showed Shayde its contents. Sitting inside was the most beautiful ring she had ever seen but somehow not for the first time, she felt as though she had seen it before. It was amazingly simple, a larger stone rested between several tiny versions of it on either side, yet what set it apart was the purplish tint to the jewels.

"The ring," Tara resumed, "that resides with the Sorenya is thought to have come from the Tuatha, yet how or why is not known.

"No one knows what happened to the Tuatha de Danaans and the reason is this; Christian missionaries, whose desire was to obliterate every glimmer of the ancient forms of faith were also those who transcribed the stories that had been passed down over generations. In doing so the legends were so greatly distorted that it makes it impossible to understand who or what the Tuatha really were. We only see them through the thick haze of time, so when we think of them now we see them as men, not the heroic demi-gods or Goddesses they could have been.

"These stories of the Tuathas intrigued Breken and she devoted all her time to learning everything about them. As she grew up, she learned that she too, was able to change her form, and cure cuts, scrapes and gashes—even certain diseases—with water. She constructed her own wand out of Rowan wood and enchanted it with every splendor she could. With it, and with the aid of her own magical concoctions, she even fashioned a magnificent set of wings to ride the wind.

"By the time she was eight, she was a very powerful witch, though she detested being called such a thing, as by this time 'witch' was now associated with the abominable stereotype. She decided to create a new name for herself and her Pagan forebears; Sorenya, which combines the words, Sorceress, Enchantress and Aenya, the name of her mother.

"When she reached the age of nine, it was apparent to her and her family that they would have to leave Ireland. Though many witch families lived and were accepted in County Cork, the witch-hunts had become more unpredictable and their safety was being threatened. They booked passage to the New World and headed for Salem, Massachusetts. Within days after they left, the town that they had called home was destroyed, burned to the ground along with its inhabitants, only a few hundred people survived.

"The Guards arrived in Salem in June of 1689. The family of seven settled into their new town. Eamon was employed by a local farmer and Aenya stayed at home to look after her younger children and tutor them and her elder daughters, while the older boys went off to school. Even though there might have been other witch families in Salem, the Guards didn't know of them and they kept quietly to themselves. Fear was still always close by in the memories of what had happened in their homeland."

Shayde's brow was furrowed in confusion, "Why did people suddenly start to hate witches so much?"

Tara turned to Dustin, "Your father's become quite an expert on this."

Dustin nodded and explained; "During most of the Middle Ages, those who practiced the Old Religion and worked with herbs and charms were largely ignored by the Church and the Inquisition. After the scourge of the Black Death however, witchcraft trials began and steadily increased in number throughout the fourteenth and fifteenth centuries. In 1427, the first major witch-hunt occurred in Switzerland, and in Valais in 1428, there was a massive burning of one hundred so-called witches. In 1486, the official textbook for trying and testing witches was written by the monks Sprenger and Kramer, the infamous 'Hammer for Witches' or 'Malleus Maleficarum'. The period of the great hysteria that many practicing witches today refer to as the 'Burning Times', occurred from about 1550 to 1650 but in many countries the practice continued well into the eighteenth century. Even though organized witchcraft trials continued to be held in most of the English colonies in North America and in Europe as well, most often they were civil affairs. Around forty people were executed in the colonies between 1650 and 1710, and half of these victims perished in 1692 as a result of the Salem Witch Trials."

Shayde looked to her mother, "So what happened to our family?"

"The Guards had managed to live peacefully in Salem for about three years when things suddenly went awry. People were getting word of the witch-hunts over in Europe, and when the plague broke out hysteria hit New England along with it. People who hadn't done anything wrong were being tried, convicted and hung for crimes they didn't commit.

"Breken's family secret had remained undiscovered until Keyan, the Guards eldest son, was accused of putting a hex on a girl named Catherine. The truth was, Catherine had fallen ill and gone into convulsions outside the school. Keyan knew that he should hide his magic, but unbeknown to anyone they were sweethearts and had been secretly meeting after Keyan's classes. Keyan, using magic learned from his mother, enchanted some water and gave it to his dying love. When Keyan poured the elixir down her throat she instantaneously recovered. Unfortunately, Catherine happened to be the daughter of the head witch hunter, John Briggs, and because there were so many witnesses, word of the strange events quickly made its way to him.

"Although Keyan had actually saved his daughter, the witch hunter refused to believe it and accused Keyan and the whole family of devil-worship and witchcraft. Without a trial, they were tied up and dragged to the local church where they were barricaded in and burned alive. Breken, who had been with Aura gathering herbs, suddenly had a deep foreboding and returned home to find her family missing. Breken ran to the horses while Aura implored her not to go, but her attempts were futile because Breken knew something terrible had happened and was undeterred. Galloping off as fast as she could go, she headed for town with Aura following in her wake. When she saw the inferno in the distance, she collapsed to the ground, inconsolably screaming at the world to return her family to her.

"Aura took it upon herself to follow the dark energy

surrounding the church to see who had done such a wicked thing. It led her to the Briggs' home. Knowing that there was nothing they could do to bring them back, she returned to Breken and begged her to flee, lest she be the next one to die. Though the idea of death was tempting to her, she vowed it would not be by Briggs' hand.

"Breken and Aura left in the middle of the night for the neighboring town of Lynn where another Pagan family was offering refuge to those fleeing the witch hunts. They hid with them for a year, waiting for the craze to pass.

"Breken was broken by the loss of her family, she seemed inexorably wounded beyond all repair. Aura did what she could to ease her ailing heart, but there was nothing that she could do that would make it better, Breken seemed to have built a wall around her soul and thoughts.

"In May of 1693, they heard word that the witch trials had finished, the hysteria had abated. Breken decided that she wanted to return home. When they returned, they found the family's house unscathed. Breken knew she would have to be even more careful if she wanted to practice her magic, so she built a secret spell room in the basement of her house away from the prying eyes of the world.

"A few months had passed when Breken told Aura of her intention to seek revenge on the man that killed her family. Aura advised against it, it was contrary to the Laws of Enchantment and the magic would turn against her. As your mother said its central tenet being: 'If it harms none, do as you will.'

"Breken however was adamant; convincing Aura she could find a way to perform a spell that would cause no harm. She studied long and hard in the books her mother had brought over from Europe. She hovered over her cauldron for weeks on end and worked with potions and spells, it sometimes seemed like she had tried every single ingredient of the earth. Aura was sent far and wide on missions to seek things out, as Breken worked into all of hours of the night, conjuring spells that might help her circumvent the rule.

"Breken realized that the only revenge she could take upon Briggs would be revenge wrought by his own hand. She planned to use all the energy that the death of her family had produced and use it to create another entity like Aura. This entity would follow Briggs as Aura followed her, and bring good or bad luck to him depending on the goodness of his actions. She would not break the Laws of Enchantment because he would have the opportunity for redemption and this was her loophole. If he continued to be bad, bad luck would dog him, and if he became good, he would truly suffer for what he had done, as he would realize the evilness of the crime he committed. That would be revenge enough.

"She channeled the winds of the four corners of the earth and summoned the energies from across the world. It was an amazing sight to see. It was as if she had roped and harnessed the northern lights with a long, invisible lasso. Brilliant beams of light came streaming in from all corners of the world into the little basement, creating a prism of light of every color of the rainbow, radiating above the cauldron. She then channeled the energy that the actions of John Briggs produced when he butchered her family, and thrust it into the light.

"In a flash the colors instantly turned dark grey. It began to swirl above the cauldron, like clouds before a tornado. Breken took an athame and pricked her finger and then took up a piece of fabric taken from the clothing of each member of her family and dabbed it with her blood. As she chanted her spell, she gave each piece to the wind one by one.

"When she was finished, she had formed another gathering of energy like that of Aura, except this was a vitality that contained all the negativity the massacre of her family had caused. She named this 'spirit' Viento. Though he would be invisible to ordinary people, to Breken and Aura he took the form of a tall man, dressed in the breeches, stockings and topcoat of the time yet with a peculiar dark translucence that meant that the features of his face couldn't be discerned. Viento was essentially an embodiment of sorrow.

"Viento was forbidden to show himself to Briggs, as Briggs had to find his own way to redemption. However, if as death approached and he had still learned nothing, Breken instructed that Viento was then to reveal himself and remind Briggs of the terrible crime he committed and that the adversities he had suffered had been needlessly caused by himself—if he had only lived a better life he could have turned Viento into a spirit of good fortune. When she was finished, she sent Viento on his way. He dissipated before her and she never saw him again.

"Breken blossomed into the most captivating, beautiful woman anyone had ever seen. She had the long red hair of her mother, bright, piercing green eyes and a soft, soulful face. Breken continued to live in Salem, though she practiced her faith in secret for fear of another witch-hunt. She loved helping people, it was the only thing left in the world that gave her meaning, so she would send Aura to search out people in need and help them anonymously. A woman in childbirth she aided with a concoction of herbs, spells, and flowers. She would send

Aura to guide home fishermen lost at sea. A farmer whose crops were dying from drought; she summoned the summer rain.

"She was so busy helping people in need that she didn't even notice that her luck was getting better. The farmer whose farm she helped save—Charlie McKarat—became her husband. They began a family and through their goodness and the help of Aura, their dynasty flourished.

"Magic has been inherited by all of Aenya's descendants; every infant born of the Sorenya revealing their magic through their beautiful luminous eyes, but only sometimes is a child born that bears the mark of a great Sorenya. This child has the potential to develop powers as wondrous as those held by Breken. She was the only one who had been able to shape-shift, read minds, cure diseases, dream of things to come and to fly by the magical wings.

"In order to determine who has inherited Breken's Gift of Light, Aura examines every infant born of this family to search for the Lily birthmark. The birthmark was an intrinsic force in Breken's abilities and any child who carries the mark will be the one to carry on the legacy. This is the child who Aura will protect most, the one that is charged with safeguarding the family story and the Gift. It is the child born with the mark of the Lily to whom the greatest gift of magic is passed down. The child that will have the deep, dark-red hair and bewitching green eyes of Aenya, wield Breken's wand of Rowan, and wear the diamond ring of the Tuatha.

"Not all the descendants of Aenya and Breken wanted to use their magical gifts, even some of those who bore the mark of the Lily were not interested in developing their skills. It was over two hundred years ago that Julienne, the most unwilling

Sorenya, decided that no child of hers or her descendants would be told of their powers until they reached sixteen years of age. They could then make a choice about what they would do with their power, whether they wished to harness it and learn the craft and sign the contract, or if they wished to turn their back on it. Since then it has been a sixteenth birthday tradition. If the child signs the contract, eyes that have been dimmed since birth from not practicing magic then begin to brighten again.

"The contract states that any one of the Magic Sorenya who choose to participate in the craft have to sign the said contract, agreeing to follow the Laws of Enchantment, and to pass down the magic and the story to their descendants."

"Did Kain sign the contract?"

Tara nodded.

Shayde looked down. Her brow furrowed as she clutched her necklace that Kain had given her, "Did he have any powers before he knew?"

"He knew something was not normal, just as you had," Tara confided. "Kain was able to read thoughts, and he was really self-conscious about it. When he first told us about it he was really concerned, thinking something was seriously wrong with him, but until he signed the contract we could say noth-ing. After Julienne, it became a Law that we must wait until our children are sixteen to inform our children of their powers." Tara smiled, "the only skill he didn't seem to mind was that he could also get into people's heads and influence them, like he did with the boys at school who tried to talk to you. He freaked the boys out so much they would never try to talk to you again. The only one whose thoughts he couldn't read were yours.

What we didn't realize is that he had a strange ability to wish something true.

"When he signed the contract we realized he would be a powerful Sorenya, even though he didn't have the birth sign of the Lily. He was able to see the future in his dreams, move things with his mind, and he was even capable of changing his form to whatever he wanted.

"Like you, Kain hated bullies. One day he was walking home from middle school when he saw one of the known bullies giving a smaller kid a really hard time. It wasn't the first time he'd seen it and this time he decided enough was enough. He went to intervene but as he did so the bully's friends arrived on the scene. Though the younger kid escaped, Kain was set upon quite badly and as he lay curled in a ball while they kicked him he wished as hard as he could that the ringleader would drop dead. Immediately the boy's eyes rolled back into his head, he fell to the ground and suffered a severe seizure, one that took his life. As the bully's friends scattered, Kain tried as hard as he could to wish him back to life. The cause of death was determined as a massive grand-mal seizure and most people saw it as a coincidence, but Kain always felt he had something to do with it. He was never the same. We told him it was only a coincidence too, but when he signed the contract he realized that his worst fears were true.

"As time wore on, he started having dreams about his death. In every dream he died in a different way. He knew that if he tried to avoid what he saw in the dream, the dream would only change again to counter it so that a different dream would come true. Although he hadn't meant to, he had done some-thing terrible with his power and no matter what he tried to do to redeem himself, the Law of Enchantment had been broken. He saw his own demise in many different circumstances and knew that no matter what he did to make amends, and how much remorse he felt, he had to come to terms with it. It was coming for him.

"In one of these dreams, Kain saw you both driving home after a football game and getting struck by a drunk driver. I think he knew if he didn't succumb to his fate instead of just avoiding it, something bad would happen to you. So he told Aura of what he dreamt and asked her to do anything she could to get you out of the truck that night. Aura did what she had to do. She jumped into the mind of Alizé's boyfriend and forced him to break up with her. Being the friend you are, she knew that you would stay with Alizé instead of going with Kain. It was the first time Aura had been able to achieve something like this.

"Kain's death was a great tragedy which we will never truly recover from. He was a kind-hearted person who never meant to do any harm. Hopefully it will serve as a warning that a powerful witch like you has to be extremely careful with your powers." Tara smiled wistfully, "Perhaps it is his final gift to you."

No words could explain the way Shayde felt. There were a million different feelings all at once. From excitement about this new knowledge, to sadness about Kain and the secret he was burdened with: the fact that he knew he was going to die young and chose to go alone to save her. She was angry that her parents kept this all from her for so long and thought that maybe, just maybe, they would've been able to spare Kain if they both had known sooner.

"I used to try to see if he could read my eyes but he never could. I have always had this feeling that there was something deeper within me, something I was looking for and could never find," Shayde said as she hugged her knees to her chest. All of the strange things that had surrounded her entire life were because she was a *witch*. It was why she could see people's auras and read their eyes, how she could dream of things to come, and how she knew something odd surrounded the night.

"So," Tara continued, "to answer the first few questions that are streaming into your head. One: we have been writing this family history since my grandma, Bria. Aura wanted to make sure that we were keeping an accurate account of The Magic Sorenya, so everyone with the Lily has agreed to help her write it. Even though the stories have been verbally passed down for generations, Aura thought it best to start keeping a written record of our family. Two: our eyes do glow too; we just have good contacts, and three: our family is worth well over forty-seven billion dollars today."

Shayde paused, and then stared incredulously at her mom. "Did you say *billion?*"

"Yes sweetie pie," Tara answered laughing. "You come from a long line of millionaires. Our family has helped start universities, medical research centers, towns, animal clinics, and of course our very own Fleur-De-Lis Medical Center and many, many more. The largest portion of our legacy now comes from an ancestor of ours who helped turn a small agricultural college into a very prestigious university, which greatly contributes to our fortune daily and is why we have so many charities we give to. I will tell you all about your ancestors some other time, they are all in here, but it is too much for one night. The fact of the matter is that none of us have chosen to live extravagantly. We like living simply and no one really knows we're worth so much. As long as you stick to your faith and continue to do good things for people, good things will come to you and Aura will stay strong. As you have heard though, should you choose to do negative things you are at risk. The tiniest thing will affect your fate. It's the weight we bear for having our power." said Tara gravely.

"Oh, I definitely want to live like you guys."

Tara took Shayde's hand. "When Aura first looked upon you she saw you were the image of Breken and this gave us hope that you would be able to fly, that gift has not been given since she lived. There is no clear reason as to why the gift seems to have died with her but Aura has been waiting with baited breath to see those wings again."

"That's strange that she thought I looked like Breken," Shayde said softly. "I have always had this feeling that I have lived before. Always."

"I know. All your life you have done a lot of things that made us think you weren't new to this world," Tara said quietly. "You picked up everything so easily, from the day you were born. You walked first, never even crawled. Your spoke very early and you were never really like a toddler; you didn't go through the terrible twos. You were a good baby, always calm and cool and you never threw fits. Unlike your brother, and we could tell when he was about throw one because you'd halt anything you were doing to run and hide underneath your bed. It was how I always knew if a temper tantrum was coming." Tara laughed at the memory of her lost son. "You have always been so much more mature than your years."

"Yeah I have felt that way often. I don't feel sixteen. I feel thirty-six."

"When you were born, the mark of the Lily was there on the back of your head, and so Aura has been with you throughout your life, protecting you, while she waited for the time she could begin helping you fulfil your magical destiny. Would you like to meet her?"

"Oh yeah!" Shayde exclaimed as she sat up straight and wiped the tears from her eyes. Tara looked to the far southeast corner of the room. Shayde followed her gaze and found the interesting mirror. Suddenly, the mirror started glowing the brilliant shades of the sunset. It beamed white at first and then gold, then it shifted to shades of red, orange and yellow. As the colors began to fade, the shape of a woman started to appear within the glare. She was as tall as Shayde, she had very long and wavy dark-red hair, held back by a pearl head-band, and her eyes were the color of moss under the shimmering movement of a mountain stream. They held the unfathomable wisdom of an unimaginable lifetime. Her nose was small and straight, her lips were full and sparkling slightly, and she was thin, and wore a white dress from some other time.

She stepped down out of the mirror, holding onto the edges as she did so. Shayde went to her, impatient to see her face to face. Aura was translucent, not quite ghostlike, more like water. She radiated light from within, creating an aura of light around her.

"Shayde my darling. It's nice to finally meet you," Aura whispered, her voice unlike anything Shayde had ever heard. It was like a voice carried on the wind, whispering through a field of wheat, with just an undertone of like the sound of rain pattering on the leaves of tree.

"It's nice to meet you, too. Thank you for protecting me," Shayde said, stepping closer to her, she resisted the urge to touch her.

"You can touch me, my princess, it will not hurt me. It might be a little strange for you though."

Shayde hesitated at first then she extended her hand and went to touch Aura's face. Her hand went through her, Aura rippled a little as if Shayde had poked her reflection in a pool of water. She felt strange to the touch as well, like warm air with the density of a fluid, but when she retracted her hand it was dry.

"So you have been with me my entire life?" Shayde asked, examining her hand as she pulled it back. "You are how my mom has known about everything I have ever done?"

"Yes. I have done everything I could to keep you safe. It is my job to protect you." Her expression was unwavering.

"You saved me the night my brother died? You're the reason I hate bullies? You were with me in the diner today, listening to Alizé tell me to tell my mom?" She couldn't help it. The questions were overflowing in her mind and she couldn't stop them from pouring out.

"Yes. I have been with you always."

"That is one of the reasons we agreed to let you go to Cape Cod this weekend," Dustin explained. "When Kruise came up to talk to you, Aura read his thoughts. She even stayed with him for a while to see if his thoughts changed after he left you. They did not, they stayed completely honorable the entire time and all he wanted to do was hang out with you, to get to know you.

Aura told me this at dinner; she was talking to me inside my head."

It suddenly made sense why her father had said yes. Despite the incredible events that were unfolding, Shayde couldn't stop her mind from flicking back to Kruise and flush with pleasure that he thought of her with respect. She felt no animosity towards Aura for telling her parents what she heard. Though Shayde had only just met her, she loved her with her whole heart. It felt as though she was drawn to her, like she had always known her, as if she was an old friend.

"It was how I knew that you had a crush," Tara continued. "It was how I could read your eyes. It is usually difficult to read your eyes, Shay. You have a built-in defense mechanism that makes it extremely hard for one to get in. It is the same gift Breken had. You do let some people get in every once in a while, but only a very few. Only I have been able to read your eyes and your grandma, Mariah, was able to once when you were a toddler, but your dad and brother, never."

She wondered how she had been able to turn it on and off without knowing.

"Come," Aura said, gliding towards the couch. "I know you have questions."

"You okay Shay?" Dustin asked her.

"Yeah, I'm okay. I feel a bit lost, but okay." She looked at Aura and sat back down on the couch next to her mom.

"Ask whatever you want my love," Tara said.

She felt the back of her head and tried to feel for the birthmark.

"It's there," Tara answered her unspoken question. "You just won't ever be able to see it unless you shave your head."

"What does it look like?"

Tara pulled her shirt down over her left shoulder and exposed her back shoulder bone. There, just faintly, was a patch of lighter colored skin in the shape of a lily. Something that you wouldn't know was there unless you knew what you were looking for.

"Oh, it's pretty." Shayde looked closer, tracing it with her fingertip. Then she focused on Dustin. "So, Aura is how you knew about the car Dad?"

"Yes. I couldn't read you, but Aura was there and saw how much you wanted it and told me about it later on that day."

She paused. Then she gazed at Aura. "Okay, so you're energy? I mean I know you are, but you look normal, aside from the fact that you look like water. I mean... Well... Do you sleep? Eat? Think? And the mirror, what's that for, have you always had it?"

"I am energy," Aura began. "But I am much like you, though I do not have or need the internal organs inside me that you do, I am just intelligent energy. Sort of like a spirit, except I was created from positive energy from the earth, from people's good karma and that is the only way I can remain. I am self-aware, I have consciousness and, as you can see, I can walk, talk, I can see, I can move about, I can shape-shift and part of that is being able to show myself in this form at will. I can read thoughts. Because I do not have a solid mass that I am able to enter into things that do. Therefore, I can get into your head and read your thoughts just as I can jump into a body and take control.

"The mirror has been around since the beginning, a gift from Aenya; it is part of who I am. Some spells I will teach you use that mirror, but it is my sanctuary. If I go into my mirror, it is like sleep is to you. I do not just sit there and stare off into space until someone calls me again, I sleep on my own and when I want. My mind goes blank and sometimes I dream, it is like you being unconscious. I can wake up whenever I wish, or when someone calls my name, no matter where they are. If the mirror was to break, I would be okay, we would find me another one. I am just particularly fond of this mirror since it has been my home for three hundred years.

"I am not all-knowing and I do not follow you around constantly without giving you a second's peace. I do give everyone their privacy and I stay out of people's minds as much as possible. There is so much going on in a person's mind that to jump into it and try to figure things out, is like jumping into a conversation someone has been having for hours with three other people that they have known for years.

"I was not born, just sort of created. I do not remember my life before Aenya, just as you have no memory of who you were or where you were before you were born. I know that I have lived in the past though, for becoming this form was so natural to me, and being this being, whatever I am, is close to human. After all, we are all just energy. I do not know how long I will be here for, but it seems that as long as you all continue to do good deeds, I will be around for a while longer."

"That makes sense," Shayde responded quietly. "I have so many questions yet I don't even know where to begin. I mean, I have always known there was something weird about me, I just had no clue it was *this* big."

"Well, on that note," Dustin said, getting up and walking over to the bookshelf. He pulled out another great big book from the top shelf and grabbed a rectangular box as well. "It's time," he said to the women.

"Time for?" Shayde asked.

"To be initiated into the Sorenya," Aura explained. "This will ignite the magical blood that is lying dormant in you now. Although you possess powers that you have already experienced, these have merely been an overflow of the really great magic within you. Once we awaken your magic, there is no turning back. You will be magical for life. Are you sure this is the life you want?" Aura asked her.

"Of course," she replied without hesitation. "It was what I was born to do, I know it."

"Okay then, stand up," Tara instructed her.

Dustin motioned for her to follow him to the table in the corner . He pulled out scroll from the box that looked as though it was made from parchment. It looked very old—yellow-brown, and dingy with age. As he unrolled it, he laid it flat on the table, using the little box as a weight to hold it open, as the edges were worn and it was accustomed to being rolled up. It took up the length of the table. Elegant, handwritten rules filled up the page and names in every script were scrolled along its margins.

"As you have probably already guessed," Dustin said, holding the other end down with his right hand, "this is the contract. It states: You commit to studying and using the craft in good faith and to the best of your ability. When your children reach the age of sixteen you will tell the story of the Sorenya, of our family, our faith, our magic, and you will teach them the craft. The child that bears the mark of the Lily will be given the ring and the wand of

Rowan. You are not to discuss the craft with anyone who is not of our faith unless a deep love has been declared between you; if you do it is considered a bad omen. Does that all sound okay?" He eyed her intently as he offered her a quill.

"It does."

She took the feather pen, bent over the old paper and pressed the pen to its surface. As she did so, it began to glow at its tip. The ink was gold and glittery. She signed her name just below her brother's, the sparkling ink illuminating the dark and lending her father's face an amber tint. It was the first type of magic she had ever seen, and she looked wondrously at her name as it settled into the page, which though the glowing had dimmed remained golden.

"Look," her father said and pointed to the cauldron. Her signature was now embossed on the cauldron, along with the other Sorenya of the past.

"Wow," she breathed, motionless with amazement.

"Okay," Tara interjected her musings. "Now come back over here."

Dustin took the pen from her and began to roll the contract back up as she walked to Aura and her mom. Tara had lit the big candles that were on stands behind the couches and turned out the overhead lights.

"Shayde," Aura began, her voice calm and collected, "I need you to stand and face me."

Shayde did as she was told as Tara joined them, another long wooden box in her hand. Shayde watched as her mom opened it, looking at it as though it were a rare jewel. Lying on a cushion of red velvet was a beautifully smooth, ash brown wand. The wand was thicker at its base and came to a point at the tip.

Tara gracefully removed it from the box, handing the box to Dustin as she pointed it at Shayde's forehead.

"I, Aura," Aura began as Tara steadied the wand at Shayde's forehead, *"charge the strength of our sun god, Nuada, to light the flame of affluence within Shayde Jennaevicia Gamic. We charge the Sorenya, through time from Breken to Tara to bestow the wisdom of their understanding upon her. From the symbol of beauty, Venus, we ask for joy, prosperity, happiness, and love. In Mars, I place our trust to keep her inner powers and energies flowing. We entrust to Jupiter the growth of her knowledge and inner wisdom. We charge Saturn with the deepening of her respect for all things living and dead. And, from our Lady Avaluna the moon, she shall receive the secrets of the currents of life that shall help awaken all that is magical within her. Blessed be."*

As Aura spoke, there was a slight tingling sensation all over Shayde's body. She felt the room's temperature start to rise, as though she was sitting under a heat lamp. She could feel every hair on her body rise up and could feel the hairs on her head growing. She tilted her head back and closed her eyes, then opened her arms to the elements, as if to welcome them home. It felt like she had been awakened from a long sleep, like she was seeing the world for the first time. Chills began to fill her and she shivered. It felt as if her heart had sunk down into her stomach and that ants were crawling up and down her veins. Tiny little beads of light illuminated her skin and she glowed in the darkness. It was the weirdest and most wonderful feeling that she had ever felt. She brought her head back up as the feelings subsided.

Silence engulfed the room, the expression on her parents' and Aura's faces made her want to see for herself what they were looking at. She walked over to the mirror and staring back at her was her same old reflection, however it was different from before. Her skin was softer, her aura was brighter, she almost had a glow to her, and her eyes were the most piercing, glowing green she had ever seen. They were still her eyes but brighter. People would definitely notice.

"You may have to wear contacts too," Tara said smiling, suddenly there beside her, staring over her shoulder into the mirror.

It was still dark in the big room, aside from the candles, but her eyes pierced the darkness like a cat's when light shines on them in the dark.

"Is that what Kain's did too?" Shayde asked, remembering how light his eyes looked after his birthday.

"Yes," Aura said. "It seems the longer the bloodline, the more powerful the Sorenya, the brighter the eyes. The family has always had the intense green eyes, but as time goes on the more radiant your eyes will become. We figured out over time that contacts help dull the brightness. We both wear them, Kain did and now you will have to as well."

"That's okay, I can deal with contacts," she responded, feeling relaxed and calm, almost sedated. "How did our ancestors hide their eyes before contacts were invented?"

"There is a spell that dims your eyes temporarily," Aura responded. "When contacts were invented it was just easier to put them in and wear them all day than to have to work a spell each time you needed to go out into public."

"I see."

When she returned to the couch, her mom held up the box containing the ring. "And this," she said as she opened it, "belongs to you. When you wear it Aura will come to you, if she isn't with you already, but you won't be able to hear other people's thoughts. It acts as a shield between you to others."

Shayde took it out and looked at it with awe. It was astonishing that it came from her ancestors, that each of the powerful Sorenya of her family had worn it, going back thousands of years. She felt like she was truly part of something now, something much, much bigger than herself.

"How come I've never seen you wear it?" Shayde asked Tara.

"Over time you will learn how to control your mind on your own without it and you won't want anything to happen to it—as it is so incredibly old. When I received the ring from my mother I hadn't seen it before, she too had put it away for safekeeping, as did I, and so will you."

Tara then handed her the wand. Hot tears ran down Shayde's face and she wiped at them with the back of her hand. It was all so overwhelming. To learn something like this, to know she may have to power to *fly*, to find out why her brother died, and then to discover that she was a *billionaire,* it was mind-blowing.

"It's okay love," Tara said, pulling her into her arms. "Cry. Let it all out."

Shayde cried into her mother's arms. "I'm sorry that Kain had to die."

Her knees became weak and suddenly they were heavily hitting the floor, so overcome with sadness again that it felt like Kain had just died. A floodgate opened and a gush of emotions came pouring out of her, her heart breaking for him all over again. She cradled her face in her hands as her mother rocked her, letting her cry as long as she needed.

After the uncontrollable sadness subsided, Aura was there at her side, motioning for her to sit on the couch.

"I know this is much for a young person to comprehend," she said soothingly as Shayde sat back down. "But we are all here for you as we are a family, and I am yours forever."

"And we don't have to think about this anymore tonight," Tara said. "It is almost midnight. You can start your learning whenever you wish," she whispered softly, stroking her hair.

"I used to teach your mother once a week," Aura said, "but some liked to do more; it's completely up to you."

"I will probably start with once a week," Shayde said through a yawn. "But since I am leaving on Friday and have things to do tomorrow, can we start on Monday?"

"Of course my darling. Whenever you wish."

"I am excited to learn. I hope I can fly," Shayde whispered.

Her eyes felt heavy. Even though she knew a big part of that had been her tears, maybe it was also the igniting of her magic blood. All she knew was that the sleepiness was plundering her ability to think straight and the suspension of consciousness was rapidly approaching.

"I know you will be able to my Shayde," she heard Aura hum, as her eyes opened and closed again. "When you were born, your eyes told me so."

And then unconsciousness grabbed her and pulled her into the depths of dreams, rendering her unresponsive and numb to the world.

SEVEN

K ruise's eyes shot open in shock as one of his first alarms went off.

As the desire to sleep more fought the comprehension that he had to be awake, he rolled over and grabbed the phone, hitting the snooze option.

It was a quarter 'til five and he didn't have to be awake until five, but he needed that fifteen minutes before—and sometimes fifteen minutes after—to become fully awake.

As consciousness surfaced, he was setting his phone back on the table when he remembered her. He quickly pulled the phone back to him and strained his eyes through the fog of sleep to see if there were new messages.

There weren't any.

He felt a tiny ping of sadness. He had been looking forward to waking up to a message from her, finding out if she was able to come this weekend or not.

He may even have dreamed about her, but he couldn't remember at the moment.

Maybe it would come back to him.

The light from the moon was weakening as the sun's rays were battling the darkness, filling the room with an eerie blue light that was still too dark for him to see clearly, but light enough to know that the day had begun.

He lay back down to try to sleep for fifteen more minutes until his next alarm went off, but as soon as his head hit the pillow it was flooded with images of her. It was pointless to try to get his mind to quiet now; by the time he finally did it would be time to wake up.

Sitting up and swinging his legs around to rest his feet on the floor, he sat there for a minute, trying to get his eyes to focus and get rid of the fog so he could function. After a few minutes he got up and went into his closet. From the right side of it he grabbed an old t-shirt from a hanger and then from the left, a pair of old blue jeans and ratty old work boots from the floor. He dressed and then grabbed his socks from the dresser, returning to the bed to sit while he put them on along with his boots.

He glanced over at his phone, wondering why he had not heard from her. What had her family ended up doing for her? Maybe they had planned a surprise party and she got caught up in the moment and was too busy to text.

It's okay, he reasoned with himself, *it doesn't matter.*

He shouldn't care this much. After all, it was only a little crush. She'll text later on in the day when she's awake. He needed to stop thinking about her. Anyway, she wasn't his to worry about yet. He had to get it under control but this strange, beautiful girl was completely obsessing him, eviscerating all his normal thoughts and replacing them with thoughts of her. They hardly knew each other; he'd had dates before and never felt like this.

Before these deliberations created a landslide in his mind, he stood and went to the bathroom where he brushed his teeth and sprayed some cologne. Even though the scent would probably only last until he arrived at work where it would be replaced by the fish smell, he put it on anyway. He finished up by lathering lotion into the tattoos on his arms.

When he was done in the bathroom, he gave one last look at himself in the mirror and left, turning off the light as he did so. He went back to his room, grabbed his wallet and hat from the dresser and unplugged his phone, stowing it away in his pocket.

Although he sometimes detested getting up so early, he loved this time of morning in summer. Quietness lurked in every corner and the air was warm, with only occasional gusts of cool wind creeping up from the sleepy depths of dawn. The sun was winning the battle and the sunrise was transforming the night sky into a beautiful canvas of oranges and pinks. Dew clung to the blades of grass and leaves on the trees, giving everything around him a hint of a sparkle in the infancy of morning. The briny air was crisp and soothing, filling him up with scents of the boundless ocean nearby.

As he drove he thought of her again. This time of day, she was probably sleeping soundly in her bed. He wondered what she looked like when she slept. Probably just as breathtaking as when she was awake. Her delicate eyelashes pressed ever so slightly against the soft skin of her face, acting like a dark curtain of mystery, covering up the anomaly that was the color of her eyes. Her delicate hands pressed up against her cheek, caressing her face while resting millimeters away from her lips. He longed to be those hands, to touch that sweet face and to be so close to those lips.

The sunrise was becoming increasingly beautiful on the horizon, though the lavender heavens were still lightly dusted with faint stars. The boats in the harbor slumbered quietly on the water that reflected the sky, floating in what looked like a melted rainbow. The surface was still, reflecting the rays of the rising sun, giving the stillness of the water a serene and unreal feeling to it. Yet however beautiful Kruise thought the splendor of the sunrise, at this moment he still thought it was incomparable to Shayde's beauty. *I really must get a grip*, he chided himself.

Luckily at this time of day there were hardly any cars on the road and he didn't really have to focus on traffic, but why was he so caught up with this girl after just a few glances and some text messages? The answer was not meant to be found yet and the truth was, he enjoyed feeling like this, it made his soul sing, so he continued to think of her all the way to work.

When he pulled his truck into the lot across from his work, he killed the engine and took out his keys.

Quimby's Fish Market was located in the heart of Palmer Cove. Locals chose to go to Quimby's rather than getting their seafood at grocery stores because the seafood was fresh, never delivered from a far away place, as Jack even employed the fishermen.

When Kruise was done with his opening duties, he sat behind the counter and started to read yesterday's paper that was sitting on the counter. It was only six a.m. He had the whole day ahead of him until tomorrow; it was going to be the longest day of his life and the clock was bound to get over a million glances from him throughout the day.

He thought about what he should say to Shayde when he did finally text her. He pulled out his phone, went into "compose new message", and stared at the blank message screen.

Different options deluged him as he tried to come up with the perfect thing to say. He finally settled on, "Good morning beautiful" and hit send before he could change his mind. He put the phone on silent and stuck it into the desk drawer. He knew that it was going to be a while before she responded.

The day was passing so slowly, he didn't know how he would get through it. Thinking about different things that they would do while they were in Cape Cod helped him to pass the time, but even that barely made the minutes move.

He decided to divert himself with planning the weekend. By the time that he was finished, he had a complete grocery list and an itinerary of what they would do from day to day. When his lists were complete, he remembered his phone that was still in the drawer. He pulled it out to see if anyone had messaged him.

A little yellow envelope was on the main screen. His heart raced at the thought it could be from her. He opened the phone, scrolled over to messages and opened it up.

Hey bro how's work?

Jay's text said.

So slow. I'm bored to tears. How was last night?"

Kruise responded, sad that it wasn't Shayde.

It was alright. I got pretty wasted. It was fun though. What you do?

Chilled with dad, ate some burgers and went to bed. Hey, guess what?

What bro?

Dad said that we could take the boat and the jet skis! Isn't that dope?

he texted back, smiling to himself.

The bell over the front door rang as an old woman in a red scarf traipsed in and began to browse. Kruise stood up and greeted her, sticking his phone in his pocket as he did.

"Can I help you find something?" he asked when she paused at an icy display case. She shrugged her shoulders but didn't turn to face him. He felt the phone vibrating in his pocket.

Impatiently he waited for what seemed like hours, while the woman scoured around, never allowing him to help her with anything. He was palpably annoyed by the time she finally decided on two pounds of salmon and a pound and a half of mussels. She handed him the money without even a smile and was on her way. He thought she would never leave.

He took out his phone again and flipped it open.

There were two new messages.

That's awesome! I can't wait for the trip! How late you working 'til?

The second one was from Shayde. When he saw her name, a clamor of passion surged through his chest.

It read,

I'm so sorry I didn't text you back last night. My parents planned this nice dinner for me and they don't allow texting during family functions. By the time it was over I passed out downstairs and someone must've carried me and put me in my bed. I'm so sorry; I really had every intention to.

He felt so relieved. Worry had plagued all day him for nothing.

He responded to Jay first, telling him what time he was off and asking if he wanted to go to the store with him later. Then he wrote back to Shayde.

Don't worry about it. I totally understand, that is a good rule to have I think. Did you have a good time?

In between the texts he was getting from Jay and Shayde, he played solitaire on the computer. Jack didn't mind if they played on the computer or their phones as long as they stopped what they were doing when customers came in.

His phone vibrated loudly on the desk.

Jay responded first, saying he'd tag along with him to the store and asked what he needed to get. Shayde's next text said that she had a great time and mainly just talked the night away.

Kruise responded to Jason first.

> I was thinking of getting some food for lunches and dinners so we don't have to eat out the entire time. Maybe we can get some money from the boys to pitch in.

Then to Shayde he said,

> That sounds really nice. I just hung out with my dad and went to bed. So did you ask your parents if you can go?

He was suddenly nervous about her answer. She had to say yes, she just had to. It was the only answer he was going to accept.

A couple more customers came in.

The second employee was supposed to be there at noon, staying until they closed at eight, and it was quarter after. It didn't surprise him that Finn wasn't there yet, he was a stoner kid that Kruise knew from school and he slacked off at absolutely everything.

As Kruise helped the customers with what they needed, he could hear his phone vibrating in the drawer. When everyone was paid and gone, Finn came staggering in, obviously still tipsy from last night.

"What's up bro?" Finn said as he stumbled passed.

"What's up?" Kruise asked, watching him as he wobbled a bit, his eyes so red it hurt to look at him. "You alright man, gonna make it?"

"Yeah for sure," he said, righting himself on the display counter. "I'm perfect man." He even had a stoner voice, like Tommy Chong's.

"Alright bro."

Kruise laughed to himself as Finn shuffled towards the back to clock in.

The suspense was nearly killing him when he finally glanced at his phone.

There were two new messages.

> I did.

> They said yeah!!

The blood raced beneath his skin and his knees weakened just at the thought. It was real now. She was coming this weekend and he was going to be able to be with her gorgeous self in person and not just in his mind. Tomorrow couldn't come fast enough.

The other one was from Jay telling Kruise to text him when he got off and he'd meet him there.

Kruise wrote back to Shayde first.

That just made my whole day! Jay and I are going to the store tonight to get food for the weekend so we don't eat out the entire time.

He was finishing up his text to Jason when Finn came back out from the office and sat on one of the other chairs they had behind the counter.

In a monotone voice Finn asked, "Busy today?"

"Yeah, swamped," he answered sarcastically. "It's been so boring dude and I'm going away for the weekend so it's passing by so slowly," he said as he sat down next to him.

"Nice, nice, where are you going?" Finn queried as he played with a rubber band on the desk.

"Some friends and I got a cabin in Cape Cod for the weekend. I just asked the hottest girl to come along and she just said yes! It's gonna be dope!"

"Heck yeah man," Finn slurred. "That's tight."

"Yeah should be a pretty good time."

He grinned as his phone went off again and he focused on the message. It was Shayde asking if there was anything that she could bring.

He responded,

No, I got it. Just bring your lovely self.

THE DAY CONTINUED TO GO BY INTERMINABLY SLOWLY. THERE HAD been only four or five customers throughout the duration of his shift. He played solitaire on the computer, talked with Finn, and looked at pictures on Facebook. He was pleased that he finally got to talk to her by text.

When the fishermen came in from their day on the ocean, he knew his shift was almost over. They went out to sea around six a.m. and usually came in around one in the afternoon. He helped unload the fish from their boat, and when they were done he sorted them out and put them away. It was the part of the day that usually went by the fastest. When he was finished with everything and had the back room swept and tidied up, he went up to the front to see how Finn was holding up. It appeared as though he was asleep with his eyes open; he was just staring out into space. It was a quarter 'til two and Kruise decided he was just going to leave early. He was always on time, had never called in, not even once. He always stayed to the end of his shift, even after, sometimes, if they were busy and needed his help. And he did it gladly for days like today, when he could leave early and go get ready for his weekend.

"Hey Finn, I'm gonna take off," he said, grabbing his empty coffee cup from the shelf. "You good?"

"Yeah, I'm cool man," he said, his eyes still apparently fixated on nothing. "Go on, get outta here. Have a blast this weekend man. Oh, and if you run into a dude named Marshall, stay the hell away from him man, he's all messed up."

Kruise was laughing inwardly; he had no idea what to say. He simply nodded and said, "Cool, will do. See ya," and snickered all the way to the door.

Stepping outside into the hot June afternoon, he breathed in a refreshing sigh of relief. The day was half over. Now if the rest of the day would just go by fast he would really appreciate it.

The sun was shining brightly in the big blue sky. Large fluffy clouds were out in abundance, the kind that were so thick they looked as though someone could actually walk on them. None were near to covering the sun though, so as the sun's rays bore down on him and with no wind to come to the rescue, the humidity and sunshine almost felt like they were penetrating his skin.

By the time he arrived at his truck, beads of sweat were already running down his face. If it was this hot outside, he couldn't imagine what the inside of the truck felt like. Opening the door the heat hit him like a back draft, he quickly turned on the engine and rolled down the windows before hastily escaping the furnace temperature.

After some of the hot air absconded, he climbed in and turned on the air conditioning.

He had sent Jay a text telling him that he was off, right before he told Finn he was leaving.

The last text that he received was from Shayde, he asked her what she was up to today and she said that she was going to Courtney's for lunch. That was around eleven. He had typed a message back to her but had forgotten to hit send. It was no wonder why he hadn't heard from her in a while.

It said,

> That sounds fun. What you up to this evening?

He decided to send it now.

Now that he was off work, he turned the ringer up on his phone and at the same time the message indicator went off.

Nice. Wanna meet at Johnny's?

It was from Jay.

Johnny's was one of the local supermarkets.

After he responded to Jay that he'd meet him there, he put the truck in reverse and backed out of the parking spot. As he put it in gear and headed towards Johnny's, his phone beeped again.

The grocery store was five minutes away from where he worked. He waited to inspect the message until he arrived there. When he found a parking spot to wait for Jay, he opened his phone.

Shayde's message said,

Don't have any plans. Probably just hang out at home; maybe go for a walk on the beach.

That sounds like something I'd do.

he responded.

There was a little part of him that wanted to ask her to hang out before the weekend. But the more he thought about it, the more he decided that it would be all the more special if their first time getting to know each other was in Cape Cod. It just seemed right.

Jay pulled into the parking lot just then and parked next to him. His face was pained, as though he had been nursing a hangover all day.

Kruise stepped down from his truck and locked it.

"What's up?" he said as Jay staggered out of his green truck.

"Not much," he said, smacking Kruise's hand in greeting. "What's goin' on?"

"Nothing much," he answered as they entered the store. "Just got done with the longest shift ever at the Q. I did get the weekend planned out though."

"Oh yeah?"

"Yeah."

As they wandered through the store, gathering the items on his list, Kruise went over the weekend itinerary he had planned.

"So, what do ya think?" he said as he concluded his run down of the weekend.

"Damn, you had a lot of time to think today didn't you?" Jay laughed. "I think it all sounds dope. Did you get money from the guys?"

"I didn't, but I was just thinking that groceries won't be too much, I'll just pay for this and have them buy my dinner on Sunday when we go to the Lobster Shack. I think it'd come out pretty even," he said, tossing some bread and buns into the cart.

The Lobster Shack was a restaurant in Cape Cod that served the best fresh lobster within miles. He had eaten there a few times in his life as he, Jay, and his parents used to vacation in Cape Cod every summer before Reanna passed away.

"I think that should work. You talk to your girl lately?"

"Yep. I've been talking to her off and on all day."

"Nice, that's sweet."

"You talk to Alizé at all?"

"We talked quite a bit last night and then a little today. About nothing really. She's a pretty cool chick."

"What'd you do last night?"

"Not much just drank over at Jordan's. Won like eight rounds of beer pong and then started losing for some reason," he chuckled at the memory.

"Probably because you were wasted," Kruise laughed at him. He stopped in the dairy aisle and added some cheese and eggs to the cart.

"Just a bit. It was a good time," Jay said as he walked alongside him, watching him shop.

They were advancing down the meat section where he gathered some steaks and burgers, when his phone chimed again. He threw the contents into the cart and pulled out his phone.

It was Shayde again.

> Yeah, I love it. I have the ocean in my backyard, it is truly amazing.

He thought of her goddess-like self, walking along the beach with the moon high in the sky, its silvery light illuminating her angelic features. It was almost as if he was there with her, rather than trailing round Johnny's with a grocery cart.

Jay reminded him that he needed to get plastic cups and ping pong balls so they could play beer pong. He had been planning on bringing his dad's saw horses and a large piece of plywood to make a make-shift beer pong table out on the beach.

When he'd got everything on his list, they headed back to the front.

"Thanks for coming bro," Kruise said teasingly as they walked to the checkout counter. "You've been a big help."

"Sure thing dude. Anytime," Jay laughed. "You just wanna split it and we'll have them pay for yours and mine?" he asked as the red-headed check-out lady started scanning their items and putting them in bags.

"That sounds good. You sure you can afford it?"

"Yeah, Dad gave me some money this afternoon for helping him with all that yard work last week."

"Oh yeah, I forgot about that. Right on, how much you get?"

"He gave me a hundo. Said he may have more work for me next week too. I'm down with it; it helps 'til I can find a job."

"For sure. That's cool. "

The total came to one-ten and some change. Jay handed him a fifty-dollar bill and Kruise stuck it in his wallet while pulling out his card. The red-head ran the card and handed him the receipt to sign. He did and then loaded up the bags into the cart.

They walked out to their trucks and Jay helped him load the groceries into the bed of Kruise's Toyota.

"Alright," Jay said, holding out his hand. "See ya at home?"

Kruise smacked it. "Yeah for sure."

Jay climbed into his little truck, started it, and disappeared down the road.

When Kruise was back in the cab of his truck, he opened his phone and eyed the last message from her.

All he could think about was walking along the beach with her, it dominated his thoughts of the upcoming weekend.

Being alone with her on the beach sounded like the best thing in the world to him.

With that thought, he wrote,

> Maybe I can join you sometime

Then he glanced at the time.

Ten 'til four.

It was quite possibly the longest day of his life.

When Shayde opened her eyes it was in her own room, she was lying on her side with her hands resting under her cheek, looking at the light from the morning sun dance with the wind behind the white lace curtains. She didn't remember falling asleep, or even how she had ended up in her room for that matter. She was taken aback, the first thought that popped inside her mind was that the strange episode that occurred last night had all been a dream. Yes, it was all a strange manifestation created by her mind.

Then she felt it.

The beautiful heirloom ring was pressing into her cheek, no doubt making an indention where her hands were. It hadn't been a dream. She held out her hand and examined the piece of jewelry. It didn't matter how long she admired it, there was no way to wrap her mind around all that it had seen in its existence. It was unfathomable.

The next thought that made her heart race was Kruise. She never had the chance to text him and tell him that she could go! Frantically she sat up and looked around for her phone. Her eyes scanned the room frenziedly, finally finding it on the nightstand.

She rolled over and grasped it, plopping back down to bed as she pulled it free from the cord.

There was one new message. It was from Kruise. It said,

Good morning beautiful.

Elation entangled her nerve endings at the sight of the word, *beautiful.* It was as if it had some other meaning when he said it, as though it became a whole new word with a meaning beyond the scope of normal minds.

Even though she had forgotten to text him—not that she had had the chance—he had sent her one anyway, one that she could wake up to.

He had sent the message at six-thirty a.m. and it was now nine-thirty.

She typed in a message that explained how she had meant to text and just got busy with the festivities of her birthday. There was no way she could explain what really happened and even though there was a bizarre haze over all that had taken place, she was sure that it was against some law if she did.

After hitting send, the thoughts of all that she had found out last night hit her like a tidal wave. Processing the information was almost too much for her to handle and so she set the phone aside, stood up, and went over to the windows that faced the ocean. She pulled the curtain aside and surveyed the ebb and flow of the sea, letting the sweet summer scents submerge her consciousness. The soft wind caressed her face and she closed her eyes, wishing the overwhelming thoughts away for the moment. She had time to figure it all out; right now she just wanted to be normal for the last couple days that she had, before truly learning all that she was capable of.

A calming breeze swept over her and it was as if all the worry and anticipation melted away and disappeared with the wind.

Sighing, she turned and went to the bathroom. As she leaned against the counter to wash her hands it came back to her once again. Everything about her reflection seemed normal, aside from the fact that her eyes glowed brighter than a flashlight in the dark. She closed and opened them again to see if they would dim but they did not. No matter how hard she wished them to fade, they stayed just as illuminated as they had in the basement. She tried to ignore them while she brushed her teeth and hair, but they were like magnets. She stared into her own eyes as though she had never seen them before. Well, she hadn't seen a pair of *glowing* eyes before.

As she was leaning over the counter, staring into mirror at what seemed like beacons in the night, she heard her phone go off again. She had to practically peel herself away from the reflection to go back to her room to check her phone.

> Don't worry about it. I totally understand, that is a good rule to have I think. Did you have a good time?

Kruise wrote back.

Good time was not the words she would have used to describe it, but she just told him that she did and asked what he had ended up doing.

Hunger rumbled in her stomach as she descended the staircase, clutching the phone in her hand as she did. It went off loudly again as she entered the kitchen, startling her mom who was sitting in the nook, typing something into her computer.

"Goodness," Tara said, clasping her heart. "You scared me!"

"Sorry Mom," Shayde answered, opening the cabinet and pulling out some cereal. "I thought you'd be at work."

"No not until later," she declared, returning her attention to the computer. "I have an intervention today and have to meet the family in a little bit to discuss it."

"Oh." Small talk seemed difficult at the moment and she left it at that, drowning the cereal in milk.

"How are you feeling?" Tara asked as Shayde joined her at the nook, her green eyes relatively normal behind her neatly framed glasses.

"I'm not sure yet. Still trying to process it all, you know. Where's Aura?"

"Probably sleeping. She doesn't hover around you all the time. Usually just when you go places and things like that. Sometimes she comes and hangs out with me. I miss her when she not by me." She took a bite from the cream cheese bagel that had been resting on a napkin at the computer's side.

Shayde nodded and yawned as she looked at her phone.

Kruise asked if her parents said yes to the upcoming weekend.

Excitement reared up as she remembered that her parents had agreed to her weekend away. After all that she had learned last night, it seemed that the incident at the dinner table with her parents was a distant memory.

She responded to him that they had said yes, smiling to herself at the tautness of the connection she felt towards him. The jittery anticipation over what this weekend could quite possibly bring was almost unbearable.

Upon hitting send, she set the phone down and eyed her mom. "So, she still can follow the other witches with the Lilies?"

"Oh yeah, she just mainly emanates around the newest one. The older witches have more life experience and she doesn't worry about them as much anymore. She still goes and visits your Grandma Mariah and Grandpa Dan."

"Oh really. That's awesome." She paused. "So what do you do about the whole money thing? Did you tell dad about it right away?"

"No, I didn't tell him right away," she explained as she typed. "He had no idea at first. I felt it was the best way to go about it. He knew I had some money, but he had no idea it was as much even then. Most of our family's ventures still add to it daily. But then, when I found out he didn't have a faith and he believed in mine, I thought it was okay to tell him. It didn't change him at all either. Both of us knew that neither of us would ever be happy without a goal to aim for, so we decided to ignore the money and get on with our lives as if we didn't have it. Having to work for what we have, in the long run it made our lives more meaningful and satisfying."

"Yeah, that makes sense," Shayde responded, taking a bite of her cereal. "I'm not going to tell anyone. Maybe Alizé, I tell her everything and we love each other like sisters."

When her phone clanged loudly and vibrated on the table, Tara looked up from her computer and smiled. "Who are you talking to already?"

She felt the blood race to her cheeks and a smile take over before she even had a chance to fight it. "Kruise."

"That's nice sweetie," Tara smiled at her lovingly and took another bite of her bagel, returning her gaze to the screen.

Shayde clicked her phone on to read the message.

The first part of his text said that her message had made his whole day. The second part explained that he and Jay were going to get groceries for the trip after work.

She knew that the day was going to be very long. A part of her wondered if he was going to ask her if she wanted to hang out later. She knew immediately that she would say yes, but if he didn't ask, she wouldn't get sad and pout. If they waited, it would make the weekend with him all the more special.

> Is there anything that you need Alizé or
> I to get at the store as well?

she responded.

As her mom busily typed away on her laptop, Shayde studied the bright sunny morning through the window. It was the perfect day to go for a run on the beach. The sun wasn't high in the sky yet, but it was still brightly shining. A run on the beach sounded refreshing, a mind cleanse was definitely in order.

Her phone sang again.

No, I got it. Just bring your lovely self

The tingles she felt when she thought of him staggered her, she felt them everywhere from her tips of her fingers and toes to deep inside her.

"So, should I call Aura awake?" Shayde asked Tara as rational thought process began to commence once again, "or does she just wake up whenever and come and find me? And will she be there sometimes and I won't know that she's there?"

"You can call her whenever you want. And yes, she will be there at times when you don't know she is but as soon as you think about her she'll let you know that she is there with you. When you don't think about her she just stays hidden," Tara responded, finishing her bagel and dusting the crumbs off her hands. "Sometimes, if you are around other people and you wonder to yourself if she is there with you, your birthmark will tingle a little. She won't show herself in front of other people."

"Oh. Well that's cool."

"When you start the lessons I would like to be there. I don't really *need* to be there all the time, but I would like to watch you learn some things. I would like to teach you some things too."

"Maybe we can do two days a week," Shayde grinned excitedly as she tipped the bowl to get the last few particles of her breakfast on to her spoon. "Or more. I'm really into this. This is totally up my alley."

"Okay sweetie, that's great. Tell Aura that when she finds you," Tara said, getting up, she crumbled her napkin into a little ball and threw it in the trashcan. "I gotta get going. I'll see you later. If you need anything call or text okay?" She leaned over and kissed Shayde on the top of her head.

"Okay Mom, have a good day."

"You too sweetie pie," Tara said as she closed her laptop and stuck it in her shoulder bag that was sitting on the floor beside her.

Once Tara was gone, Shayde finished her cereal, rinsed the bowl off in the sink and stuck it in the dishwasher.

When she was done, she decided to text Courtney to see when she wanted her to come by and also searched her mind for something to say back to Kruise.

She opened the message folder and picked Courtney's name from her favorites.

Hey lady, you up yet?

she typed in and hit send.

Then she opened Kruise's last message. She stared at it for a long time, trying to decide what the best thing to say back to him was. Even though it was a simple text, finding the right words proved more difficult to her than they would have normally.

Aw, you're so sweet. So, how's work?

she decided on saying.

She laid the phone on the counter while she went back up to her room to change. When she was finished, she had put on her running shorts, shoes and a light shirt. She was pulling her hair up into a messy bun as she descended the stairs when once again, she heard her phone alerting her in the kitchen. When she reached the kitchen she grabbed her phone from the counter along with her headphones.

> Yeah, just getting up now. What you doing?

Courtney replied.

> Getting ready to go for a run

she responded, sliding on her sunglasses as she headed out of the back door.

> Still want me to come by?

She pulled up the armband that acted as a holster for her iPod and stuck her phone into it as she reached the gate to the beach. She was securing the headphones in her ears when her phone vibrated.

It was Courtney again.

> Sure. Wanna come over for lunch when you're done running?

> Yeah for sure. I'll text you when I'm on my way

Shayde wrote back.

She clicked her phone to sleep and opened the gate.

She turned her music up and prepared to run, but then her phone vibrated twice. She fished it out and clicked it to life.

There were two new messages.

One of them was from Courtney saying the plan sounded good. The other one was from Kruise.

So boring. What are you up to today?

Kruise said.

Just going for a run and then to Courtney's for lunch.

After she hit send, she returned the phone to the armband.

She started to run along the beach at a slow and steady pace, just at the waters edge. Running was one of the things that she loved the most in this world. Worries melted away like heat in the rain, evaporating to the back of her mind. It was still early enough so that it wasn't unbearably hot, and every time she started to feel a little warm, a cool breeze would sweep up and kiss the torridity right off her face, it was as if the wind was looking out for her. The soft, damp ground absorbed her foot-falls, and a rhythm between her feet and the sand developed. As she ran, the music serenaded her, her mind started to drift to thoughts of him.

Different scenarios infused her mind. Nervousness hitched itself to her thoughts when she imagined her first kiss. What would it be like? Hopefully she wouldn't be awful at it and do something *extremely* embarrassing. Having a few beers beforehand would probably take the edge off a little bit but still, how was she to know exactly what to do and when?

She looked out to the sea, and wished away her worried thoughts. The large blue ocean was teeming with waves that broke on the shore to rhythmically surge back and forth, but even this could not peel him from her mind. All she could see was his face, his staggering eyes, his soft, full lips, and his shatteringly perfect smile. Clearing her thoughts was proving to be more of a difficult task than she had originally thought, but on the other hand she reminded herself, there was a good chance she might view something that was actually going to happen. But so far everything she was seeing seemed more like a daydream. Maybe the ring prevented her seeing the future too. That was okay with her; she didn't want to know. She enjoyed not knowing, she wanted to experience the situation as it unfolded and let things happen naturally.

Her mind wandered again to the events of the previous evening and all the stupefying things she had discovered about her family. But she didn't feel any different than she had yesterday. It was as it should be, she supposed. Something in the back of her mind already knew. The memory from Breken was in her blood, tucked away in the back of her mind, and finding it again was similar to visiting with an old friend. It was like knowing someone a long time ago but over the years the relationship had faded. Now it was all a matter of getting reacquainted.

She felt a surge of elation when she thought of Aura and all that she had in store for her to learn. Discovering that she had *magic* in her blood was astonishing in itself, yet it felt like things were as they should be. Something seemed to click into place when she learned of her ancestors. All her life she had been different and now she knew why. It was like a giant fog had been lifted off her and it was a wonderful relief.

Things that she never even dreamed possible were happening and all at once. A wonderful new boy that she had her eyes on all year, a life full of a magic past, and wings hiding somewhere in her blood, beneath her skin. It was surely going to be an interesting and, hopefully amazing, summer.

Before she knew it, she had run a mile down the beach. She had been so wrapped up in her own thoughts that she had forgotten she was running. She stopped to catch her breath and check her phone.

No new messages.

Kruise must be busy at work.

She breathed a little sigh and tucked the phone away again. When her breath was back at a steady pace, she began to run in the direction that she had come.

Aura was in her mind suddenly and she wondered when she would see her again.

At that moment, the back of her head started to tingle where her birthmark might be. She wondered how Aura would come to her. Could other people see her or would she just look like she was talking to herself?

I am here Shayde, Aura's voice came whispering into her head, *but I cannot appear to you now as I do not want anyone to see me, I look like a ghost to normal humans and I do not want to frighten anyone. So I will talk to you in your head, if that is okay.*

They were just like her own thoughts. Aura had answered the questions Shayde was sure she heard.

It was weird.

Yeah, its okay, Shayde thought back to her. *So you were the one who told me to tell my parents in my head last night at dinner?*

Yes, that was me, she laughed the most peculiar laugh. *Do not forget that you need to get contacts soon. Your friends might notice.*

Oh yeah, Shayde thought. She had forgotten about her eyes. Good thing there wasn't a lot of people out yet and that she had put on sunglasses. *I will get some after lunch with Courtney. Good thinking.*

That is why I am here. And just so you know, they will still glow from underneath the contacts when you work spells and other things.

That's okay, I'll be in private while doing that. I'm just worried about being around people and having them glow.

Yes. The contacts will take care of that. So, when did you want to start learning?

I was thinking that we could start on Monday, after I get back from my trip this weekend.

That works for me. I have much to teach you, my darling.

I am so excited to learn! She grinned. *Then maybe we can do it on the weekend too. Mom wants to show me some stuff I guess, and watch how I learn.*

Yes, she only got to teach Kain for a short time. He still had so much to learn.

So what was his ability that made him hurt that kid? Do I have that too? I mean, not that I would use it, just so I know what to do in a situation like that.

I am sure you do, if you have Breken in you. I do not know if Breken possessed the same power because she never thought to try it, but I am assuming she did. All the power within all of the Sorenya stem from her and Aenya's magic. She just did not live long enough to learn it all. That is why as the time goes on, the newer Sorenya discover more and more about what they can do, as you build on the already known magic. You may have a few of the same powers as them, or perhaps all of them and more. You do have the most powerful Sorenya in you, which may ignite some magic that we have never seen. Then again, you may only possess a few of their magical qualities. We never know until we start learning. Kain had the power that made whatever he visualized come to pass, or as he said, 'wished it true', and because of this power, he accidentally manipulated the energy surrounding that boy and made it work for him. Because it was energy, it was deemed natural causes because, well, it was all natural. They just did not know that Kain had used nature to do his bidding.

So will we be able to figure out if I have that quality without actually hurting somebody?

Oh yes, of course. Aura reassured her. *We will only practice with inanimate objects and that will tell us if you have the power to make them do something just by picturing it in your head. Then, you will know if you can do it in general. Then we will work on channeling your thoughts so, if a bad situation does occur, you will be able to navigate your mind away from the bad thought.*

She felt a little bit better. It was frightening that she may have the power to accidentally do the same thing her brother did and pay for it with her life. She breathed in a deep, refreshing breath of air.

Do not worry Shayde, we will teach you everything you need to know so that you do not make the mistake that Kain did.

Shayde nodded as she reached her house. Turning off her music as she opened the gate, she pulled her phone out and glanced at it.

No new messages.

Kruise must really be busy at work. She had been hoping that she would get to talk to him again today.

It's not a big deal, she reassured herself. Surely she would hear from him again.

When she stepped inside, the fantastically cool air-conditioned house brushed her face and neck with its icy kiss. Pulling out her earphones, she plopped down on the couch to catch her breath.

When her heart rate slowed and her breathing was normal, she headed upstairs to shower, texting Courtney on her way about what she was doing. After hitting send, she glanced at the time, hoping it would say three or four, and when it only read noon, she sighed. It was, without a doubt, the longest day of her life.

It was a fast shower and when she was finished, she went into her room to throw her dirty clothes in the hamper and check her phone.

There was one new message from Courtney saying she'd see her soon.

Shayde ran back downstairs and after retrieving her purse, she put her sunglasses back on as she headed out of the door.

Courtney lived across town from her. It would usually take only fifteen minutes to get there. Today, it took her half an hour because of the lunch rush.

For now, Courtney shared a little duplex with her mom and step-dad. It wasn't going to be for much longer as she was planning to move into Cherie's house in the next week. Cherie lived in a large, three bedroom house that her parents owned. She used to share it with her brother and sister but they had moved out of state for college. Cherie now occupied the house alone and was only paying her portion of the rent. Her parents told her that she needed to find roommates to make up the difference or she would have to move out so they could find someone who could cover the whole rent; otherwise they were going to have to sell the place. When Cherie told Courtney, she jumped at the idea to move out of her mom's house.

"Hello?" Shayde yelled into the darkened and cool condo.

"Back here," Courtney called from the back patio, most likely smoking.

She walked through the house to the patio and sure enough, Courtney was lounging on her lawn chair in the sun, smoking a cigarette and talking on the phone.

"Yeah, I know... It'll be okay, really... Just tell him what you decided," Courtney said into the phone. "Okay, well just come over, Shayde just got here."

Shayde sat down on the chair next to Courtney's and as she finished up the conversation, dug out her own phone to check it for messages. When she saw that there were none, she wondered if he was just really busy or if he had gotten bored of their conversation.

"Okay... Okay... Okay, bye," Courtney said into the phone then clicked it off. "Sorry. That was Cherie. She's gonna come over here in a minute."

"Is she gonna keep it?"

"Yeah, I think so. She doesn't want to abort it and she doesn't want to give it up for adoption. She doesn't think that she could do that."

"Yeah, I could see that."

"So, how was last night?" Courtney said, taking a drag off her cigarette.

"Good. I just had dinner with my parents and an old family friend I haven't seen in a while. It was a good time. Not really much else though."

"Did you get anything else?"

"Yeah, I got this." She pulled off the ring and handed it to Courtney. "It's been in my family longer than anyone knows. All the oldest girls get it on their sixteenth birthdays."

Suddenly Courtney's thoughts came pouring into her head.

Oh, it's so pretty. It looks really old. I wonder what kind of stone it is. She's so lucky to have gotten a car and a ring. I think it's a diamond. It looks expensive. I wonder where my diamond is. I haven't seen it in so long...

Shayde shut her eyes and tried to think about something else to turn it off, pressing her finger tips to her temples beneath her sunglasses as if it would help. She didn't like being in other people's heads. It felt like spying.

Turn off, turn off, turn off, she commanded with all of her mind's power, clenching her muscles as hard as she could and squeezing her eyes as tight as they would go.

Then she opened them one at a time.

Courtney's thoughts were silent, but she was staring at Shayde like she was crazy.

"You okay?" Courtney eyed her quizzically.

"Yeah, totally, I just have a migraine," she lied.

"Aw that sucks, I'm sorry Shay. Want something?" Courtney asked, handing Shayde her ring back.

"Nah, I'm cool," she said, sliding the ring back on and releasing all the tension that was keeping the voices still. "I took something at home, just waiting for it to kick in... Anyways, Cherie's heading over?"

"Yeah, she should be here soon. She's been super emotional. I talked to her last night for a long time, trying to help her sort out her thoughts. I hate Nate for what he does to her. I hope this baby at least helps him grow up," Courtney said acidly, taking in a deep drag of her cigarette.

"No kidding. I've never even heard of anyone like him before in my life."

When the phone went off loudly in her purse it felt like her heart had been electrified. She fumbled clumsily around the bag until she found it.

> Hey lady, how was last night?

It was from Alizé.

Shayde was pleased to hear from her but she did feel a little let down that it wasn't a message from Kruise.

Courtney looked up from her own phone. "That your boy toy?"

"No," she said, a little sadder than she had intended. Then to Alizé she said,

> Last night was good. Just hung out with my parents. What did you do?

"Aw," Courtney replied, stubbing her cigarette out in the grass. "Have you talked to him at all since yesterday?"

"Oh yeah, we talked last night and a little this morning. He's just at work, probably busy. I just like talking to him."

Courtney's phone buzzed to let her know she had a new text message.

"Who are you talking to?" Shayde asked her.

"Oh, this boy I have been talking to."

"Oh yeah, who?"

"His name is Ryan. I met him at work a while ago but he quit to start a new management position somewhere else. We've always been friends, but since Mark and I broke up he's been very flirty."

"Do you like him?"

"He's cute. He's really sweet and he's older too, more mature. He's got a good job and a good head on his shoulders. I'm just taking my time with this one. I don't wanna rush into things you know?"

"How old is he?"

"Twenty four."

Shayde's phone buzzed again and she flicked it open. Alizé replied that she just hung out at home and asked if she had talked to her mom.

"That's cool. Have you guys hung out yet?" Shayde asked, grinning as she responded to Alizé.

I did! They said yes!

"Not outside of work yet. He wants to hang out this weekend, maybe go to a movie or something."

"That should be fun."

"Hello?" Cherie's voice came from inside.

"Out here," Courtney yelled at the screen door.

She appeared at the door, slid it open, and joined them on the lawn.

"Hey," Shayde told her.

"Hey," Cherie said sadly.

"What's the matter?" Shayde asked her.

"Oh, hell, what's not the matter is really the question," she hesitated. "I told Nate."

"And?" Shayde sat up, fixing the sunglasses on her face.

"Well, he told me to get rid of it. He said if I abort the kid he'll be with me," she broke down and sobbed.

"What! Are you kidding me?" Courtney exclaimed.

"So what are you going to do?" Shayde asked worriedly.

"You're not going to abort it for that stupid jerk are you?"

"Oh no! No! He can go to hell as far as I'm concerned. I will raise it on my own." Cherie took off her sunglasses and wiped her eyes with the tissue she had in her hand. Her eyes were swollen and red from crying.

Shayde thought about how much she abhorred Nate.

"I'll help you," Courtney consoled her. "We'll make the third room in our house the nursery and I will help you, you won't be alone."

"What did he say he'd do if you kept it?" Shayde asked.

"He said that he would never talk to me again. He wants nothing to do with his kid," she muttered.

"God, I *hate* that guy," Courtney replied fiercely.

Shayde's phone sounded and Alizé's message exclaimed how excited she was and asked if she wanted to drive.

"I know," Shayde returned. "I cannot stand him, Cherie. You need to just get rid of him. I know you're going to have a baby by him, but really girl, he's no good. For real."

"I know, I know. I... I just, I just," Cherie stammered, "I just *love* him so much. I... can't understand why he just won't love me back. He won't, it's almost like he can't. I *hate* him." She cradled her head in her palms and sobbed.

Shayde and Courtney both stood up and went to her. Courtney crouched in front of her and Shayde hugged her from behind.

"I know sweetie, I know," Courtney reassured her. "You can't help who you fall in love with. I am so sorry you are going through this. I have no idea how to make you feel any better. Just know that I am here for you no matter what, okay?"

"Me too, love, me too," Shayde added. "I got your back no matter what you decide to do. We will all help you with the baby when we can."

Shayde wished there was something she could do. She hoped beyond all hope that this thing with Nate would either get better or he would stop tormenting her friend and go away.

"Thanks you guys. I love you. I'll figure this all out," Cherie said, wiping her eyes again. "But anyways, Shayde, how was your night last night?" she asked, changing the subject, obviously not wanting to talk about it anymore.

"It was good," Shayde said, walking back over to her chair. "Just hung out with the family."

"That's nice; did you get anything else from them?" Cherie asked her, sadness still lurking inher voice.

Shayde knew better than to take the ring off this time, she didn't want to know what was going on in *Cherie's* mind. She stood and walked over to her again.

"I got this," she said holding her hand out for her to see. "It has been in my family for generations."

"That's it? That's what the huge surprise was?" Cherie asked, her disappointment clear in her voice, examining the ring on her hand. "I hoped they were gonna tell you that you're a millionaire or something."

Shayde laughed at the irony. "No ma'am, just this ring."

"Oh, I mean it is very beautiful, I was just expecting more by the way they were going on about it."

"Me too," Shayde lied. She went back to her chair and flicked her phone on to reply to Alizé, saying that she did want to drive and to meet her at her house.

Her stomach flitted with excitement.

"So are you all packed?" Cherie asked Courtney.

"Not quite," she answered, not looking up from texting. "I should be done by the end of today or tomorrow though, so we can start to move me in for sure this weekend. I have to work tomorrow morning and Saturday and Sunday night, so I figured I would finish packing tonight and tomorrow night, and start moving in Saturday and Sunday morning."

"Cool, sounds good. You sure you wanna live with a screaming baby?" Cherie asked, wearily.

"Of course! I love babies!" she exclaimed.

"Yeah, now, when you don't live with one, but what about at two a.m. when it wakes you up from crying?"

"I'm a sound sleeper. That's your department," Courtney giggled. "That is the part that I ain't doing! I'll help with everything else when I can, but sleep is something I am not willing to give up."

"I know," Cherie said. "Hopefully Nate will come around and help me with that part." She sounded hopeful.

"Don't get your hopes up okay," Courtney said earnestly.

"We all know him and know that he's incapable of being nice to you. Just please don't count on that."

"I know. I'm not."

Shayde knew that she was lying. She could see it in Cherie's eyes that she truly believed Nate was going to come around. Even through the shield of the ring she could see it in her eyes; Cherie's daydreams of her, Nate and the baby.

The hopeful thoughts about helping her friend discouraged her once again. She detested Nate and had to try to dispel the daunting thoughts that crossed her mind when she thought of his face.

After a long while of talking together, they headed inside to make sandwiches and then returned to the back patio.

They took turns talking about the different men in their lives. Cherie talked about Nate, Courtney talked about Ryan and Shayde talked about Kruise, who still hadn't texted her back yet.

When they said all that they could say, Courtney decided to over some important things about dating with Shayde.

"It happens with guys," Courtney stated. "They just don't think like girls do. Girls read everything into anything that a boy says and boys just brush stuff off, even if it is important.

"If he doesn't text for a day or so, everything is fine, it is all completely normal, however, if he doesn't respond to you for days on end, then he's not interested and stop trying. You don't want to come off desperate and clingy. Wait for him to text you all the time. Never send the first one until you are classified as a couple, then feel free to text him whenever you wish. Until then, leave everything up to him. Let him make the first move and leave him wanting more.

"Don't take things too far on the first night, or even the second and third, always leave him wanting more. When this weekend is over and you leave him, wait for him to contact you and wait for him to set up the next date. Maybe, even when he does ask you to hang out again, have something going on, be busy so he knows that you are popular and wanted, it makes guys go crazy."

"Okay, I think I got it. I'm still really nervous about my first kiss," Shayde almost whispered. "Were you guys nervous about your first kisses?"

"Oh yeah, totally," Courtney exclaimed. "I think everyone is. It's something that you will remember for always and you want it to be perfect, yet you never had the practice so you know it will be kind of awkward."

"I know, I'm afraid I'm going to slobber all over his mouth," she blushed with embarrassment, and then laughed a little.

"You won't, it won't be like that," Courtney reassured her. "It will be soft and slow and you will have time to prepare. Just relax your lips and follow his lead. Don't try to lead him, wait for him to turn his head, or when he first comes in for his kiss, peck him then wait for him to part his lips first."

A glint of worry tempered with desire flickered across Shayde's mind as she considered Courtney's advice. Different images surfaced in her mind that made her blood scorch beneath the surface of her skin. *Lips. Kiss. Part.*

"Don't worry hon, it will be okay. You will make it," Courtney giggled at her, "and then next week you will wonder what you were ever worried about."

She just hoped she would remember everything her friends were telling her.

After lunch, Shayde went over to Wal-Mart to get her contacts, then headed home so that she could make a start on her packing for the weekend.

When she arrived home, the first thing that she did was head up to the bathroom to put in her new contacts. The glowing subsided the instant they were in and she wondered how such a small thing made such a big impact. Satisfied that her eyes no longer looked like a radioactive accident, she went into the garage to fetch her luggage and then headed upstairs where she started to brainstorm on what the contents of her luggage should be.

She got so caught up with packing that she had forgotten all about her phone for a while. When it did cross her mind, she walked over to her purse and pulled out her phone.

There was one new message.

Her heart raced.

It was from Kruise.

> That sounds fun. What are you up to this evening?

In her last text she had told him she was going to Court-ney's for lunch and that was hours ago. Either he had gotten really busy and just now had a chance to respond or he had written it in and forgot to hit send. She did that often.

> Don't have any plans. Probably just hang out at home; maybe go for a walk on the beach.

she responded.

She wondered if maybe he would ask to come along. Of course she'd say yes.

A troubling thought entered her mind. What if he did ask and then she had to kiss him tonight and not this weekend? She wasn't prepared for a kiss tonight; she thought she had the entire weekend to prepare.

Keeping her mind occupied on something else was the only way to soothe her nerves. She started grabbing things from her closet and stuffing them in the suitcase when her phone buzzed again.

> That sounds like something I'd do

Kruise wrote.

It was apparent that he wasn't going to ask her to hang out tonight and so the nervous bubbles faded.

After she replied, she continued to pack her suitcase.

It was okay that he didn't ask her to hang out tonight. It would make the weekend with him all the more special. Maybe they could even go on a moonlit walk along the shore together.

And just as if he had read *her* thoughts, he replied,

> Maybe I could join you sometime.

Kruise's alarm went off at seven a.m.

A shock wave of excitement blew away all other thoughts besides the ones of her. He bolted up, shut off the phone and was out of bed. He had taken a shower and shaved last night but he took another one anyway. He brushed his teeth and when he was done with the finishing touches, he grabbed his remaining toiletries and returned to his bedroom. He quickly dressed in camouflage cargo shorts and a black t-shirt with a skull on it. When his socks and shoes were on, he grabbed his pillow and blanket and the bag that he had packed the night before, shoved in his toiletries, put on his hat and was out the door.

It was only a quarter past seven when he plunged down the staircase with his effects.

Setting the handful of possessions down by the front door, he headed to the garage to get the tent, a few coolers, the sawhorses and the large piece of plywood for beer pong. Danny was coming over at seven-thirty to hook the jet-ski trailer up to his jeep and help Kruise get the boat hooked up to his Tacoma.

After adding the other essentials to the pile by the front door, he put all the groceries into the coolers and stood for a second; searching his mind for anything he had missed. Satisfied that he had it all, he opened up the door and began to haul it to the truck, making sure he left room for Jay's things. As he was shoving the last of his pile onto the truck's bed, Danny pulled up in his lifted black Jeep Wrangler.

"Sup dude?" Danny asked, slapping Kruise's hand in greeting when Kruise approached his vehicle.

"Not much bro, just getting my shit loaded, about to go wake up Jay."

"Cool. Well let's do this. I still gotta go get Amy."

"Yeah for sure," Kruise responded, backing up to clear the way for Danny.

After he reversed the jeep up to the trailer with the jet skis on it, Danny hopped down and helped Kruise hook it up.

"Alright, see ya in a bit," Danny said when they were finished.

"Yep. Later," Kruise answered, heading back towards the house as Danny climbed back in his jeep.

As the sound of Danny leaving echoed in the quiet neighborhood, Kruise entered the house and bounded up the stairs to Jay's dark cave of a room.

He crept up to the bed quietly and then yelled as loud as he could in his ear.

"FIRE! FIRE!!!"

Jay shot up, swinging. Kruise ducked out of the way, laughing.

"You're a dick, dude," Jay said angrily.

"Don't get all butt hurt, it's gonna be okay!" Kruise laughed. "C'mon, get up; get ready so we can go."

"Ah piss," Jay grumbled. He was not a morning person.

Kruise carefully made his way to the window, losing his footing on a book bag and righting himself on the desk, only to stumble again on the piles of clothes that were scattered all over the floor. When he reached the blinds safely without falling, he opened them and let the morning light pierce the dark room with its golden rays, revealing flecks of dust that had been aggravated by his clumsy meandering.

Jay grunted with abhorrence and gruffly tumbled out of bed.

Kruise laughed as he quickly departed, now able to see the floor and the obstacles before him.

While the coffee percolated, he anxiously fidgeted with his phone, trying to concentrate on a game of solitaire, but instead he kept looking at the time, each minute seeming longer than the next. When the coffee was done, he poured some into his blue to-go mug and was adding the cream and sugar when he heard the stairs creak. Jay emerged with his backpack and some blankets, Kruise shut off the coffee maker and met him at the door. He opened it and followed Jay out to the truck.

"Ready?" Kruise asked him.

"Yeah for sure," Jay said, throwing his bag in the back with some blankets and pillows. "Bringing some extras in case the cabin's suck," he said, motioning towards them with his head.

"Ah, I see," Kruise grinned. "I grabbed some too, along with my tent. I think I'll probably just camp on the beach."

Kruise climbed into the driver's side and Jay the passenger and as he revved the truck to life, elation surged through him. Neither one of them said much as they made their way towards the restaurant; Kruise was numb with anticipation of seeing his red haired beauty and Jay was probably still half asleep. He didn't wake up early too often.

They were the first to arrive at the diner. Kruise parked the truck and they got out and quickly walked towards the entrance.

A short blonde girl was standing in the lobby, smiling a false smile not unfamiliar in the service industry.

"Good morning!" she said with a pseudo charm. "Welcome to Benny's. How many are in your party today?"

Kruise counted faces in his head. "Um, there will be eight of us."

"Alright awesome," she replied, grabbling menus from the side of her counter. "Let me just go set something up and I'll be right back."

Kruise nodded at her distractedly and then turned to look through the windows of the front lobby to the parking lot, searching for the little green bug. He was so fixated on the procession of cars that were slowly trickling in that he didn't even notice the blonde's return.

"Okay," she stated, jolting him out of his trance, "I can show you to your table."

Jay and Kruise followed her to the right of the counter and

turned left towards the back. There were two tables put together for them and the two boys took their seats. He began to look at the menu that had been handed to him by the blonde girl yet he wasn't reading the words, he was envisioning Shayde's face and what she would say today.

Another blonde, this one taller with long, curly hair, appeared at their table next.

"Hi there," she said in a welcoming tone, this one a little less false than the one at the front. "My name is Megan and I'll be your server today. Can I start you guys off with some coffee or juice?"

"I'll take some coffee please," Kruise said.

"Sure thing," she responded, she turned to Jay. "And for you?"

"Just OJ please."

"Sure. I'll go grab those and be right back."

As Kruise was trying to focus his attention back on the menu, he heard Jordan and Hannah's voices suddenly at the table with them.

"Hey," he said, shaking Jordan's hand.

"What's up?" Jordan replied.

"Not much. Just ready to get on the road."

"Yeah for sure," he said, taking a seat across from him, next to Hannah.

The waitress was there again, setting their drinks down and taking more orders from Jordan and Hannah. No sooner had she gone when Danny and Amy arrived as well.

While Megan took the newly arrived couple's drink order, Kruise sat sentinel, his eyes fastened on the door. He had given up trying to find something to eat; he was too excited.

Kruise checked his phone to see the time. It was only eight-twenty but part of him started to panic that she may not show up. Megan arrived again with the rest of the drink order and asked whether they wanted any more. He was about to tell her that they were expecting another two, when he looked up towards the lobby and almost gasped.

There she was.

To his dismay, he could not tell if he was dreaming or awake, her beauty was so otherworldly. He couldn't believe that she was there for him, this beautiful creature, and he watched almost bewildered as she sauntered across the threshold to the hostess stand.

She looked absolutely stunning, as she had in his memory and all the other times that he had seen her, yet there was something different about her today. He swore her eyes looked brighter. He could see them from across the room. Maybe it was just because the crush he had on her had grown so immensely over the past forty-eight hours, but those eyes pierced through him in a way that they never had before. His heart contracted and he thought he might just go into cardiac arrest.

The hostess showed Shayde and Alizé to the table where the six of them were seated. When she arrived at the table, Kruise stood up. He risked gesturing for a hug; and to his relief she leaned into him and he pulled her into his arms. It was only a couple of seconds long, but his heart stuttered at her touch, and it felt like his stomach had melted when he breathed in her sweet smell. He quickly let her go before he lost complete control of his senses. She sat down next to him, and Alizé sat down next to her.

"Shayde, Alizé, this is Jordan and that's Hannah," Kruise pointed at the couple, "and you already know Jay."

"Nice to meet you," Hannah stood up and shook the girls' hands.

"You too," Shayde smiled at her.

"What's up?" Jordan said, giving them both high fives.

"Yo!" Jay said in a sarcastic tone.

Alizé chuckled. "Yo, what's up!" she said derisively.

"And this is Danny and his girlfriend, Amy," Kruise continued. "Guys, this is Shayde, and this is Alizé."

"What's up?" Danny said.

"How's it going?" Shayde asked Amy.

As the girls carried on about how they knew each other from school, he was acutely aware of her sitting so close to him. So close, in fact, that he felt he could feel her aura, and when she grazed his arm with hers he almost lost it.

He wanted her. He wanted her bad.

I'm going to behave, he told himself, and he would not do anything but try to kiss her this weekend. But that was the one thing that he was not going to leave Cape Cod without, a kiss from this beautiful girl.

After breakfast was finished and conversations were rounded up, Kruise mentioned that they should get on the road to beat the afternoon lunch rush. They paid their tab and, one by one, emerged into the parking lot.

Kruise walked Shayde to her car.

The bug suited her as much as he had thought it would.

"Okay, so just follow me then," he said, he had a powerful urge to kiss her on her cheek—or her flawless lips.

"Okay, will do." Shayde smiled a smile that weakened his knees and made parts of him go numb.

"Okay, I will see you there." He gestured to her for another hug.

Automatically, she leaned in, wrapped her arms around him and squeezed ever so lightly. When she let go and climbed into her car, he could have sworn he heard her sigh.

A smile covered his entire face as he turned and walked back to his truck. There was absolutely no doubt in his mind that she liked him back. He didn't know how he had gotten that from the simple hug they had just shared, but he was, without question, sure that it was true.

The drive wasn't bad at all, there was hardly any traffic and it took a little over two hours to get there. He thought of her the entire way there and looked in his mirror to see her, over and over again, wondering if she was thinking of him too. Jay navigated their way to the cabin using Google Maps so fortunately he didn't have to try to suppress his thoughts about her and her unerring appearance, because frankly he didn't think that would have been possible.

The cabin was located on a picturesque little street that was backed by the ocean. Rows of quaint cottages lined the street on both sides, mostly white with red roofs and white picket fences surrounding their front gardens.

Kruise pulled into the driveway of one and killed the engine.

The two boys jumped out of the truck and gathered as much luggage and supplies as their hands would carry, the rest of the group following suit, grabbing their luggage as well. Jay and Kruise walked towards the cabin as the other members of the crew began to gather on the walk, waiting to be let in.

"She said the key should be under the rock by the door," Jay announced, setting his things down temporarily and lifting a rock that had "Home, Sweet Home" painted on it. He found the key and unlocked the door, leaving it open for the gang to go through. Kruise waited for Shayde and Alizé, who were still gathering their essentials from her car.

When the girls had retrieved their things they caught up with Kruise, who opened the screen door for them and let them in. Shayde smiled and thanked him as she walked past. He retrieved his belongings from the ground and followed them in.

"Big room's mine," Danny claimed immediately as they all converged in the living area.

"What makes you think so," Jordan challenged him.

"'Cause I called it first, dude!" Danny retorted.

"I say we flip for it," Jordan said.

"I say Shayde and Alizé get it you guys, they don't know us all that well," Kruise declared. "You guys can flip for who gets the little room and then whoever doesn't get that can sleep on the hide-a-bed. I don't mind sleeping outside, I brought my tent. I'll just camp on the beach."

"Yeah, okay that sounds cool, who's got a quarter?" Danny asked.

"Here," Shayde said, grabbing her wallet out of her purse and pulling one out from the change pocket.

Amy took it. "Okay, who's heads?"

"Me!" Danny yelled.

Amy flipped it up in the air and caught it; she placed it on top of her hand and studied it. "Tails!"

"It's cool. I don't care where I sleep," Danny said, seemingly indifferent. "Who knows where I'll actually pass out anyways," he chortled.

Amy rolled her eyes and handed the quarter back to Shayde. Hannah and Jordan headed into the little room and Shayde and Alizé started towards the master.

Kruise was leaning against the door jam, smiling at Danny's cheekiness when Shayde stopped abruptly in front of him.

"Thanks for that," she said softly.

"No problem." He eyed her intently, wanting to put her up against the wall, grab her face between his hands, smother her lips with his and blanket her with kisses. She stared into his eyes for just a few seconds without saying anything, and he froze.

She's never looked at me like this before, he thought.

Then she turned and walked into her room with Alizé.

Kruise almost grabbed her and kissed her just then. But he didn't.

Breathing in a deep, agonized sigh, he grabbed his bag and headed out towards the patio. Setting up the tent outside took no more than five minutes; he then put the beer pong table up in the sand by the fire pit. After that he was finished outside, so he went in to put the groceries away. When he was done, he found Jason to help him get the keg out of Jordan's truck. They unloaded it and put it in the bathtub.

They were going to need to get ice for the keg and firewood for the fire pit.

As Kruise was coming out of the bathroom, Shayde was

emerging from her room, concentrating so much on her phone that she walked right into him.

"Oh, hey sorry, my bad," Shayde said.

"No, it's my fault, so sorry," Kruise replied. "Hey I was just gonna run up the street to go get some ice, would you like to come with me?"

"Yeah, for sure, let me get my purse." She turned and disappeared into her room, returning again within seconds. "Okay, ready."

"Cool, wanna drive, you know, since you're new and all?" Kruise teased her.

"Shut up!" she said playfully, lightly punching him in the arm. "But, yeah I would like to drive."

"'Kay, cool. Let's go," Kruise said, and led the way.

Shayde followed him out to her car and let him open the door for her.

"'Kay, where am I going?" she asked after the car was started and in drive.

"Just go out how we came in and go right at the stop sign."

"You've been here before?" Shayde asked, following his instructions.

"Yeah, I've been coming up here since I was a kid. I haven't been here in a long time though."

"Oh no? Why?"

"Ever since my mom passed away, my dad hasn't wanted to come again," Kruise said sadly, glancing out towards the ocean.

"Oh, I'm so sorry."

"I know, its okay. I am sorry about your brother."

"It's okay. I didn't realize that we had that in common. When did she pass?"

"When I was eleven. Six years ago."

"Ouch. I can't imagine going through that," she said apologetically. "I am truly sorry."

"Things happen, you know. Anyways, it's nice to be back. I have missed it," he said, admiring the scenery.

"It is beautiful here, thank you for inviting me."

"At this next light go left. No problem, thank you for coming. I hope you don't mind crazy drunk boys. My friends are morons when they drink."

"Oh, not at all. Alizé is pretty wild when she drinks too. It's always a good time though. I don't drink too often so who knows how I'll be when I let loose," she laughed as she turned left when the light went green.

"Yeah, I only drink every once in a while. The boys, they drink more often. Okay, see it up there on the right, that's where we're going, to that gas station there."

"Yeah, I see it," she said, slowing down and turning.

Pulling into a spot, she turned the car off and got out leaving the top down.

"So you do drink a little then?" Kruise asked as they walked into the gas station.

"Oh, yeah. I drink once in a while. I like it; it's always a good time."

"Awesome," he smiled at her. "I wasn't sure if you did by how—" He trailed off, not wanting to dredge up any old memories that would make her sad. Seeing her sad was the last thing that he wanted.

"Oh yeah, I just don't drink and drive. And I don't let anyone that I'm friends with either, I'm pretty much a Nazi about it. Just so you know, for future reference." Smiling, she looked at him and winked.

Her smile was deranging, there was a chance that he wouldn't make it out of the store without tasting her lips. He would surely break.

"Oh, totally, I totally understand that," he said, collecting his composure as he went up to the counter and paid for the ice and firewood. "Did you need anything?"

"No, I'm good," she smiled.

They walked back outside and he grabbed a large bag of ice and a big bundle of firewood and threw them in the back seat, while she climbed in. The car hummed to life, and they started off back to the cottage.

"So, what do you do, you know, for fun?" Kruise asked her, studying her face as she concentrated on the road.

"Um, I write poetry, I read, I run, I like to exercise and do yoga. I like to walk and run on the beach, lay on the beach, swim, pretty much anything that has to do with the beach," she giggled. "I like to ride my bike, too, with my dog."

"Nice, I like to ride too; I usually ride my bike places instead of driving."

"Yeah, I did too, 'til I got my license."

"And you like dogs? I am a total dog lover."

"Oh yeah, that is awesome! Do you have one?"

"I do. He is a Great Dane. His name is Guido."

Shayde glanced at him and laughed. "I like that name! I have an American Bulldog named Knotti."

"Knotti! I love it! That's great. Maybe sometime we can get together and bring our dogs to the park or something?" he offered.

"Heck yeah, I'm so down! That would rock," she said as she found her way back to the cabin and parked.

She pressed the control to return the vinyl roof, turned off the engine, and removed the keys. Kruise grabbed the items from the back seat and once both doors were shut, Shayde pressed the button to lock it.

"Thanks for coming with me," he said as he opened the door for her.

"Welcome," she said sweetly, and stepped inside.

For now, Kruise set the wood in the living room, and then went to the bathroom to spread it ice over the keg. He grabbed the tap that had been left on the bathroom shelf and secured it in place.

He walked to the kitchen to get the plastic cups he had bought and grabbed himself a beer on his way outside. Everyone was hanging out on the beach already so he joined them and announced, "Keg's tapped."

Everyone cheered and walked inside single file, getting a cup from Kruise along the way.

He was half tempted to charge Shayde a kiss for hers—but he didn't.

"Here you go," he smiled as he gave her a cup.

"Why thank you," she said playfully as she grabbed her cup and fluttered past him.

The wind carried her scent to his nose and he breathed it in deep. Nothing in the world smelled as lovely as she did.

He followed them in.

"Hey, is anyone hungry?" he asked the queue. "Should I start the burgers?"

"You brought food?" Jordan asked.

"Oh yeah, I forgot. Jay and I went to the store last night and bought a bunch of food for the weekend so we don't have to eat out the whole time. I figured then we could go out to eat Sunday before we go home and you guys can all pitch on mine and Jay's dinner."

"That's cool, bro." Jordan held out his hand. "Thanks for doing that."

Kruise smacked it. "No problem man. So, is everyone hungry?"

"For sure," Jay said.

"Yeah, me too," Shayde agreed.

The remainder of the group concurred they were all indeed hungry.

Nodding, Kruise headed back towards the kitchen where he rummaged in the freezer for the burger patties. After retrieving the package, he began to thaw four at a time in the microwave. While he was waiting, Shayde came in with her beer.

"Need help?" she asked.

"No, but you can keep me company," he smiled at her as he switched plates, taking the thawed patties out and sprinkling seasoning from the spice rack onto them.

"This place is great," Shayde said, her gaze scanning the kitchen. "You guys found this on Air B&B?"

"Yeah, I think it's someone's home that they rent out for the summer, and some of these they rent out for the winter. The owners have houses in other places and just come here for vacation; they rent it out for the time that they aren't here. It's a pretty good deal. My parents, Jay and I used to do it every summer when we were kids, before Air B&B even."

"That's cool. I've never rented an Air B&B before. My family and I always just used to go camping and stuff."

"Yeah, it's cool. I like camping too, though," he responded, the microwave beeped, he retrieved the burgers and sprinkled them with spice as well.

Wiping his hands on a cloth, he then turned on a radio that was sitting on a little stand and put it on the windowsill so they could hear it outside.

With plates in hand, he motioned for her to follow him.

"Will you grab that for me?" he asked her, inclining his head to the firewood by the door.

She nodded and picked it up.

"Have you been to this exact one before?" Shayde asked.

"Nah, I don't think so," he said as they made their way out to the porch. "These little rental houses are all over the place but then who knows, maybe," he laughed.

Shayde giggled with him.

Setting the plates down on the shelves beside the grill, he sparked it to life. Afterwards, he gathered the things he would need to start the fire and walked out to the pit with Shayde on his tail.

Tingles ran the length of his body thinking about being next to her in the dark, watching the fire burn, mesmerized by her eyes.

"What do *you* like to do for fun?" Shayde interrupted his distracting train of thought as he set the wood down and they took their seats on the benches around the pit.

"Um, I like to ride, go camping and play on and in the water. I like to go for walks on the beach... I sound like a bad blind date video," he laughed at himself. "Um, basically the norm, I like to chill with these dudes and go over to Jordan's to people watch. People watching is one of my favorite pass times. Get stoned; drink beer, chill with my friends, that kind of stuff." He gazed at her and she was just staring at him with a smile on her face.

His heart raced.

I'm a jackass; she thinks I'm a jackass.

"I like to people watch too," she said quietly and he immediately felt better.

"Do you? That's cool," he smiled to himself while looking out to the ocean.

What is she thinking about? Are the same thoughts swarming around her head that are in mine? Should I kiss her? he wondered to himself.

They were alone, they were talking on a beach and it was the opportune moment. There was a moment of silence between them and all that hung in the air was the unspoken question—when will we kiss? He was positive that her eyes were actually glittering. Either he just thought she was the most beautiful girl on earth or she actually had eyes that sparkled. He let out a nervous little laugh and cocked his head to the side. She smiled in response and focused on her beer. A strand of her gorgeous hair was swept out of place by the wind. Reflexively, he lifted his hand up to sweep it back behind her ear. Her gaze met his and he inched his face forward.

"What'cha doing?" Danny's annoying voice broke into the moment.

Kruise cursed under his breath as he gave Danny a pseudo smile.

Danny sat down with his beer and was followed by Amy.

Not too long after them Jordan and Hannah came up with their beers, and Alizé and Jay brought up the rear, taking seats on the benches around the fire pit.

"So, who's down for a game of beer pong?" Danny asked the group.

"We'll play you," Hannah said to Danny.

"Sweet, I'll go get a pitcher of beer and some cups."

"I'm gonna go check the grill," Kruise addressed Shayde. "Be back in a sec."

Her kind eyes smiled at him as she nodded her head.

"Hey, where's the balls dude?" Dan asked as the two boys stood up to go to the house.

"Damn, you guys playing already? It's only noon," Kruise said disparagingly. "Put those burgers on the grill and I'll get them for you," he said as he walked to his tent while Danny put the burgers on.

He unzipped the tent and rummaged through his bag until he found the pack of ping-pong balls he had bought and threw the package to Danny.

"Thanks," Dan caught it, having successfully put the burgers on the grill.

"Sure."

Kruise made his way back out to the fire pit, his eyes drawn to her. She was just as enticing viewed from behind.

"Miss me?" he asked, as he hopped over the bench.

Shayde jumped a little, she had been taking a drink of her beer. A little spilled onto her lap.

"Oh, I'm sorry," Kruise exclaimed as he settled in next to her.

"It's okay," she said, swallowing, she held her beer out towards her feet as it dripped. "How was it?" she joked

"Oh great, I found some balls for Danny and he put on some burgers," he chimed back.

"Sweet, sounds like a good time."

Danny came back out from the house, holding the package of balls in his teeth, the cups in one hand and the pitcher in the other. Amy ran up to him and grabbed the pitcher and cups and he transferred the balls to his hand. Amy went to the table and started laying out the cups while Hannah filled them up and Danny opened the package and removed two balls.

Kruise and Shayde remained seated while the rest of the bunch started to gather around the table.

Jordan and Hannah took their places at the far end and Danny and Amy got into position opposite them.

"Have you ever played?" Kruise asked her, watching the proceedings.

"No, never. I like to watch though. I'm afraid I'd get too drunk," She giggled and the sound did something to his stomach.

"It's too early to start playing now but later, will you please play? I'll drink most of the cups," he bargained.

He could see her considering the matter. She was contemplating the ocean and he could tell she was running a scenario through her mind. His eyes glided from her perfect eyes to her soft cheeks, her smooth arms, down to her delicate hands that were wrapped around her almost full beer. There was a ring on her finger that he hadn't noticed until now. Although he knew he had never seen the ring before, it was strangely familiar, like he had seen it somewhere or it had been in a dream of his once.

"This is sweet," he said, pulling her hand into his and admiring it. "Birthday present?"

"Oh yeah," she answered, her attention regained from her reverie. "From my parents. I guess it's been in my family for years."

"It's very pretty. So... are you down?"

She eyed him and smiled. "Sure."

That smile is gonna be the end of me, Kruise thought as he stared at her for a few seconds. The breath in his chest escaped him; she was truly breathtaking in every sense of the word.

"What?" she asked him innocently.

"You're just so beautiful."

His heart raced. She looked back at him, unmoving, her green eyes locked in his. He felt himself inch forward once again, those sweet luscious lips enticing him, drawing him forward like a magnet. Her face was angled towards his, inclining towards him. He closed his eyes, his stomach quivered as he drew closer and closer...

"HEY!" Jay's loud voice came booming between them, making them both jump.

Kruise cursed under his breath again in annoyance at his friend. He knew that Jay had interrupted them just to be irritating. Jay smirked at Kruise as he walked around the fire pit and sat down, he was trailed by Alizé. Kruise saw Alizé give Shayde an apologetic look that conveyed she hadn't realized that they were about to kiss.

"What's up guys?!" Jay said in a grating, childish voice, taking a chug of his beer.

"What's up dude," Kruise grumbled through gritted teeth.

"Nada just signed up for next game."

"Nice. I'm gonna go check the burgers," Kruise said, and stood up.

He heard Jay strike up a conversation with Shayde as he walked back to the grill. The burgers were about done. He went inside and collected the things they would need to dress the burgers and laid the contents out on the counter.

"Food's done," Kruise announced to everyone from the doorway.

"Nice!" Jay jumped up and started towards the house. "Coming?" he called to Alizé.

"Yeah, come on Shay, let's go," Alizé suggested to Shayde.

Everyone filed into the house and one by one they all came back out with plates filled. They sat around the unlit fire pit and ate lunch and talked amongst themselves, drinking beer. Kruise observed Shayde maybe a million times and wondered what was going on in that beautiful head of hers. He hoped that she was having a good time, it looked as though she was. Each time that he studied her, that dazzling smile was dancing on her face, lighting her already sparkling eyes.

The group exchanged stories about their lives, anecdotes about each other and mutual friends, and she laughed often. His friends were just naturally funny and stupid. As they finished their burgers, the paper plates were thrown into the pit to be burned up later. The girls seemed to be getting along as though they had always been friends. As the day progressed they had made two little groups creating a circle, the girls on one side and the boys on the other, connected by Shayde and Kruise on one side and Jordan and Hannah at the other.

The girls were caught up in conversations about school and hair, outfits and shoes, and other girly things of the sort.

Shayde was sitting so close to Kruise that, while he was discussing what they planned on doing tomorrow, he was acutely aware of her. Sitting so close beside him, he could feel the warmth of her skin touching his and it made his blood boil.

The conversations had been flowing like the beer they'd been drinking for what seemed like hours. Suddenly Amy jolted up and announced she wanted to finish their game of beer pong. Making her way back towards the table, the people who had been playing followed her.

The summer sun was starting its decent towards the horizon, casting lavender rays of light that streaked across the opal sky and the deep blue ocean.

They had talked the day away.

Kruise stood up and started to build the fire.

TEN

Shayde was having a magnificent time so far. She was sitting next to one of the most handsome guys that she had ever seen, drinking a beer and laughing with her new friends. She truly liked the company Kruise kept. They were all genuine, very down to earth individuals. They all had unique personalities but they still complemented each other. Shayde found them easy to relate to as her friends were the same way. She had a feeling that her friends would get along famously with his.

As he was building the fire she surreptitiously glanced at him. No matter how much she tried, she couldn't figure out why he liked her.

He could get someone that looked like Dawn or Courtney.

Why on this green earth he wanted her was beyond her comprehension. She had confidence, she knew she attracted some men, but she never thought she could have attracted this one. The one and only guy she ever wanted. It was too good to be true. He was way out of her league. Someone like Kruise deserved the prettiest girl in town and to her, she was far from it. But this was her night she resolved, and she was drinking in every moment of him.

Aura was with her, she had the ring on, but she was probably floating in the energy around her.

Everyone here tonight at the cabin had good auras. Shayde could still see them with or without the ring; she had learned long ago how to turn that one off and on by herself.

Alizé was across the fire from her, in a deep conversation with Jay. All the others were still wrapped up in their game of beer pong.

"There," Kruise said, after he took the ping-pong ball packaging, lit it and stuck it amongst the kindling. The fire began to catch.

Shayde clapped for him. "Yay!" she laughed. "Good job!"

"Thank you, thank you! 'I... have made fire!'" he said, imitating Tom Hanks in *'Castaway'*.

Shayde giggled at him as he grabbed his beer from the ground and sat down next to her.

"So, tell me about you," she said, taking a drink of her beer.

"Um, well, what do you wanna know?" he asked, holding his cup in front of him with his elbows on his knees, looking at the fire.

He looked so gorgeous. So kissable. Never had she wanted someone to kiss her so badly. She had been afraid of kissing, but not tonight. No, on the contrary, she wanted him so badly that she was tempted to grab his face and kiss him right there and then.

But she didn't.

"I want to know everything," she said almost menacingly, raising her eyebrows as she admired him.

He laughed at her. "Everything huh?"

"Everything!"

"Okay, well I'm really not that interesting."

"Where did you grow up?"

"I grew up in Salem. I've lived in the same house all my life."

"I grew up in Salem, too! I wonder how come we've only just met."

"I don't know. I went Carlton Elementary School."

"Oh. Kain and I went to Bentley. They're just across the harbor from each other."

"Yeah, they are. That's strange. What part of town do you live in?" Kruise asked.

"Um, I live off of highway one-fourteen, in Canary Cove," she said, hesitantly.

"Nice. Those are some nice houses. Jay and I used to beg our parents to take us trick-or-treating in there," he laughed shyly.

He didn't seem intimidated by the fact that she lived in a rich development.

"Yeah, we've lived there for six or seven years. I was raised off of Turner Street though, by the House of the Seven Gables," Shayde said softly.

The House of the Seven Gables was one of the oldest

surviving seventeenth century wooden mansions in New England.

"Yeah, I know where that is. Been there a few times on Halloween," Kruise said.

"So, you and Jay, you're brothers? I thought you were just friends." She wrinkled her brow in confusion.

"No, not by blood, but close. My parents took him in around second grade. He was my best friend and his mom was a drug addict. She used to shoot up in front of him and he would tell my parents about it, like it was normal. My parents called CPS and got him put into protective custody. Then his mom lost everything because she pawned her whole life away for the drugs, and my parents adopted him. So, yes he is my adopted brother."

"Oh wow. That sucks he went through that but it is cool your parents were there for him. I knew you guys seemed close. My mom is a drug addiction therapist. She works with families like that and tries to get them off drugs. She tries to save them."

"That's tight. I don't think his mom could be saved even if she wanted to be. It's okay though, he doesn't miss her. All his memories from then are filled with bad stuff. He has better memories with us." He looked lovingly over at his friend.

Kruise was compassionate. From an outside perspective, it seemed as though he didn't have a soft bone in his body, but when she looked into his eyes she could see that it was just a front. Inside, he was a softy; sweet and loving and she liked that about him.

"What does your dad do?" she asked, taking another drink of her beer.

"He's a machine operator at a plant that makes stuff like

baseball jerseys, hats, and soccer uniforms—that type of thing. It's hard to explain, but it's way cool. What about your dad?"

"He's Vice President of a software engineering company."

"Damn! That's crazy! So, that's how you guys live in Canary Cove," he realized.

"He's really normal; he worked his way up from being a janitor there when he was in college. You'd like him; he's a lot like you. His arms are fully sleeved and he rides a chopper," she said, happily.

"No way?! That's dope dude, I love tattoos, as you can see, and it is my dream to build my own chopper. My dad has one that he built himself. That's cool as hell Shayde." He smiled at her and she could feel herself melt.

That smile could light up the whole world.

"Thought you'd like that. He's way chill. Just a total down to earth guy."

There was a loud commotion from the crowd at the beer pong table and from the looks of it Jordan and Hannah had just lost. Danny was jumping around in the sand like a monkey then he doubled high-fived Amy, lifted her up and carried her a small ways, bouncing her for his victory dance.

"Who's next?" Danny hollered over at Alizé and Jay as he set Amy down. Jordan and Hannah smiled and slapped the high five Danny offered, then grabbed their cups and wandered over to the fire pit. Alizé and Jay stood and walked over to the table as Danny ran in to fill up the pitcher.

"And you and Alizé have known each other for a while?" Kruise resumed.

"Yeah, we met in sixth grade and have been best friends ever since. When I lost my brother, she never left my side and I will always love her for that. She's like a sister to me," Shayde answered quietly, remembering those dark days that followed her brother's death and shuddered at the thought.

Kruise must've seen her shiver because he wrapped his arm around her shoulders.

"Cold?" he asked.

"Yeah," she lied, as she didn't want him to take his arm away.

"Yeah, I couldn't have gone on without Jay either. After my mom died, we three kept each other going. It was the hardest thing I've ever had to do." Although he spoke matter-of-factly, there was a definite pain behind his words.

Just then her phone's message indicator sounded.

She had to lean over to get the phone out of her purse on the ground next to her and he took his arm away. She felt bereft at its absence.

"Boyfriend?" Kruise teased.

"Parents," she corrected him, embarrassed. "That was their stipulation about me coming, that I have my phone on me constantly, respond immediately, and text often."

"That's cool," Kruise said, looking down at her text when she tapped the screen to awaken her phone.

It asked how she was doing.

She typed back to her mom that she was good, hit send and put her phone away.

"They don't bother me at all; I know they're just overly protective of me. I just have to respond quickly in little answers so they know I'm still alive." She let out a nervous, embarrassed laugh.

"It's okay; you don't have to explain yourself. It's totally cool," he said, and put his arm back around her.

A giggle almost escaped her as she snuggled up next to him, breathing him in deep. He was so warm, she really just wanted to wrap herself up in him.

The sun had finished its descent into the ocean and little stars were starting to peek out from the darkness.

Shayde took a large swallow of her beer.

Jordan and Hannah were sitting across from them, cuddling, looking at the fire and talking.

"Wanna go for a walk with me before we play?" Kruise asked sweetly.

"Sure." Her blood boiled beneath her skin, knowing the kiss was so close that she could feel it. "I just gotta go tell Zey that I'll be right back."

"Okay."

Shayde couldn't help the prance in her step as she walked over to Alizé and tapped her on the shoulder.

"Hey girl, I'm gonna go for a walk, be back in a bit," she said, trying to contain the excitement in her voice.

Alizé regarded her with an immense grin on her face. "All right, be careful, use protection!" she teased Shayde.

Jay laughed at her side.

"ZEY!" Shayde glanced behind her to see if Kruise heard. He was already a few yards away looking thoughtfully out towards the ocean so she hoped he hadn't.

"Just playing girl, go get you some."

Shayde grinned ruefully and walked away. Remembering she had to keep the phone close by her, she collected her purse and then made her way to Kruise. He held his hand out for her to take and even at this slightest little touch, the butterflies in her stomach went crazy.

"What's your favorite type of movie?" Kruise asked as they began their journey along the shore.

"I like horror movies, even though I can't watch the bloody parts. I have to cover my eyes and watch through the cracks in my fingers," she giggled at herself, "then I have nightmares afterwards. But I love them, especially the ones about ghosts."

"That's funny!" He laughed back. "I like horror films too. And action of course."

"Of course!"

"What kind of music do you like?"

"I like all types. If you were to put my iPod on shuffle and listened to it, you would hear every genre. Music is something I cannot ever live without."

"Me neither. I like the heavier music though. But my iPod is the same. One minute we're listening to something hard like death metal and then we're jamming to Tupac."

"I love Tupac! He is such an awesome lyricist. His music tells a story and the flow of his words are expressed like nothing else on earth. He truly is a legend in his own rhyme."

"Word, I agree," he said and abruptly stopped when they were out of view of the others. As he turned to face her, she inwardly gasped at his sudden and intense glare.

"Your eyes are truly a wonder I cannot quite grasp," he said softly, almost a whisper, moving a stray strand of her hair from her eyelashes.

"Thanks," she blushed, and turned her head to admire the ocean, she was so nervous.

Suddenly his hands were on her face pulling her gaze back

to his. He leaned in slowly and silently and as he grew closer she closed her eyes and let her mind go blank; she didn't want to over-think this. The beating of her heart was so rapid, she was sure he could hear it. When he reached her lips with his, her body turned to mush. Her breath quickened and grew heavy, he paused and held her there for a minute—so that she could feel his breath on her face—and then he parted his lips. When she felt his tongue ring on her tongue her knees almost gave out.

Following his lead she did what he did, tasting his mouth again and again. It was not at all what she was expecting. Her entire body felt alive but numb at the same time. She had an intense feeling of euphoria as she wrapped herself up into him, holding onto his muscular torso, pressing herself against him. He had her cradled in his arms so close, yet not close enough. She wanted to get nearer to him but knew it wasn't possible while being clothed; she was as close to him as she could get.

They stood there in the dark, under the stars, on a beach in their own paradise and kissed each other with such softness, such subtlety, she felt how a princess might feel when her prince came to rescue her. He softly ran his fingers through her hair while he continued to kiss her. Then he slowed down, his breath abating, and he cradled her face in his hands while his lips brushed hers over and over again. She didn't want him to stop, but he did. When she opened her eyes he was looking into hers, and she could see something in them she hadn't ever expected to see. He had feelings for her that he had never felt before. When he kissed her, she had awakened something in him that had been sleeping for a long time. It was written in his eyes. And what surprised her was that she wasn't afraid that she felt it too.

They stood there and gazed at one another for a long time. Shayde felt like it was hours, she was so completely lost in his eyes.

"What are you thinking?" he asked curiously, still holding her close to him.

"I'm not sure, I can't put it into words, my head is still spinning," she admitted shyly.

"Mine too," he confessed.

And then he kissed her again, harder this time, even more passionately. She let herself melt into him, wrapping herself around him, and breathed him in deep and long, savoring the moment, his lips, and his body. If ever there was a moment that she would remember for as long as her days, it would be this one. As she kissed him back, gravity suddenly betrayed them and they were lying upon the sand, her legs beside his, still wrapped in his arms. He continued to kiss her slowly, caressing her face and her long neck, following his finger trail with his lips, along her jawbone, down her neck, under her ear, then back up to her lips again. This was the most romantic kiss that she had ever dreamed of. The million times she ran this scenario through her mind, she had never envisioned it like this. Maybe that had been her nerves, but now all trace of them were gone and all she wanted to do was to kiss him, forever.

She lay there and kissed him for as long as she could, with her leg wrapped around one of his, lying beneath him, kissing his soft lips over and over again. It felt normal, natural, as though she had been kissed before, in another life, but in every life it had been him. Her body was alive with wild butterflies she never felt before, in places she never realized she could.

Then he slowed down and pulled his face away from hers for a moment. "We need to stop," he said, with the most beautiful smile plastered across his face.

The way that he looked at her made her melt.

"Why?" she moaned, grabbing his head and pulling him back to her, retrieving more kisses, each one stronger than the next.

He tried to pull away and then gave up, his breath growing more erratic and heavy, but then reason asserted itself and he forced himself to let go.

"'Cause right now I can refrain from tearing your clothes off and taking you on this beach but if you continue to kiss me like that I'm afraid I won't be able to stop myself. You're too powerful, I'm enjoying this even more than I thought I would and I didn't think that was possible." His sweet laugh escaped his lips.

She hesitated slightly, maybe she didn't want him to stop, but then she thought better of it. They needed to be something more to each other than just a kissing partner on the beach. Something told her they would be more to each other, but not right now.

"Okay," she said regretfully.

Kruise kissed her lips one more time, then her nose, then finally disentangling himself he got to his feet. He held out his hand to her and helped her up, as he did so he picked up her purse that had been flung to the ground in the heat of the moment. He handed it to her and Shayde took it unsteadily, her head was swimming, she felt as though she had been swept away to another place.

Being in that moment with him had changed her somehow, and she didn't know what had changed or how, but there was something different. She felt like a new person. One day she found out she's a witch and it felt like nothing had fundamentally changed within her, but one kiss from this handsome man transformed something deep within the realms of her soul.

THEY WALKED BACK TO THEIR CABIN HOLDING EACH OTHER CLOSELY AS they walked. It felt as if she had always known him; she was so comfortable with him. They continued where they left off, talking about their lives and asking each other questions.

When they arrived back at the cabin, everyone was crowded around the beer pong table. It appeared as though Alizé and Jay were winning; they only had one more cup to get. Alizé was aiming as Shayde and Kruise walked up, she tossed it and it landed in the last cup. She yelled with victory and Jay high-fived her then flipped Dan off with both hands.

"Ah ha ha!!! You suck!" he yelled.

"Screw you dude, ya only just came back from losing the entire game. Rebuttal!" Danny yelled back washing the ball off in the water cup and aiming intently, he tossed, and missed.

"AH HA HA HA!" Jay laughed loudly, thoroughly amused.

Then Amy took her ball and aimed. They still had four cups left; there was no way they were going to come back now.

She shot and missed.

"Yeah!" Jay shouted.

"Good game," Amy said as she and Dan walked over to

Alizé and Jay and shook their hands. Grabbing the remaining cups and pouring the leftover beer into their own cups, they walked off towards the fire.

"Kruise, Shayde, ready to lose?" Jay called out.

"Only if you are dill hole!" Kruise mocked him, walking up to get the empty pitcher to refill it. "I'll be back," he said to Shayde.

"I'll go too, gotta piss," Jay said as he followed Kruise in.

When the boys were inside, Alizé smiled and peered at Shayde as she was setting up her cups. "So?" she said, anxiously awaiting the boys' return.

"Oh my," Shayde responded. "That was amazing!"

She couldn't stifle her happiness and she grinned inanely. She felt a little childish by how she felt about him already, but she couldn't help it.

"Yeah? What happened, tell me everything," Alizé pressed.

"We were just walking and talking and then he stopped and looked at me with his beautiful, eyes. He told me my eyes were amazing and I got all shy and looked away, then he grabbed my face and kissed me like the movies. It was the most romantic moment of my life." As Shayde remembered, the feelings came flooding back.

"OOOOHHHH! I'm so happy for you!"

Shayde felt her cheeks go red. "Yeah. It was not at all how I thought it was gonna be. It was so much more sensual than I had ever anticipated."

"Really? He seems like he would just be rough and tough, like his appearance."

"No, not at all. Underneath it all, he is really quite a sweetheart. He wears a mask; a tough shell for his outer exterior but inside, he's soft and sweet. Like an M&M," she giggled.

"You're a retard."

"I know. I really am. I have never felt this way about someone. I'm scared."

"Don't be. It's your first love, let it happen. Even if it ends up hurting, it'll be worth it. Just live in it now, you'll miss it when it's gone."

"What do you mean, *love?* I don't *love* him. I only just met him. I like him, though. When it's gone?" She couldn't help the questions that were rapidly pouring out of her, she was suddenly worried. "What do you mean? You don't think he likes me back like I like him?"

"Shayde, no, calm yourself," Alizé laughed. "I'm just saying; sometimes your first love doesn't last. You never know what the future holds. Just live in the moment and breathe it in deep. Learn how to love from it, and hold on to it while it's yours because, speaking from experience, once it's gone you will miss it with every ounce of your being."

Apprehension quashed her jubilant mood as Alizé's advice sunk in. Her face crumpled in distress as she thought about how she didn't want to lose him, not now, not ever—she had only just found him.

"I didn't mean anything by it Shay, I'm just saying don't take anything for granted. No regrets."

"No regrets," Shayde repeated as the boys emerged from the house.

Shayde didn't know why Alizé had said what she had, and it bothered her. Was there a deeper meaning to her warning, and why did her best friend deem it necessary to mention it now? Was there something Alizé knew that Shayde didn't? Anxious thoughts were tangling themselves in her heart and yet, when she looked up and saw his smile, they immediately disentangled and dissolved away.

The boys came back up to the table, laughing at something one of them had said in the house. Shayde hoped Kruise hadn't told Jay what just happened between them, but seeing as she had just told her best friend, he probably had told his as well.

Oh well, she thought as she joined Kruise at the opposite end of the table, *at least it was worth mentioning to the most important person in his life.*

Her first game of beer pong went surprisingly well. Even though she and Kruise lost in the long run, she was okay with that as she was starting to get tipsy, even with Kruise drinking nearly all the doomed cups.

"Hey, good game!" Alizé called to Shayde as she and Kruise finished their last sips of beer.

"Thanks! You too!" Shayde responded as Kruise's hand met the small of her back to escort her back to the fire.

"Who's next?" Jay shouted over his shoulder as he headed towards the house to fill up the pitcher.

"We are!" Hannah returned.

"Good game," Kruise said as they made their way back.

"It really was. That was so much fun. My first game of beer pong."

"I still don't believe that it was your first time. You're way too good for it to be your first time."

"Yeah it was," she said matter-of-factly.

There has been a lot of firsts happening tonight, she thought to herself.

As they reached the fire, she sat down and he took a seat next to her, pulling her into him. Even though it was summer, there was a cold gust that came up off the ocean's surface every now and then. She shivered at one of these little drafts and he drew her closer to him, rubbing her arms for friction to help keep her warm. She was only wearing a thin little sundress.

"Wanna go in?" he whispered softly into her ear. Little goose bumps arose on her skin; caused not by the wind—but by his soft breath on her neck.

"No, I want to stay out here. It's so beautiful and peaceful."

"I'll go get a blanket," Kruise said as he jumped up. He kissed her on the top of the head and bounded off before she could protest.

She looked into the fire while she waited for him to return. How beautiful fire was, with its soft colors glowing, flowing every which way in different shapes and different patterns. She could stare at the facets of a fire for hours, hypnotized by its movement, mesmerized by its blinding beauty. The fiery tongues licked at the night air as if they were thirsty for the dark.

She couldn't look away even if she tried; she was so lost in the fire's blaze. Then Kruise snapped her out of it by wrapping a blanket around her shoulders as he planted himself down next to her.

"Ah, you scared me," she said sweetly, taking a drink of her beer. "Thanks for the blanket."

"Anytime." He flashed his beautifully white teeth at her and her heart quivered a little.

They sat by the fire and talked into the night. They drank their beer, laughed so hard her abs and cheeks started hurting, and they would stop to kiss each other every so often when they couldn't stand it to be even an inch away from one another any longer. Shayde knew that she was starting to get drunk because her head was light and her eyes tingled. Every time he kissed her she felt a prickling sensation all over and when she kissed him she felt like she may never be able to stop. Finally, she tried to get up to go to bed. As much as she didn't want the night to end, with the alcohol in her system, she didn't want to end up saying or doing something foolish, in front of a bunch of people she didn't know well enough to know they wouldn't use it against her.

She inched away from him little by little, trying to convince herself that she really had to go.

"I should go in," she said softly.

"Okay sweetheart. I'm not far behind you anyway."

She gasped when he said the word "sweetheart", she didn't know what it was about the way he said it, but when he did, it sounded magical. When he leaned in to get his goodnight kiss, he grabbed her face with his hands and started slowly, softly drawing her in, engulfing her with his presence. Feeling herself melt into him, her heart almost fell out of its place it was beating so hard. She changed her mind a thousand times before going in, telling herself to stay with him a little longer. The way he was making her feel, she would surely not make it through the night with her virginity intact. But she couldn't pull away. The longer he kissed her, the further away she got from her reasoning. It felt like he was the witch, like he had bewitched her with a spell that cast wonderfully weird sensations all over her body. Feelings like these were never known to her before. She tried to let go again and when he started to relinquish her lips, she pulled him back with her hands and bit his lower lip some more, tasting his mouth again. She started to let up again, slowing her kisses, her breath, trying to snap out of it, but he wouldn't stop either. The more she tried to pull away from him, the more he chased her lips and begged for more. How was she to say no to someone like him? He was breathtakingly handsome and he was all over her. His lips tasted like something out of dream, like a breath of fresh air or thirst quenching drink, refreshing her soul so much that she didn't want to let him go. Not now, not ever—but she had to try again.

"Okay," she said in-between kisses. "I... I gotta... I gotta go in."

"'Kay," he responded, slowing down. "Okay, you should... you should go then."

"'Kay," she moaned pulling away. "I'll see you tomorrow."

"Okay," he whispered, kissing her one last time. "Sweet dreams."

"You too," she said, smiling at him as she rose. She kissed him one last time, caressing his face with her hands, and then turned sadly and slowly on her heels to go tell her friend—who was still ruling the table—goodnight.

Scooping her purse up from the ground, she looked at him again with longing, biting at her lower lip. He gazed at her with an intensity she hadn't felt from him before, it enveloped her. It begged her not to go at the same time telling her to go in. When she was finally able to find her feet again, she turned her head sadly away from him, breaking their connection, and she began to walk towards Alizé.

When she reached Alizé she gave her a hug.

"G'night friend."

Alizé turned and hugged her back. "Night love, sweet dreams."

"You too," Shayde told her and turned to leave. "Night guys," she said to everyone else.

"Night Shayde," they all chimed at different times.

Slowly, she made her way back to the cabin, glancing at him one last time as he walked towards the crowd at the table. She blew him a kiss and he caught it and put it on his heart. Her body tingled at the gesture. Sending one last smile his way before she entered the house she opened the sliding glass door and disappeared inside. As she closed it, she sighed sadly at the slight ache that she had at leaving him.

She turned on the light to her room and looked around. Everything looked dull and ashen, though she knew that the light from the overhead ceiling fan should have cast a brilliant glow to everything in the room, now textures were less complex to her and the colors seemed to fade right before her eyes. She wondered if it was just because of the contacts, the alcohol she had consumed, or if it was the new boy in her life.

Does this happen to every teenager? she wondered as she made her way to the bathroom.

After she was done, Shayde found her way back to her room and plugged in her phone. There were no new messages so she sent a good night text to her dad and clicked the phone to sleep.

She changed into a pair of yoga shorts and a tank top, turned out the light, and climbed into the bed. The sheets met her skin with a soothing chill and fresh smell and she settled into them, while listening to the muffled sounds of her new friends laughing on the beach. She wished she wasn't such a pansy when it came to drinking and partying, but she knew herself too well and knew that if she had drank one more she would have been drunk. Having not been drunk enough times in her life to know exactly how she would act, she opted out of making a fool of herself the first night she and Kruise hung out together. She did still wish she was out there with him but knew she had made the right decision.

Are you here with me my friend? she thought to Aura.

"Always my love," Aura's voice came through like the wind.

"Did you see everything?"

"No. I knew what was about to happen and wanted you to experience it alone," Aura had materialized and now lay beside her. She glowed faintly in the dark like a ghost.

"You didn't stay by me, to protect me or stop me in case I got carried away?" she asked, confused, gazing at her from the other pillow.

"It is your life, Shayde my darling. You must experience life on your own, without my help. I have been around for a very long time and have seen many first kisses. It is a special moment in any young woman's life and I gave you your privacy to experience it all on your own. I did check his thoughts before the two of you left though," she smirked a little. "Still perfectly honorable."

"Where did you go then?"

"I went back to your mom to say hello and give her an update. Her thoughts were swarming with worries; I had to make her feel a little better."

"Did you tell her what I was doing, the boy, the drinking?"

"I told her about it all, except for the kiss. She knows what young people do. She knew it was coming and she told me to leave you to your privacy and let you experience it alone. She does not want to spy on you."

"So she's not mad? Why is she so worried?"

"She is not mad. She was a young woman once too, exactly like you except more wild and crazy. She would still be out there drinking like a fish!" Aura laughed. "She is worried because she is your mother and loves you more than her own life. It is not you she does not trust, it is the world. You will not understand a mother's love until you have a child of your very own. From the moment of conception a mother will never be free from worry for her child. It is more powerful than any energy on earth, so intense it makes you ache from the inside out. You are her baby and she has already lost one of her babies. You know how badly it hurt you when you lost your brother. Well, that was her *baby*. That pain cannot be comprehended. She had to live through it because she still had to be there for you. If anything were to happen to you too, she would not make it, she would not want to."

"I understand. I don't like to make her worry."

"Yes, I know that, but know that it is inevitable. You see, you have to live your life in your own way. You have to make the mistakes that she made, but in your own time and, as your mother, she knows that there is no other way around it. She gave you wings, hypothetically and maybe literally, she has to let you learn how to fly. The important thing is that she *trusts* you. She knows that you are very smart and will always do the right thing, as you have tonight. You knew that if you stayed out there with him you would do something you would regret, so you forced yourself away from him, as much as it pained you to do so. Your mother knows that you have that power within you, that you are wise beyond your years and know how to handle yourself and the world."

"That makes me feel a little better. And this Kruise thing? What are these strange things I am feeling for him?"

"That is *love* my darling, of a different kind."

"So this overwhelming pressure I feel on my chest when he is near me is normal?"

"Oh yes! Is it not grand!? That is young love, first love..." She paused. "True love."

"You say it like it is a good thing. I have only just met him; just barely kissed him tonight, today is the first day hanging out with him. I'm a total dweeb if I love him already. He'll think I'm crazy, that I have gone mad if I think I am already in love with him so soon."

"Tell yourself whatever you wish that gets you through the day. When it comes down to it, what you and Kruise have is special. Not many people meet a person with whom their auras mix so well with. Your auras were dancing, they go together so well. It is almost as though you belong together, like you have been together in another life, they were so at home with each other."

"That's weird. What you're saying is weird to me. I can't wrap my brain around him yet and now you're telling me this. I have to process the night first before I try figuring out what I am feeling. I love you but I'm spent. I think I'm going to go to sleep now."

"Okay my love. Goodnight my Shayde. May you dream the sweetest dreams," Aura said as she faded away.

"Goodnight Aura. See you tomorrow."

She didn't know if she was just tipsy and was imagining everything Aura was saying, or if it was all real. She felt sleepy and just wanted to close her eyes and let things happen as they did and not try to figure them out just yet.

Closing her eyes, she pictured his face—his handsome, soft, unerring face. She touched her lips as she remembered his kisses. No words could explain the way he made her feel and she couldn't wait for the morning and to spend the whole day with him. She felt like someone special to be in his presence and to get to spend time with him.

Slowly she drifted off to sleep thinking of him and their first night together.

ELEVEN

K ruise watched her as she entered the house, still draped in the blanket he had placed on her. He stood up despondently and joined everyone at the table, taking up the pitcher of beer and refilling his cup.

"What's up?" Jay greeted him, with a slight slur. He and Alizé had won about five games in a row and were still going strong. They were playing against Danny and Amy again.

"Nothing much, how's it going Jay? You feeling good?" Kruise teased him.

"Hell yeah! Feeling great! Me and this girl can kick some ass at this game!" Jay enunciated carefully, trying hard to form his words.

"Nice Jay, that's awesome," Kruise laughed as he focused on the house.

Her light came on for a few minutes, probably while she changed, then it flickered out again. The image of her invaded his mind and subjugated all other thoughts but those of her.

Is she thinking of me too? he wondered. *Did I make a good impression?*

These feelings that he had for her were strong and he knew he wanted to be more to her, but he couldn't be sure how she felt about him.

Deciding to let it go for now, he knew the weekend would pan out for him one way or another.

He stayed outside for a little while longer as everyone else grew more and more trashed. Hannah and Jordan were the next to go inside, returning to the house after shaking everyone's hands goodnight. Kruise paired up with Danny for one more game when Amy went off to bed, *finally* beating Alizé and Jay. Alizé decided it was her turn to go inside afterwards and said goodnight to the remaining few. When Danny retired as well, Kruise started picking up the cups on the table.

Jay stumbled around a little bit, searching for something on the ground as Kruise stacked the cups together.

"What are you looking for?" Kruise asked as he laughed at his drunken friend.

"A good place to lie down," Jay's words were garbled together.

"Where did you put your things?" he asked, as he grabbed Jay who was tipping a little farther to the left than anticipated.

"Not sure. Don't think I ever moved them from the place I put them down. Not sure where that is right now."

Kruise laughed again, he walked him to the benches by the fire and sat him down.

"I'm going to go look for your things. You can just crash in my tent, there's room, it's a two person."

"Cool bro, thanks."

Kruise tossed the cups into the fire before he jogged to the house to find Jay's things. When he found them lying in a pile by the front door, he returned to his tent to make Jay's bed for him. Finally, Kruise helped Jay walk the distance to the tent where Jay fell down on top of the blankets and immediately began to snore.

Returning to the fire, Kruise put it out with sand, using the pitcher from the beer pong game. When the fire was a mere smolder, he went back to the tent, took off his shoes and climbed into his makeshift bed. Although it would prove difficult to fall asleep because of Jay's snores, Kruise knew it was more Shayde's face occupying his consciousness that would prevent it. Thoughts of her green eyes and soft lips were tempting him to stave off tiredness; they were the last thing he saw when he was finally tugged away from reality.

When he opened his eyes again, the little tent was like a sauna, the morning sun was lancing down on it, making him sweaty and extremely uncomfortable. He dug his phone out of his pocket and flipped it open.

Seven a.m.

Wonderful, he thought.

There was no way he was getting back to sleep now, so he decided to get up. He crawled out of bed, unzipped the tent, and clambered out. Stretching in the morning air, a nice cool breeze came off the ocean and swept over him, melting the stuffiness away. He looked appreciatively out to the sea, embracing the quietness of morning, the gentle lull of the subtle waves coming up to the shore and then softly retracting once again. Mornings by the sea were the best on earth.

After standing in the cool breeze for a moment, he decided that now was a good time to go in and take a shower before everyone else woke up. He ducked back into the tent where Jay was still snoring loudly, snatched his duffle bag and proceeded into the house.

The shower was quick, and after he was changed he started for the kitchen to make breakfast. Even though it was still early and his friends wouldn't be up for a while, he was hungry and there was nothing else to do.

The wonderful smell of breakfast burritos must've pulled Danny out of his slumber because he suddenly emerged from the living room, clad only in boxers, looking half asleep and half drunk.

"Damn dude, looks good," he mumbled.

"Help yourself. It's all ready."

Danny didn't hesitate to grab a plate and a tortilla and start making a massive burrito. After grabbing a fork, he sat down at the small table just as Amy was getting out of the hide-a-bed.

"What's up gorgeous," Danny said to his girlfriend.

"Hi," she said sleepily.

"Get some food mama, and come join me."

She walked up to the counter. "Yum Kruise, this looks so good."

"Thanks dude, help yourself," Kruise said while he stirred the last batch of potatoes in the oil.

Amy took out a plate and a tortilla and built a smaller burrito, joining Danny at the table afterwards.

"Yum, this is awesome dude," Danny said with a mouth full of burrito.

"Smells good," Kruise heard Shayde's unmistakable singsong voice behind him. He turned around to face her and forgot how to breathe for a millisecond; her beauty caught him off guard.

"Morning." He smiled and walked up to her, spatula in hand, giving her a good morning hug and swift little kiss on the lips.

"Morning." She smiled back.

"Hungry?" he asked her as Alizé came into the room behind her. "There's food for everyone, help yourselves."

"Nice, I'm starving," Alizé said as she headed towards the food and dug in.

Alizé finished making her plate and joined Danny and Amy at the table. Just then Jordan and Hannah emerged from their room.

"Why the hell is everyone yelling?" Jordan said sarcastically. No one had even raised their voice. They all laughed at him. He walked up to the food and started making himself a plate, Hannah followed suit.

Shayde finished making hers and stood in the kitchen with Kruise, eating while standing up. He finished cooking the last of the potatoes and added them to the rest on the counter. After Hannah was done making hers she joined the other three at the table. There was just enough left for Kruise and Jay, whenever he woke up.

He put the dishes that were dirty in the sink and made himself a plate.

"Jay still sleeping?" Alizé asked as she took a bite of the burrito.

"Yeah, he was pretty hammered last night. He passed out face-down with his shoes on, on top of the sleeping bag, after he tried to pass out on the beach," Kruise laughed.

The room erupted in amused laughter.

"Last night was a blast," Danny said, his plate already almost empty.

"It was for sure," Shayde said. "This is so good," she said, pointing towards the burrito with her fork.

"How does everyone feel?" Kruise asked, standing up at the counter eating with Shayde.

"I feel okay, I didn't get too wasted," Amy announced.

"I feel like crap," Alizé said grumpily.

"It's 'cause you ran the table all night long!" Shayde reminded her.

"I don't feel too bad," Danny announced. "A little hung over but not terrible."

"I feel fine," Shayde added. "But I didn't drink that much at all."

"Yeah, I'm not too bad," Kruise said. "I had a nice buzz but didn't get too hammered. I just couldn't sleep in that scorching tent. I don't know how the hell he's still sleeping out there. It was like a hundred and ten degrees at seven this morning, it's gotta be even hotter now." He stretched his neck to look out through the little window to see if there was any movement in the tent.

"That would suck. Why don't you sleep inside tonight?" Shayde asked him.

"Nah, it's all good. I like sleeping outdoors, especially by the ocean. I usually get up early anyway."

"Ah, I see."

"So, what are the plans for today?" Amy asked Kruise after taking the last bite of her burrito.

"Gonna get the boat ready and when everyone is up and ready to go, head down to the marina and do some boating and jet skiing," Kruise informed them while chewing on a bite of potato. "I was thinking we could just pack our lunches here and have a picnic on the boat."

"YAY!" Shayde exclaimed. "That sounds like an excellent idea!"

Just then the sliding screen door opened and in walked Jay, drenched in sweat.

"Whoa dude, you look haggard," Jordan said to him as he stumbled in.

"It's so damn hot in that tent dude," he said as he eyed the food. "Whatcha'll eatin'?"

"Breakfast burritos. How ya feeling?" Kruise asked.

"Terrible. Maybe it wouldn't be as bad if I hadn't taken a nap in a sauna," he said, laughing at himself.

The group chuckled back.

"Eat dude, it might make you feel better," Kruise said, inclining his head towards the food as he took another bite.

Jay grabbed a tortilla and started making himself a burrito with the leftovers.

One by one as they finished eating, they rinsed their dishes in the sink and then neatly stacked them in the dishwasher.

"Alright, we're gonna go shower," Danny declared, "Does anyone need in?"

"Nah, I just pissed outside," Jay said, as he sat down at the table with his burrito next to Alizé. They both resembled indignant souls who regretted their choices of the previous evening.

"Cool," Danny said and he and Amy headed towards the bathroom.

"How you doing?" Jay asked Alizé.

"Not as bad as you but not great either." She laughed.

"You gotta take a shower before we go?" Kruise asked Shayde who was rinsing her plate off in the sink.

"Nah, I don't think so. I'd like to take one after, to get all the salt water off of me."

"Good call," Kruise nodded.

After they finished eating and cleaning up the breakfast mess, they gathered their things and prepared for the day. The boys loaded the trucks while the girls changed and fixed their hair and makeup, and when they were ready everyone climbed into a vehicle.

Shayde jumped into Kruise's truck and sat between him and Alizé. As the truck was only a single cab, Jay jumped in the bed and the other four climbed into Danny's jeep.

They drove to the gas station to purchase more ice along with other things to drink and then headed out to the harbor. They put the jet skis on the water first, then the boat and then they parked the vehicles. Danny and Amy manned the jet skis while everyone else climbed into the boat.

And they were off.

Kruise accelerated slowly, with Dan and Amy following behind, until they were out of the no wake zone, then he floored it. The boat responded with a loud roar and they sped off into the wide open water while and Dan and Amy played around in the wake.

He loved being out on the boat, the open air blasting by, the smell of the salty air, the cool water that spritzed his face just when it started getting too hot.

When they dropped anchor, Jay popped open a beer and took off his shirt to sunbathe in the back of the boat with Jordan and Hannah. He handed a beer to Kruise who took it, he only planned to drink one on the water and that was going to be it for the day.

He surreptitiously watched Shayde who was heading to the front of the boat with Alizé. He couldn't take her eyes of her and she just so happened to be directly in his line of sight, so he didn't have to. She put her things down, kicked off her shoes, and slid her sundress off, revealing an intoxicating bikini. It was bright pink; a one piece on the left side that divided into three pieces in the center and tied on the right side of her, exposing just enough of her tan skin to tease him. Even though he could still see her sexy, flat stomach underneath it, they were annoying little distractions. It was like a piece of cloth dangling in front of a Monet, seeing only a piece of something so beautiful made you yearn to cut away the fabric and see the entire picture. She looked like a goddess. He wanted to kiss her all over. Her soft, tan skin sparkling in the sun; she was flawless. He couldn't wait to taste her lips again; she had the sweetest kisses he had ever tasted in his entire life.

As his friends took turns playing in the water on the jet skis,

Kruise chatted with Jason while Shayde and Alizé sunbathed. In between turns on the jet skis, they made sandwiches from the items in the cooler and ate lunch in the sun. When they were through, Hannah and Jordan went back out to play on the water. Danny, Amy, and Jay were playing a game of cards and Alizé and Shayde had returned to their sunbathing posts. When Kruise finished his lunch, a dip in the water called to him. He took off his shirt, remaining only in board shorts, and took a running dive off the side of the boat. After swimming around in the cool water for a few short laps, he swam around to the front of the boat where Shayde was dozing in the sun.

"Hey!" he called up to her to get her attention.

She peeked her head over the bow. "Hi," she said in her sweet, sexy voice.

"Come swim with me," he pleaded.

"'Kay, be right there."

After giving him the most dazzling smile that he'd ever received, she disappeared beyond the bow of the boat.

"Boo!" she yelled, popping up behind him in the water.

Startled, he turned around to meet her exquisite gaze centimeters from his face.

"Hey beautiful," he said seriously, momentarily disconcerted by the feelings she evoked in him.

"Hi," she said again shyly.

"How's your day?" he asked, stroking a stray strand of wet hair out of her eyes and tucking it back gently behind her ear.

"Really good. I am having the time of my life, I never want this weekend to end," she said, swimming up even closer to him.

They were in front of the boat, close enough so that they

were hidden from everyone and in the shade a little, out of the scorching sun.

"Me neither," he said, holding on to the anchor rope to stay afloat, he scooped her up and pulled her onto his lap so her legs were on one side of him. She wrapped her arms around his shoulders as he cradled her in his. He was so close to her face he could feel her warm breath on his lips.

He went in for his kiss, starting slowly, just brushing her lips at first: her soft, wet lips kissing him back in a way that drove the butterflies in his stomach wild. Then he parted his lips and kissed her with a passion he had never in his life felt before. His entire body burned, sweltering from the overwhelming way she made him physically feel. He had a severe crush on this girl, his body ached for her—but it was more than that. Being with her was like being caught in a light, tropical rain; it was warm and refreshing, soothing to the soul. When he was with her, his heart felt like it was finally home. Until the day that she walked into that classroom, he always felt inadequate, half of a whole. It was as though he had been missing something, even before he lost his mom, yet he never knew what it could possibly be. But the day she walked in that door, his world stopped moving and something clicked into place in the universe. It was as if her heart was magnetic and he was being pulled to her, uncontrollably. They were meant for each other and there was nothing else to it.

He continued to kiss her long and arduously and she kissed him back, just as long and just as hungrily. Even though they weren't at that point where they could tell each other how they felt about one another, their kisses spelled out every word. He not only wanted her in a way that he had never known, he was starting to need her, and he could feel it in her kiss, that she was starting to yearn for him as well. She wasn't just kissing him back; she was drinking him in, soaking up every atom of him and using it to feed her soul. He worshipped every inch of her and kissed her in a way that told her so. He wasn't just attracted to her, his heart needed her, and he realized it always had. This wasn't just a girl he wanted a fling with; she was a girl that he needed in order to live. Now that he found her, he had no idea how he had been surviving without her. And the fact that he had only had one full day with her didn't scare him at all. He felt like he knew her, like he had been with her in another life, and things were happening exactly how they should.

He started to slow the kissing down, he was only human and he knew he was close to losing control, but he could not quit kissing her altogether. As if sensing his withdrawal the more passionate she became, and when she started to let go it drove him beyond crazy. Finally he pulled his face away and buried it in her neck.

"God I want you so bad," she said, surprising him that she was the one admitting to it first, kissing the top of his head.

"You have no idea," he said as he kissed her neck.

"Oh, I think I do."

He could sense her smile as she fought to control her breathing.

"WHAT'RE YOU TWO DOING?!" a booming voice came from above.

Of course it was Jay, his obnoxious self, interrupting their romantic interlude.

"Nothing Jay, go away!" Kruise pulled his face out of Shayde's neck and looked up at him from the water below.

"You guys want a turn on the jet skis? I know Shayde hasn't gone yet, but if you guys don't wanna go next I can take Alizé out."

Kruise beheld her piercing green eyes. He called them piercing because when she looked at him, they pierced into his heart and caught it, hook, line and sinker, every time.

"Would you wanna go try it out?" he whispered.

"Um..." She contemplated for a second, biting her lower lip. "Yeah, but maybe let them go first?" She smiled, seemingly a little embarrassed at the request.

"You guys go ahead," Kruise shouted up to him. "We'll go next."

"Word," Jay said and disappeared.

The second Jay was gone Kruise had to kiss her again. After gazing into her eyes for just a few seconds, he thought he would either go mad from not kissing her or go entirely crazy from kissing her. He was bound to lose one way or the other. So he dove head first into her world; her enchanting, bewitching world and started to kiss her just as passionately as before. He could hear the jet skis returning on the other side of the boat but didn't want to stop kissing her, to open his eyes or pull away. She wrapped her hands around his shoulders, up into his hair, twisting her fingers in it, pulling his head closer to her, though he thought he couldn't get any closer if he tried. With the hand that wasn't holding them afloat, the other one held her close to him, enclosing her little waist so she didn't float away. Without letting up on her kisses, she twisted herself so that she was straddling him, he knew that he was bound to go mad now. Their passion was building and the heat was rising immensely, he didn't know if he could stop himself now from taking her right there in the water, with their friends just feet away from them.

"Wait!" He was the one who interrupted them this time. "Wait. We should stop," Kruise sighed, he didn't want her to do something she would regret later, or himself for that matter. If they were to give in to the heat of the moment, it wouldn't be right. Their first time together had to be as special as her, not on the side of the boat with people so close by. He wanted to lay her down, to kiss her from head to toe, to get wrapped up in her limbs and drown in desire the right way. Being no stranger to the wet and wild tango, he knew he wanted his first time with her to be different; he didn't want it to be tacky.

"What's the matter?" she asked softly. "Did I do something wrong?"

"No," he laughed at her. "No, quite the opposite actually. You are driving me mad and I was about to do things to you that you've only seen in movies."

She giggled. "What if I wanted you to?"

"Really?" he asked, kissing her nose.

"Yeah," she exhaled a deep, hungry exhale, cradling his face in her hands.

"I've never met anyone like you," he let slip, staring longingly into her eyes.

"I've never met anyone like you either, I'm enchanted by you." Her voice was a soft whisper.

"You are the one who is enchanting sweetheart. You have me under some sort of spell; I can't get my head right when I'm around you."

"No spells, I promise." She grinned at him.

"Then I don't know what it is about you but I am completely bewitched. Things like this just don't happen to guys like me."

"Things like what?" she asked, innocently.

"Just meeting someone and having these feelings that I have for you in an instant. It's something you only read about in books and see in the movies." He was shocked by how easily it came out.

A smile emerged and her face lit up with it. "I know exactly what you mean. I feel the exact same way about you." Her eyes beamed when she said it.

His heart melted as she spoke the words, it was almost magical.

"I want our first time to be more personal than this. As bad as I want to take you right here, I want it to be special, not just on the side of a boat like two horny teenagers."

She laughed her sexy little laugh. "But we are two horny teenagers!" she snickered. "But I know what you mean and I respect that you feel that way, I didn't think about it that way. But you are right; this wouldn't be a good place to lose my virginity."

"You're a virgin!" he exclaimed, his tone shocked.

She batted her eyes as her face turned scarlet. She looked down, embarrassed. "Yeah, why do you say it like it's a bad thing? I have never had a boyfriend and you're the first boy I've ever kissed," she said, almost a little defensively.

"No, Shayde, that's not what I meant, I didn't mean it to sound like that. What I meant was that you are so beautiful I didn't expect it at all. A girl as gorgeous as yourself surely had your pick of any guy you wanted. I just assumed and it was wrong of me, I'm sorry."

The thought that she had never even kissed anyone floored him, she was so natural at it; he couldn't tell she was new to it.

"It's okay," she said sweetly. "I assumed you weren't a virgin either."

"You assumed right." He glanced down ashamed, but he wanted to get it out of the way because of the awkwardness. "I —I was your first kiss?" he asked smiling, looking at her softly.

She met his gaze. "Yes… and it could not have been a more perfect, romantic first kiss any girl could've ever dreamed of."

Visions of last night's kiss consumed him. The two of them locked together in a moment of passion, under the moonlight, on a beach, with the ocean murmuring in the background. It had been a sensational kiss, the most passionate and romantic kiss he had ever experienced.

"It was pretty perfect for me too. You are really good at kissing, never having done it before. I am quite shocked I have to admit."

Relief washed over her face, as if she had been worried about something.

"Good. I was so nervous; I just wanted it to be perfect, without knowing how to do it."

"It was the most perfect kiss I have ever had," he said, kissing her nose again.

"Really? Aw, yay! I was wondering how I did all night."

"You did great." He laughed at her a little; she was so sweet and innocent. "Okay, well let's get out of this water, shall we, before we prune up."

"Good call."

They swam to the stern, where the ladder was attached to the boat, where he stopped her before she began her assent.

"One more, so I can make it through some more of the day."

He pulled her into him and tasted her with one more long and passionate kiss that stirred up a shock wave within him, then he let her go and climbed up behind her.

Alizé and Jay were still not back yet from their jet ski adventure, and the rest of the gang were playing cards.

Retrieving a towel from his bag, Kruise covered her with it as her bottom lip started to quiver and goose bumps broke out all over her soft, tan skin. Pulling one out for himself, he wrapped it around his shoulders and pulled her into him to warm her, loving the feeling of her so close to him.

"Hey, how was your romp in the water?" Jordan teased.

"Ha ha, very funny," Kruise said back. "Hey, have you ever ridden on a jet ski before?" he asked Shayde, quickly changing the subject.

"No I haven't. Is it hard?" she asked with her head still resting on his chest, her shivering starting to subside.

"Not at all. It's super easy, you just grip the throttle and go. You can ride with me at first if you want."

"No, it's okay, I'll try it out. It looks easy and if all the other girls did it, so can I."

"Okay sounds good," he said as he saw Jay and Alizé coming back from their joy ride.

They pulled up just as Kruise was dried off and warm again. He helped them back onto the boat as they exchanged life vests. The one he put on from Jay was cold and damp and made him shiver as he helped Shayde buckle hers. When they were both fastened and ready to go, they headed down the ladder and onto the jet skis.

He climbed onto the green one and held her hand as she got on the red one.

"Okay this," he pointed at the string leading to the ignition, "is the emergency shut off switch. You wrap this cord around your wrist nice and tight and should you happen to tip, crash or get thrown off, this will pull out and the engine will automatically shut off."

"Okay," she said looking at what he was pointing at.

"All you do is turn it to start it, and it should fire right up."

She turned the key and it revved to life.

"Okay, good. Now the right is the throttle, the left is the break, like a bike break. Twist the throttle towards you to go, the more you pull it back, the faster it will go. When you're going really fast turn easy, slow and wide, otherwise it can hit a wake just right and tip you."

"Okay."

"That's it. Ready?" he asked as he started his up and wrapped the string around his wrist.

"Ready."

He twisted the throttle and took off slowly, waiting for her to find her groove. She quickly caught up to him then zoomed passed him with confidence. He punched it and caught up to her, riding alongside her. She was all smiles as he coasted next to her, not a hint of worry on her face. When he spotted a large yacht out in the distance, he altered his course and motioned for her to follow him as he set out to capture the impressive wake the boat was leaving behind. When they approached the robust, white-capped waves, he started zigzagging across the heaving water. She followed his lead and caught some air herself, screaming with excitement as she bounded up and down over the swells.

"Having fun?" he yelled at her when they returned to the open ocean.

"Oh my god yeah! This is awesome!" she said laughing.

"You're awesome!" he laughed back at her.

She smiled and took off into the wind full speed ahead to the right. He revved the throttle and began to chase after her as the cool wind whipped at his face. He stayed close behind her at first; chasing her in every direction she went. Once he finally caught up to her, he coasted along at her side and cruised on the beautiful ocean. They had lost all track of time when he noticed dark clouds looming, threatening to engulf the glorious blue above them, and he decided that they should head back to the boat in case a thunderstorm was close behind.

When they returned to the boat, everyone was laughing and having a good time, playing cards and drinking beers. As soon as Kruise and Shayde joined them on the deck, thunder boomed so loudly that it seemed to shake the entire world, and the lightning that followed lit up the dark clouds like a flare, as if warning the people of earth to take cover.

Once again, the weather people who had said there was no chance of rain this weekend were wrong.

As Kruise put his shirt on and wound up the anchor, a light drizzle followed the next round of thunder. Amy and Danny pulled on the life jackets to bring the jet skis in and they headed back to the marina. Shayde put on her clothes and sat in the co-captain's chair. As they were pulling the boat in next to the dock, it started raining harder. Jay and Jordan jumped out to go get the trucks while everyone else piled onto the dock. They pulled the jet skis out first and then the boat just as it started to pour. Everyone climbed into the vehicles and they headed back to their cabin.

Once they unloaded everything, they took showers and changed into dry clothes. It was still raining outside so they agreed on watching a movie while the storm passed by. Kruise sat on the far side of the couch with a blanket and patted the seat next to him playfully for Shayde to come cuddle with him. Jay and Alizé joined them on the couch, Alizé sitting down next to Shayde in the middle while the guys occupied the ends. Amy and Hannah made a bed on the floor for the remaining four and they found a movie on Netflix that they all wanted to watch.

About a third of the way into the movie Kruise finally saw Jay put his arm around Alizé in his peripheral vision. It was about time that they started getting closer. Jay hadn't been with anyone since Jessica had broken his heart and Kruise was glad to see him back in the game.

Snuggling in close to Shayde, he inhaled the air around her, breathing in every molecule, savoring every moment that he was able to spend with her. Paying attention to the movie was proving to be very difficult with her so close, even though he had wanted to see it. He could only concentrate on her. The sweet-smelling lotion that emanated from her skin permeated the air and blended with the scent of her conditioner producing an aroma which was unique to her. It entered his nostrils enticingly. It was such a beguiling mixture, he yearned to bottle the smell up and have it on him always. She was leaning on his right side, her right hand enclosed in his left, his free hand gently caressing her beautifully soft arm. Her beating heart thudded against his ribs, quickening the beats of his own as he struggled with the thoughts evoked by her being so close to him. Her soft skin was the only thing on his mind. As he pretended to watch the movie, he thought of her face, even though she was right beside him. Memories of their day together flooded the shores of his being and his stomach galloped when he thought how perfect and right the entire day had felt. Sadness tugged at the back of his mind when he thought that tomorrow was his last day with her for a while, and not knowing when he would see her again ate into him. He didn't want this weekend to end.

Kruise had been thinking so intently about his feelings for Shayde, it was only when he looked down at her beautiful face that he saw she had fallen asleep. Finally, he was able to see what she looked like when she was sleeping. Just as he thought, she looked how he imagined an angel must look, if there were such things as angels. He glanced up and realized that he was the only one awake. Jordan and Hannah were cuddled on the floor sleeping, as was Danny and Amy. When he glanced over at Jay and Alizé, she too was fast asleep, nestled neatly on his chest while he slept sitting up.

He hadn't even noticed that the rain had stopped and the sun was coming out. Everyone had had a long day of drinking in the sun. Looking at his sleeping beauty one last time, he drifted off to sleep as well.

When he awoke it was getting dark outside. Shayde was still sound asleep on his chest. The movie had ended and was now at the title screen, repeating the same music over and over again. He tried to get up quietly to go start dinner but when he moved her arm she woke up and looked at him.

He smiled at her. "Hey," he whispered.

"Hi." She smiled back. "I passed out?"

"Yeah, we all did."

She scanned the room and saw that everyone was sleeping. She giggled. "That's funny. Long day in the sun'll do that to you."

"Yeah for sure. You hungry?"

"Famished. What are we having?"

"Steaks and mashed potatoes. I was going to do baked potatoes but I should've started them long ago."

"Mashed is good too. Need help?"

"Sure," he smiled again and together they left the couch and proceeded to the kitchen.

Shayde grabbed the bag of potatoes and when Kruise handed her the peeler, she sat down at the table and began to peel them into a plastic bag. Kruise retrieved the steaks from the fridge, tenderized and then seasoned them.

People from the living room began to emerge shortly after.

"Need any help guys?" Jay asked.

"Um, you can start the grill if you want," Kruise told him.

"Word."

"What about me, can I help with the potatoes?" Alizé offered.

"Sure," Shayde answered.

The girls worked on the potatoes while the boys rattled on outside. Danny started a fire with the dry firewood that Kruise had stuck under the patio, thankfully out of the rain, and then he and Amy started playing their own little game of beer pong. Jordan and Hannah stayed in the living room for a while, watching something on TV.

When dinner was ready, they each made up their plates and returned to the fire pit to eat. Even though everything was slightly damp from the rain, it was better to be outside than in. The storm had passed but there was still an after-rain chill in the air, so they were dressed in the warm clothes that they had brought in case of rain.

The last two days had been magnificent and a melancholy descended upon Kruise as he thought that it was their last night in their own private paradise.

"This is sad," he said, more to himself than to the group.

"I know," Hannah seconded. "It's our last dinner here."

"We should do something like this again soon," Dan added.

"For sure bro, I've had a blast so far," Jay said.

"I know, me too. I don't want it to end," Shayde said sadly.

"Maybe we can do it again next month," Kruise suggested. "And then one more time before the end of the summer. We can always go camping too."

"That's true," Jordan joined in. "I'm down with that."

"Alright then, it's a deal. When we get back we'll start planning the next trip."

Everyone agreed.

They talked, some of them drinking slightly warm beer leftover from the night before and ate their meal. They had gotten ice for the keg on the way back but it hadn't cooled enough yet.

After dinner, the beer pong started up again with Alizé, Jay, Danny and Amy. All Kruise could do was smile inwardly at his friends. It was a perfect end to a perfect day.

Kruise and Shayde sat by the fire and talked. There was nothing that he didn't want to know about her. He asked her about everything in her life. Being just as curious as he was, with every question she answered, she would ask one of him in return. They laughed so hard at things that his face would cramp up from smiling.

As they were talking, he had an inward discussion with himself on what he was going to do with her. Liking was beyond what he felt for her and making her his girlfriend was the thought that sat front and center in his mind. The adorable creature that sat before him was not going to escape from his life without a fight. Like he had said to himself before, this girl was special and he didn't want it to be a weekend fling, or a summer fling either. He didn't want it to be a fling period, he wanted a relationship with her, and hoped with all of his being that she would want the same.

Nervousness suddenly caught him off guard. What if she didn't want to be with him? What if *she* only wanted a silly fling?

He wondered whether he could go through with it. He would have liked a beer but that would hinder the plan brewing in the back of his mind, knowing she would not get in the truck with him after having even one. His expression must've done something odd because she regarded him with concern in her eyes, her face a picture of confusion. "You okay?" she asked anxiously.

"Oh yeah, I just got a little headache is all. Must be from the all the sun," he lied. After a moment's pause, he asked, "Wanna go somewhere with me?"

"Sure, where?"

"It's a surprise. Just follow me."

He jumped up, grabbed her hand, and led her to the house.

They walked through it, out to the front and climbed into his truck.

"Don't worry; I haven't had a beer since the boat." Kruise turned and smiled at her.

This was all an impulse but it was something that had to be done and now. There wasn't time to dwell on it any longer.

They drove for about fifteen minutes, to the outskirts of town. Kruise knew exactly where they were going but Shayde didn't have the slightest idea. Finally, he took a right into a parking lot that was surrounded with deep, lush forest. He put the truck in park and ran around to open the door for her. As soon as she stepped down, he walked her towards a pathway into the trees.

"Where are we going?" she asked, with no hint of worry, only curiosity.

"Just follow me," he said with a devilish grin.

They walked along the dense path for a while and then finally came to a clearing. Shayde stopped dead in her tracks upon entering the paradise. The clearing contained a beautiful pond, almost the size of a lake. It was bordered by soft, green grass that was specked with wild flowers. There was a myriad of birds of all types singing their songs to each other, nestled ubiquitously in the tress, the grass, and water. The pond was midnight-clear and still, acting like a mirror to the colorful sky. The sun was setting, making the twilight sky purple and pink with hints of orange and dashes of blue. Specks of stars were starting to peek out here and there, glittering in the perfect sky.

On the far side of the pond a small stream trickled softly into the water over a dam of branches. The gentle sounds of water falling and birds chirping filled the atmosphere. On the bank closest to them, there was a little fishing dock that protruded a few feet over the pond. It was the most peaceful place Kruise had ever been to. The fireflies were starting to come out too, lighting up here and there, their glittering bodies darting about the place, making the air appear to sparkle. He looked over at Shayde who gazed in awe.

"Pretty ain't it?" He held her hand as they walked further into the beautiful place.

"Oh my goodness," she said taking out her phone to snap a few pictures. "This is the prettiest place I have ever seen."

Leading her out to the fishing dock, he sat down at the end of it, took off his socks and shoes and dangled his feet into the water. She followed his lead, flinging off her flip-flops and sitting down next to him.

"What is this place," she asked him, still amazed.

"Well it was just a clearing in the woods where a stream ran through it. But see over there," he pointed to the dam, "the beavers dammed the stream and created this beautiful little pond. The locals told my parents about it one summer. Local people come here to fish. It's an ideal fishing hole with all the fish that come streaming in from the Adirondacks. We came here once and my mom fell in love with it, and then we came back every summer we were here around this time. I haven't been here since my mom died."

"I'm so sorry," she said quietly.

"No, don't be. I couldn't think of a more perfect person to come back here with. I wouldn't want someone as beautiful as you to miss out on a place like this. It seems like you belong here."

"Why do you say that?" she asked quizzically.

"Because this place is magical," he paused, stroking her hair, admiring her with longing. "And so are you," he said and he kissed her long and soft, not heated and frantic like earlier. He kissed her like his soul needed her embrace to flourish.

"You are so sweet," she told him breathlessly after he let her lips go free.

"You are."

He was holding her face in his hands, running his fingers through her hair. Her irises were deep chartreuse, rimmed with the color of a tropical sea, mimicking the bays that were only found in the islands. He pulled her in to kiss her and he felt her melt like putty in his hands. "I was thinking..." he stopped to assemble his thoughts.

"Yes?" she asked when he paused for too long.

"Shayde, I have never met anyone like you in my life," he started, his voice taking on a serious tone as she gazed attentively into his eyes. "When I'm with you it feels so right, so natural and I know this may sound crazy... but I think I'm falling for you." He stopped so he could gauge her reaction.

She looked back at him with such intensity that he felt he might shatter under her gaze. She didn't say anything, all she did was lean in and kiss him passionately. Then she stopped and stared at him again. "Kruise, I am falling for you too. I've felt it since I first saw you. It's like you're pulling me in. I feel like this is supposed to be."

He couldn't believe how she seemed to take the words right out of his mind. "I was thinking the same thing. Shayde I want you to be mine. I don't wanna share you with anyone. I already feel protective over you. I was hoping you felt the same way."

"You want me to be your girlfriend?" she asked softly, blushing.

"If that's okay, yeah. I want you to be my girl," he said in his matter-of-fact tone.

"Of course I'll be your girl. I finally found someone who seems to complete me." She focused on her hands then looked back up into his eyes profoundly.

"Me too. I have strong feelings for you already and I'm not afraid to see where they lead. No one in my life has made me feel this way. My heart is at home when I am with you. I feel happy and I haven't been this happy in a long, long time."

"Me neither."

He kissed her again softly. It was a long, sensual embrace. She was his. His heart was beating so hard that he thought it might burst out of his chest. Now he could continue falling for her, not hold anything back because he knew she felt the same way. They sat in their private paradise, in their precious moment, and kissed each other for almost an hour. There wasn't even an urge to ravage her, all he wanted to do was to kiss her, forever. He drank her in and when his lips started to go numb and his jaw started to cramp he slowed his kisses down and pulled away from her, holding her face in his hands and staring into those bright green eyes.

After a moment or two of comfortable silence they began to talk and laugh again about life. Dangling their feet over the side of the dock with their toes submerged in the tepid water, they laughed and reminisced about their lives.

They were so pre-occupied in the intimate setting that they had lost all track of time. When Shayde's phone beeped they were suddenly pulled into the here and now, where darkness had fallen. She pulled it out from her shorts' pocket and clicked in on.

"It's Zey," she said. "They wanna know where we went."

"Okay, tell her that we're on our way back."

She typed it into her phone as he stood, putting his socks and shoes back on. He helped her up as she stuck her phone back in her pocket and slid on her flip-flops.

"I don't wanna leave," she said, her tone edged with disappointment.

"Me neither." He pulled her close to him as they walked back towards the woods.

WHEN THEY ARRIVED BACK AT THE CABIN, THEY JOINED THEIR FRIENDS who were playing more beer pong.

"Where'd you guys go?" Jason said as he threw the ball.

"To that little pond," Kruise told him.

"I called it, did I not call that?" he asked the group.

"Yeah, you called it for sure," Alizé told him, zeroing in on her next shot.

"Did you guys go make a bunch of babies?" Jordan teased.

"Nope. I did make her my girl though," he announced to everyone nonchalantly.

"WHAT!" the group said in unison.

Everyone stopped what they were doing to gawk at the new couple. He glanced over at Shayde who was smiling and blushing at the same time.

"Yup, she's all mine. Just wanted it to be known," he announced proudly and gave her a kiss on the lips.

"Nice, good for you guys," Alizé said and regarded her friend happily. "You two will be good for each other."

Shayde smiled back at her.

He was as happy as he ever thought he could be and seeing her smile made the world and everything around him as right as rain.

TWELVE

W hen Shayde opened her eyes, she was still in Kruise's arms and her insides turned to mush at the notion. The mere thought that he was her boyfriend now hit her like a live wire hitting water, and all the pieces of her being became electrified.

The time that they had shared together last night would be a memory that would never leave her and be a veil through which she would view her life for as long as she lived. After that wonderful, romantic moment on the pond, she felt like she was living in a dream, and the fact that he was all hers was something she could not even come to terms with. After the pond, they stayed up until all hours of the night and played beer pong, winning almost eight games in a row together, and she kept up with Kruise this time. She decided to let herself go wild, after all, she was young and he was her boyfriend now. Their reign as champions was finally lost when Alizé stepped back up to the plate and ripped them apart.

Both girls were having a great time. She had been able to talk to her friend a few times last night when they went for bathroom breaks together. Alizé told her that Jay kissed her on the boat when Shayde and Kruise were out on the jet skis, and that he had kissed her often since. Alizé really liked him, a lot more than she ever thought she would and Shayde noticed they were more affectionate towards each other, giving kisses along with high fives throughout last night's festivities.

Shayde and Kruise stayed up talking until the sun came up. They sat on the beach cuddled together and watched the sun's ascent; coloring the sky with crimson, peach, and apricot. A canvas of color reminiscent of a painter's palette was strewn across the heavens, its brilliance reflected in the undulating waves of the sea, creating a world around them that took on an almost magical, awe-inspiring hue of yellow. The universe went quiet at that very moment, only the soft, low murmur of the brewing waves could be heard. Together they observed Mother Nature's radiance as she enveloped them.

Alizé and Jay had retired to the tent after their last game of beer pong and Shayde thought it would be nice for her boyfriend to sleep next to her. After the sun rose and she could fight sleep no longer, she walked with Kruise to the house and climbed into the big comfy bed, pulling him with her. After giving each other a long kiss goodnight, she lay on her left side while Kruise held her from behind and she drifted off to sleep in his arms.

Shayde still hadn't taken the ring off and she knew that it was one of the best decisions she ever made. She liked being surprised at Kruise's loving words towards her; she knew that she had to let him be the one to share his most intimate thoughts about how he felt. Though she wouldn't have had the insecurity of not knowing if he liked her or not if she had taken off the ring, she knew it was the right choice. They had discovered their feelings together and here she was, lying in his arms, now his *girlfriend*.

It had to be around noon or one o'clock, her parents had texted her a while ago asking how things were going. So far she had kept her promise and hadn't forgotten to keep in contact. Aura and Shayde hadn't really talked since the other night as they lay in bed. Shayde reached out to her through her mind once yesterday, to check in, and Aura had just laughed and told her there was no need for her to keep checking in, she was always nearby and would show herself if she needed to.

Kruise was still in a deep sleep from the sound of his breathing and Shayde just lay there, not wanting to move. This was her new favorite spot in the whole world.

Just then, the door opened and in ran Jay and Alizé. Before Shayde could react, Jay yelled; "WHAT'RE YOU DOIN'?!?!?!" really loudly in Kruise's ear. With eyes half closed Kruise bolted upright and punched Jay square on the nose. Jay fell back against the door as blood ran down his face and Alizé's eyes widened and her jaw dropped.

"Oh my god, dude I'm so sorry," Kruise apologized

sincerely, leaping out of bed to see if his friend was alright. "It's a reflex."

"Whatever ya dick, that's what you say every time!" Jay laughed a little while Alizé ran to get him some toilet paper.

"This has happened before?" Shayde asked, amused.

"Yeah 'cause he's a dick and can't take a joke," Jay said, his voice squeaky and muffled from holding his nose shut.

"Whatever dude, you're the one who doesn't learn and keeps trying to wake me up like a robber," Kruise laughed. So did Shayde.

"A robber, dude? C'mon seriously!" he mumbled as he held his head back, braced against the wall. When Alizé came in with the toilet paper, he pressed it to his nose.

"So what's up?" Kruise asked nicely, as if nothing had happened.

"We were coming in to wake you up," Alizé retorted with an annoyed inflection. "We thought you might sleep all day if we didn't."

"What time is it?" Shayde asked her.

"Almost two."

"WHAT!" Shayde exclaimed and sat straight up. "Oh my god I thought it was closer to one. Holy crap, we slept the day away."

"It's okay baby doll, we stayed up 'til the sun came up talking. I would trade a day of sleep for that any time," he said sweetly and kissed her cheek.

Shayde's stomach fluttered in response and she instantly felt better, her anxiety dissolved. "Good point," she told him.

"So, let's get up people and get dressed," Alizé ordered. "We wanna go."

"Go? Go where?" Shayde asked them.

"I thought we were going to go into town for lunch and walk around, see the sights. Don't you remember?"

Shayde had no recollection of these plans.

"No, did I say that that's what I thought we should do today?" she asked, confused.

"Yeah, we all did; during our last game of beer pong together. We thought we would try to get up early and play on the beach for a while and then go downtown for a bite to eat and walk around 'til it was time to head home."

"I kinda remember that," Kruise said, lying on his stomach, shirtless, clutching onto the pillow. He squinted one eye as he tried to remember the conversation.

Shayde laughed at him. "Does squinting your eyes like that help recall the lost memory?"

He looked at her with his wonderful smile. "It does, actually."

They laughed hysterically at one another.

"Alright you two weirdos, let's get moving," Alizé scolded them. "The day is already half over."

"Okay, be right out," Shayde told her, nodding towards the door, hinting for her to leave so she could get dressed.

"Okay, but hurry. No making out alright? Seriously guys, I know how this new relationship stuff goes, can't keep your hands off each other for five frickin' minutes. We've been waiting for you guys to wake up all morning, let's just keep that in mind, shall we?" Alizé stared at them with sweetness but a look that said, "If you take too long I'm going to punch you in your face."

"Yes mom, be right out," Kruise said derisively.

Alizé and Jay rolled their eyes and walked out, Jay still holding the tissues to his nose.

"Ugh, I thought they would never leave," Kruise eyed her, and then pounced on her like a cat on its prey.

Shayde giggled loudly as he buried his face in her neck and kissed her all over.

"Your face hurts," she laughed out loud.

"*Your* face hurts!" he said back and looked at her with playful menace. He hadn't shaved since the night before they left and had a five o'clock shadow that prickled her. Then his smile faded and he kissed her with one of *his* kisses; the kind that melted her whole being and left her weak in the knees. She kissed him back fervently wrapping her legs around his and pulling him close to her.

"We really shouldn't take too long," she said softly, trying more to convince herself than him. "I feel bad for sleeping this late as it is."

"Okay." He kissed her. "Let's go..." he said as he brushed her lips again. "C'mon, are you ready?" Once more his lips touched hers.

"Stop it," she said as she kissed him back. "You're mean."

"You are."

Shayde grazed his lips one last time and sat up. "Okay, I really need to shower though," she said studying her suitcase and thinking about what she was going to wear today.

"MMMM, can I come?" Kruise asked her, kissing her hands, her fingertips.

"No! I don't think that is a very romantic place for one's first time."

"I won't do anything, I promise."

"That won't matter 'cause I probably would," she laughed.

"Oh yes? You can do it, just don't think about it. Mind over matter."

"That won't help. You'll be *naked* and close to me. I wouldn't be able to handle it," she concluded.

Just thinking about him naked made her want to rip his clothes off. She remembered how he looked clutching that pillow moments ago and thought how wonderful it would be to be that pillow just then. His sexy arms, his toned chest, his hot abs, clutching her, becoming a wonderland just for her to explore and to do whatever she wished to. In her head, he was all over her right now.

"You have no idea," he breathed.

"See what I mean. It's a bad idea."

"Aw." He pouted.

"Someday, I promise I will take a shower with you. When I'm not in such a fragile state and virginities aren't at risk anymore." She kissed him and started to get up.

"Okay, you promised!" He pulled her back down and gave her one last hungry kiss.

After picking out an outfit that consisted of black shorts and a dark red tank top, she gathered her toiletries and a couple of towels. Kissing him on the lips on her way out the door, she made her way to the bathroom where she took a quick shower and dressed.

When she returned to the room, he was gone. He must have left to go get ready himself.

She threw her things back in her bag, grabbed her phone from the charger and clicked in on to check for messages.

No new messages.

Tucking the phone away in her back pocket, she made her way to the others.

They were hanging out by the fire pit, talking and laughing about something while passing around a joint. Kruise was sitting with his back to her and when they saw her approaching, he turned around and his face lit up when his eyes found her.

It made her feel good.

She sat down next to him.

"Okay, we ready?" Kruise asked everyone.

"Yup, let's go," Danny said, stubbing out the joint and sticking it in the brim of his hat.

"I'll drive too," Shayde said as they made their way to the front.

"'Kay, I'll ride with you," Kruise responded.

"Yeah, us too," Alizé added for her and Jay.

The rest of the gang piled into Danny's jeep and they headed into the little town.

Dinner had been delicious, the best seafood that she had in a while. Kruise ended up buying her dinner for her, which she didn't agree with but he said he had planned it that way. He bought food for the group for the weekend so they would buy his dinner, so he could buy hers. It had been his plan all along. Their first date, he said, even though he said he wanted their first *official* date as couple to be just the two of them. She was okay with that, even though she already considered the weekend to be their first date. It had been the most romantic time of her life.

After dinner, they walked around the town for a while, stopping in different stores and buying mementos of the weekend. They also had their picture taken at the olden times photo shop. The picture came out well and everyone received a copy of it.

Shayde was having the time of her life just being with her new friends, and her new man. Alizé was too. They fit with the group; it was like they had always been friends. She couldn't wait for Dawn, Courtney and Cherie to meet them either. The girls may not get along so well but they would definitely fit in with the guys.

Kruise made sure to kiss her often throughout the day. He even bought her a little keychain memento for her new car that said "Cape Cod" on it and had a spinning lighthouse. It was the cutest thing; she put it on her key ring the moment he bought it for her.

When the town had been seen and they had walked back and forth along the pier at least twice, the sun began its slow descent and they all agreed that they should get back and start packing up.

When they returned to the cabin, they moved about nostalgically with their heads slightly hanging. Nobody wanted to leave but they knew it was time. They eventually headed off in their own directions and started to pack.

After Shayde and Alizé were finished packing and had zipped up their suitcases, they tidied up their room a little bit and then deposited their bags in the living room. Shayde went into the kitchen and cleaned it up, putting all the dishes away and wiping the counters down well. Kruise came in with his bags and smiled the smile that melted her.

"You didn't have to do that," Kruise said to her, after he had set his bags down in the living room. He walked up to her, wrapped his arms around her from behind and kissed her neck.

She shivered. "I know but I wanted to. You cooked the entire time we were here, it's the least I could do."

"Well, thank you," he said gently.

"You're welcome." She turned around and wrapped her arms around his neck.

"Hi," he said in a luscious whisper.

"Hi," she smiled, caressing his hair with her hands.

"I don't wanna let you go."

"Then don't."

"Oh, I won't. Trust me. I'm just gonna miss you when you're not around me anymore. I liked waking up to your beautiful face."

Her heart jumped up into her throat. "I know what you mean. I'm gonna miss you just as much."

"So, when will I see you again?"

"Um... Whenever you want," she smiled shyly.

"Okay, how about tomorrow?"

She hesitated. "Well, except tomorrow," she furrowed her brow and eyed him apologetically. "I got this thing with my family tomorrow but I'm free the next day."

"Okay, Tuesday it is. I'll plan something, no worries. Leave your day open."

"Okay, I will." Pulling his head into her, she kissed him subtly. Kissing was becoming natural to her. As he returned her embrace, it gained intensity with a burning passion behind it. They knew it would be the last time they would be able to touch each other's lips until Tuesday. A part of her didn't know if she would make it until then. They kissed one another as long as they could, until someone came in to interrupt their moment.

"Hey!" It was Alizé. "Sorry to interrupt you guys but we really gotta get going Shay, I told my mom I'd be back before dark."

She pulled away from him and glanced at her friend. "'Kay, I'll be right there."

"'Kay, thanks. Sorry."

"No worries honey, I'll be right there."

"Okay."

"I better go." Shayde gazed at Kruise forlornly.

"Okay." His eyes were flecked with hints of anguish. "Text me whenever you want. Really."

"You too." She smiled at her boyfriend and pulled him close for a hug goodbye.

"You need help out?" he asked when he let her go.

"No, I think I got it. I only have the one suitcase, but thank you."

"No I'll get it for you, it's no problem really." He kissed her nose and then led her into the living room where everyone was finishing up their packing and cleaning.

Grabbing her suitcase for her, he headed out to the car while she said goodbye to her new friends.

Kruise was putting her bag in the car when she stepped outside. Alizé was wrapped up in Jay's arms, kissing him good-bye. Shayde walked up to Kruise. He shut the trunk and he escorted her to the driver's side of the car.

"Okay, this is it," he said dismally.

"I know. This sucks. Why can't we just live here, all of us?" she giggled but it was tinged with gloom.

"It would be a good time." He smiled and then whispered in her ear, "Thank you so much for coming. You have no idea how incredibly happy you've made me."

"Ditto." She closed her eyes and laid her head on his shoulder. She heard him smell her hair and she smiled at the gesture. "Thanks for inviting us."

"Drive safe okay? Text me the minute you get home. You know how to get back, right?" he asked her as she lifted her head to look up at him.

"Okay, I will. And yes I do. You too."

One last time their lips met quickly, followed by a hug before he opened her door for her and she climbed in. As soon as Alizé was in as well, Shayde started the car and rolled the window down right as he was popping his head in to swiftly kiss her cheek.

"Bye baby doll. See you soon."

"Bye-bye."

As soon as he was standing by Jay on the curb, she flipped the car around, waving to him and blowing him a kiss as they pulled away. When he was out of sight, her chest ached a little from being away from him already.

THE DRIVE HOME WAS A BREEZE, HARDLY ANY TRAFFIC. SHE AND ALIZÉ talked about the weekend and how smitten they both were over their guys. Alizé and Jay already had plans to hang out on Monday and go see a movie.

As soon as she hit the highway her phone went off. She had Alizé check it for her, it was Kruise already.

"I miss you already. Don't text back, I know you're driving. I just wanted to say I miss you and text me when you get home."

She smiled at the thought of him and really started to miss him.

On the drive home there was plenty of time to let her mind go free and wander through whatever subject she wished. Alizé had fallen asleep a quarter of the way into the journey. Shayde thought about everything that had happened. The weekend seemed like a crazy, wonderful dream. One of those vivid dreams that you never want to end and your heart aches a little when it does. Although she remembered every little detail, aside from some blurry moments last night, she had a sense of unreality; memories were misted around the edges, and there was a layer of fog that made her feel like it was too good to be true, like it never really happened. She focused on her keychain over and over to remind herself it had been real, committing every moment that they had this weekend to her memory.

Even though she never had a boyfriend before and logically this could all very well be an infatuation, she trusted her heart and knew that what she was feeling was real. She was inexorably and completely head-over-heels in love with him. And it didn't scare her at all. She knew by the way she ached from being away from him, the way his smile melted her being, the way his every touch threatened to throw her over the edge, into out-of-control madness. She had just dove head first into complete and utter love with him. Although she had heard it before in love stories, seen it in movies and read it in books, she never believed in it until now.

Before this weekend it had been a total myth to her. How could you fall in love with someone in one day?

Now she knew. It was possible. The way that she felt about Kruise in that diner, although she didn't know it then, she knew it now, *it was love*. He was like a magnet that beckoned her heart to come. His world called out to her and she was prepared to become entirely lost in love with him.

THIRTEEN

The very next day, bright and early, Shayde began to learn magic. The first spell she learned was how to make an elixir out of water. This didn't require any ingredients at all, only that of a powerful being along with intense concentration, and the water itself of course. The magic within her blood was potent enough that when she channeled it through her mind and projected it out through her eyes, she would be able to turn the water into a healing agent. Once she'd learned how to do it, it would be embedded in her mind and when she needed to do it again, all she needed to do was channel the memory and make the water do as she wished. The elixir was strong enough to cure cuts, gashes, bruises, broken bones, and even certain diseases.

She filled the cauldron up with water and her mother told her to focus on it, picturing it becoming the most powerful medicinal agent she could think of. As she did, it began to thicken and flecks of what looked like gold started to whirl within it. Dustin took a silver, jewel-imbedded athame and ran it along his forearm. Blood seeped out of the wound, enough to make Shayde feel lightheaded and woozy, but she fought the feelings, stifling them enough to focus on the spell. Aura instructed her to take a cup full of the water and rub it on her father's wound. She did and the moment the water touched the wound, it began to heal immediately, leaving only the blood that had spilled from it.

The next things she learned were how to move things with her mind, shape shift and finally, how to protect and project her thoughts.

Aura told her to visualize a barrier between the world and her innermost thoughts. She imagined an enormous erection of brick being built in her mind, encasing all the things that she didn't want to share. She still had the power to implant any of her thoughts into any person she wanted—unless they had the magic to protect them like she had.

The next day, Kruise and Shayde spent the day together as planned. He had put a romantic day together for them; they went for a picnic in the park, a walk on the beach, a mid-day movie and dinner by candlelight at a delicious Italian restaurant called Bella Sara. She met his dad, Simon, that day, too, and was really nervous about it. But he was a sweet, charming man who reminded her a lot of Kruise, though he seemed dejected, his aura colored by his grief. Shayde could tell that he had a broken spirit and was kind of coasting through life in a sad fog. She could almost feel his pain. Despite his sorrow he tried to show her kindness and make her welcome, she realized where much of Kruise's kindness came from.

During the next few weeks, she spent hours upon hours with Aura, learning whatever she could about magic. She also began learning how to counter her ability to wish things true. They found that like Kain, she was able to implant her thoughts in other people's minds. What Kain had failed to do though, was to control his thoughts, with terrible consequences. Before she knew it, almost three weeks had passed since the weekend in Cape Cod. Shayde spent every free minute she had with Kruise when he wasn't working or when she wasn't learning the magic, though it seemed every time he wasn't working, she had a learning session planned. Her only excuse was that she and her family did a lot of adventurous things in the summertime. Using the, "I can't text when around family" rule became a norm for her, and she felt really bad about it, but she was not to reveal her secret to him until they established a deep love for one another. Although they had both admitted they had strong feelings for each other, their love hadn't been declared. Shayde knew this had to be done according to the Laws of the Enchantment before Kruise could be truly part of her life. Her parents were going out of town for their anniversary and were allowing her to have a get-together—providing that they didn't break anything, stayed off the white carpet in the sitting room and cleaned up after themselves. It was then that she was planning on telling him how she really felt.

Aura told her the night before their get-together that it was time to see if she could fly. This magic would need a day of preparation, as well as spells that included multiple components of concoction. They were to do it on a day when the moon was full because the high energy of the moon and the gravitational pull would work in their favor.

On the morning of the full moon, Aura woke Shayde before the sun came up. She instructed her to draw a bath, and place seven lavender incense sticks around it so that when they were lit the ash would fall into the tub. Shayde had taken a piece of paper the night before and drawn a beautiful set of wings on it; they were similar to how she imagined angel wings would appear—except they were white with a deep purple hue. As she lit the incense sticks around the tub, she imagined those same wings emerging from her own skin. With each one she lit, she pictured a different stage of them growing out of her.

Aura then instructed her to stand out on Tara's balcony with her back towards the east. While the incense burned, Tara taped the drawing of the wings onto Shayde's back. She was wearing a black tank top, a color that would soak up every bit of light from the sun. As the sun came up, Aura whispered ancient, magical words which Shayde repeated with her arms outstretched, her wand in her right hand and her eyes closed tight in full concentration.

"Min paiz kassani pissas vole mana sol," she said, which meant, "May the elements surround us with the sun's power."

As the sun rose and its rays rested upon her, she cleared her mind and thought only of flying. She closed her mind to everything she knew, everything around her, and thought only of those wings emerging from her back. Her mind went blank until she saw herself in the clearing that she had gone to with Kruise. She watched herself, standing on the edge of the dock gazing out across the water, wearing a white silky robe, surrounded by fireflies. The robe slowly started falling down past her shoulders. There was a blinding light and all she could see was the outline of herself, the robe falling slowly down, revealing more unbearably bright light until finally that's all she could see. As it started to subside, she saw folded on her back the most magnificent pair of wings she had ever seen. They not only looked like the picture she had drawn but better beyond words. They looked like a pair of angel wings, soft and feathery, brilliantly white, but all the feathers had delicate highlights of purple which made the wings luminesce. She saw herself unfold them into an incredible wingspan, spreading out about seven feet each way. Shayde saw herself bend her knees and jump off the pontoon. Wings outstretched, they caught an up draft of air and she watched herself fly away.

When she opened her eyes, she was back on the balcony with her mom and Aura.

She looked to her right and to her left.

No wings.

"It didn't work," she said despondently.

"No, honey that was only the first part," Aura responded reassuringly, "the next part of the spell needs a full moon."

Shayde breathed a sigh of relief.

"We're not done yet," Tara said and walked Shayde back into her bathroom where the incense burned.

The purple sticks were almost finished burning, the bath water covered in floating ash. Aura instructed her to submerge herself in the murky water, clothing and all. The bath she could've done without. It was luke-warm which was off putting, but she did as she was told and sat in it with her head tilted back, resting on a folded washcloth while another one covered her eyes.

"Why do you think this hasn't worked for generations?" Shayde asked Aura and Tara as she soaked in the tub.

"We are not sure as to why," Aura answered. "I suspect that the Sorenya that couldn't, had something in their lives that hindered their ability to let themselves fly. You have to give your whole self over to it, body and soul. I think sometimes there are external forces that break the concentration needed to fly."

"Is that what happened to you Mom?"

Tara hesitated. "I don't think my relationship with Mary helped," she said after a moment of silence.

"Your sister Mary?" Shayde asked removing the cloth from her eyes to look at her mom perched on the closed toilet seat. "The aunt that I have never met?"

Shayde had only heard Tara talk about Mary a few times in her life. She knew that her mom had a sister and that they had a huge falling out a long time ago and hadn't spoken since, but that was all that Shayde knew. Tara refused to go into detail about it, and the few times she had brought Mary up the tension in Tara's voice was thick enough to cut with a knife. Shayde learned to never bring it up again.

"Cover your eyes again and I will tell you the story," Aura instructed.

"Aura, is this necessary?" Tara frowned.

"Yes, my darling, she needs to understand you, there should be no secrets between you, especially now."

"If you insist, but I can't listen. I'll be back when you're done."

"Sorry Mom, I don't need to know, it's not important." The water in the bath splashed as Shayde reached across to her mom to reassure her.

"Sweetheart, Aura's right, you need a clear head." Tara kissed her on the forehead and left the room.

"Go on then, cover you eyes and I will begin."

Shayde did as she was told and returned the cloth and waited for Aura to continue.

"Tara was born first and then Mary," Aura began. "From the day Mary was born Tara adored her little sister, she would rock her to sleep, look after her, read to her, but as they got older things changed. As soon as Mary could walk and talk it was clear she resented her older sister, she would make up stories that Tara had hurt her and would try to get Tara into trouble. She would steal and break her things, she was quite awful. No matter how caring and forgiving Tara tried to be to Mary, Mary's resentment never lessened—in fact it got worse. It didn't help that Tara was excruciatingly beautiful both inside and out, people were drawn to her, they automatically liked her. Unfortunately Mary was very plain-looking and grave all the time. Your mom had scores of friends; Mary didn't. Tara would try to include Mary in her circle of friends but it was as if that made Mary even angrier. By the time they were both teenagers they had little to do with each other. It saddened your mom but there was little she could do about it so she gave up trying and just got on with her life.

"When Tara turned sixteen and learned of her birth right, she was elated that she came from such an amazing line of extraordinary people, but her joy was marred. She finally understood the significance of bearing the mark of the Lily, but rather than feeling excited she was afraid. Tara knew Mary didn't bear the same mark and realized that this would be the final wedge between them. She knew her sister would despise her even more when she found that yet again Tara had an advantage. When I told your mother that there was nothing she could do to change Mary's feelings, she reluctantly accepted the craft and the responsibilities, but we both realized she would never be able to fly with the weight of that fear and sadness upon her."

"So what happened to Mary?"

"When Mary turned sixteen and learned of their heritage, she realized that Tara had the Mark of the Lily and it seemed she couldn't contain her resentment any longer. She beat Tara up atrociously. She broke her jaw and a couple of her ribs, broke a mirror and slashed her face—it was if she were trying to scratch off Tara's beauty. Tara was hurt so badly that grandma Mariah had a hard time healing her wounds at first, but she managed to do so without leaving any scars. Tara was broken-hearted; she couldn't come to terms with being the object of such hatred. Mary vowed to never to have anything to do with her sister or magic. I think Mary decided that unless she could be a better witch than Tara she would rather not be one at all.

"Tara went about her life as best she could and continued her lessons with me alone. She reveled in the magic and wanted to learn everything that I had to teach her. She learned it all too, and was an excellent witch. She possessed the abilities of all the past Sorenya as well—aside from flying, the idea was too tainted for her.

"When Mary turned seventeen, she fell very ill, but she refused to let us use our magic cures. When Doctors said that she needed a kidney transplant, your mom did not hesitate to see if she was a match, but Mary refused even to take an organ from your mother. When the doctors informed her they did not have time to search for another donor, your grandma and grandpa begged her to take it and she finally accepted. Even then, Mary couldn't bring herself to speak to your mom, and when Mary turned eighteen she went to college with the money she was given and has had little contact with our family since.

"It affected your mom quite badly, she felt responsible for the rift in the family. It broke her heart to see her parents so hurt. No one blamed your mom for her sister's rejection of them, but your mom just couldn't shake the idea that she was the cause of it and perhaps she could have been a different sister. To escape these feelings she started drinking at college and experimenting with drugs. It was when she became addicted to cocaine that she realized she was really going to hurt her family, she knew she needed to get past these feelings or she would destroy herself and everyone around her. She beat the drugs and it's why she became a Drug Addiction Counselor."

At the sound of the door opening Shayde removed the cloth again and looked up to see her mom had returned.

"I'm so sorry you had to go through that."

Tara sat back down on the toilet and smiled wryly, "It's in the past now my love. There's nothing we can do now, no need for tears and pain."

"But it's because of her that you cannot fly," Shayde whispered, her heart breaking for her mother.

"Yes, but I knew I'd have you. I had a dream once that

showed me I'd have a daughter that could fly, and to me that makes up for it. The wings may not have happened for me, but the magic *you* create will be all the magic that I need."

Shayde smiled at her mom and wiped away a tear. That was the all the affirmation she needed to hear to give the extra confidence to pull this off.

"Okay," Aura returned attention back to herself. "I need you to concentrate on that vision you had outside once more, but this time in the first person."

Replacing the cloth, Shayde's mind went blank again, but she saw the exact same vision she had seen before. She was having trouble wrapping her brain around it. After what seemed an age, Aura told her to get out of the tub and dry. Changing and showering weren't an option, she was to sit and literally soak in her thoughts all day long.

From there they went to the basement.

It was there that Tara handed her a large burgundy book with gold stitching and told her to find the spell for flying. It was an old book and the pages were a dull brown, tattered and flimsy from age. Shayde skimmed through the book until she came across the spell entitled, "Aviation Conjuration". Under the title was a list of ingredients and instructions. She gathered the items accordingly and laid them all out on the table that her mom had pulled towards the cauldron.

Tara handed Shayde the silver, jewel-imbedded athame. With it she carved the word, "wings" on the top of a wide orange candle and beneath it she made an engraving of the sun. Then she carved the word "fly" horizontally around the candle's column. Finally, she etched a moon on the underside.

The next step was to prepare a success oil, using High John

the Conqueror root, Orris, Patchouli, Myrrh and Sandalwood. Shayde ground the ingredients up with a wooden muddler until they were almost a puree texture and then rubbed paste clockwise around the orange candle while focusing on the words and their meaning. She set it on the table and lit it, letting the vapors that were burning off of the candle surround her. The remnants of the success oil were to be thrown into the cauldron.

As the room filled with an orange tint, Shayde filled the cauldron up with water. After it was full, she took a white rose and pulling the petals off one by one, dropped them into the cauldron, whispering "to fly" as each one touched the water. She anointed the candles next; the green one invoked the Goddess Venus, and the white; Enlil, the God of the air. As she anointed the candles, she read the following words from the book, "*With the oil of rose I do anoint these candles. Now may they perform magic of flying free for those who use it.*"

She placed them on the table with the orange one and lit them. "*Blessed be,*" she whispered as she did it, throwing the remaining oil into the cauldron.

The spell then called for a droplet of blood to be given. Taking the athame, she pricked her finger, held it over her mixture, and repeated after Aura;

"*Venus, Goddess of Love and Beauty, Enlil, God of the Air, I ask you to bring to me the one true gift that I am destined to have and awaken the wings of Breken to thrive in me.*"

When the blood dropped into the mixture, a fiery red smoke burst from the cauldron which cast a beautiful scarlet glow throughout the basement.

Tara handed her the wand. "Call it to you."

Shayde held out the wand. "I command you to enter my instrument of magic!" The red substance obeyed and swiftly glided towards her, taking up residence inside the wand.

The last and final candle to be lit was a yellow one for luck. While lighting it, she repeated, *"As the flame is lit, so may it burn to you my request."* After doing so, she laid it on the table with the others.

After all the instructions were followed, she closed her eyes and imagined with all her might those wings emerging from her skin. She cupped her hands in the mixture and rubbed it on her arms, her legs, her shoulders and her hair, not knowing why she did this or even if she was supposed to. That was the end of the first part of the spell. She was supposed to leave the candles to burn out and the next stage didn't begin until the moon came up, so the three of them left the basement and returned to the first floor.

Since the next ingredient of the spell included the moon and it was only half past noon, Tara and Aura thought it best for Shayde to rest and save her energy for the most important phase—the emerging of the wings. Her mind was in a state of delirium as it had been all morning. She wasn't sure if it was from the magic or from being tired, but either way she tried to keep her mind clear and not let anything pollute it. Finding time to text Kruise was a must though, and she apologized for being so distant. She explained that she just had a lot going on with her family and that she couldn't talk for a while, but she said she would call him as soon as possible and that she missed him. She hit send and then clicked the phone off.

As she lay on the couch her eyes became heavy, and fighting to keep them open was getting harder and harder. Before she knew it, Tara was above her waking her up in the dark living room. She sat up sleepily and rubbed her eyes.

"It is time," Aura said.

Chills ran up and down her spine. She knew she was going to do it, she felt it in her bones. Before they headed back out to the balcony, she grabbed her picture of her wings from the table. Aura instructed her to stand with her back to the full moon. Tara taped the picture of her wings onto Shayde's back again and Aura had her chant more ancient, magical words. Shayde stood with her arms outstretched and eyes closed tight in full concentration while Tara positioned the wand so it was pointing towards the rising full moon.

"*Min paiz kassani pissas vole mana luna,*" she repeated after Aura,

"May the elements surround us with the moon's power."

The moon glowed brilliantly, its austere light reaching down to caress her, and the only thought that surfaced was of those wings. She closed her eyes and saw herself standing on the dock, looking out across the water, but this time she approached herself from behind and she entered her own body. Everything was peaceful and the sky was purple again, glittering with fireflies. She felt weightless, so that if she were to jump up, she could surely fly. Then she looked to the right and left and saw those amazing wings stretching out above her head.

She could not believe her eyes.

When she opened them again, she was back on her balcony. Tara and Aura were standing in front of her; Tara was weeping, while Aura had the most beatific smile on her face. As the red smoke from the wand evaporated, she felt a strange sensation. Suddenly her shoulder blades flexed independently and when she looked up, there were her wings, larger than life and more beautiful than she could have ever have imagined. A strange numbness engulfed her, she could not believe what she was experiencing. There seemed to be new muscles in her back now. She moved the wings back and forth a little, trying to fathom what it was that she was governing. She pulled one forward and touched it with her fingertips as if to make sure they were real though she knew they were. They were soft to the touch and she could feel both the wing beneath her fingertips and her fingers touch her wing. She wrapped them both around her and smothered herself with them, caressing them with her face. Then she extended them stretching them as far as she could. She observed Aura and her mother, both were unmoving, unblinking and speechless.

"Go for it," Tara told her after a moment, stifling a sob.

Tentatively, Shayde crouched a little, unsure about the whole thing, and then after taking a deep breath she bounded up into the air. She reached high into the sky above the roof of her house, but she couldn't figure out what to do next so instead of rising higher and higher, she only rose to the top of a tall tree. She came back down, landing on her feet in her backyard, but it didn't hurt, it was as if they had grown springs. When they hit the ground, she bounded right back up, higher than before. She tried to flap the wings but this only rocked her awkwardly back and forth.

The people on the balcony must be having an interesting show, she mused as she came back down to the earth.

When she hit the ground again, she folded her wings and sprung into the air another time. As she peaked and began the decent, she tilted her body parallel to the ground and unfolded the wings. They caught a gust of wind and sent her soaring off into the sky. She hit it just right so that she was riding the wind, flapping her wings here and there in a slow methodical way; she flew out over the ocean, the cool salty air brushing at her face. Pride engulfed her at the realization that she was actually flying! Pointing her nose straight, she climbed the wind to fly around clouds. The feeling of freedom had never been so intense in her entire life. It was like riding the largest roller coaster she could imagine, yet boundaries were nonexistent. There were no words to describe the way that she felt.

She turned around and headed towards the bright lights of the city, staying high enough so that people would only think she was a bird if anyone noticed her. She flew above the town that she so loved and gazed down at it with awe. Millions of lights sparkled throughout the town, like tiny fireflies lighting up a midsummer's night. The boats in and around the harbor twinkled on the sea, casting haunting rays of light upon the water. This felt like a dream. It had to be a dream. The wind reached up and kissed her face and sent her sailing into the clouds. She flew straight up as high as she could, then stopped, folded her wings to her back and bee-lined straight down. It was exhilarating, her stomach jumped up into her throat as she free-fell to earth. She then stretched out her wings and caught the air to go back up. It was like jet skiing to an amusement park then going on the steepest roller coaster on earth, but much, much bigger and better. She wished that Kruise was able to enjoy this with her.

It wasn't a foreign feeling, as if she had never done this before, it was if she had been doing it her entire life. In all her dreams of flying, it felt the exact same way that it did right now. It was as if her wings and the breeze were old friends and were finally together again, as if they had never parted ways. The feeling of her new wings, united with the wind, taking her wherever she wanted to go, was better than any other feeling she had before—aside from the feelings that Kruise inspired in her. So far, being able to fly like this was the only thing that came close to how she felt about Kruise. It was almost as if his love for her had drawn the wings out of her body, as if they were searching for him.

After she flew about the town and visited every place that she wanted—from the air anyway—she decided she had better get back home as her mother was probably worrying about her, it being her maiden flight and all. Spotting the familiar sights that would lead her home; she followed them from the air, whooshing in and out of the clouds as she did.

When she found her neighborhood, she decided to come in through the back to avoid being seen and flew over the houses to the ocean so she could follow the beach home. When she spotted her house and grew closer to it, panic gripped at her. She realized she didn't know how to land yet. Aiming for her backyard, she slowed the rhythm of her wings, but the wind had her and she was heading in fast. She made it over the fence but as she stuck out her feet to land she bounded back up into the sky; Tara and Aura, growing smaller and smaller as she contemplated what to do.

She headed back to the ground and waited until she was a few feet from the earth before bending her legs and curving her wings around her to try a parachute effect. Instead of landing softly, her knees hit the ground hard she tumbled a few feet and landed on her face.

"Shayde!" Tara exclaimed and jumped over her balcony, landing beside her on her feet like a cat. "Oh my god! Are you okay?"

"Yeah, I'm fantastic!" Shayde was out of breath, there was no disguising the utter delight in her voice.

"You scared me!" Tara screeched, picking her up slightly and pulling her up into her embrace.

"Mom, I'm okay, I just don't know how to land yet," she said, panting. "Did you just jump off the balcony?" She giggled.

Her mom laughed back. "Yeah! I thought you were hurt. What was it like? You are so lucky, and I am so proud of you!"

Shayde looked up at her mom, trying still to catch her breath. "It was the most amazing thing I have ever done in my life. No words can tell you how it feels. It is absolutely the best feeling in the entire world."

Tara's eyes welled up with tears as she brushed the dirt and grass away from Shayde's face.

"Well done," Aura said, floating down to them.

"Thank you for everything you guys, I couldn't have done it without you," Shayde said standing again and dusting herself off. "Okay, how do I put them back in now, and do I have to do that ritual every time I wanna fly?"

"No," Aura answered. "Now that you have awakened them, they should come whenever you call them. Just picture them emerging from you like you did before. And when you want them disappear do the reverse." Aura was gazing at Shayde's wings. She reached out with her transparent fingers as if to touch them, lovingly tracing the outline of their shape that seemed to glow in the night. "Truly amazing. I have not seen a sight like this in over two hundred years, Shayde. A beautiful sight for sore eyes."

As Shayde watched Aura study her wings with such wonder she realized that Aura was even more beautiful than the last time she had seen her. Not only was she glowing, as she always was, but there was a new presence about her, energy seemed to emanate from within her.

"Do my wings give you power too?" Shayde asked when Aura finally pulled away.

"Oh yes," she said with her eyes still fixated on her wings. "They are one of the most powerful things on earth. The fact that you used the elements around you, the gravitational pull, the solar power, you pulled them to you and it increased your own energy, which ultimately added to mine... I feel refreshed, as if a long thirst has finally been quenched."

"It shows. You are positively radiant." Shayde contemplated Aura with a new understanding. Even though she had known that good deeds gave Aura power, she had not known that the wings would do the same. It was a wonderful feeling to know that what she had accomplished had made Aura so positively angelic.

As Aura reluctantly withdrew, Shayde looked down, closed her eyes and pictured her wings receding into her back, melting into her skin. There was a subtle tingling sensation that increased to an oscillating flutter. The sound of the feathers brushing against each other as they folded whispered in her ears, until the only sound that remained was the waves. Remnants of feeling where they once were, pulsated a little but faded fast and then were gone.

. . .

LATER THAT NIGHT, AS SHAYDE WAS LYING IN BED, SHE THOUGHT ABOUT her wings and still couldn't wrap her brain around the fact that she had done it. After so many of her ancestors before her tried and failed, she had made it happen. The ultimate dream had just come true, *she flew*. The urge to tell Kruise was very tempting, as she wanted to share this overwhelming joy with him.

Picking up the phone and flicking it on, she looked at the time. It was well past midnight and even though she missed her handsome boyfriend so much, she knew calling him was not the best idea because he was surely sleeping as he had to work in the morning. She was going to see him later on tomorrow evening but she still wished she could hear his voice right now. It was going to be the first time they had seen each other in a week and it was also going to be the first time that all their friends were getting together. The anticipation of what more firsts may lay ahead brought excited little butterflies to the pit of Shayde's stomach.

She decided to text him something to wake up to.

> Thinking of you. I'm sorry I never called. I'll make it up to you later on tonight, I promise.

She clicked her phone to sleep, plugged it in, rolled over onto her side and closed her eyes. Worried thoughts entered her mind as she contemplated just how she was going to bring up her huge secret to him. How he was going to react to it? Would he would think she was crazy and dump her right then and there? Or would he be supportive and agree to keep her secret and be with her no matter what?

Even though she just flew, the last thing running through her mind was not her wings.

It was her handsome boyfriend.

FOURTEEN

·• ☽ *·•*

It was almost quitting time.

Kruise was excited to get off work.

It had almost been a week since the last time he'd seen his alluring girlfriend. She had been so distant ever since they left Cape Cod. Every time he sent her a text it would be hours before she responded and it seemed the moment she left the beach, her interest in him withered. Not wanting to be the jealous, overbearing, paranoid boyfriend right off the bat, he just let her be and waited around for her to come to him, even though it was still torture. Allowing himself to fall head over heels in love with this girl that he barely knew and had really only *just* met, and then to have her become distant and almost removed from their relationship, hurt his pride a bit. The few times that they had hung out since the Cape Cod, she was always exhausted from doing things with her family. There was always something going on with her, but he knew their lives weren't going to rebuild themselves around each other just yet.

He had heard from her more often today than he had in weeks. The text that he woke up to from her in the morning made his entire day into a good one. She texted him all day, which was extremely unusual as of late, and he loved every minute of it. They were figuring out the details for their week, and he was getting to spend all of it with her, starting with a gathering of their friends at her house.

Her parents, whom he just met last week, seemed to like him and trusted him with Shayde. They were going away for their anniversary and told him to take good care of her. They didn't mind if Kruise stayed at their house the entire time, as long as they acted like responsible adults. He really liked her parents, Tara reminded him of Shayde and not just in the way she looked but how she acted. Kruise had hit it off with Dustin without a hitch; he hoped he would be much like Dustin when he was older. They'd all had dinner in Shayde's back yard, eating barbecued ribs sitting on their patio, being serenaded by the ocean. Kruise watched Dustin and admired him for what he did for his family. Even though he was a protective father, he still made it a point to be friends with Shayde. He had handed Kruise a beer and cracked one open himself, offering one to Shayde too. It was his way to show that he was cool with treating them like adults but in return they would have to behave like responsible ones.

As soon as Kruise got off work he met his dad to get beer for them. They decided on getting another keg and Danny was bringing a bottle of Jager, or two. After Kruise collected the beer he headed over to Shayde's house for dinner. Their friends were going to turn up later.

On his way over, he could hardly slow his pulse down. Feeling as hyper as a schoolboy leaving class, stifling laughter was proving difficult for him to do. It had only been a week, but that week had felt like an eternity to him and he missed her so much he was almost in pain. Even though he hadn't had the moment to tell her yet, he was obviously unconditionally and desperately in love with her, and hated every moment that they were parted, but what would be her reaction to his declaration?

Kruise knew that he was Shayde's first kiss, first boyfriend, and—if things continued to go as they were—it seemed as though he would be the one who take her virginity too. But he realized there may come a time when she wanted to spread her wings and fly away, see what else—or who else—was out there, and that thought scared him. There was something about her that he loved more than even he understood. It was as if their relationship was something out of a fairy tale, he couldn't wrap his brain around it just yet.

Trying not to stress about it too much, he felt better as he pulled up to the gate to her community and punched in the code. As it swung open, a text came through.

> Just come in when you get here. I'm upstairs getting ready. My parents are already gone.

Shayde said.

Containing the excitement in his heart from communicating it to his foot, he still yearned to break the law and go 45 instead of 25 just to get to her faster. Finally, when he saw her car, the tingles in his system went insane. Pulling the truck up to her house, he looked up to her window and smiled. He was only moments away from her.

Hopping out of the truck, he quickly grabbed his bag from the back and practically ran up to the house.

When he was inside, he shut the door lightly behind him and slipped off his shoes. He surveyed the upper landing and saw that her bedroom and bathroom light were on. The house was filled with the aroma of fresh shower and he took a deep breath and held it in. The smell of her was over-whelming. He started up the stairs to her room.

As he reached the landing he spotted her in the bathroom, leaning over the cabinets with her face at the mirror, putting on some mascara. She was wearing little white shorts, that made her legs look incredibly tanned, and a lacey black and white spaghetti-strap tank top. Her hair was down and wet and her toes were done in a French manicure. He couldn't move he was so enchanted by her beauty. She turned around to gaze at him and he almost fell over the edge she was so radiant.

"Hey," she said sweetly, smiling a smile that almost knocked him to his knees.

She put the mascara on the counter and ran up to him, jumping up into his arms and straddling him; he dropped his backpack and caught her. Wrapping her arms around his neck, she kissed him like she had never kissed him before. It was as though she missed him, like she had been yearning for him too, as though she had been lost without him. Feeling the exact same way, he returned her hungry embrace with his, the agony that being away from her had caused him undeniable in his kiss. He felt the butterflies almost burst out of his stomach they were so intense, hardwired to his thoughts of her. Letting himself drown in the moment, he kissed her as though he would never get to again. Her breathing became rapid and his heart rate quickened; he wanted to rip her clothes off, expose all of her skin, and take her right here in the hallway. But he couldn't. Not until he told her he loved her. He slowed down his kisses until they were mere pecks and put her back down on her feet. As he did this she continued to kiss him over and over again, not letting up.

"Hi beautiful." He pulled away long enough to say, in between kisses.

"I missed you so much," she whispered.

"I missed you too, baby doll. More than I could tell you," he said looking deeply into her eyes until everything else went dark and they were the only two in the world.

She kissed him again softly, and then let go.

"I'm almost done getting ready. You can put your stuff in my room and I should be right out."

"'Kay."

He gathered his bag from the floor as she turned on her toes and headed back into the bathroom. Walking into her room he flung his backpack into the corner, and while he awaited her return he admired all of her pictures. There were mainly just snapshots of her and Kain. Other than that, her room was pretty bare, aside from some ballerina pictures hanging above her bed. The bareness reminded him a lot of his own room; she appeared to be a lot neater then him though.

He flopped down on her bed and took out his phone.

It was a quarter to six.

All of his friends were going to head over around eight or nine.

Shayde walked into her room with her dirty clothes and threw them in the hamper by her closet. Then she grabbed some lotion from her dresser, sat down next to him and started to cover herself with the sweet smelling nectar.

"Hi," she smiled as she looked at him, sensuously rubbing lotion onto her right leg.

"Hi," he smiled back. "What time are your friends coming over?"

"Um... I think they are gonna start to head over around nine," she said, now massaging her left leg.

"Cool, that's when my friends are gonna head over too. Alizé was at my house with Jay when I left. They said they'd be here in a little bit after they ate."

"Oh nice! Okay cool, well I'm cooking *you* dinner tonight. I hope you like chili. I have been simmering my famous chili all day long." She grinned again as she continued to moisturize her arms and face.

"I love chili! Especially with tons of cheese and crackers, yum!"

"Good. I make it with grilled cheese too. I think the two go together marvelously." She giggled.

Grilled cheese and chili, he thought to himself while smiling, *a woman after my own heart.* "That's the only way to eat it," he said adoringly.

"Really? You eat it like that too? I thought I was the only one that did that!"

"Nope. I do it too!" He laughed at the delightedly shocked

expression on her face. He found himself staring keenly into her eyes.

She stared back at him as she finished putting lotion on her arms, then stood up and threw on some black flip-flops. He liked her style. It was one all her own, she didn't try to follow the trends, or dress flashy, she had an individuality and he loved that about her.

"All right," she said as she brushed out her long hair again. "Hungry?"

"Famished."

"'Kay, let's go eat."

Dinner was eaten in the little nook by the open windows as they talked into the evening. Time passed by so quickly he was so lost in conversation with her, never before in his life had he met someone he could do that with. Everything was discussed, from school, to their families and a lot about their friends. The story about Cherie and the so-called man she was caught up with was one story that really upset Kruise, and even though Kruise didn't know Nate or Cherie, he knew he didn't like Nate at all. Before they knew it, the doorbell was ringing.

As everyone showed up, Shayde went to the white room and threw on some music. Kruise was hanging out in the back-yard with his friends when the girls came out to fill their cups. Shayde introduced him and they all shook his hand and said hello. He saw a pale girl that appeared unbearably sad and he knew right away that it was Cherie. He felt terrible for her.

The night started off well. Everyone was mingling with everyone else. Little chat groups were being formed here and there and he and Shayde made it around to all of them. Kruise was having a good time just being around her, laughing and meeting her friends, making memories and letting loose.

As everyone socialized with each other, some headed inside, some remained outdoors. Kruise and Shayde settled on the patio deck. The night was warm and there were a few dark clouds in the sky. They looked like ink-soaked cotton balls and the stars glimmered entrancingly between them. The waves were gently lapping the shore, and the sounds of music, laughter and alcohol inspired chatter echoed throughout the backyard.

"Okay, who wants some shots?" Danny hollered as he came out onto the patio with a giant bottle of Jager in his hand. "Got any shot glasses, Shay?" he asked her.

"Yup, I'm pretty sure we do somewhere. I'll go get them." Shayde stood up and disappeared into the house.

Kruise's eyes followed her longingly. As good a time as he was having with everyone, he really just wanted to be alone with her. She returned quickly, gripping shot glasses of different sizes and colors in each hand. Kruise bolted up to help her the minute he saw her coming out of the door. Taking them from her, he set them down on the glass table while Danny opened his bottle and began pouring the shots.

"Who wants one?" Danny asked, putting the cap back on the bottle and offering them one by one to those who had gathered.

"I'll take one," Jay said, grabbing it and standing back, waiting for everyone to get theirs to cheers.

"Me too," Alizé said, taking one too.

Danny held up another and Courtney took it. "All right, I'll take it."

Dawn grabbed two for her and Brayden and when Danny offered one to Jordan, he shook his head and it was Hannah who took it from him. He handed one to Kruise who accepted it and then Shayde, who hesitated.

"C'mon, take it!" Danny pressured.

"You don't have to if you don't want to," Kruise said to her softly. His friends could be overly persuasive sometimes.

"No, it's okay, I'll try it," she said, grabbing it from Dan and holding it up like everyone else.

Danny took his, held it up, and said, "Here's to new friends."

Everyone let out a "whoo-hoo!" and knocked their glasses together. Courtney plugged her nose while she took it, Shayde just squinted her eyes tightly, and Kruise grinned at her. He shot his back and then caught a glimpse of her as she opened her eyes and grimaced, shaking her head at its harshness.

"Good?" Kruise joked, laughing at his girlfriend.

"Oh yeah, it's the bomb," she said, sarcastically.

He kissed her on her cheek and set his shot glass back on the table. She sat back down with him and admired all of her friends.

It looked as though she was having a good time and this made him happy.

Cherie sat down next to her and they started chatting about her situation. Kruise didn't want to listen in, he could barely restrain the animosity he felt towards Nate as it was and he might not be able to hold his tongue, but he heard them every once in a while and none of it was good. Dawn and Brayden took the other seats around the table and talked amongst themselves.

Kruise sat back and enjoyed the midsummer's night air, the cold draft beer in his cup, the gorgeous girl at his side and all his friends, old and new that surrounded him. He felt good. Not a drunk kind of good, just a content kind of good. Glancing in through the window, he could see Alizé and Jay sitting in the nook, cuddled close. It warmed his heart to see Jay happy again.

Jordan, Danny and Hannah were talking by the back door. Danny was taking another shot of the Jager with Courtney, who lit up one of her cigarettes. Danny then walked up to the beer pong table that Jay had brought from home and set up on the lawn. He must've asked Courtney to play with him because she followed, Jordan and Hannah not far behind.

Before he knew it, half of the night had gone by. Danny and Courtney were still running the beer pong table and Kruise could tell that everyone was starting to get drunk because their voices grew louder. They became more talkative, more prone to saying things that they normally wouldn't and being more honest about things. Although Shayde had never really drunk a lot around him, he could tell that she was feeling good but not drunk. She was more relaxed, less shy and she liked to talk a lot. He smiled at his prize; everything she did was okay with him.

Danny took a timeout between games and grabbed his bottle of Jager, which was half gone by now. He walked over to the deck where a few of them still sat, poured more shots and started to hand them out again, this time everyone took one but Cherie, who turned away looking nauseated.

They cheered, clinked their glasses together and shot them back.

Danny and Courtney returned to the beer pong table as reigning champions. Shayde had volunteered her and Kruise to play the next game. When they were up, she jumped out of her chair and bounded over to the table, leading Kruise by the hand. Kruise followed behind her and kissed her cheek as she started to put the cups in formation. Everyone else had gone inside to play a game of cards in the nook.

Danny put his bottle of Jager, which was almost gone at this point, on the pong table and ran in to get his other one. He came back out as Courtney returned with the pitcher of beer and started filling up the cups. Danny filled up four shot glasses while Courtney finished up and handed the pitcher to Shayde. Shayde then started filling up hers and Kruise's cups while Danny passed out the shots. Kruise waited for her to finish and then handed her the shot glass. He was semi-surprised when she took it from him, assuming she would start to regulate herself at some point in time tonight—though he couldn't care less whether or not she did. He loved her company, drunk or not. They held out their glasses and air-toasted from opposite ends of the table, shaking their heads from the potent taste afterwards.

Kruise and Shayde started out strong, Shayde making it into the same cup as him first try and getting balls back. Then he shot and made it into one cup, as did she into another cup, and the duo down at the end had to drink two more cups and send the balls back yet again. Shayde was getting ready to shoot when Kruise noticed that Danny didn't look so good. He was swaying slightly and staring at the table as if he couldn't focus. Suddenly his lips went white and he turned drunkenly to his right. He stumbled off into the yard and out onto the beach.

Kruise went after him to make sure he was all right. When Dan reached the sand, he fell to his knees and vomited violently. Kruise stood by him and waited it out, knowing that he would be better in a minute. He heard a whisper and looked over his shoulder to see Shayde standing at the gate, checking on them.

He hesitated. "Everything's okay baby doll. We'll be back in a minute."

"Okay." Her worried look told him she wanted them back soon. She turned and headed back slowly to the table.

He waited until Danny stopped heaving; crouched behind him he rubbed his back. When it seemed the heaving subsided, he helped Danny back up to a standing position.

"You okay bro?" he asked.

"Yeah, I'll be all right."

Danny took his hand and staggered a bit to get back onto his feet. They started walking back towards the yard, Kruise supporting him from one side so he didn't fall over.

Kruise knew his friends liked to party and knew that from time to time they got stumbling-around wasted, but it worried him when Danny did it. When Danny drank alcohol like he was, it put him at higher risk because of his diabetes. Kruise knew that Danny was going to go a little more crazy than usual. Amy was the one who usually watched over him and was the only one who could get him to listen even partially, but she was out of town, and even she couldn't stop him from doing what he wanted if he set his mind on it. Kruise knew that Danny wouldn't listen to him no matter how hard he tried.

They returned to the table and Danny took his place. He grabbed the ball from the water cup, swaying and with one eye closed he aimed and shot. He missed. As Courtney was taking her place and aiming the ball, Danny stumbled up to the bottle to pour more shots of Jager. Shaking his head in disapproval Kruise looked at him, then down at the table. He could feel Shayde staring at him and he glanced over at her.

She mouthed the words, "Stop him."

Kruise shook his head and shrugged his shoulders, telling her he couldn't.

Danny offered shots to them all; the only one that took one with him was Courtney.

They continued to play their game and it seemed now that Danny had vomited, he was drinking more to put what had escaped from his system back in. Kruise was worried but continued to play the game and have a good time, knowing that Danny was stubborn and would carry on, regardless of what he had to say. He had seen it a million times before and had almost got in a fistfight with him over it once.

They played for a little longer and then Courtney and Danny finally lost to Shayde and Kruise. Danny grabbed his bottle and in a drunken slur asked if anyone wanted more shots. When everyone declined, he stumbled off towards the house. Kruise gave Shayde a victory kiss and then they followed Danny across the garden hand-in-hand.

The sky had darkened with the clouds, a low rumble of thunder could be heard and then lightning began to flash in the distance. They sat on the patio a little longer with each other until it started to sprinkle with rain, then they headed into the house with everyone else.

At this point in time everyone at the party was nice and buzzed. The card game at the table was full of commotion and laughter. Shayde and Kruise hung out in the kitchen for a little bit and then she asked if anyone liked to play pool. Jordan, Hannah, Cherie, Dawn, Brayden and Courtney jumped up at the offer and followed her down to the basement to play. Shayde came back up a few minutes afterward and joined Kruise at the nook with Alizé and Jay. Danny was standing up at the counter with his eyes closed, swaying.

"Is he okay?" Shayde asked as she sat back down, and Kruise could tell that she was worried.

"He'll be fine," Jay replied. "He does this often,"

"Really? Isn't it really bad for him?"

"Yeah, but it's Danny," Kruise answered. "There's nothing you can do,"

There was a big boom of thunder that shook the house and the rain started to pour down. Kruise, Shayde, Alizé and Jay tuned to look outside and watch as the rain took over their world. They all were mesmerized as it covered everything with a blanket of water.

"Damn!" Alizé exclaimed. "It's really coming down."

They watched in silence for a while as the yard, the patio and the grass became swathed with a shimmering coat of water.

When Kruise turned back around Danny wasn't there anymore. Worried that he was vomiting in the white room, which is exactly something Danny would do, he stood up to search for him.

When he looked back on it, the next few minutes must have happened very fast, but as Kruise went through them they seemed to be in slow motion.

As he left the table, a flash of lightning lit up the world and a boom of thunder followed, knocking the power out so everything went black. Shayde's house must have had solar power reserve because small lights lit up along the baseboards, illuminating the house a little. He started to walk around the island and as he did, he saw Danny, looking sallow and lying in a pool of his own vomit. His eyes were open but rolled slightly back in his head, his face was blanched, his lips were turning blue and he was twitching.

"SHIT!" Kruise felt his face drain of blood and his heart started hammering blood into his veins. "Someone call 911," he shouted as he ran to kneel by his friend. All thoughts on what to do left his mind.

Shayde, Alizé and Jay jumped up from the table and ran over to him.

"He's going through a diabetic keto-acidosis," Alizé said. "Do you know when he last checked his sugar levels?"

"No I don't know," Kruise yelled. "We have to do something fast, his body is shutting down..."

"Where is his insulin?" Alizé yelled back.

"Over in the mud room off the garage, in his backpack." Kruise stood up as Alizé ran off. Jay was holding Danny's head, talking to him in a whisper, telling him to hang on while tears rolled down his face.

Kruise saw Shayde slowly walk over to the kitchen sink, her demeanor showed no panic at all. It was as if she was in a trance as she put in the plug and started filling it up. He was beginning to get agitated that no one was calling 911. He was about to call out to her but what he saw took away his power of speech. He froze. Shayde's eyes were positively glowing, like cat's eyes caught in headlights. Her lips were moving as if she was saying something to herself, though it was inaudible.

Kruise stood up carefully and quietly walked towards her. As he reached her he could hear her whispering something but couldn't make out the words; they sounded foreign. He peered into the water; it had a glow that reminded him of Goldschlager, the alcohol. It was slightly illuminated and looked as though little gold flakes were floating in it. Shayde ceased her strange mumblings and turned off the faucet. Cupping her hands, she placed them in the water and gathered up some of the strange substance. She walked over to Danny slowly, so as not to spill a drop of the liquid. Following her to Danny's side, all Kruise could do was watch in wonderment. Alizé came running into the room, dropping Danny's backpack to the ground in shock when she saw Shayde's strange appearance. It was if everyone apart from Shayde had turned to stone. She knelt down and looked at Jay; he nodded as if in reply and immediately he lifted up Danny's head and gently tipped it backwards so his lips parted. Shayde put her hands up to Danny's mouth and poured the liquid down his throat.

As the glowing water advanced down his esophagus, the skin on his neck began to glimmer as if lit from within, gradually extending to his chest. Before he knew it, Danny's whole lifeless body was illuminating the darkened room. Kruise couldn't move. He felt as though this was all a strange dream, it couldn't possibly be real.

The light had calmly retreated to a slight swirl around his pancreas when suddenly his chest lurched upward, as if his heart were trying to escape. No sooner than it had appeared, the light moved back up his throat and seeped out of his mouth. A big sphere hovered above him for just a second before it burst into a million tiny glowing specks that illuminated the room like lightning. As it faded away, Danny's body fell back to the floor, seemingly lifeless once again.

Then he coughed a little, opened his eyes, and looked around.

"Ww-what's up g-guys?" he stammered wearily but cheerfully, as though nothing had happened.

No one said anything, they just stared at Shayde.

Kruise could not even process what he just witnessed. All he could think of was that he needed air. Turning on his heel, he headed towards the door. He felt nauseous as he ran outside into the pouring rain. The sound of someone running after him reached his ears but he could not focus on who it was. The gate to the ocean was suddenly in front of him, he flung it open and half-walked, half-jogged out on to the beach.

"KRUISE!!!" he could hear Shayde call after him.

He stopped dead in his tracks; the rain had already drenched him from head to toe, and turned around abruptly to face her. His movement caught her off guard and she came to a sudden halt, stopping inches from his face.

"What are you?" He couldn't keep the bewildered fury from his voice.

"I'm a witch," she said matter-of-factly, beads of rain collecting on her face, drenching her beautiful hair. She was positively radiant in the rain, eyes still glowing from the event. Even though he was livid with her, he wanted her right then all the same.

His blood was boiling and he couldn't process what she had just said, what she had just done.

"A WITCH?" he said, his voice cracking.

"A Sorenya actually." She looked at him like that was supposed to clear everything up.

It took all he had to not laugh hysterically.

"A Sorenya," she continued, "is the name for the people of magic in our family. We are good people, all witches are, we just have a bad rap."

He hesitated. "How long have you been a witch?"

"Since I was born. It has run in my family longer than anyone knows. I only just found out though, on my birthday."

"WH—what... H—how...?" he stammered, not being able to find the words.

"I've been trying to figure out a way to tell you. It's why I have been so distant since we got back. I had to start my lessons, learning the magic."

"Magic?" His eyes widened as he hesitated. "Am I under a spell?" He regarded her now with a resigned sadness. He had felt so strange since he met her and the way she made him feel was positively foreign, he hoped with all his heart that it was not a spell.

"No spells," she smiled sweetly and he found himself believing her instantly. "I found out on my birthday and didn't start learning 'til after Cape Cod. It's against our faith to put spells on people..." She paused. "There is so much I have to tell you. I just hope you accept me for who I am and don't break up with me for it."

His heart broke a little at the thought. His expression went from confusion to utter devastation. So much was swimming through his mind; he didn't know what to say, how to feel, or where to start. All he could do was look in awe at this strange, beautiful creature with glowing eyes. Her face was suddenly in his hands and he was kissing her with an intensity that bordered on anger. Even though he wasn't angry with her at all; he was struggling to come to terms with all that had taken place, it was as if he was trying to find a solution to these emotions in her very being. The kiss was more than passionate. He loved her more now than ever and he knew it was because he finally understood her. As hard as it was to process, it all made sense.

She *was* magical.

He held her face in his hands and kissed her long and hard. She wrapped her arms around his neck and was caressing his wet hair, kissing him with determination. Her kisses were hungry; his will to stop was growing weaker and weaker. He felt breathless, powerless and light-headed. Even though he was drenched from the rain he wasn't cold at all, he was quite the opposite and it felt like he was overheating.

Suddenly he stopped and gazed at her through the pouring rain.

"I LOVE you Shayde. More now than ever before."

Relief washed over her face. "I love you, Kruise. I feel like I always have."

He kissed her again but this time with gentleness, all the anger had subsided and he was left with an overwhelming feeling of adoration, tenderness and delight.

As they started to slow down, she stopped this time and looked at him. The glow in her eyes was starting to fade and rivulets of rain were dripping down her face, collecting on her eyelashes. "What am I gonna tell them?" she asked, inclining her head towards the house.

"Well, you're probably gonna have to tell them, too."

"I'm not supposed to tell anyone who isn't of our faith and hasn't declared their love for me." She let out a nervous giggle.

"Well," he said, shrugging his shoulders, "they know something is up. I would just explain it to them and tell them not to say anything. Luckily, most of them were in the basement when it happened."

"Yeah." She contemplated. "Are you, Jay or Danny religious?"

He tilted his head in confusion at the question. "Why?"

"Well, it's the closed-minded people that we worry about most. Organized religion often makes people extremely dogmatic and frightened of new ideas they don't understand. They have an inherent insecurity which makes them demand that everyone thinks the way they do or they feel they're undermined. They need the affirmation of a group perhaps because they are not confident in their own belief to stand alone. Although we too are a group who share a belief, that of paganism, our faith is very personal. We do not group together in order to persuade others to think as we do, in fact it's the opposite. We strongly believe that everyone has to find their own spiritual path, be it a belief in a god or nature itself."

Kruise smiled wryly, "Put it that way, no, we're not religious."

"I don't think I'll be in too much trouble then."

"Trouble with whom?"

"Too much to explain right now. I will tell you all about it tomorrow when everyone is gone."

"Okay, let's head back in, I'm starting to prune," he laughed and kissed her one more time. They both were sopping wet.

"'Kay." She pulled him by the hand and he wrapped his arm around her waist.

The curiosity that lingered in him now grew stronger with each passing minute. He had been fascinated by her before, now fascinated was beyond what he was by her. There wasn't a word that fit.

They arrived at the back door and he heard her take a deep breath before opening it.

Soaking wet they entered the kitchen, leaving tracks of sand and water across the entryway. It didn't seem like Shayde minded too much right then. The house was still dark save for the emergency lights and it seemed, from the laughter coming from the basement, no one downstairs had even known about the incident.

They took off their muddy shoes before walking into the living room. Danny was lying on the brown couch resting. Alizé and Jay were sitting next to him, cuddled close, they eyed Shayde as she came in and sat down on the floor. Danny was conscious, looking extremely tired.

Kruise sat down cross-legged on the floor next to her.

"So," she started.

"Yeah, what the hell was that?" Jay butted in before she could speak, with a half-kidding, half-serious tone.

Kruise could tell that the three of them had been trying to figure it out amongst themselves and couldn't come up with anything.

"Okay, let me explain, and please listen with open minds," Shayde said, nervously.

They looked back at her with blank expressions.

"What you just witnessed was magic. I am a witch, or

better yet, a Sorenya. I have magic in my blood and have had it since I was born. My whole family is magic. I only just learned about it on my birthday and I've been practicing it since we got back from the beach. We are good people, we are not evil. We just live in secrecy for fear of being misunderstood and feared. People who don't understand us pass judgment and deem us evil, devil worshipers. Our faith has nothing to do with god or the devil as our religion doesn't have a heaven or hell, or a god or devil. It's not something we believe in. What we do believe in is hard to explain and I won't go into details at this point. All you need to know is that I am a good witch, I do things like you just witnessed, to help people and so does my family. They have been helping people for more than three hundred years. I hope you don't say anything to anyone, as I am not supposed to share my secret with anyone who is not of the same faith. I apologize for any discomfort I have caused you. I hope that you still accept me as your friend and love me the same as you did before." She finished and stared down at her fingers clasped in her lap.

The only sounds in the room were the crickets chirping, the rain hitting the windows and roof, and the muffled, adolescent laughter coming from the basement.

"So there really are witches in Salem," Jay chortled. "What else can you do?" he asked with sincere curiosity.

Kruise knew his friends wouldn't judge her and would love her just the same.

"Well, I shouldn't really disclose that information just yet, not until I find out how much trouble I'm in for doing magic in front of you. I promise to share that with you when the dust settles."

"Why would you be in trouble?" Alizé asked, her eyes fixed on Shayde with wonder. "You saved his life."

"Well, it's the secrecy thing that I told you about. A lot of my people have died for our faith. It is not easily accepted by society," Shayde said sadly.

"Thank you, Shayde, for saving my life," Danny interjected, like he had been waiting to talk. "They told me what you did and I didn't believe it. But they insisted. I wish I could've seen it, they said it was truly magical," he said sincerely, his dark eyes hiding behind his hat.

"You're welcome, Danny..." she paused. "And just so you know, I didn't just cure your keto-acidosis, I cured your diabetes."

Kruise's entire body erupted with chills at her words.

"You what?!" Danny sat straight up, dumbfounded, eyes wide with disbelief.

"Yeah, it comes with the territory. If I heal someone who is severely sick with something, the water subjugates all that ails you. The elixir we make cures almost everything."

Everyone was quiet, contemplating what they just heard. Dan's eyes welled up with tears.

"I've been battling type-one since I was nine." The tears overflowed and slid down his face. "And then you come along and save me. I owe my life to you Shayde." He dropped off the couch next to her and hugged her, crying silently into her wet hair.

As hard as he tried to fight them off, Kruise's eyes welled up with tears as he watched Shayde hug Danny back. She closed her eyes tightly, but still tears spilled down her face. He could tell she was overwhelmed with everything, and happy she had saved him. They sat there in a silent reverie for what seemed like decades, no one moved a muscle.

Then Dan let go, stood up, wiped the tears off his face with the back of his hand, and cleared his throat, getting rid of the evidence that he was ever crying. He walked over to the couch and lay back down. This time Alizé stood up and went to her friend, eyes red with tears.

"I always knew you were special," she said, taking Shayde's face in her hands, "and though this is inconceivable, it sort of is. I love you and all that you are. I would never stop loving you, for any reason, especially one that defines you as a person. You will always be my best friend, my sister and I'll have your back no matter what. You do your thing girl." She kissed her on the lips and went back to join Jay on the couch.

Shayde was weeping now and Kruise wrapped his arm around her shoulders and pulled her to him. She buried her face in his wet t-shirt and sobbed. He knew she was crying because she had just thwarted the demons that Dan had battled for years, because she finally told her best friends and her boyfriend a secret that had been tormenting her, and because she was overwhelmed with this intense situations that had shook up her world, when all was calm and quiet before. And all he knew was that he was unconditionally in love with her, and his love was deep and unyielding.

He couldn't wait to learn everything about her.

FIFTEEN

Shortly after the emotional episode, the power came back on. The incident had sobered everyone up and none of them were in the mood to drink anymore. Danny passed out on the couch where he lay. Alizé and Jay hung out next to him on the other couch and popped in a movie. They ended up falling asleep there. Cherie grew bored and wanted to leave, since she was sober, and she offered to take Dawn and Brayden home. Jordan only drank a few beers and was okay to drive him and Hannah home. Kruise and Shayde went upstairs to change into dry clothes after everything had happened. They hung out downstairs on the floor and watched a little of the movie the others put in, but Shayde started to get sleepy and wanted to go upstairs.

She could not believe the way things had happened tonight.

When she saw Danny lying there on the floor, some sixth sense kicked in and took over. It was as though she shared a consciousness with whatever had taken over, she moved as if she were a marionette and someone was pulling her strings from above. She had a feeling it had been Aura but wanted to let things lie for now and try to process the bigger things at hand. Some of her friends now knew her secret. Alizé accepted her for all she was, her supportiveness had made her cry. Shayde saved Danny, cured him of his diabetes and that gave her a feeling of utter accomplishment. He was the first one she used her new powers on, the first life she had saved. Kruise now knew her secret. And he *loved* her. She was expecting him to dump her right there and then on that beach, she didn't expect his reaction, let alone him telling her he loved her. But oh, how she loved him back. The way he looked at her out in the rain, when he told her he loved her, she knew he meant it right down to his very core. Now that it was over and he finally knew her secret, she was excited that she didn't have to hide anything anymore, although she still had to talk to Aura and see how much trouble she was in. Not wanting to think about that right now, she pushed away worried thoughts to relish the moments with her boyfriend who loved her.

They went upstairs and lay down on her bed, in the dark, listening to the sounds of each other's breathing and the soft music she had on in the background. The rain had stopped around the time that their friends left. She lay with her head on his chest, his arms wrapped around her. She listened to the sound of his heart, never had that sound been so musical to her. She could lie there and listen to it forever.

"What are you thinking?" he asked her.

"About you," she answered.

"What about me?"

"How crazy I am about you."

"I'm crazy about you too, baby doll."

She absolutely loved it when he called her baby doll. It was the sweetest sound that she ever heard.

"You sure that you don't think I'm crazy?" She smiled.

"I don't think you're crazy. I think you are amazing."

Her heart fluttered. "I think you are. *And* I think that *you* are crazy for thinking that I'm amazing. I'm nothing special."

"Oh, but you are. You are the most special person in the world to me; my everything. I've always felt as though I was missing something, like I was incomplete. And as cliché as it sounds, the day I met you I finally felt whole," he mused, kissing the top of her head.

Melting further into him, she still couldn't believe that the one person she wanted in this world wanted her back, and *loved* her.

"You are my world, too, Kruise. I don't know what I would do if I lost you. My world would fall apart."

No fear remained when it came down to telling him how she felt now. There was nothing that she could say, do, or be that would warrant him leaving her. She knew that now.

"You're not gonna lose me. Don't ever think that. You're stuck with me now."

"Good. Because you are stuck with me, too."

A thought occurred to her at that moment. Getting up, she

walked over to her nightstand and pulled out her wand, Kruise watching her from the bed.

"What are you doing?"

"I wanna try something. Come here..." she said, and opened her door. He stood up and followed her.

"Where are we going?" he asked her.

"You'll see."

Figuring that she was already in trouble and may as well make it worth it, she led him by the hand, pulling him into the hallway to her parent's room, then out to the balcony.

"Okay, now what?" he asked her, confusion written all over his face.

"Just stand still and watch."

Standing on the exact same spot she had been on when she awakened the wings in her skin, she faced her back towards the east and closed her eyes. She pictured her wings coming out of her back as they had the first time. They came out a lot easier this time and as she opened her eyes, she saw him standing there, gazing at her like normal.

Great, it didn't work, I look like a moron, she derided herself.

However, upon looking to the right she discovered that it had, in fact, worked. Her glorious wings were there, outstretched towards the heavens, beautiful and bold as ever.

"What?" she asked him, puzzled as to why he wasn't screaming, or fainting... or running.

"You never cease to amaze me. Earlier on tonight I wouldn't have believed my eyes, but you have shown me that anything is possible. It's only right that you have wings, as you are my angel and they suit you well."

Only he would say something like that. "Thank you," she

smiled at him, "but this is not what I wanted to try. Come over here, stand where I am."

"You don't mean—"

"I'm gonna try. I don't know if it'll work. I'm the only Sorenya since my ancestor Breken, able to fly with their own wings; no one else has been able to duplicate them. If I just imagine it hard enough, I might just be able to give you wings as well. Okay, take off your shirt."

He appeared bewildered but he obeyed her and with wide eyes he removed his shirt. Closing her eyes, she imagined them at their pond standing on the dock together. She could feel her wings on her back but when she looked at him he had none. She forced herself to visualize them lighting up beneath his skin. She saw them pop out from his shoulder blades like a new plant, little shrubs of light. They grew until they were large enough to be visible over his shoulders. When she asked him to unfurl them, she was almost blinded by their beauty. They were just as big as hers, if not a little bigger as he was taller and needed a longer wing span. When she crouched down to pounce and glide into the air, he was right beside her.

She opened her eyes and beheld him, her jaw dropped and tears welled. There, standing before her, was the most handsome man she had ever seen, He stood with a magnificent pair of blue wings outstretched and glorious, ready to take to the skies.

She'd done it.

Neither of them spoke, they just stared at each other; these winged creatures, and smiled.

"Wanna go for a ride?" she said finally.

"I've been waiting my whole life for this moment," he said, wiping a tear that escaped his eye with one quick movement.

"Okay. It's gonna be kinda rocky at first. I had trouble flapping my wings at the right moment. The secret is; crouch down and then jump into the air. Once you are in the air, keep your wings folded and let yourself fall to the ground. Once you feel a nice gust of wind, spread them wide and you'll catch an updraft of air and take off."

Nodding his head, he looked at her and grinned. His expression was both eager and dumbfounded.

Shayde crouched down, ready to do it right this time. Kruise followed her lead and hunkered down. She jumped up... bounding into the air. She left her wings folded on her back this time and then as she came hurtling towards the earth; she snapped them open, caught the air and glided up towards the clouds. Once she found her rhythm, she glanced back to see where Kruise was, but he wasn't behind her. Her heart skipped a beat and she started to panic as she searched all around for him. Then, out of nowhere, he dropped right in front of her from above.

"Oh god, you scared me," she yelled to him.

He already had the hang of it. Boys always had to be show offs.

"Whoo-hoooooo!" Kruise yelled as he dipped and dove and spun around like a total boy.

"Having a good time I take it?" she asked, laughing.

"Hell yes! This is the most awesome thing I have ever done in my entire life," he yelled at her from ahead, whirling and twirling about.

"The first time I did it all I wanted to do was have you here to experience it with me. I never thought in a million years that I would actually be able to make that happen." Her voice was a little shaky with tears that threatened again.

"You are truly amazing my Shayde. Truly and utterly amazing."

He slowed down to fly by her. Soaring high above the earth with Salem unfurling below them, the world became their playground as the skyline sprawled out inexorably before them. Anywhere that they desired to go was now at their fingertips and it was exhilarating. Even more so was the fact that she was able to enjoy this experience with her first and greatest love in the entire world. When the sun started to threaten to break apart the night sky, she decided they should head on back to the house. As much as she wanted to live in this moment for the rest of her days, she didn't know how long the wings would last, if they had a time limit or not, and she didn't want to find out the hard way.

"We should head back," she told him sadly.

"Yeah, I was just thinking that. The sun is gonna come up soon and people may start to see us."

They inversed their flight path and headed home. As they grew closer and closer to her house, she started to panic again.

"Uh—now a warning."

"*Now* a warning?" he said, his voice stricken with panic.

"I'm not really sure how to land yet," she said hesitantly.

"Oh, okay, that's not bad. We'll wing it. Ha ha, get it? Wing it!" he laughed, amused at himself and Shayde laughed with him.

"Okay, just don't stick your feet out flat because you'll just spring back up into the sky."

"Oh, okay. Well let's try this," he said. She looked at him and saw immediately what he intended. They would stick their feet out at an angle to the beach so as to skid to a stop. Apparently, she still caught glimpses of things even with the ring on.

"Oh yeah, okay," she said before he'd said anything.

"What—?" he asked.

"Nothing, it's weird. More of my witchy stuff. I can read peoples' eyes. It's just this weird thing I do," she said with an awkward giggle.

"Oh."

He didn't sound surprised. After a night like tonight, one wouldn't blame him for not being shocked; the eye reading thing was the least of the weird things she had shown him.

As they headed towards earth together, she flung her wings straight back, like an eagle who was going in for a kill, and angled her feet way out in front of her. Then, as she neared the sand, she dug her heels into it and skidded to a stop. She came to a halt and turned around in time to see Kruise coming in for his landing. It was truly amazing. His glowing blue wings outstretched behind him, and there was a look of a serene calm on his face. As he skidded towards a controlled stop, he found his balance and keeping up his momentum, ran to her, tackling her hard into the sand. Shayde squealed with laughter. He kissed her with one of *his* kisses, engulfing her within his wings.

They were in a little glowing bundle of wings, kissing each other with a soft fierceness. He looked at her, breathless and took her face in his hands.

"I love you... I love you, I love you, I love you. Without wax."

She giggled. "I love *you*! And what?"

"It's an old saying. It stems from the Roman and Greek artistry. When a sculpture had a crack or a flaw, the artists would fill them in with colored wax to match the marble, which would mask the imperfection. Therefore, the sculptures that were perfect, unfaltering and absolutely perfect were 'without wax'. It means my love is absolute, unconditional, undoubting, unhesitating and unquestioning."

Everything within her dissolved at his words. She felt exactly the same.

They kissed each other for a while longer. From an outsider's perspective, it would've looked like two angels on the beach, kissing beneath a tent of wings at twilight, stars sparkling as brightly as the wings.

Sadly, they parted their lips and decided to head in. He arose first and helped her, wings outstretched to help out his balance.

"Can we do this again sometime?" he asked her.

"Oh yeah! I wouldn't want to fly without you."

They walked past the gate and towards the door to the house. When they arrived at the deck she looked at him regretfully.

"Okay, ready?" she asked him.

"No. Do I have to?"

"No. But people may start to look at you funny."

"Okay." He caressed his left wing gently with his right hand, as if to say goodbye. "It's so weird that I can feel that."

"I know. Crazy huh?" she smiled at his amazement, glad that she had been able to share this with him.

"Okay, do it," he said, almost bracing himself.

She looked at him and his wings, closed her eyes as tight as she could, and wished his away. Slowly, they shriveled up until they were little specs of light beneath his skin and then they were gone completely. He felt his back awkwardly, to see if they were still there.

Then she wished away hers.

They went back inside, wiped off their sandy feet, and climbed up to her room. Shayde lay down on her bed and then sat up a little, with her back resting on the headboard as he sat down next to her. He wrapped his arm around her shoulders and nuzzled his head in the nape of her neck.

She could not stop adoring him, his marvelous beauty, his soft, strong skin, his captivating hazel eyes and his perfect mouth. Nothing made her feel the way his mouth made her feel. She sat up and gazed at him, he returned her gaze just as intensely. Staring searchingly into his eyes, she saw herself reflected in them, his first true love, she saw that he yearned for her, he ached for her.

She started to kiss him, softly at first, just grazing the edges of his lips. Then, as she parted her lips and he tasted her mouth, her body turned feverish. She grabbed the back of his head ferociously and pulled him towards her, landing underneath him. His kisses grew more intense, hotter, with a purpose. They knew they had reached their boiling point and it was okay, this time, to explode. His hands started to wander, all the while still kissing her. Down her arms, around her waist back up to her face, staking out the territory, finding out where his boundaries were, if there were any at all. When a small moan escaped her mouth as he glided one hand over her breast, he knew she was his to conquer. No one had ever touched her like that before and she struggled to contain herself. He moved his hands down to the bottom of her shirt and started to pull it up slowly to see if she would stop him. When her kisses remained unfaltering he continued to raise it up and over her head. No one had ever saw her naked before but she wasn't shy or embarrassed with Kruise. All she wanted was him, all over her. She still had her bra on so she sat up, not letting up on her kisses and took it off for him. His hands started to explore the newly uncovered territory and she moaned again with ecstasy at the new sensations. He already had his shirt off so she went for his pants, fumbling around to get his belt off and when she couldn't figure it out he undid it for her. He took off his pants so that he was left in boxers alone. She went back to his mouth and fed more of her hunger with his lips. Her body felt hot in ways she'd never imagined. She pulled at the button of her shorts and unzipped them, slid them down her legs and onto the floor. They were almost completely naked, aside from her little white panties and his boxers. Going mad with his cravings, he raked his fingers through her hair, wrapped his arms around her body, pulled her up to him and laid her back down, as if he was straining to survive. She could feel his bare chest on hers and the feeling made her eyes roll back in her head. His rippled abs rubbing against her bare skin tested her sanity to a breaking point. When she slid down his boxers, he responded by ripping her panties off, not even trying to take them off nicely and then they were naked together, inches away from being one. His kisses ceased for a second while he reached down to grab a foil packet from the pocket of his jeans. As he frantically ripped it open, took out the contents and put it on, he continued to feel the silk of her skin under the tip of his tongue, feeding off her, enticing her drive. She could feel the steam of his breath around every curve; the heat was rising intensely, teasing her, burning her insides. Then, when she couldn't take it anymore, she beckoned him to explore the depths of her body.

Magic. That would be the only acceptable word to describe what she felt as the two of them coalesced. Sparks flew, volcanoes erupted, the earth shattered and mountains moved. Contrary to what she'd imagined, there was no pain for her. They entwined together as if they had always meant to be that way. She felt like he fit her, like a puzzle piece. As he glided in and out of her, she wrapped herself up in his pleasure, letting herself go completely. Every pore opened up to him, every inch of her belonged to him, her very soul was making love to him. He made her heart fly, and she knew then in that moment, it had always belonged with him. Her heart, her virginity, her soul, they had all been his. And now they were home. He was her soul mate and this was the way that things were always supposed to be.

For the first time in her life she felt sexy, she felt free. Although she had just learned how to fly, being with him was the most intense magic she ever felt in her life, it was disorienting. Her whole body tingled as he gnawed at her being, bringing her to a precipice at the edge of the world. As he started to slow down, she knew he was getting closer to the brink and she wanted to jump off with him. She was right there too and she pulled him down to whisper; "I love you."

He sighed. "Without wax."

And they both erupted into earth-shattering ecstasy.

*S*H...*AAAAAAAAYYYYYYYDE.*

She awoke to a voice in her head.

It came like a whisper from a dream. It startled her at first. She opened her eyes, stared at the ceiling, and tried to decipher whether it was a dream or reality, blinking wildly to try to keep her heavy eyes open.

Shh...aaaaaaaaaayyyyyyyde, Aura beckoned her out of the fog.

Shayde sat up slightly. *Yes?*

Come here please, down to the basement.

Hopefully she wasn't in too much trouble.

Okay, I'll be right there.

Kruise's arm was still around her. The sun was high in the sky so it had to be well after noon. The shades were drawn but her room still flickered with daylight here and there. Moving softly to get out of bed, she made it without rousing him. Searching for her clothes, she found her shorts, but her panties were ripped and laying on the floor. She slid her shorts on and when she found her shirt and bra, she slipped them on and tip-toed to the door.

She passed through the living room to the basement door; her friends who had been asleep on the couches were gone. As she headed for the sub-basement, she was worried and trying to think of what could possibly happen. Opening the big wooden door, it creaked loudly on its hinges as she shut it behind her. The light was on already so she just headed towards the couches. When she sat down, Aura appeared at her side.

"Whoa!" she shrieked. "You scared me."

"Sorry darling. I forget I am still new to you and cannot go popping about as I want to," she giggled a little.

"So, how much trouble am I in?" she asked, cutting right to the chase.

"Luckily none."

Shayde's eyes went wide with shock as she waited for her to explain.

"You did what you had to do—with my help of course. That boy *was* dying and I knew you wanted to save him but were taking too long. I jumped into your body to help things along a little. But once I led you to the water, you were the one who did the rest. It is you who saved him."

"So, I'm not in trouble for exposing us?"

"No. Luckily, none of your friends are a threat to us." Aura's expression remained hard, unchanging. "They all have open minds and believe in the good in people. The rules that your father told you about are more or less guidelines. You are not supposed to tell others of what we do, yes, but that is because of what has happened in the past. We sometimes have to expose ourselves in order to save people, but the less people that know about us the better. That does not mean that you cannot tell anyone of who you are. If you are truly loved by someone, they will accept you unconditionally for all that you are—flaws and all. They will love you, all of you and will not pass judgment on you. You are a wise woman, Shayde, surround yourself with these people all the time. You can see the good in people and that is all that matters. You thrive off the good in people, as I thrive off the good in *you*.

"Anyone who loves is welcome with open arms into our faith. They can be of any religion and we would embrace them all the same. That is what makes us different. Your friends love you and would do anything for you.

"What I cannot overcome is what you did today. I am not *angry*, I am speechless. I have not witnessed the wings of Breken in so long; I have seen countless Sorenya try with all their hearts to make it happen and fail, who have cried out in desperation at their failure and wept under the night sky, begging the stars to help them. Then you come along. You not only re-create the wings of Breken with ease, you gave them unto a mortal man, who is not even of our blood. I knew as soon as I saw it in your mind that you were going to succeed. I cannot tell you how incredibly proud you have made me."

Shayde absorbed all that Aura said and was relieved that she hadn't let her down. That was the last thing that she would have wanted.

"I was surprised to see how fast Kruise learned though. Those wings emerged as if they already had a path to his soul; it was almost as if he had something deeper running in his veins." Aura mused.

Shayde's brow furrowed. Did Kruise have magic in his blood somewhere in his family's history?

"I couldn't believe that he picked it up that easily too. He even showed me how to land. But you probably already knew that. Do you really think he is magical?"

"Not that I can see. If he is, he has no recollection of it. What matters now is that your friends are okay with the way you are. You still should not do any more magic in front of them, unless absolutely necessary. The wings I can accept for you and Kruise, as long as you do not fly during the day or when people can see you. You are not to try to give wings to anyone else who is not of our blood or faith again either."

"No, I won't. I totally understand. So it's okay if Kruise and I go flying again?!" she said enthused.

"Yes, as long as you follow the rules. We do not need people in Salem thinking there are witches here again."

"Okay. Got it. I will make sure to never fly when there are a lot of people out."

"Good. You may want to take your mom flying sometime. I think she would enjoy it more than you know."

"Oh I will! The second she gets back. I was actually hoping it would work so I could take her flying. I know it would mean the world to her!"

"I know you were. You make me very proud Shayde. You are an excellent Sorenya and I trust that you will always do your best to make the right choices. I am happy that you have found a man that you love so much. I can see it in both your hearts that you are in tune with each other. Your auras are still dancing." She smiled an indulgent smile.

Shayde grinned happily. It *felt* like their auras were dancing.

"You may go now, that is all I wanted. Get some rest."

"Okay Aura. Thank you," she said, wishing she could hug her friend.

"One day maybe. One day we shall be able to hug," she said, plucking the thought right out of Shayde's head. Shayde nodded faintly and headed towards the door.

As she put her hand on the handle to open it, Aura spoke again.

"His love you for you is enormous. Much bigger than you think. I know you have not had any experience with love and even though you may worry it is infatuation; it is much, much larger than that. Just keep listening to your heart, it will never steer you wrong. You did the right thing by giving your heart to him. It is in a safe place."

Shayde paused, looking down at her hand on the door, feeling a contentedness within her that she had never known. She smiled as she considered what Aura had just told her, and her heart sighed.

"Thank you," was all she said.

She opened the door and went back upstairs.

As she crept back into her room, she slid in silently next to her sleeping boyfriend. He hadn't moved, and was still naked and warm beneath the sheets. Softly she snuggled in next to him and drifted back to sleep.

THEY WOKE UP TOGETHER A FEW HOURS LATER. HER PHONE MADE A small beep, signaling she had received a new message.

Flicking it on, she saw that there was one new message from Courtney.

Call ASAP. Bad things happened last night after we left. At hospital now.

It was sent at nine that morning. It was now almost two in the afternoon.

Shayde's heart jumped into her throat and she started to panic. Kruise could feel her tense up.

"What is it, what's wrong?"

"I don't know, it's from Court. It just says something bad has happened and they were at the hospital. I have to call her." Her shaky hands found Courtney's contact details and hit call.

It rang... and rang... and rang...

"Hello?" Courtney's voice finally came through, sounding exhausted and raspy like it would from lack of sleep.

"Hey, what's up?" Shayde asked, standing up and walking towards her window. "Where are you?"

"I'm at home now."

'What happened? Who's hurt?" Shayde was pacing with worry now.

"It's Cherie. She's okay now, don't worry. She lost the baby though."

"Oh no!" Shayde responded, dropping her head back to look unseeingly at the ceiling. "How?"

"When we were at your house playing pool, Nate was texting her all night. He was drinking, saying mean stuff to her. He wanted her to drop what she was doing and leave to come get him and bring him back to our house. She kept telling him no, no, she ain't leaving; she's having fun with her friends. He got really mad and started blowing her phone up, so I told her to turn it off. When we got back to the house, he was waiting outside. They started yelling at each other outside so I told them to come in to argue. They went down to her room and I could hear them screaming at each other from the living room.

All of a sudden it got quiet, and then he ran up the stairs and bolted out the door. I ran down to see if she was okay.

"Oh my god Shayde, she was lying on the floor, clutching her knees to her chest. She was moaning and crying hysterically. I asked her what happened, and she said that Nate got pissed off that she still wasn't gonna get an abortion and kicked her in the stomach really hard. When she started bleeding I rushed her to the hospital. He kicked her so hard he ruptured her uterus and she ended up losing the baby." Courtney's voice broke, "They had to do a full D&C procedure right then and there so she wouldn't bleed to death. She's still there now resting but she's not doing so well."

Shayde's jaw dropped, unable to believe her ears. "Oh my god... Oh my god." It was all she could muster as it grew harder to breathe while the rage set in.

"I know. I want to kill him. No one knows where he is, I told the ER staff what had happened, I think they've called the cops, but they said that since she wasn't that far along he would probably only get either domestic violence or aggravated assault. He needs to be charged with murder as far as I'm concerned."

"That is crap. That bastard needs to sit in jail a long time for what he did. Is there anything that I can do?"

"She doesn't want her parents involved; they didn't even know she was pregnant yet so I'm going to pick her up tomorrow morning. I think she's out of it at the moment. I wanted to stay but she just wanted to be alone. Maybe tomorrow or something you can come to see her."

"Okay. Well tell her that I love her and if she needs anything to call me no matter what."

"All right sweetie, I will. I'll call you later or tomorrow to see what you are doing."

"Okay hon. Bye-bye." She clicked the phone off and looked over at Kruise who was fully clothed now and was sitting on the bed, listening.

"Everything all right?" he asked her.

"No. Nate kicked Cherie in the stomach last night and she lost the baby."

"What! Are you kidding me?"

"No. He's such an asshole. God, I hate him so much," she cringed, trying with all her might not to wish him dead. She was furious.

"No kidding. What's gonna happen to him?"

"The nurses in ER told Court that the only thing that would happen to him, would be for him to get charged with domestic violence or aggravated assault because she wasn't that far along."

"That's crap. What a crock. It's still a human being. Granted a very little, see-through, tadpole-looking thing, but a human none the less."

"I know, I'm so fuckin' mad."

It was getting harder for her to stifle the destructive thoughts that were assailing her mind. Focusing on something positive was being drastically hindered by the fury that she felt when thinking of Nate's pudgy little face. She paced back and forth in front of the window.

Come here please. Aura's voice intruded into her tumultuous thoughts. Shayde stopped her pacing and looked out the window. *What about Kruise?* she thought back.

Bring him. I know that he loves you. He is here to stay. And he has already flown with you, there's not much else that will come as a surprise to him.

Okay.

She turned around to look at him and he was just sitting there, studying her, trying to figure her out.

"Come with me… please," she said, walking up to him and holding out her hand.

"Where are we going?"

"Remember yesterday when I told you there was much more to explain and that I would try to clear things up today?"

He looked confused. "Yes?" he half-questioned, half-answered.

"Well, I'm about to clear things up. C'mon, let's go." She pulled him off the bed and headed towards the door.

"But where are we going?"

"Downstairs. Just try to save your questions 'til later."

Together they descended the flights of stairs, went past the pool table and game room in the basement to the little storage area.

She opened the hidden door underneath the stairs and headed down the dark steps to the sub-basement. When they reached the old wooden door she glanced at him and found a look of utter confusion on his face, but also a hint of anticipation. As she opened this door to the room and led him in, he looked around in amazement. She walked him over to the couches in front of the giant cauldron, sat down and pulled him down onto the seat next to her. Kruise sat silently, in awe of his surroundings.

"Okay. This may come as a shock to you, or it may not, but

she will be able to explain things way better than I would be able to."

"Who?" His eyes searched around the room with trepidation.

"Wait... Aura, come out now." She looked over at the mirror.

He followed her gaze and watched as the mirror became bright with luminous colors, and out came Aura.

Kruise shook his head in disbelief.

Aura undulated towards them, Kruise's eyes remained fixed on her, unblinking.

"No, I am not a ghost. I am energy. I belong to Shayde and her family, and have for hundreds of years," Aura replied, answering his unspoken question. "I am not going to tell you the entire story of our family, as it is long, drawn-out, and would probably be very boring to you. I will just *show* you the gist of it so that you may understand Shayde better. Is that okay with you?"

Kruise looked at her, befuddled. "Sure, yeah."

Floating up to him, she came to a stop right before him and as she extended her hand inches away from his forehead she said, "Close your eyes. This will not hurt at all." As he closed his eyes Shayde knew that Aura was beginning to project visions into his head. This was one instance where she decided to read his mind so that she could see what he was seeing. Aura started at the very beginning with the magical Tuathas of Ireland. Next, she showed him how she came into being and what she was to the family that she emanated from. This was followed by images of certain incidents of magic that past Sorenya had demonstrated but hid anything disturbing like the massacre of Breken's family and Kain's incident with the bully. She left out the majority of things that Shayde could do with her mind for Shayde to reveal as and when she wished. It was basically to show him what they did as a family and how they helped the world around them.

When she was finished she floated back and studied him. He still had his eyes closed.

"Open your eyes," Aura instructed.

He opened them slowly, calmly.

"How do you feel?" she asked.

"Weird. That was the strangest, coolest thing I have seen in a while. Wow!" He looked through her, reliving what he'd just seen, an astonished smile swept across his face.

Shayde hugged him and laughed. A smile crept across Aura's face too.

"You like that? That was the first time I've ever tried it. I didn't know how well it was going to turn out," Aura said.

"Yeah, no, that was cool. Wow," he said again. He was obviously at a loss for words.

"Okay, good. Now you know what we do." She paused. "Now, Shayde, you and I need to figure out what to do about Nate. What he does to that poor woman is unacceptable and we have to do something about it."

"Yeah for sure," Shayde agreed. "What should we do?"

Aura stared at her, concentrating on something.

"Oohh, I have an idea!" Shayde jumped up.

"What is it?" Kruise asked, intrigued.

"Be right back," she told them as she sprinted to the door. She bounded up the steps three at a time. When she arrived at her dresser, she hastily grabbed her wand and bounded back down all three flights of stairs again.

"Okay," Shayde said as she returned breathless.

Neither one of them had moved.

"Okay, what are we going to do?" Aura asked.

"Um, let me think it through some more."

Cradling her head in her hands, she tried to think of a way to stop Nate hurting Cherie. She couldn't hurt him as she'd like to, that would go against the rule of 'do no harm,' and she couldn't get rid of him either. She knew that Cherie was going to keep going back to him, and that no matter what Nate did to her, that he verbally abused her, broke her heart and then trampled on the pieces, she would always take him back. He slept with different women, and *dated* different women and gave her their diseases. Then he killed the baby he made in her. In spite of all these things, she was putty in his hands and would do whatever he wanted. Shayde knew that if she were to harm Nate or if anything bad ever happened to him, it would hurt her friend beyond comprehension and she did not want to hurt her friend.

Repulsion filled her mind when she thought of insolent Nate and his ugly, blotchy face, his disgusting, feeble self. From the moment that she met him she knew that he was an ugly person inside and out. His aura was dirty shades of brown, black and dull yellow.

That's it! she thought. "I got it!" she exclaimed, jumping up and running to mirror.

Standing in front of it, Shayde pulled out her wand, pointed it at the mirror, closed her eyes and pictured Nate's face. She pictured every detail: every single eyelash, every last hair on his head, every clogged pore on his face. Then she visualized his aura and when she saw it, she wished it into the wand. When she opened her eyes, the wand was slightly glowing. She looked into the mirror and pointed the wand at it.

"In!" she commanded.

The wand started to fume in shades of brown, black and yellow. The smoke then began to waft towards the mirror. As more smoke came out of it and into the mirror, it started accumulating at the bottom of the glass, gathering to form in the shape of a pair of shoes. Then legs clad in jeans appeared, then a torso—in a Metallica t-shirt—a neck, and finally a head. The smoke then disappeared and there, standing in the mirror in front of Shayde, was Nate. It looked exactly like him, except this Nate didn't move or speak.

"Now, show what's bad," she commanded the apparition in the mirror.

Suddenly, there was a burst of energy, yellow, brown, and black specks resembling droplets of water, appeared to have been drawn from the apparition and had now gathered around it, hovering there, somehow emanating from it but at the same time separate from it. She took the wand and poked it in the mirror.

"Come to me!" She commanded. The wand acted like a magnet to the specks of light that were surrounding Nate. She plucked one droplet out of the mirror at a time and released them to form a ball of light hovering in front of her. One by one, she added to the ball making it bigger and bigger. Once the last droplet was plucked, she scanned the room for something, yet wasn't exactly sure what it was.

She glanced over to her right at Kruise and Aura, who were just watching her, then to her left. Her face lit up. Placing the wand on the floor, she cupped her hands around the big ball of light and started walking it slowly towards the fireplace. Reaching the hearth, using all her body weight, she flung it into the back of the grate. She ran to the switch and flicked it on. When the fire ignited and engulfed the ball of light, it began glowing brighter, becoming so bright that it started changing colors.

Suddenly it exploded into a million tiny pieces and the flames turned green. Shayde watched the fire until it reverted to a normal color, then she turned it off and returned to the mirror.

She picked up the wand and commanded; "Return to your home!"

The figure in the mirror deteriorated, turning into smoke and floating away, hardly recognizable as the figure that had arrived. She smiled, satisfied, and walked towards her audience.

"Very good Shayde," Aura told her. "That was good thinking,"

"What did you just do?" Kruise asked slightly puzzled.

"I took all the bad out of his aura. Now, he will value the good in people rather than judge them by just their appearance and what they have. He will see Cherie for who she is, not what she looks like and he'll stop hurting my friend."

"Oh... Nice," Kruise said simply and held out his hand for her to high-five it.

"Yeah!" she said, jumping up to smack his hand. "Go me!" she giggled and sat back down with him.

SIXTEEN

The last few days had been interesting for Kruise, to say the least. It was all quite strange, not to mention foggy, as if it had been a dream. Processing it all was challenging as it was almost impossible for him to wrap his brain around it. It had to be a dream, things like this just don't happen. But at the same time it didn't feel like a dream at all—for even in dreams it's easy to recognize that they are in fact dreams. No, it all felt very real, as if it was normal, natural; as though it was always meant to happen that way.

After Shayde fixed Nate, they spent the remainder of the day cuddled close, watching movies. They were completely and totally in love with each other, and he was happy. During the night, they entwined together passionately, and even though the release of the pent up excitement of the first time was sated, it was replaced with something even more special, something deeper. With each new discovery about one another, it was as if their love and need for each other intensified.

The next morning Shayde called Courtney and Cherie's house to see if Cherie was okay. Courtney was really mad. When she'd arrived to collect Cherie at the hospital, the Police were there; apparently Nate had walked into the station last night and confessed to what he had done. The police had turned up to take a statement at the hospital early that morning, but Cherie just refused to press charges, denied everything. They didn't know what to do, this sort of thing hadn't happened before.

When Shayde finally talked to Cherie later that day, Cherie was adamant that something strange and wonderful had happened to Nate. The fact that he had turned himself in and confessed everything meant that he had really changed. He was so remorseful; he looked as though he had been crying. In all the time that they had known each other, Cherie had never seen him cry. He said that he was so sorry for doing such an evil thing; he couldn't understand what had made him do it. He told her he loved her more than anything in the world, he had no idea why he'd been treating her so badly when she was such a wonderful, beautiful person. He seemed so genuinely sorry that although it was going to take some time for her to trust him, she had to take that chance.

Courtney wasn't convinced, she just thought that Nate knew he'd gone too far and was playing Cherie so he wouldn't have to go to prison. She wasn't happy that Shayde seemed to be giving Nate the benefit of the doubt too, but then she hadn't been down in that basement with them.

Now, they were standing in the marina about to watch the fireworks go off with Alizé and Jay and Courtney and her date Ryan. Cherie was being looked after by Nate at home. Alizé and Jay were hanging out a lot but still hadn't established anything. They enjoyed each other's company and had a good time when they were together.

As they were chatting together awaiting the holiday's festivities, Kruise's phone alerted him that he had a new message.

He clicked it to life.

I'm sorry.

It was from his dad.

It felt like his heart stopped beating. Frozen for a second, he found his pulse again and opened up his favorite contacts, found his dad and hit call.

It rang... and rang... and rang... then went to voicemail.

He hit end then called again and waited.

"What's the matter?" Shayde asked him worriedly.

"Don't know. It's my dad. He sent a strange message."

"What'd it say?"

"Just said, 'I'm sorry'," Kruise said, with the phone to his ear, still waiting for Simon to answer.

"Oh no. What could that mean?"

"I don't know but I have a bad feeling. C'mon, we gotta go."

Shayde told her friends that she had to go and she'd be in touch soon.

Kruise and Shayde ran across the marina to where he had parked his truck while he tried over and over to reach his dad. He hit unlock and they both jumped in. Throwing it into reverse and then into gear, the tires squealed loudly as he weaved frantically in and out of traffic. When he hit the main road home, he put the pedal to the metal and punched it. They didn't say much to each other on the drive home. Shayde sat silently in the passenger seat, probably trying to think of what it could be that was happening. He was still trying to reach his dad when he pulled up to his house. He slammed on the brakes and jumped out of the truck, leaving the keys in the ignition. He noticed Simon's bike was outside as he bounded across the grass, up the steps and through the door. When he entered, the living room was quiet and dark. Running up the stairs to his dad's room, all was dim except for the light coming from his bathroom. He ran over to it with Shayde on his tail.

There was his father, lying face down on the floor in front of the toilet in a puddle of vomit. An envelope lay at his side.

"DAD! DAD!" Kruise yelled, shaking him violently, when he was unresponsive he yelled, "SHAYDE!"

She must have already known because she was moving methodically in a trance, filling the sink with water, duplicating the actions she had taken for Danny. When the water was fully glowing, she cupped some liquid into her hands and ran over to Simon as Kruise opened his mouth for him. The water trickled down his throat and it began to glow. It went down into his chest, through his body, then back up his throat and exploded out through his mouth. Simon began wheezing slightly which was followed by a bout of coughing.

"DAD!" Kruise yelled as he shook him some more.

"S-son," Simon stammered.

Kruise turned him around and pulled him by the armpits and dragged him into his room. Shayde grabbed his feet and helped him get Simon onto the bed where Kruise propped him up on some pillows. A look of death was on Simon's face; pallid and clammy, causing a churning in the pit of his stomach. Kruise had no idea what was happening, but he knew he didn't want to lose his dad too.

"Dad, can you hear me," he said, crouching on his feet by the bedside, holding his dad's hand.

"S-son..." He tried again.

"What is it Dad? What happened?"

Shayde knelt by Kruise awaiting his response as well.

"G-get h-her AWAY from m-me," he stuttered, glowering at Shayde with such hatred in his eyes that it looked like he would harm her if he could.

"Dad, what? Why?" Kruise asked beseechingly.

"Sh-she-she's she's a w-w-w-w WITCH!!!!" Simon spat out the word as if he didn't want it in his mouth.

Kruise shook his head. "Dad, c'mon, what? What happened to you?" he implored.

"Y...your, gr...grandma M...Marilyn ha...a...had a heart attack," he said, starting to heal more from the elixir and was less drowsy and shaken.

"Oh my god, what?! Is she okay?" Kruise asked as his eyes started to sting with threatening tears.

"N...no son, sh...she's n...not. Shh...she's in I...ICU."

"What! Why didn't you call me?"

"I...I didn't know where you were, whether you were at w...work or with—*her*. There wasn't time anyway, when I got there she'd come around but it was as if she was hallucinating, she was freaking out, they had to give her something to calm her down. When she was calmer she...she told me that after she f-fell from the pain, she looked up to see a m-man hovering over her," he grimaced. "The man called himself Viento. H-he told her he was created b-by a witch over three hundred years ago and nurtured by her descendants ever since. He was instructed to show himself to all of the first born of all the generations of our family, just when we are close to death. It is here that we are told that it is he who took our first love from us, and that we are the cause. Your grandma was devastated; he said that the moment we felt like we couldn't be happier, when we were truly, totally in love, he took our loved one. She was saying she shouldn't have loved my father so much, it was her fault. I've never seen her in such agony.

"Then it hit me, that's why I lost my Reanna, I just knew what she was saying was true. I went straight home and took out Reanna's rosary beads, she loved those beads. Do you remember them? She went mad with fright when she found you sucking them when you were a baby, poisonous as hell. I crushed them and ate what I could; it was enough to meet this monster. He came to me almost right after I took them and told me the same as he'd told your grandma. I was so angry, I wanted to find these witches before the poison finished the job, so I got on the computer and went on ancestry dot com to find out who they were and where they went. Turns out they remained in Salem and are here to this day. They're the reason I lost my dad, my wife. *She's* the reason your mother is dead, son," he said accusingly, gaining more strength but still looking pale. He struggled to lift his head off the pillow but managed. "GET OUT OF HERE WITCH!!!"

Kruise couldn't believe what his dad had said. But how would he know that she was a witch if he wasn't being truthful? It couldn't be true. Tears welled up in his eyes and he turned around to face her. She was as white as a ghost; hand over her mouth, staring at him in disbelief.

"No, not our family, we can't—It's not true, Breken never did such a thing," she protested before he could ask her anything.

"Did you know about this spirit?" Kruise cut her off, his voice cracking with utter devastation.

"Yes, but—"

"WITCH!" Simon bolted up and screamed at her with indignant hostility.

"SHAYDE! You knew about this and you didn't tell me?" he said, searching her face incredulously.

"Kruise, it's not like that really—"

"Get out," he said quietly, looking down.

"But Kruise, just listen—" She started to sob, trying to pull at his hand.

"GO!!!!! I. DON'T. WANT. TO. SEE. YOU. RIGHT. NOW!" Kruise swatted her hand away.

A look of absolute anguish descended upon her face as she stood, she turned and ran out the door. Kruise fell to his knees and sobbed at his dad's side.

CHAPTER
SEVENTEEN

Shayde couldn't breathe because her very heart was being crushed. As she stumbled out of the front door and out on to the street, she didn't know where she was going, but she didn't care. Everything had just lost all its meaning and nothing in the world was making any sense right now. All that she knew was that her world was falling apart and the debris was slowly suffocating her. She was so utterly destroyed she couldn't get her bearings and she needed to get home but she was so lost. How did this happen? As soon as any sort of understanding would surface about the past few minutes, it would disappear as fast as it came. Trying to get her mind right was futile. All she could think of to do was to get away from his house. When she was down the block and around the corner her phone's message indicator sang to her.

A flicker of hope ignited in her mind. Through tear stricken eyes she flicked her phone on and looked at the text. It was from him.

It's over

was all it said.

The pain hit her heart and threatened to rip her apart as she fell to her knees on the sidewalk. She tried to scream but no sound came out of her mouth. Hot tears poured out of her eyes, her rib cage felt like it had shattered and the jagged pieces were puncturing her lungs, her heart, out through her skin. There was no possible way to breathe, it was impossible to gather air into her lungs, and she clutched at her chest to try and make it stop hurting, trying to get the throbbing to stop. But it wouldn't. It was as if she were drowning. Pulling her knees to her chest, she curled up in a little ball and looked up to the moon, begging it to set her free from the pain. If this grief was what came with love, she wanted nothing to do with it. She wanted to run and hide from the crippling feeling, but there was nowhere for her to hide.

She lay in the street for longer than she cared to know. Far off in the distance she could hear the booms of the firework display. She didn't know what time it was and didn't care. All that she knew was that her reason for living was gone. Something had gone terribly wrong and now he was no longer hers.

It all felt like a dream. Like a very bad dream.

Trying to dislodge the terror that being without him

brought, she told herself she would wake up from this nightmare, in her room next to him and it would all be all right. It was all an awful dream and nothing more. There was no way that loving him was over.

The next thing she knew she was in her room and it was completely dark. She sat up in her bed and looked around.

He wasn't there.

Was I dreaming?

A moment of joyful hope hit her heart and as she arose she looked around for her phone. His backpack still sat in the corner and the sight of it stung her a little but she tried not to think of why. She continued to search for her phone. It wasn't on the charger on the nightstand. It wasn't in her pants' pocket on the floor. Finally, she flipped over the covers that had been blanketing her.

There it was.

Then she hesitated. Did she even want to know? Slowly, she reached for the phone and clicked it on, finding the message button and inbox folder.

It's over

It was the last message she had received. Her eyes filled up with tears and she held the phone to her heart and sunk to the floor. She put her head back on her bed and cried harder than she had in her entire life, harder than she did when she lost her brother. Her world went blank and her body filled with a gut-wrenching pain, all she could see was his face. Her heart pounded with it, hammering poisoned blood into her bloodstream.

A debilitating fire took over her body, yet she felt so cold that she was shivering. The ache in her chest became more and more painful with every breath she took. The puncture wounds in her lungs opened back up and stung her with every beat of her heart. She kept seeing his gorgeous face and his smile. The feeling of his lips on hers haunted her and she touched them to stop the pain from reaching them. Her tears soaked the side of her face, her neck; they were falling down her arms, down her chest. They were unstoppable. Breathing out of her nose was now impossible and she had to take deep breaths in-between sobs that made the ache in her chest worse. Clutching it harder helped to ease the pain.

I'm fine; she told herself, but it was futile. Sitting there in her room, completely lost, her very being reduced to nothingness, these intense emotions ripped through her and threatened to break her apart and overturn her very existence. And it was cold. She didn't know how to go on, how to get past this loss. Her world had known sadness before, but it had never known total devastation, destruction to her spirit beyond all comprehension. Every molecule in her body ached for him. Every droplet of sweat and every ounce of her tears bled for him. She fell to the floor and screamed louder than she ever had in her life in an attempt to get some of her anguish out, like it would relieve some of the pressure that threatened to crush her alive. It hurt like hell. The sobbing eventually quieted as she soon lost the strength to scream anymore or to even cry out loud. Her will had been broken, her spirit severed from her heart.

SHE WOKE UP TO DAYLIGHT. SHE HAD NO IDEA WHAT DAY IT WAS, OR the time, but she was still lying there with her hands clutching her phone to her chest. With a sullen look, she checked the phone to see if it was still on. Thankfully it was dead. She didn't want to know if *he* had tried to contact her, or worse, if he hadn't tried at all. Her chest started to throb at the thought of him again and she began to dread the emptiness. She didn't think she could do it anymore. It was too hard, she loved him too much. With unprecedented anger, she sat up and threw the phone against the wall as hard as she could and saw it break apart, leaving a huge chip in the drywall where it had met its demise. She fell back to floor and sobbed, holding on to her heart as if to keep it inside her. Millions of little pin pricks ran up and down her, stinging her skin and cutting into her soul. Everything had lost meaning, her life, her heart, her soul, all gone. She was incapacitated with agony and didn't think she would ever make it off the floor.

SHE LAY THERE THINKING OF ANYTHING ELSE BUT HIM, SO AS NOT TO wake up the aching in her chest, listening to music playing softly in the background that she didn't remember turning on. She was trying to keep her thoughts sedated; she stared at the wall from her position on the floor by the side of the bed. She looked from the wall to the shards of phone strewn across the floor, and then back to the wall again, over and over. When different songs came on the radio she listened to them intently, trying desperately to become someone else, to live in another body away from one that was suffering, crumpling into nothingness. Cautiously, she tried not to relate to any of the songs that came on, solely living in other people's moments. She had grabbed her stuffed bear from the floor, the one from Kain that usually sat on her bed, and clung to it with all her might pretending it was Kain she was hugging, until finally a numb calm swept over her.

Then, in the background, a song came on that had been playing the night of their first kiss. She had feared this was going to happen eventually but hadn't the strength to get up and change the station. She tried desperately to repress the memory but fragments of what she felt during that first kiss still pierced through. It was her guillotine. Any trace of rationality dissipated and her body started to quiver silently, heaving in pain. The discomforting spasms grew into torturous convulsions as she thought of the moments she associated with the lyrics of the song. Anguish gripped at her heart and squeezed at it with treacherous torment, imbibing her. The misery that lay in the open puncture wounds and lacerations from her severed soul throbbed with excruciating pain. Her breathing became more erratic with convulsions of sobs. She gripped onto her bear as if maybe he could help manage the pain, even in the tiniest way. She struggled to gasp for air; the hurt was asphyxiating her, strangling her will to survive. As she suffocated, she felt herself weaken; the strangulating ache debilitated her as it smothered her spirit. Her abs began to burn from the intense force of her mourning. She wasn't going to make it through this and no one could do anything to stop it. She lay there paralyzed with her pain, and absorbed it, soaking every ounce of it into herself.

IT WAS DARK AGAIN; SHE MUST HAVE PASSED OUT FROM THE PAIN. SHE still had no recollection as to day she was in now. Her eyes stung with dryness caused by all her tears. The mysteries of the last foggy days were hanging around her like a dreary mist, but she knew enough not to try to remember, she wanted to be numb again, she would rather feel nothing than feel that excruciating pain again. Lying still, she hid from her agony; it was all she could do to cling to the calm.

WHEN SHE OPENED HER EYES IT WAS LIGHT AGAIN.

The music was still on, her bear clutched to her chest and the bits of phone were still scattered about. The familiar dreaded clawing of the nightmare scratched at the surface of her consciousness, forcing her to think of him, taunting her to move and awaken the sleeping giant. She refused to move, remaining on the floor; as still as a statue. She began to regulate her breathing to fast, short breaths, so as not to expand her lungs too much, and reopen the wounds that were for now sleeping. She felt a vibration which she vaguely remembered would be the rumble of the garage door opening. She tried to think of what that could mean but couldn't wrap her brain around it and gave up. All meaning had been lost.

She lay there with her ear to the floor, the same place she had been for days and stayed motionless. There was a voice calling her name. It sounded familiar but that still didn't mean anything. Footsteps followed the voice that seemed to be coming up the stairs. They grew louder and louder until she heard her door open.

"Shayde?" the familiar voice said.

There was no way she could talk or move, it would hurt too much.

"Over there," she heard another familiar voice that sounded like the wind.

"Shayde!"

Suddenly she was being lifted off the ground and carried somewhere. She couldn't focus on the face, her vision was blurry. The strong arms carried her into a bright hallway. Grimacing from the pain that the sunlight caused her eyes, she felt as though she was awakening from a drunken stupor, trying to piece things together, to make sense out of nonsense. The strong arms had laid her on a soft, cushiony surface.

"What happened?" a soft, sweet voice asked someone in the room.

She covered her ears, fearing that she might hear something she didn't want to think about. Her eyes remained closed as well and she focused on remembering the sound of Rise

Against—one of her favorite bands—playing a song that wouldn't remind her of him. After a little while, she felt the surface tension change on what she was lying on. Suddenly someone was next to her, wrapping their arms around her. She felt tired. Even though she might've been sleeping for days, she felt sleepy and the unconsciousness was welcome, for it was a chance to feel nothing at all again.

EIGHTEEN

Aura had no idea what to do with Shayde. She had at least been able to take over her unconscious body and get her home and changed, but afterwards it was as if Shayde's suffering had enabled her to put up a brick wall in her mind that let no one enter, not even Aura. Aura could not even show herself to Shayde, to try and comfort her. All she could do was let her lie there in her anguish, and it killed her.

Aura mulled over what could've possibly happened to distort the aim of Breken's spell so. She never ordered Viento to kill anyone; why had he said that to the Wright family? Breken's spell had covered all bases and certainly the law of 'Do no harm,' or so she thought. Aura remained in the mirror for some time, contemplating, trying to go back in time and see where they went wrong, but to no avail. She was not all knowing, she could only search her own memories, and those of the Sorenya blessed with the mark of the Lily for answers.

Aura was going to have to find Viento himself, but she had no idea how to do that and she didn't want to go to Tara just yet; not until she figured out how to solve the problem first. Aura decided that she was just going to have to go, dissipate into the air and ride the wind to the Wright's house.

She entered into the darkened home, moving from room to room, calling to him in her mind and audibly with her voice.

There was nothing.

She hid in a darkened corner and waited for him to appear, willing him to show himself.

After waiting for what seemed like hours, she still sensed nothing. He never showed.

She tried to think of where he might dwell. He was told by Breken to disappear after he revealed himself to Briggs on his deathbed, but where would he go? All energy that was drawn together to create them had to have somewhere to reside. As Aura would go into her mirror, Viento had to have a place to dwell too, but she was at a loss as to how to begin to figure out where.

She drifted back to her house and returned to the basement, retreating into her mirror to clear her mind. Memories of the night that she was down in the basement with Breken conjuring up Viento, flooded her consciousness. She tried to go back, to relive it, to find the cracks in the spell, the space between the lines.

Then she found it; a glimmer of hope, a possible path to the answers.

She faded away again and traveled on the cool night air to Fleur-De-Lis Medical Center.

Aura suspected that Viento's relationship with the Wright's was not very different from her relationship with the Sorenya, except that he meant to do harm rather than good, he fed on the distress he caused the Wright's when they were about to die. Realizing this, Aura hoped that like her, Viento could be summoned by the family that his very essence was created through.

She found her way to the ICU.

The building was dark save for the dim lights at the nurse's station. She followed her senses until she found Marilyn Wright. Her "room" was more a cubicle of curtains. Marilyn lay motionless in the hospital bed, surrounded by machines that beeped in a peculiar chorus. Her room was dark except for a glowing screen with her vital signs displayed on it. Aura looked down upon her and knew this would be difficult to do with all the equipment surrounding her. Aura closed her eyes and dispersed the energy that formed her; enough to enter into Marilyn's body. When she lowered herself into it, she felt stiff, awkward at first. She lay there, emptied her mind, and then concentrated as hard as she could.

Show yourself, Viento.

Remaining stock-still, she waited, but there was nothing.

Viento, I command you to show yourself. She waited. Suddenly she felt the energy in the room shift and the temperature drop. There was a long pause.

Are you here, spirit? Aura thought to him again.

"I am, and who are you?"

When she opened Marilyn's eyes to look around, there was still nothing, just darkness.

It is I, Aura, spirit of Breken.

She couldn't use Marilyn's voice as she had a ventilator pipe down her throat, so Aura communicated through her mind.

"And why is it that you are here?" His voice had the same texture as Aura's, yet it was harsher, deeper and more corrosive.

I have come to find out why it is that you harm this family, kill their first-born's first love. That was never your instruction.

"Things do not always work out the way you want them to, Aura." His voice was ubiquitous yet nowhere at the same time.

What does that mean, Viento? Tell me what you have done?

"I am setting right a wrong, a grave betrayal. It started with the witch lover, Catherine, who brought the curse of ill fortune upon the family and was punished for it. When Briggs took her first love, then her life, and finally in madness his own; my existence changed, my purpose shifted and now it will never be enough."

Viento stepped out from the dark shadows; his once faceless appearance was now that of an older man in his late forties. He had a gruff beard, his eyes were a lustrous grey and he had a stooped stature with a paunch. He still wore the same clothes that Aura remembered when he was first formed but he had taken on John Briggs' facial features and form.

But you are not Briggs, you are Viento.

"I was able to soak up the very essence of John Briggs when he took his life, and he then became a part of me. When we take the life of every first-born's first love, they are punished again for the betrayal of this family. When I reveal myself to that first born at the point of death, they are punished twice fold. The agony of their grief only surpassed by their torment of their guilt."

Aura was devastated at his words. She didn't know how to fix this. And then something dawned on her that chilled her to her core.

Shayde was Kruise's first love. Kruise was Simon's first born... Shayde was doomed.

"Aw, you see it now don't you, witch?" he said derisively.

Aura's colors began to darken as she could think of nothing else but to get away from this entity, this... thing and try and find a way to save Shayde before Viento would turn his attention to her.

She evaporated and fled back to her house. Down to the basement she went, to search the books on every shelf, seeking a way to stop him. Luckily, one of her powers was that by merely placing her hand in front of a book she could soak up the information within them, absorbing the words from their pages. It took her minutes to read a book of a thousand pages. She scoured through them, one by one, until she came across something that made her gasp.

It was in a book of ancient remedies under the heading; *A Cure for a Negative Conjuration of Energy.*

Stricken, Aura read that the only way to get rid of a conjuration of energy was by the hand of the witch who created it or failing that, if a witch from the same bloodline sacrificed herself for her family's past mistakes, the negative conjuration would be forced to collect the good energy. One positive energy would neutralize the other negative energy though the conjuration would still exist.

Aura colors wavered again.

Whatever happened, they would have to lose another member of their family, whether it was Shayde or someone else, all for just one past mistake.

She made a snap decision, disintegrated and drifted away.

The sound of the garage door closing and Tara and Dustin's voices upstairs awoke her. She shot up through the ceilings to warn them of what was going on with Shayde. As they hastily made their way up the stairs, Aura followed.

"Shayde?" Dustin said as he walked into Shayde's room.

"Over there," Aura pointed to the side of her bed.

"Shayde!" Dustin ran to his daughter and pulled her up into his arms. He headed out the door, to take her into their room.

"What happened?" Tara asked Aura, concerned.

Dustin carried Shayde into their room and laid her down on their bed.

"It's bad," Aura said, solemnly.

"What?! What's bad Aura, tell me what is wrong with my daughter?!" Tara's voice was stricken with panic.

"It is Viento. He still exists; he didn't disperse after Briggs' death. He goes to the Wright family when they are nearing the end of their lives and tells them he was sent to them by a witch family from the sixteen hundreds who have told him to kill the first love of every first-born child of a generation. It is Kruise's family, Kruise is a Wright... Viento killed Kruise's mom, Reanna. When Kruise's dad, Simon, found out about this, he poisoned himself to meet the man who took his wife. Shayde saved Simon and when he came to, he told Kruise it was Shayde's fault his mom was dead. They threw her out of the house and then Kruise broke up with her. She has not moved since Sunday night."

"But why would Viento do this?!"

"After Breken and I created him, he did as he was bid and followed Briggs, collecting all the negativity that Briggs brought upon himself. If he had dealt with it well, all would have remained well and good. If he didn't, it would be punishment for his crime but not one Breken had given herself, so avoiding the law of 'Do no harm'. Eventually when Briggs fell ill and Viento revealed himself to him, Briggs refused to see that he had committed any wrong against the Guards or that any ill fortune he suffered was of his own making. He believed that in order to save his family from the misfortune that had dogged him; he would sacrifice his daughter and eldest child Catherine, who he accused of cursing the whole family through her love of the witch, Keyan. He took her life and then his own. In doing so it seems that Viento soaked up the very essence of John Briggs as well, and they became one and the same. It also made him stronger than we'd ever anticipated.

"It distorted the commands we gave Viento. Briggs punished Catherine twice, firstly by taking the life of her first love Keyan, and secondly by accusing her of causing it. It is a twisted logic but it is the logic of Briggs. Now it is the first love of the first-born child of every generation that is taken, and when Viento reveals himself near the end of the life of a first born Wright, it is now not the sin of the massacre of the Guards they are charged with, it is the sin of love—the so called betrayal of their family."

"Poor Kruise, oh my poor Shayde. Surely we can explain to him?"

Aura hesitated, "It's worse than that Tara... Shayde is Kruise's first love."

Tara went stock still, quietly comprehending Aura's words. Stricken, she ran over to her daughter with a sob and cradled her close. Dustin held Shayde's hand and stroked it. She was lying motionless, with her eyes squinted tight, mumbling something to herself.

"What do we do, Aura?" Tara asked her as she rocked her daughter.

"I researched it as much as I could; because the balance of the universe and the 'law of do no harm' is sacrosanct, the only way to get rid of a negative conjuration of energy is by the death of the witch who created it. If this isn't possible only the death of the last witch to be born of that witch's blood line can destroy the spell—the death of the bloodline would in effect be the death of the witch, albeit later in time. Failing that, if any witch from the same bloodline makes this sacrifice, the negative conjuration is forced to collect the good energy created by this selfless act. One positive energy will neutralize the other negative energy, though the conjuration will still exist."

"What?! So what are we supposed to do?" Tara asked, her face dissolving into one of hopelessness.

"I'm not sure. I went to Mary—"

"You went to *Mary?!*" Tara interjected; the tone that was edged with sadness now was drenched in anger. "What the fuck would Mary do to help us, Aura," Tara yelled at her, getting up from the bed.

"Tara, calm down." Dustin said, trying to calm his wife.

"No, it is okay," Aura said, drifting back to the wall. "She has every right to be angry. This situation is beyond our control now. I do not know what to do."

"What did you tell Mary?" Tara asked, stopping at the foot of the bed.

"I told her what was going on. I thought she might help us."

"Why would she? She never cared before."

"Her time has come and gone, she is here because of you. I thought she might see that."

"You cannot say that Aura, it's wrong."

"We cannot let this continue, Tara. We are the reason he exists. We cannot let him kill any more innocent people."

"Then it has to be me," Tara said, falling to her knees. "And it has to be before he comes for my Shayde."

"No!" Dustin cried out.

"There is no alternative, I can't survive the loss of another child and we can't let this go on for the Wright's, it's not fair." Tara smiled at him wistfully. "You know I'm right."

Dustin stood and went to her, tears running down his face.

"I know," Aura whispered. "I do not have an answer."

"What did Mary say?" Tara said through silent tears.

"Not much of anything."

"But you told her that mine and my daughter's life were at risk?"

"I did."

Tara sat and lamented into her hands. Dustin tried to comfort her. Tara mumbled something that was inaudible but Aura knew what she was thinking.

She was at a loss on what to do.

CHAPTER

NINETEEN

· ⁎ · ⁎ ☽ ⁎ · ⁎ ·

Shayde stared at the seeds in her hands and then looked into the mirror.

It was dark outside and nothing but a lit candle cast any sort of light within the bathroom.

Tears trickled from her eyes and down her cheeks.

She had heard every word Aura said to her mom. When Tara yelled at Aura, Shayde quit singing to herself to listen to what was going on. Now she knew what she had to do.

Viento had to be destroyed, the Wright family had to be protected and she was the last of the bloodline. She had to act quickly; she knew what her mother would do, even if she hadn't heard it with her own ears. Her mother would sacrifice herself for her and it would be futile. Tara could have more children and save the bloodline, Breken's legacy was far more important than Shayde's life. Shayde was doomed by Kruise's love for her and she was glad of it, she couldn't live without him anyway.

The diamond was no longer on her finger.

The reflection of herself in the mirror was solemn and sad as she whispered goodbye to her own eyes.

I am taking my own life to save the family of the man I love, she told herself. *May they never suffer another loss from our spirit again.*

She put a handful of Rosary Peas in her mouth and swallowed them with a glass of vodka.

CHAPTER

TWENTY

Downstairs in the basement, Tara was gently stirring an effervescent liquid in the cauldron. Beside her, Dustin lay on the couch unconscious from the effects of a sleeping potion she had made for him. Luckily, Shayde hadn't needed any because she was already sleeping soundly when Tara went to check on her before she came downstairs. She gathered some of the liquid into a ladle and funneled it into a small vial. When she was finished, she bent down a kissed Dustin lightly on the lips and then climbed the stairs and left the house, walking steadily towards the ocean.

The moon shone brightly in the night sky, lending a silvery tint to the navy blue horizon behind it. The lustrous waves surged up towards her as she approached them, as if in greeting. The water was chilly to her feet, yet there was a strange numbness throughout her body. When the water reached her knees she stopped and admired the stars.

I take this poison into my veins for the Wright family. May Viento never harm their family, or their loves, ever again.

Tara took the cork from the vial whispered "Blessed Be," and emptied the contents into her mouth, drinking it in one large gulp.

Standing in the waves for a while, she felt the ocean kiss her thighs and take her scent to sea.

Aura floated out to Tara just in time to see her collapse into the waves.

TWENTY-ONE

The wind was hitting his face at full force now. As he glided down the bike trail at high speed, Kruise thought of nothing while he listened to his music. It was all he had been able to do for days. He had to keep his mind away from the agony that breaking up with *her* had been.

When she ran out that door, he had collapsed to the floor. He couldn't believe what he had heard. The death of his mother had been the single most traumatizing event in his entire life. Not just the fact that he lost his mom, his best friend, but the fact that he had to watch his dad try to survive without her. Her death had broken Simon beyond recognition and he fought daily for the will to get up in the morning and live another day. The only reason that Simon kept himself alive was for his kids.

Kruise knew that the death of his mother wasn't Shayde's fault directly, but it was because of *her* family. They were the reason Simon lost his beloved father so young. It was why Marilyn lost her mom at a young age as well. It all made sense now, and it stung like hell. It was like a dagger twisting in his heart that her family was responsible for this pain, and what was even worse was that she *knew* about this spirit and didn't tell him. It was a life-altering revelation. He was still in shock by it all.

Even though a part of him resented her from his core, he still loved Shayde beyond all reason. She was his first true love. The ache from breaking her heart the way that he did demolished him and ravaged his entire being. It had wrecked him. Left with the overwhelming devastation breaking up with her had brought him, he wallowed in it and it threatened to drown him. He did not care to carry on. He knew he would never find another like Shayde, but he knew he could never be with her again.

The only way that he could function, was by either riding his bike all day or sleeping. He couldn't let himself think about her. It hurt too bad. Songs would come on that would remind him of her and he would hit skip and try and clear his mind. But sometimes all he could do was drink her away. He would find quiet places to go and drive out his rage so it didn't suffocate him, so he didn't leave his anger to fester and eat him alive from the inside out. He would smoke joints on the cliffs and look out at the ocean and scream into the sky. Trying to live without her was tormenting. His heart needed her by his side to live, and trying to adjust to living without her was harder than it had been to learn to live life without his mom.

As he rode his bike and listened to his music, he saw someone up ahead at the side of the trail. He wondered why someone would just be standing out in the middle of the forest. He squinted to see who it was and as he grew closer, he realized it was a woman dressed in a white gown with long red hair. Her figure reminded him of Shayde's, and at first he thought it just might be her. When he was close enough to see a face, she disappeared. He blinked his eyes a few times beneath his sunglasses to see if it had been a trick of the mind. When he reached the spot she had been standing, he slowed his bike down and stopped. He noticed a trail of bent grass leading away from the track towards the trees. Dismounting, he walked his bike along it until he reached the edge of the forest. The trail of bent grass was replaced by bare footprints on the sandy ground. Leaning his bike up against a tree he followed them deeper into the gloom. Eventually he saw light coming through the canopy of trees directly in front of him, and when he arrived at the opening the footprints disappeared. He realized he'd arrived at a beach where the ocean met the forest.

The fact that he didn't find her didn't bother him at all. The private little beach clearing was an optimal spot to sit, smoke and try not to think. There was an array of boulders on either side of the beach that prevented the public from easily accessing it. It was a rather spectacular find and he was going to commit it to memory and bring his friends here, though they weren't the first people to come mind, dark red hair and bright green eyes flashed into his consciousness automatically, but he quickly dispelled those thoughts as soon as they scratched at him.

What a chore mind reprogramming was.

He walked towards the rocks that were jutting out into the water. The big boulders on either side of it made a perfect spot to sit and feel the waves lap at his feet. He could sit on one and put his back up against another. So, he leaned back, pulled out a joint from the brim of his hat, lit it and started to get lost in the gentle lull of the sea.

Then, out of the corner of his eye, he saw her again.

He turned his head sharply to the left to catch her with his gaze and when he did, she did not move. It wasn't Aura or Shayde, though she resembled both of them. She was beautiful, more so even than Shayde. She was about Shayde's height and with the same piercing green eyes, but her face was older. She had long, wavy hair that reached down to her waist, and she was wearing a long white dress that appeared very old fashioned but he couldn't place the era it was from. Suddenly, he recognized her as one of the faces from the visions that Aura had put into his mind. She was part of *them,* and he didn't want any part of *them.* But this strange beauty was hypnotic and all he could do was stare.

She walked—or rather glided—over to him.

"Hello, Kruise," she said, with a thick Irish accent.

When he tried to speak he couldn't find his voice.

"Do not be frightened."

"Who are you?" he said when he finally found his voice.

"My name is Breken McKarat. I have something to tell you," she said as she drifted closer to him.

He leaned back as she put out her hand, trying to touch his forehead. "What do you want?" he asked sternly.

"Let me show you. It will help you understand."

He thought about it for a moment then stood up, the being

floated backwards out of his way. "I don't want any part of it anymore."

"You do not have to be. But you *will* see what I have to show you, you have the right to know. Now sit back down."

He didn't have a choice. His body was being moved for him. Anger roared inside of him but could find no release. Without being touched his body lurched forwards and then back, hard, thumping onto the rocks. His eyes shut and his mind went blank.

Suddenly he was in a room, the walls were made of logs and the floor was dirt. He looked down and didn't see his hands. It was like he was the wind; he didn't have a body and was everywhere and nowhere at once. There was a group of kids sitting around a table eating something from wooden dishes. There was a mother and a father, and four children, dressed in clothes from another time, laughing and talking with Irish accents. He couldn't understand what they were saying but he could tell it was a cheerful conversation. Suddenly, there was a loud crash that interrupted their merry chatter. The door came thundering down off its hinges and a group of men stormed in and immediately started castigating them. They began beating the mother and father with batons; even the children were thrown to the floor and kicked. Then they were hog tied, blindfolded and dragged from the house. Kruise followed frantically, screaming for them to stop but they couldn't hear him. He watched helpless as they were all thrown in the back of a horse-drawn cart. The ride was dark and bumpy. The children were screaming for help and the mother was crying hysterically. The cart stopped. Some men—it must have been five or six—dragged them from it. Stumbling they were led up some steps and picked up and thrown hard onto the ground in a place that echoed. There was another loud thump, and then a cacophony of banging nearby with what seemed like large cudgels. One of the kids managed to free herself from the blindfold and scanned the room. She started screaming. The dad freed himself of his ties with help from one of his sons and they all started to untie each other. They were in the town's chapel. The thunderous noise was the windows being boarded up with thick boards. They started to panic, each one running to one of the windows to try and open it, to no avail. Suddenly it was deathly quiet. They looked around waiting for something to happen, then the sound of liquid being splashed all over the outside broke the silence.

And then the quiet returned.

WHOOOOSH.

Kruise felt sick with fear. The entire perimeter went up in flames. The orange and yellow tongues licked at them through the cracks in the boards as they began to scream.

Then there was darkness.

WHEN LIGHT RETURNED AGAIN HE WAS IN A FOREST WITH A SMALL RED headed child, and *Aura.*

Trying to call out to her, he discovered he still had no voice, he was a ghost. He followed them silently as they walked back towards the little brown house he had just seen. He didn't want to see that room again, so he watched from a distance as they found the door had been broken down, the house empty, and the remnants of a struggle. He saw Aura evaporate and the little girl run out into the yard, calling out to her family. Aura returned he could see she was agitated as she spoke to the little girl, they seemed to be arguing. The little girl ran towards the horses in their pasture despite Aura's pleading gestures. She jumped on one, bareback, and rode away. Kruise followed her with dread in his heart. They arrived at the blazing inferno that used to be a chapel, she jumped off of her horse and fell to her knees. She screamed at the night sky, tears streaming down her face and Kruise felt like he would break apart from her sadness.

The light faded to black.

He saw the little girl lying on a cot, staring at the wall, staring at nothing. It was like looking through a time-lapse camera, he must've watched her for days and she did not move. She would only sleep, then wake up and sob, then sleep again. He almost cried from her agony.

A gloomy haze swept over him.

They were in a new little house with a dirt floor, but they were in a basement. He saw Aura and the little girl. The little girl was doing something with the cauldron that sat in the center of the room. He could hear her speaking.

"Tis I, Breken, with everything that I am.

'This is my sadness. I ask thee to leave me now, thou are not welcome here anymore and I shed no tears in parting.

'This black cloud represents all the pain the man who murdered my family created, the man called John Briggs.

'All thy wits shall be turned to black,

'And over thy face the loathsomeness shall creep,

'All that is bad shall be swallowed up here, and will follow thee wherever thou goes.

'And these things shall be 'til thou releases thyself through selfless acts.

'And the light will then return.

'And the bad will turn to good.

She took the athame and pricked her finger. Then, she took the pieces of clothing and dabbed them with her blood. She gave them to the wind one by one and said a name with each one,

'Within thy heart remember the names,

'Aenya, Eamon, Keyan, Brayen, Nolan and Bridget.

'All of which thou savagely burned even after one had saved thine own daughter. And thou plunged him into the fiery pits of thy own hell.

'I spread these spirits and set them free.

'I ask this negativity be thy own shadow 'til thou sets thy own self free, the power of the elements will hold thee in its hands.

'I pray thee welcomes good energy into thy life and that the spirit of change embraces thee with open arms.

'Blessed Be.'

Darkness engulfed him again.

KRUISE SAW A MAN LYING IN BED. HE RECOGNIZED HIM AS ONE OF THE men that came storming into that little cabin and atrociously beat that family. He was coughing up blood, reading the bible and praying with a rosary. A faceless spirit similar in form but not appearance to Aura, stood before him and appeared to say something to him. The man jumped up, looking mad with rage. He began shouting at the top of his lungs about the devil and how the witches had sent their demon from hell to torment him even more. Stumbling outside, he grabbed an axe from the woodpile and then ran back into the house and into a small bedroom. A young woman lay sleeping beside a younger child. He made the sign of the cross before driving the axe into her skull. Kruise closed his eyes in horror, when he opened them he saw the man leave the room and he followed to see who else he might harm. Instead, Kruise watched in shock as the man took a long length of rope, threw it over the rafters and hung himself.

The spirit appeared again and a vortex appeared within it. Kruise couldn't see what was being sucked into it but the cabins atmosphere changed. It was somehow lighter but he couldn't explain it. When the energy had finished dissipating, the spirit looked at him, into him, and he now had a face, the face of John Briggs.

The light faded to dark.

HE BEGAN TO SEE DEATHS—WOMEN AND MEN DYING IN VARIOUS WAYS. Falling from horses, drowning, shotgun blasts, victims of robbers, sicknesses, murders, accidents, suicides... then he saw his mom. His heart broke again at the memory of walking in and finding her.

THE SOMBER LIGHT CAME AGAIN.

There was his beautiful Shayde. Sorrow permeated her and although sadness fractured her face, she was just as captivating when she was sad. The room that she was standing in was dark and she was gazing into a mirror, tears grimy with mascara ran down her face. He could hear her thoughts as she looked desolately into the mirror.

I am taking my own life to save the family of the man I love. May they never suffer another loss from our spirit again.

He watched her take a handful of seeds and put them into her mouth, washing them down with what appeared to be a glass of water, but thicker.

She drank the entire glass, wiped her mouth and walked back to her room. Grabbing her keys from the dresser, she pulled something off the keychain and clutched it to her chest, along with the picture of them at Cape Cod, she lay down on her bed and closed her eyes.

His heart raced.

Tears flowed from his eyes as he tried to scream at her but he still had no voice.

The tenebrous fog was upon him again.

He saw Tara on a beach at night. She had some sort of vial in her hand. The thoughts in her head came pouring into his, as if they were his own.

I take this poison into my veins for the Wright family. May Viento never harm their family, or their loves, ever again.

Then he saw her pop the cork off and swallow the liquid. Two seconds later she collapsed in the waves.

Suddenly it was light.

When Kruise opened his eyes it was a bright, sunny day and he realized that he was back on the beach. Exhausted, he slipped from the rock and fell to his knees on the sand. He raised his head to look at the wavering image above him.

It hadn't been her family's fault. His family had started it.

"Shayde?" he asked from the sand.

"You had two people willing to give their lives for your loss—"

"Is she—" he interjected, but was not able to finish the sentence.

"It was your ancestor that killed my family Kruise. It is against our law to harm another. I created Viento, so that your ancestor John Briggs would at least experience the same amount negativity as he gave out. He was sent to follow Briggs and imbibe himself with all of the energy—negative or posi-tive—Briggs' actions produced, to act as a force of good luck, or bad, depending on that energy. Energy draws energy of its own ilk. This way Briggs would be directly accountable for his actions, which he failed to be for actions against my family. If Briggs was not cured of his badness by the end of his life, I believed that I could at least show Briggs that his bad luck was of his own making and make him to recognize it. I'd even hoped that he would realize the wrong he committed against my family, so his guilt would be his punishment. As you saw, it went horribly wrong. Briggs would not accept this, and again he blamed others for his own failings. Worse still he blamed his own daughter, his first child, whose first love was Keyan Guard; the eldest son of the family that he had burned alive.

"Just as Viento has stored all the negative energy Briggs had brought upon himself, Briggs' suicide caused Viento to imbue himself with John Briggs himself, and the undertaking he was given was tragically altered. He was then destined to kill every first born's first love."

"Oh my god, Shayde?" he breathed, realizing now the full wrath of the curse that Briggs set in motion. "Please tell me she is not gone…" he cried, all his blood seemed to be evaporating inside him.

"The only way we would be able to stop him, was for a witch of our blood line to sacrifice herself, and in doing would so counterbalance his negativity. This would not destroy him completely, he'd still follow your family and whether he was good or bad would be up to you. But if the last witch in our bloodline took her own life, this act would obliterate him altogether."

He couldn't hear anything else. It was hopeless. All he could think about was her, everything about her flashed through his mind—the way that she loved him, the way he loved her. He was utterly destroyed.

When he didn't hear anything for a long time he looked up. The ghostly image was fading. "NO! DON'T YOU GO! YOU HAVE TO TELL ME IF SHE'S GONE!" he screamed at the evaporating air.

The image of Breken waivered then faded a bit and shifted and shook. It looked like she broke apart into three pieces. There was a blinding light and he shielded his eyes with his arm. When he glanced around it was gone. After he scoured around and saw that there was nothing there, he stood up and jogged into the woods searching. It was quiet. Panicking, he ran back out to the beach only to find the same emptiness. There was nobody there. He fell back to his knees and collapsed into sobs.

The sound of a branch breaking made him turn around. Through blurry tears, at first he couldn't tell who it was standing before him.

Then he saw.

It was Shayde.

He closed his eyes and rubbed them to see if he was imagining things. Slowly, he opened them again and peeked. She was still there, looking at him, smiling. He wiped the tears from his face, jumped up and ran to her. When he reached her, he scooped her up in his arms and held her as tight as he could. She felt hot and she smelled like the summer rain.

"I am so sorry Shayde. I know you didn't know, please forgive me, I should have known, should have trusted you," he cried into her shoulder, his hand clutching at her long red hair.

"I understand Kruise. Breken never meant for your family to get hurt, for your mom, we didn't know that the spell had gone wrong." Her voice was filled with regret.

Kruise pulled away a little so he could gaze into her eyes. "When I thought you were dead I almost died too. It almost killed me when we broke up, but to think of you no longer existing, it—" he stopped, unable to finish, remembering the ache in his chest at that dreadful moment. "I need you to live. Without you... life is meaningless."

"I almost died too. Not because of the seeds or because of Viento. I almost died because I lost you. I would rather die than feel that pain again, I wanted this life to be over so I could find you again," she wept, "It's as if you and I are bound by something that even death can't break. I can't explain it but I know deep in my bones that in every lifetime we have found each other."

He wiped her tears away from her face with his fingertips. "Well I'm just happy I'm with you in this one for now." Suddenly, a thought crossed his mind. "Oh no, Shayde, if you're here that means... your mom?"

"I'm okay," came a voice from the forest.

They turned around as Tara and Aura emerged from the trees. Kruise kept Shayde's hand locked in his.

"Then who—?" he looked confused.

"I have a sister, Mary," Tara began. "We haven't spoken in years. She was found dead in her apartment. She left a note saying to call our number right away and inform us of her death. It was a close thing, I'd given Dustin a sleeping potion and he very nearly didn't take the call. The note also said that Mary was sorry for all the grief she caused me. That she was thankful I had saved her life and was forever indebted to me for it. She hated her life; she always had, then hated herself even more for what she did to me. When she found out I lost Kain, she said that her heart broke for me but she didn't have the courage to call. Then, when Aura went to her and told her that my only child was at risk unless someone of the same blood died, she knew right then that was what she had to do. She never forgave herself for what she did to me, every incident. She felt it was her way to repent for the pain she caused." Tara looked down as tears started dripping down her face. "She gave her life for your family, for ours." Tara fought back the tears.

"Aura and dad found my mom just in time and saved her, and then they saved me. Luckily, the seeds take longer to kill you than the potion does. They revived my mom in time to save her, then they went into my room to tell me but I was almost gone. My mom saved me," Shayde said softly.

"Oh my god, I am so sorry," Kruise looked at Tara. "I—"

"We are sorry for your loss, Kruise," Aura told him. "You can never get your mother back. That, we will never be able to repay."

Kruise shrugged and smiled sadly.

"Viento is still around," Aura continued. "He is better now and will start bringing luck to your family eventually. We will stay by your side and help you and your family make him lighter. It will never happen again, this we promise." Her tone was serious, her look unwavering.

"I don't blame you for her death. You're not in debt to me. I am not mad at you."

"You and Shayde will be together for a long time. We have plenty of time to make him good. It is our responsibility and we will see to it that you two will never be in danger from him again," her eyes sparkled as she said this.

"Okay." He went to give Tara a hug, never letting go of Shayde's hand. "Where did the other one go?" he remembered, peering over Tara's shoulder for her.

"Oh," Shayde said. "Well, mom figured out that when the auras of the three of us combine, we can summon the aura of Breken from within us. It was amazing to see what Breken saw first hand. I'd only heard about her life through our written history. To be honest I'm not sure I'd want to see the death of the Guards again though."

"Me neither." Kruise shook his head as if to get rid of the memory.

"It was worth it to get you back." Shayde smiled at him and he returned the smile.

"Oh yes," Aura interjected. "I almost forgot." She looked at

Tara and she nodded as Aura evaporated. Tara closed her eyes for a second and then her body lurched forward. When she opened her eyes, she walked up to Shayde and wrapped her arms around her. Kruise still refused to let go of her hand. With Tara's body, Aura nuzzled into Shayde's neck and they broke into sobs. Shayde grabbed on to Aura and squeezed as hard as she could. They held each other for a while.

I must've missed something, he told himself.

Then Tara let her go, stood back and closed her eyes. Her body shifted and Aura appeared at her side again. The three of them were silent for a minute, admiring each other, smiling.

Tara wiped her tears away with the back of her hand. "Okay, well, we're gonna go now. I guess you two are going to walk back. You've got a lot of talking to do. I'll take your bike Kruise, if you'd like, and you can pick it up later."

"Okay. That's a good idea, thank you," Kruise answered.

"I'll see you guys later," Shayde said, going to give her mom a hug, Kruise's hand still glued to hers.

It was now his turn to hug Tara.

"Bye kids. Be safe. Call me later from his phone okay?" Tara told Shayde as she started to walk towards the forest.

"Okay Mom, I will." She blew them a kiss.

"Bye you two," Aura whispered and disappeared into the trees.

"What happened to your phone?" he asked when they were gone. He turned to face her and grabbed her other hand so he had a hold of them both now.

"Um, well, it's broken. I threw it. I need a new one," she said, seemingly a little embarrassed.

"Yeah. I almost broke mine too but I thought better of it

'cause I didn't wanna miss a call from you," he admitted, looking deep into her eyes.

"You, *wanted* me to call you?" She sounded shocked.

"Well, yeah. I only went crazy without you. I never want to lose you, ever again. I was beside myself. I was so lost."

"Me neither. I broke apart. I never ever want to feel that way again. We belong together."

He took her face in his hands and kissed her.

"I'm sorry about your aunt," he said with remorse.

"It's okay, thank you. I never knew her. She didn't like our family. She hurt my mom pretty bad," Shayde said, looking down sadly. "What about your dad? Do you think he will ever forgive me?"

"There is nothing to forgive, Shayde. You did nothing wrong. In fact, you saved his life. He will be grateful to you, I promise."

"But how are you going to get him to listen? He's not going to believe you when you try to tell him about the past." Her voice was filled with worry.

"Shayde, it's okay. We'll figure it out okay? Nothing is impossible. We'll wing it." He looked at her and smiled. "It's funny how a single moment can change your life," he said to her, his lips almost touching hers.

"It is... A spark can become a flame and ignite your world." She paused, drifting off some place else. He wondered where her thoughts had taken her. "So, am I—" Shayde began again and then stopped.

"Are you what?" He brought his head back to study her eyes inquisitively.

"Nothing." She looked down grinning.

He pulled her head back up. "Shayde, will you be my girl again? I'm sorry I broke your heart and I will never hurt you again, as long as I live. Please forgive me for my ineptitudes and my frailties." He gazed pleadingly into her eyes, showing the love that had never left him.

"Of course, you are my true love. True love is when your aura finds another aura it can dance with," with tears in her eyes she looked laughingly into his. "I love you so much, I—I can't breathe without you."

"I can't breathe without you either baby doll. I love you so much... without wax."

He bent down to kiss her, wrapping himself around her. He had missed her so much; she was *everything* to him—so much so that this kiss brought him physical pain.

He loved her so much he ached.

THEY KISSED FOR A WHILE AND THEN SAT DOWN TO WATCH THE sunset. Shayde sat between his legs and leant back against his broad chest. He wrapped his arms around her and held onto her tightly. They sat there silently, watching the sun fade into the horizon. They had all the time in the world. The sky started turning all the brilliant colors of the rainbow. He kissed her head, then her ear, then her cheek.

The love of his life was back in his arms.

And he was never going to let her go again.

EPILOGUE

Shayde was running, she didn't know where she was.

As she looked around at the landscape she noticed that everything was very odd- looking. The sky was purple, the ground was lavender and even the trees were a strange amethyst color. Wherever she was, it was night and there were three moons sparkling in the plum-colored sky. She knew she was fleeing from something but she didn't know where she was running to. There was the sound of something chasing behind her, but every time she turned to see what it was it moved out of sight, she could never catch a glimpse of it.

The scenery never changed.

It was like she was running in place.

She could still clearly hear whatever it was behind her but it never came into view—it was always in her peripheral vision. She tried turning towards the noise but couldn't get her body to change direction. Terror gripped her at the same time as curiosity. She was scared but she wanted to know of what.

Suddenly she saw bushes up ahead. They were the same color as the rest of the foliage she had seen, a strange purple color and they had a cotton like texture. She took it as a good sign because at least the scenery was changing now. She ran for what seemed like hours only gaining a few feet when something glittery shone up ahead. Unequivocally she knew she had to get to it, whatever it was. The need seized her and wouldn't let her go. It was imperative that she get to it. As she tried to grasp it she fell, the hard ground tearing into her knees. She felt a stinging sensation and looked down, there was blood pouring from her hands. The wave of dizzying nausea threatened to take her down but she stifled it, still intent on trying to reach whatever it was in the grass. It was just out of reach.

As her fingertips grazed the edge of the shiny object, her vision blurred and she couldn't tell where it was anymore. She felt for it with her hands, frantically patting them over the grass.

Then she heard something move off to her side.

Her eyes caught something that was standing off in the distance, she knew it was staring at her, watching her, she was saturated with a feeling of dread. Whatever it was, it was evil, she felt it down to her bones. All she could make out was the outline of a person, but it was all shadow. There were no features, no arms and legs or head, just a mass of something.

The urge to get up and run away from it flooded her but when she tried to get up she couldn't find her legs. She started to crawl away from it but as she did, it began to move towards her.

She tried to get up again but her legs wouldn't move. They felt like they were a thousand pounds a piece. As horror hit her, she crawled as fast as she could towards one of the bushes to hide. The sound of the evil that was coming closer was terrifying and she trembled at the thought of what it might be.

It grew closer and closer still...

At the last minute she found her legs, stumbled up from the ground and tried to run, but she felt she could only get her legs to move a half an inch at a time. The sound was approaching fast. She tried with all her might to run but felt she was still only moving as fast as a snail.

It was right behind her now.

Shayde tumbled to the ground and quickly turned around to see the dark figure looming above her. She panicked hysterically and looked for something to hit it with.

There was nothing.

The black shadow lurched for her. She tried to hit it with her fist, but when she expected to connect with its face her hand went limp and she only tapped it lightly. She tried it again.

No luck.

Looking around again, she saw the shiny object in the distance. When she turned back around, the shadow person had reached her and was grasping for her, a wretched arm unfolding out of its huge mass. She kicked at it with all her might and her foot connected with its center, knocking it down. In the split second that it fell, she hastily scurried over to the object and grabbed it.

It was her ring.

She stared at it with curiosity.

What was it doing here?

The shadow monster leapt at her again.

A bolt of light shot out of the ring and hit the shadowy monster at its center. There was a sizzling sound where the intense light had touched it. The hole in the middle of the beast was expanding; a red, lava-looking substance was eating away at it. The creature made the most awful, ear-piercing screech she had ever heard, and it began to retreat, like mist in a rainstorm, and then... it was gone.

She admired the ring in utter bewilderment, as the light that had beamed outward from its core, faded and dimmed to its normal appearance again.

The light from the moons were fading as they navigated their way to the other side of the cosmos. The purple sky began to take on a darker hue as tiny stars lit up its canvas, looking as though someone had crushed them and threw the stardust up to the heavens.

She crouched down and bounded up into the sky, her wings spreading out and extending in anticipation of being caught by the wind. She flew up a few yards and glanced upon the ground to where she had been earlier, still unsure of where she was. Looking ahead, there was a large body of water, which appeared to be a purple ocean of waves and she glided over it, taking it all in.

Suddenly she heard something off to her left.

When she looked over, she saw that it was her best friend Alizé, she looked stunning. She was smiling at Shayde, flying next to her in the purple sky on a *broomstick*. Her eyes were a piercing blue and they glowed like a beacon in the night. Then, she heard something else. She looked over to her right and saw Courtney, Dawn, and Cherie. They too were flying on broomsticks. They were positively radiant, as though they were going to an important and very exciting ball. Courtney's eyes were a glowing hazel, Cherie's were a bright greenish-brown, and Dawn's were the color of a haunting dark brown.

They all smiled and flew alongside of her, their eyes piercing the darkness directly ahead of them.

Shayde awoke with a start; she bolted upright, her eyes opened wide as she fought to make out her surroundings. Her face felt moist and as she raked her hands through her unruly hair, it was drenched and heavy with perspiration. The room was shrouded in darkness, except for a faint shimmer from the full moon outside coming in through a crack between her curtains.

She felt a warm hand on her back and it made her jump, a slight whimper escaped from her lips.

"You okay?"

It was just *Kruise*. She felt better.

"Yeah. Bad dream," she said as she lay back down and cuddled into his arms.

He wrapped his strong arms around her and kissed her on her forehead.

Thoughts of the strange and very vivid dream clouded her

mind and she couldn't help to wonder what it all meant, that is if it meant anything at all.

She pulled him closer to her, feeling safe once again and closed her eyes. Taking a deep, long, soothing breath of air, she immediately drifted back to sleep.

ACKNOWLEDGMENTS

This book has been published three times. The first time, it was done through and agent and a publishing house. While the publishing house went under and my agent cut ties with me, I still learned so much from them both and want to thank them, wherever they are. The second time was through a vanity publisher who just scammed and robbed me of my time and my money. I don't wish to thank them and hope they rot in hell. The third time was done completely 100% self published and in order to do that, I had to learn from the hundreds and thousands of indie authors out there. I want to give them all the thanks. Every bit of advice, every book put out there independently, every thing I have done has been because you all forged the path for me. Indie authors are tireless angels who only want to share their stories with the world. Support them always.

ABOUT THE AUTHOR

Inara Gage is an indie author based in Northern Colorado. She resides with her son Gauge, her matador Khaleesi, kitty Bash, and bunny tWitch. After the first two failures of publishing, she went all the way through grad school to learn how to market herself in this crazy, incredibly hard, and immensely trying self publishing world. While this book is her first baby and she learned so much from all the trials and tribulations with this one, she has authored five more books since and hopes to continue putting stories out into the world that you all will love and enjoy.

This was her first book. But. Since all the fuck ups, it is like the fifth edition of it.